The Accidental Explorer

by

George Deeb

CONTENTS

PROLOGUE

June – <u>2006</u>

"I want to go with you." sixteen year old Erika Aimsler said, her words whetted by tears.

In a room full of family and friends, they were the only two there. Anthony Travellor's heart was breaking. He stroked his niece's chestnut curls, as he held her. He couldn't have loved her more if she had been his own child. Her mother Gabrielle, Anthony's older sister, had never hesitated to leave her only child with him when she and her husband wanted some alone time. They had called him Erika's second daddy, and Erika was always excited to spend time with her uncle. Now they were gone, and Anthony was going to leave Erika with her aunt and uncle on her father's side. From where he was going, he might not come back. Anthony hugged her as tightly as she did him.

Erika had stayed with him after an avalanche in the Austrian Alps had taken the lives of her parents. He had taken an emergency leave from work, and spent all his time trying to ease her pain and grief. But he did let her grieve, and he grieved with her. And he let her cry – and he cried with her. He took her to visit with her cousins whenever she wanted to, which was almost every night. For the next two months they healed together. Slowly the sun had begun to shine in their world again.

Now the time had come for Anthony to go. As sad as it made him, he knew that this was best for Erika. She would be with people who loved her. An aunt and uncle who would be there every day, and cousins to grow up with. In the next few months he wouldn't be around or in contact. He promised to call her as soon as he could. They had set up their laptops to

Skype with each other, and had tested it every night last week, even though they were just in different rooms of the house.

In case he never got to make that call, Anthony had arranged his will so that she would inherit everything he possessed if he didn't make it back. His attorney would handle the legalities until she turned eighteen. It wasn't much in total, but it was everything he owned. Money wouldn't be a problem for Erika – her father had been a very wealthy man, and her inheritance from her parents would kick in when she reached the age of twenty-one. A college fund and all other necessities had already been set up. But if he didn't make it back, he wanted her to have something that came from him.

"Why do you have to go?" she pleaded. "Why can't someone else go instead?"

"There are a lot of good people who are doing their jobs already. They're out there trying to make it safer for their families, and for us. This job is my job, and I'm the one who has to do it."

The answer didn't make the young girl feel any better. She understood what her uncle was telling her, but she didn't like it. She wanted him to stay with her.

"But it's so long." she cried, her body shaking with her sobs.

"I know it is," he said, but where I'm going there won't be any communications. Not until we set it up. As soon as I am able to, I will call you first. You're my first call. OK?"

"OK." she replied quietly – but it wasn't. Not with her. She knew there was no choice. She was starting to feel the way she did when she found out her parents had died. Her crying got worse, but she couldn't help it.

"It's time for me to go.", he said, as he held her face and kissed her forehead. "I love you. Don't ever forget that."

"Come on sweetie.", Erika's aunt Jen said, putting a hand on each shoulder in an act of both reassurance and restraint.

"I'll walk you to the car." said her uncle Phil, and both men left the house.

Anthony wiped tears from his eyes, as he got into the car. This was the best place for his niece while he was gone. She would be around people who loved her. He had been given legal guardianship of Erika, per her parents request, and no one had contested that. It was a case of very bad timing. His only sister was dead, and Erika was his only family. He had to do what was best for her – for her future.

Chapter 1

The Ganaphe´

1

July – 2006

What good is a warranty in space?

'Damn it!,' thought Captain Artau-sil-Munen, *'this can't be happening.'* The Orysta was practically brand new. It just had its second maintenance check less than a vheen ago. Everything exceeded operational requirements. Hell, the shine hadn't even worn off the hull yet. It still had that new ship smell. His lapse in concentration lasted only a fracin before reflex took over, and he touched his display console to call up the emergency checklist procedure that he had practiced so many times in training. The ship's main computer displayed several checklists as icons on the screen, based on its determination of the existing problem. Munen selected the one he needed and it enlarged and displayed on all of the consoles on the ship's bridge. The crew followed him through the appropriate section of the list, each person doing their required operations. It didn't help – they couldn't control the breach.

With great power came great risk, and this ship's engine was the most powerful one made for civilian space transports of any kind. A mining ship like the Orysta needed that power to haul its heavy cargo. A full ship required a lot of power to accelerate to the inter-galactic speeds needed to make space travel practical. His mind still kept telling him it was impossible, but the engine instruments showed without doubt that the exchanger unit was venting extremely hot plasma.

"Throttles to minimum." he commanded.

Intul-sil-Califas, the copilot, slid his finger down the throttle indicator on his control panel, from top to bottom. The ten power level indicators changed from blue to gray as he did so, with the bottom one going orange, indicating that thrust level had been commanded to idle. Munen waited for the accompanying reduction in engine noise – it didn't come.

'Instruments must be malfunctioning.' he thought for a fracin, but knew it was wishful thinking. Cross-check measurements from other instruments confirmed the temperature in the engine compartment was still rising, and was already affecting other sub-assemblies. Apparently one of the first to be affected was the engine control computer – he couldn't shut down the engine. Throttle control indicators showed the engine was set to idle, but thrust measurements showed that was a lie. Worse, the automatic safety backup systems also were not working. The engine was running away, and the sealed containment chamber was beginning to bulge as the increasing temperature caused the material to expand. The throttle indicators on his, the copilot's, and the engineer's consoles began to flash, indicating a control system failure. His mind fought against accepting that this was really happening.

"Cooling system failure!" stated the ship's main computer, in its pragmatic female voice.

Chief Engineer Benua-sil-Plessa checked his console, and confirmed the failure.

"Backup is working," he said, "but it's not able to control this

9

amount of heat."

The backup system was never designed to cool a runaway engine.

Munen glanced at the Engineer's display, and what caught his eye made him smirk to himself. The black boxes were recording everything from instrument measurements, video cameras, and sensor data caught by units around the ship – some in locations people couldn't go, and even biometric data on all of the crew members. When the main computer determined that destruction was imminent, the recordings would be launched away from the ship. *'At least someone will be able to learn from our deaths.'* he thought.

"COOLENT LEVEL IS DROPPING!" came a yell over the intercom. "We've got a leak – it's a big one. Can't tell where it is yet."
"Temperature still rising!" said the copilot.

Engine noise was increasing. Munen could feel a subtle, but definite vibration through his seat, and it was growing in strength – a warning caused by the runaway engine.

"EMERGENCY CHECKLIST. ENGINE SHUT DOWN PROCEDURE." Munen yelled.

It would take several mirlots to complete the procedure, and all the sub-procedures. As he and Califas went down the checklist, item by item, he was glad his associates were so competent. Glad for all the hours the crew had trained together. Their coordinated actions carried them quickly through the checklist. So why wouldn't the engine shut down? It was doing just the opposite, generating increasing power with each fracin that passed. The noise level was rising, and he could feel the vibration increasing in the ship.

Vibration caused by a Gravity Force Reaction Drive engine was not a good sign. A properly operating engine would give out a hum or whine, but unless you rested your hand on part of the unit you would never know it vibrated. A noticeable vibration meant the internal assemblies were operating out of sync. They were fighting each other instead of cooperating – which meant the main engine control computer was not working. Whether the engine held together or tore itself apart now depended on how well the crew at the maintenance dock had done their job.

"Sensors indicate hull distortion. Plus one point three arcleesons." came a clear, rarely heard male voice over the comm – It was the main computer's voice, and it had changed!

This was a bad sign. It was a standard feature on all commercial and military ships. Munen wasn't sure if it was the ship designers or military psychologists that had determined that during conditions of great stress, a strong male voice would be heard more clearly and was less likely to be ignored.

"Confirmed," said the Engineer, "and hull distortion is increasing."

It didn't matter what your job on a ship was, there were some things outside your expertise that every crew member learned to understand. Even the cook knew what hull distortion and pressure level was, and what it meant if it got out of control. Munen could feel the sweat on his face. *'Why would the hull bulge,'* he wondered, *'when the problem is in the containment chamber? If it reaches plus five arcleesons we're all dead.'*

It was strange, but because he was so busy following the emergency procedures, he didn't have time to be scared – and he should have been. Very, very scared. A hull breach in space has the lowest survival rate of all known mechanical failures. Such an event was also very rare – which was one reason it had a ninety-eight percent fatality rate. The only reason it wasn't statistically one hundred percent fatal was because a few lucky individuals had survived in sealed compartments. But even this was not a sure thing – someone had to rescue you before you ran out of air.

In the center of all the display screens on the bridge, was a bright red, repetitively collapsing circle that reminded Munen of a solar system collapsing into a black hole – the automated distress beacon had activated. Then Munen thought he heard, more than felt, the thump that signified the first emergency beacon had been launched by the ship's main computer. In it was the recording of all the ship's systems status up to the time it launched. As each additional beacon left, it would carry data updated to the time of its launch. Alarms were going off on all panels and speakers throughout the ship. He had already blocked out of his mind all the alarms that went off initially, and he was only aware of the beacon alarm for the first few fracins it sounded because he was so focused on the emergency procedures. Just another piece of background noise – acknowledge it in your mind when it first goes off, and then shove it aside.

"Shutting off audible alarms." said Califas.
"Thank you." Munen replied. His copilot was a very competent man.

The cockpit got slightly quieter.

"We need to vent the engine room, Engineer." he said into the comm, while looking over his shoulder at Benua-sil-Plessa, the Chief Engineer.

Plessa nodded confirmation.

"Report engine compartment clear." commanded Plessa into the comm.

There was no response. One of the engine room technicians should have responded.

"REPORT ENGINE COMPARTMENT CLEAR." he repeated loudly. Still no response.
"What is going on…?".
"I'll go look!" said the navigator, cutting him off, as she jogged off

of the bridge. Navigation was not a priority at the moment, and Mersuul-sil-Vaana had to make herself useful. It wasn't in her nature to be an observer.

"THE ENGINE WILL TEAR ITSELF APART IF WE DON'T GET IT SHUT DOWN." said Califas in a loud voice. They had to talk loudly now, to be heard over the increasing engine noise. "WE HAVE TO CUT OFF FUEL TO IT – ONLY WAY TO STOP IT!"

"AGREED." Munen said. "FUEL CUT OFF CHECKLIST."

"I DON'T THINK WE HAVE TIME FOR A NORMAL SHUTDOWN." yelled the copilot.

'Of course we don't,' Munen thought, *'how stupid of me.'*

"FUEL SOURCE TERMINATE EMERGENCY PROCEDURE – GRILIK AUTHORIZATION." read the copilot loudly, from the checklist.

Munen took a deep breath. *'Grilik Authorization'*, he thought. That was the procedural phrase meaning this was going to cause a lot of damage to the ship, and all responsibility for it would be his. The damage would be unavoidable. The sudden shutdown of fuel flow would cause uncontrolled cooling of conduits and junctions, which would crack and split and be unrepairable. The only fix would be to replace the damaged items. It was going to be very expensive.

"FUEL SOURCE TERMINATE EMERGENCY PROCEDURE." he responded, as he placed his hand on the instrument display screen and commanded "POWER REACTOR EMERGENCY SHUT DOWN – GRILIK'S AUTHORIZATION."

An array of lasers traveled from the heel of his hand to his fingertips and imaged the external features, as the computer scanned to confirm his identity. Infrared light sources then pulsed underneath, and sensors created an internal map of his blood vessels and sinews from the reflected light. Voice print identification was also performed. This was compared to Munen's physiological measurements the ship's main computer was taking in real time. White light then outlined his hand and turned green to indicate the computer recognized Munen and his authority.

The voice of the computer came over the comm, "*Identity confirmed – Artau-sil-Munen, Grilik of Mining ship Orysta. Terminating Reactor operation – Emergency Shut Down – Grilik authorization.*"

'*How calm you sound,*' Munen thought, '*and why not? No one ever fired a computer.*'

At the Engineer's station were several display panels showing different diagrams of the ship's internal structure, so that different systems could be monitored at a glance. The orange lines that had indicated the path of the charged particle flow from the Level Translators to the engine and other smaller generators faded from the screen, followed by an almost complete silence as the engine shut down from fuel starvation.

Munen could now hear the rapid breathing of the others. He could feel the thumping in his chest. It was done. It was over. They had come through the emergency. They had survived it. No damage to the hull. No one injured. He felt a bit of anti-climactic shock from the sudden change in the situation. What they were going to do without an engine was another matter. Being adrift in space was definitely not a good thing. He was half holding his breath, waiting for everything to suddenly fall apart again. It did.

"TEMPERATURE STILL RISING," said the Engineer loudly, forgetting that the ship was now quiet again, "AND HULL SENSORS STILL INDICATING INCREASING HULL PRESSURE IN ENGINE COMPARTMENT! – PLUS 2.7 ARCLEESONS DISTORTION – INCREASING!"

There was a lot of residual heat left in the engine room, and without a cooling system to pull it away, it was still affecting the ship. The massive heart of the ship that was the engine had a tremendous thermal mass, and all that built up heat energy was radiating out from it.

"We'll have to vent the area!" said the copilot. "Engine room?" he called over the comm. There was no response.

"Is anybody th..."

"IT'S CLEAR!" Vaana yelled as she came running back onto the bridge, panting heavily. "Engine room is clear and sealed! Comm is down in that whole section of the ship."

"VENT IT!" Munen yelled.

"Ready to vent engine room!" replied Plessa.

Venting part of a ship, any part of a ship, is not as simple or automated a procedure as most others. It exposed crew and ship to too much danger, to be something allowed to be done easily. Both the Copilot and the Engineer had their part to do to accomplish it. Exposing the interior of a ship to space did several very bad things. Everything in the exposed area could quickly became the same temperature of space – very close to absolute zero. The hull suffered reverse, and non-uniform stress, when only one section of a ship was exposed, as they were about to do. Pressurized areas are constantly stressing outward, and vented areas are not – a relatively negative stress on the hull.

"Access ways and hatches – Secure." read Califas, from the checklist.

Plessa scanned the bulkhead status indicators on his panel, and activated the appropriate controls. This triggered very loud and very bright visible and audible warnings at each bulkhead location. No conscious person could miss the alarms. Ten seconds later the bulkhead doors were hydraulically closed, and secured with electromagnetic latches. Panel indicators for each entry location went from green to red. Red to indicate the entry way was sealed. Red to indicate no access or egress. Red to indicate that if anyone was left in the engine room, they would now be trapped and unable to get out. Red to indicate death.

"Access ways and hatches – Secured!" confirmed the engineer.
"Vent safety seals – Blow off." read the the copilot.

Sometimes, old fashioned brute force was the safest and most effective way to do a job. Safety seals on vents were too important to be easily released by an accidental touch on a control panel, a mistaken flip of a switch, or undetected pulse of a short circuit. They were held on over the vents by explosive welds. The welds were made of misoravis, a crystalline material as strong as that used to form the ship's hull. It is metallic in nature, and can be used to weld dissimilar metals together – an important characteristic in itself. Its most important property is that it is a very stable material, that can safely be melted by normal welding processes. Once it has solidified, it provides a high resistance to electric current.

When a very high voltage signal in the proper frequency range is applied across a section of a 'miso-weld', it overcomes the intrinsic barrier potential of the material's atomic structure, and it changes from a super resistor to a super conductor. Electric current through it then increases at an extremely rapid rate, causing a structural breakdown at the atomic level. The ripping apart of the atoms in the crystalline structure releases great amounts of binding energy. Once the reaction begins it continues in a cascading effect, increasing so rapidly, and completely, that a tremendous amount of heat is generated almost instantaneously, and the material explosively decomposes. Misoravis is, in effect, an explosive charge that can be safely hammered on, heated to melting, or basically maltreated, yet be triggered into destruction by the push of a switch.

To make it an even more foolproof system, the power and signal sources are mounted next to the seal. When a properly encoded signal is received, the embedded processor within the source supply unit applies the necessary voltage to the weld.

Chief engineer Plessa placed his left palm on his control panel. It was scanned, then outlined in green. With his other hand, he then touched each of the vent seal controls for the engine room. On the bridge it sounded like multiple claps of thunder. The ship shuddered as the selected welds exploded, physically blowing off the seals from the vents, and propelling them away from the ship. With the vent seals gone, the valves could be opened to release the compartment air to space.

"Vent safety seals – Blown!" confirmed the engineer. "Ready to vent."

"Alright," said Munen, "let's try a controlled vent. See if we can minimize the damage to the ship."

Califas nodded his agreement, and both men looked at the engineer. Still keeping his left palm on the screen of his control panel, Plessa touched a linear control indicator with his right index finger, and slid it down a third of the way. Valves slowly opened, and the sound of air pushing out to space could be heard.

"Controlled venting – Activated." replied the engineer. "1000 quint liffs per mirlot."

They waited for the changes to take affect. Several mirlots passed before Plessa reported.

"Temperature dropping. No change in hull pressure yet... Wait!... Hull sensors indicating minor drop in pressure... a little more... it's coming down!"

Vaana was out of her seat, practically hopping in excitement over to engineering.

Anxiously looking over Plessa's shoulder, she yelled "DISTORTION DOWN TO 1.2 ARCLEESONS – NEGATIVE TREND – YES!"

She was a very excitable young woman, and she had a very big smile on her face. It was infectious, and soon the rest of the bridge crew were smiling as well.

"*Secondary cooling system failure!*" stated the computer, its voice once again sounding female – it had determined that the danger of the hull rupturing no longer existed.

"It doesn't matter," responded Plessa, "the engine is off line, and compartment temperature and pressure are dropping." There was relief in his voice.

"Let's get maintenance working on it," Munen commanded, "although if I know Valian, he already has his crew ready to start repairs."

Munen knew his crew well, as a ship's captain should, and each man was a dependable and motivated part of the whole. Most were cross-trained in several fields of expertise, and all knew what to do without having to be told.

"I'm heading back to see if I can help. I'll see about getting comm back on line." Vaana said, as she left the bridge again.

"We should distribute the portables to the crew, and use the radio to communicate until the comm is back on line." said Califas.

"Is comm down only in engineering? Let's find out where it's out, and get the radios there." said Munen. "How long will backup power keep the lights on?…"

There was a lot to do, to get the ship back in operation.

2

We'll all die sometime

It wasn't good news, but then again they were all still alive. The exchanger unit is where the major work of converting power levels in the engine is done. Going from raw reactor level power to controlled thrust stream power is a volatile and dangerous process. Unlike a military ship where the exchanger is designed to bypass a lot of the intermediary power levels (if necessary) and go almost instantly from a dead stop to full thrust, a commercial vessel like a mining ship uses all the intermediary power levels during acceleration. Accelerating in this manner is loosely similar to a gear box going from low gear to high, one gear at a time. The trade-off is a much shorter operational lifespan for the military ship's exchanger, versus a much longer MTBF (Mean-Time-Between-Failure) for the commercial ship's exchanger which comes with the accompanying reduction in operating cost.

During normal operation the exchanger is sealed, and it is quarantined from the crew for safety reasons. Catastrophic failure of the exchanger results in only one thing – destruction of the ship. Such a failure had not been recorded in many tanrhas, since the development of the Echo class of engines. Exchangers had developed into one of the most important parts of an engine, and also one of the most reliable. The Orysta had not been destroyed, but the leaking plasma stream had damaged the exchanger control unit, the internal containment unit, and the engine control computer – and that was just some of the larger stuff. Multiple smaller and interconnected systems were also damaged. Some beyond repair. This situation had been discussed and analyzed over and over again, by all the crew members. In a situation like this, you wanted all the available minds working on a solution.

Several emergency beacons had already launched – you never want to depend on just one message in a bottle, even if the bottle has its own navigation and communication system. Beacons had only a limited propulsion system, which was designed to position them at a stable point in space – a point not immediately affected by planetary gravity or other forces that could pull them to their destruction. More would be launched at intervals determined by the ship's main computer, to form a trail from the point of engine failure to the arrival at the planned destination.

It would take time before any help arrived – if it ever did. The history of space travel had too many instances of lost ships, never heard from again. You don't depend on hope when you are the crew of an inter-galactic ship – of any type. The Orysta was well equipped. It had a machine shop, mining equipment, some raw materials, and a skilled crew. They could literally build another ship if they had to, but they couldn't manufacture the sophisticated equipment that made one easier to run. And they couldn't manufacture an engine capable of inter-galactic travel.

The plan was straight forward. They would land on the first suitable stellar body, re-enforce any weakened sections of the hull, repair as much damage as possible, replace damaged safety systems with spares, bypass anything that couldn't be repaired, and if that wasn't enough they would manually control any other systems. A lot of the crew were ex-military, and if there was one thing you learned in the military it was how to work with minimal or damaged equipment. But before any of the major repairs and fabrication could be done, they had to get the ship landed – without breaking it. A ship adrift in space was exposed to too many dangers.

The odds weren't very good. All the factors involved with the loss of their engine were stacked against them. The timing was uncanny. They were at maximum-cruise-normal speed when the engine failed. Now they were carrying too much momentum, too close to the destination, with no effective and controllable way of dissipating the energy. And then there was the IGT!

They were presently in the Vialactea galaxy, which by inter-galactic law meant they were restricted in their actions. This was an occupied galaxy, and although the native species had not yet perfected space travel, they did have the technology to detect space travelers. By law, they would have to do everything within their means to avoid contact with the natives, or exposure of their presence, as long as these actions did not endanger the crew. "THE CREW" is what the law stated in simple and unambiguous terms, and this law had sent a lot of good people to prison, as well as costing companies a lot of value in fines. When the law was first instituted, some had thought the protection of their ship was implied by the law, but this was only true if it directly affected the safety of the crew.

There was a well known saying throughout the Interconnected Galaxies Treaty (the IGT) signatories – "The law has no mercy for the ignorant or the stupid." To be qualified to be a member of an inter-galactic ship's crew, every crew member had to be knowledgeable in inter-galactic law. It didn't matter if you were a doctor, an engineer, or a cook. Every member of every crew of every type of ship was regularly tested on their knowledge. Changes in the law were disseminated to all member species, and a vessel's legal database was verified and updated as part of its normal maintenance procedures. Every operational space dock was liable for legal action if they failed to update a ship's law database. If the new law was complicated, or had potential to be misunderstood, the crew of any docking ship were given instruction on its meaning and associated penalties. No one was exempt, and your participation in the instruction was logged by computer, sent to the Distributed Registries Exchange and your employer's base of operation.

The Distributed Registries Exchange, besides being a location where a lot of inter-galactic documentation was accessible, also handled the confirmation, registration, and transmission of legal agreements, trade exchanges, and disputes and resolutions. They were also the entity that gave legal registration to new discoveries and creations (know as "Ds and Cs",and often written DandC). These were extremely important for business. A DandC gave an individual or company the legal protection to develop and market a new product or idea, without having it stolen by others. In some galaxies the DandC was better than having a large diameter energy weapon when it came to protecting your rights and profits. Established law in this field had been so sharply honed and defined, it left no room for legal maneuvering, manipulation, or interpretation. Anyone who tried to illegally violate the DandC of another was either a great fool, or a criminal. Violations of DandC had caused devastating and expensive wars, so there was no tolerance for violators. Even species that normally didn't get along with each other, would come together to apprehend and prosecute (or destroy) these violators. It didn't matter if you didn't like your intergalactic neighbor, as long as there was peace between your worlds. Throughout the IGT membership, DandC law was one of the primary tenets of inter-planetary relationships, and was never taken lightly. Neither was any law that dealt with non-treaty galaxies, and those were the laws that had direct effect on the Orysta right now – that is, those laws and the fact that they had no engine.

Originally it was going to be a simple, and straight forward mission. They had done many of them before. You traveled to the selected location, mined the ore or element quickly, and left quietly. In non-treaty galaxies there were no resorts, bars, vacation spots, or off-ship entertainment, because there was "NO INTENTIONAL CONTACT!". That was IGT law, so there was no reason to stay longer than necessary. Once on site the crew was usually divided into four shifts, and the operation would run around the clock until the job was finished. When the hold was full or the raw material ran out, you turned the ship around and headed home.

But now they were adrift. Backup maneuvering thrusters were available, but had a limited operational lifetime, and once used up they were gone. There was no way to recharge or replace them in space – they weren't designed for that. They were strictly emergency equipment – except that now, they had become primary equipment, and they were a poor substitute. They could be turned on, and they could be turned off – and that was it. Old technology, that created thrust by burning a hybrid fuel propellant, the thrusters were usually installed and replaced at prescribed maintenance cycles without ever being used. Now the wisdom of having them was very apparent to the crew of the Orysta. Advanced technology can sometimes breed complacency.

There was some good news – and of course, more bad news. The good news was that the engine room was back to normal temperature, and re-pressurized. Also, their drift path was taking them straight to the Orysta's original objective. It was the orbiting moon of the only planet sustaining life in this solar system. A survey mission had detected rare minerals and metals on this moon. Enough to have made this a very profitable journey. But mining was no longer the priority – survival was.

The bad news was that even under these circumstances they had to follow the law to the best of their ability, without jeopardizing the safety of the crew. "Safety of the crew" had a very limited legal interpretation, as many companies and crews now paying the penalty had found out. That meant absolutely no intentional contact with the indigenous species, which

22

meant they were on their own. They were approaching from the opposite side of the moon, so would be concealed from detection by the inhabited planet. But, since it was calculated to be a survivable impact, intentionally missing the moon to avoid crashing was not an option. Doing that would expose them to detection by the planet's inhabitants – which would put them in violation of IGT law. The same restriction held for orbiting the moon before landing – safer, but again making them more detectable. The level of technology of the inhabitants was not well known.

It would take time, but once they were landed and the ship secured, they should be able to make the repairs and modifications needed to safely get them headed back home. That meant that they would have to camouflage the ship so as not to be spotted as the moon rotated. There would be no rush on most of the system repairs, since without the main engine being fully operational the journey back home would take a long, long, long time – plenty of time to fix things along the way. The engine was the priority, but the odds of repairing it were low. Regaining partial thrust was not in doubt, but that's a very slow way to travel between galaxies. Hopefully a rescue ship would soon be sent.

3

All hands meeting

The final meeting before landing the ship on the the moon was to keep the crew informed and up to date, as well as to make necessary adjustments to their plans. Munen heard the thumping sound from the hull, and knew another beacon had launched – that was good. But Plessa had reported that not all the emergency beacons had functioned after launch, and several had not launched. That meant the physical trail of beacons had gaps, and would be hard to follow. Still, all the failed units had not been followed by a second failure in the sequence, so the gaps probably were not so large as to prevent rescue personnel from determining their path. Also, the mining company knew where they were headed, and would supply this information to rescue and military forces. They were very lucky to have reached their planned destination – not all ships in similar situations had been. There is always something reassuring about having ground below your feet, even if it is ground without a breathable atmosphere.

The main computer had also been making blind broadcasts since the accident. These were encrypted for security purposes, but official Rescue and Military personnel would have the ability to decrypt them. This was done for the safety of the crew and ship, and of course the profits. The problem with this galaxy was that there were no communications relays, and the chance of the Orysta's signals being received was very small.

There were bad actors out there that would love to find a crippled ship to scavenge, and the crew were never left alive. Mining ships were especially targeted, and best when their hold was full of cargo. Pirates often would stay hidden until the mining was completed, and then attack the ship – much more profitable for them. The penalty for piracy was summary execution. There was no discretion in the matter. Personnel of any IGT vessel that had captured pirates, be they Captain or cook, were legally required to execute them – in the quickest, and not necessarily the most humane manner. The act could not be countermanded by any authority on the vessel. This was normally not a problem since captured pirates only became prisoners because they were trying to kill you and the pirate was disabled in battle and immobile on the ground. In regards to pirates, captivity was a misnomer that usually meant the nearest crew member would, without regret, terminate the disabled pirate with the most convenient instrument at hand.

The encrypted transmissions were also a way for businesses to protect the location of their mining operation. New discoveries were usually distant from home base, and a lot of time passed between discovery and actually getting equipment on location. When a valuable deposit was discovered, the only real claim to it was when a crew was on site and working. Mining operations like this one did not file a mission plan, as civilian transports did. The filed plan would have alerted authorities if they hadn't returned home in the planned time frame, and initiated a rescue operation.

The mining company would eventually realize they were overdue, and send their own rescue ship, but would not immediately notify Rescue authorities – they would have to divulge the location of the find if they did. Better to check it out themselves and maintain confidentiality – there were a lot of reasons why a ship might be long overdue that were not life and death situations. Once the location was made public, and a rescue operation started, any of a number of other competitors would either send out a ship, or divert one in the area to find out if the product had been mined – and if not, they would mine it themselves, legally, saving the cost involved in finding it. Every crew member realized this when they accepted the job. So the Orysta crew members were not very worried or depressed about spending three to four times as long on the job as planned, because one way or another they were certain they would not have to make the whole journey back at sub-galactic speed. True, they would only earn base pay on this first trip, but if everything went well they would be back to complete the operation.

Inter-galactic transmissions were not possible from Vialactea, but there were relay stations established in every well traveled galaxy and every large void in between, and each relay station would re-transmit to the next, and so on until every galaxy in the IGT would receive the signal. Any inter-galactic ships that received it would relay the transmission as well – it was an automatic computerized protocol required by the SFT (Sanction of Free Transit clause) in the IGT. If just one relay or ship received the Orysta's signal it would get to the authorities and the mining company.

All of the crash pods on Orysta had been tested, and all were functioning – one for each crew member, and four spares. All equipment and supplies had been secured in the best manner possible. Communications to all parts of the ship had been re-established by one means or another. They had supplies to last them for quite a long journey home, which would probably be the case with the engine partially or non functional. Preliminary evaluation indicated that partial thrust could be achieved after some repair and modification – it was another good/bad situation. Good they would still be alive to make the journey, and bad that it would be such a long one if no one found them first. On the other hand, with the engine unable to develop full power, fuel consumption would be minimal, and there would be plenty of it to power all of their other needs. In all, they were in better shape than most case histories on the books. Good and bad. And there were a lot of other things that could prevent their rescue – but that was something to think about after landing.

4

This is not going to be a gentle landing

They still had too much forward momentum. There was no atmosphere on this moon, so there wouldn't be any frictional deceleration. The forward thrusters alone wouldn't have enough power to slow them down enough, so they were going to perform a maneuvering deceleration. This required that the ship be pivoted around in ninety arcleeson increments, and the thrusters on that part of the ship facing the moon would be fired until depleted. On the final pivot, the forward thrusters would be fired to complete the deceleration – as much as they would be able to. Some circumference thrusters would be needed for the landing maneuvers, and would be reserved and only used as necessary to position the ship for landing. All this would be done as the ship continued to move toward that moon. They would only have one chance to intercept it.

Even if everything went perfectly, they had no fine attitude control. Automatic control by the main computer had been damaged. Munen had never before given much thought to how many systems were routed through the engine compartment. With only partial computer control of the ship's systems, everything would have to be done manually. The main computer would monitor the approach, calculate the required maneuvers, and provide verbal and visual information and guidance to the pilots.

'*Training – training – training.*' he thought, as he looked over at Califas and gave thanks once again for the man he was working with. Intul-sil-Califas was as capable of flying the ship as he was, and no doubt would soon be offered the captain's chair on another vessel. They went through the practice scenario again.

During the speed reduction maneuvers, they also had to change the ships direction slightly. To take every possible advantage of all the influences affecting the ship, they had to point the nose of the ship against the direction of the moon's rotation, and change the longitudinal attitude so that the top of the ship pointed in that direction of rotation. They would then perform a flare maneuver at the correct altitude, to change the direction of momentum to match the rotation. This would reduce their speed relative to the moon's surface. It wouldn't be a major reduction, but every little bit would help in the final outcome.

Then there were the constantly changing factors that would affect their landing. As they got closer to the moon, the pull of its gravity would accelerate the ship – the opposite of what they needed. As they got even closer, the gravity of the planet that the moon orbited would also affect them, adding to the acceleration force. They would in fact be carrying too much momentum. With the present orientation of the ship, the moon's rotation was from right to left. The ship had to be pointed to the moon's right edge, and rotated axially ninety arcleesons. When they flared, the bottom of the ship would be facing the surface of the moon, and the nose would be pointing in the direction of rotation.

Every loose item on the ship had been secured by the crew. By any definition, this was going to be be a crash landing, but the impact should be survivable. In fact, if everything went correctly, the damage to the ship should be minimal. However, it would be a shame to survive the landing, only to be injured or killed by a flying gorbel racket or bliml pitcher. But something would break loose, no matter how careful they were – it was Ilmert's law – "If it can go badly, it will go very badly". All the equipment, tools, and various objects on the ship were designed for normal environmental forces, but the abrupt deceleration of a crash landing was not normal.

As an extra precaution, all crew members would be wearing environmental suits. All crew members that were not necessary to perform the landing would also be in their designated crash pods. These pods were designed to surround the person with impact absorbing material and could supply air and communications. In situations where the crew member sustained radiation damage, the pod became a medically sterile environment where life functions could be reduced to near death levels. This would sustain the person while minimizing tissue death, giving them a better chance to be rescued and treated. Normally, even the flight crew would be in the pods, but this was going to be a manual landing without either an engine or full systems control by the computer. The flight crew had to be at the helm for this one. Although the command and engineering seats had full body restraint capability, they had no life support functions. If the helm was breached, or lost normal life support, the pilot, copilot, and engineer would be killed.

5

Form follows function

The Orysta was a beautiful ship. Beautiful, that is, in the eyes of those who understood its function. Shaped like a rectangular box with tapering ends, on a width to length ratio of five by thirteen, not counting the overhanging extension above the helm view port, the engine nozzles at the rear, and extensible thrust directors around the periphery of the rear, it was designed to haul cargo – lots of cargo if they were successful. Mainly it was a huge empty box wrapped by equipment bays and living quarters with a very powerful engine attached. It was up to the crew to fill that box with valuable materials. The amount of room taken up by the habitable spaces for the crew to live and work, was very small compared to the overall size of the ship.

An inter-galactic mining ship had no need of aerodynamic sophistication. There was no pointy end or large lifting surfaces to restrict internal space or add weight. It only traveled through an atmosphere when the destination made it necessary, and then it only needed to be a powered glider. Maneuvering was achieved mainly by using the tremendous thrust of the engine. In an atmosphere, the Orysta produced a lot of drag, which it used in conjunction with that thrust to turn, slow down, and stop very effectively in tight surroundings. It also had retractable airfoil surfaces that extended along the full length of the bottom edge on both sides. Looking extremely stubby when compared to the overall size of the ship, these could supply enough lift to take some advantage of atmosphere for large radius turning. This technique was used when surveying vast land masses for raw materials. In fact, since they ran the entire length of the ship, the total effective surface area of the airfoils was very large. No, the Orysta was not designed for atmospheric travel – that was a secondary consideration. But in open space, where it spent most of its time, there was no drag to fight or use to advantage – only mass to move. In open space it didn't matter what shape that mass was.

The Orysta's landing gear were large and extremely strong structures. They consisted of hydraulic, pneumatic, and mechanical sub-assemblies that worked together to protect the ship. For those who appreciated what was involved, they were true works of engineering art. Often a mining operation required landing the ship on very rugged, broken, non-level terrain. The gear had to take the abuse of landing on these uneven surfaces, and then support the ship with its often heavy loads. Looking like hairy skids attached to shock absorbers, they were designed to gradually dissipate landing impact forces before damage occurred to the superstructure of the ship. The "hair" like structures were long, and strong fingers made of gordaelate, which dissipate energy by flexing, and pushing against each other to catch and hang onto pointy surfaces such as jagged rock faces. Both hydraulic and pneumatic absorbers softened the contact and settling of the ship's weight. These could be adjusted to level the ship in two axes, up to forty arcleesons. When the gear performed their job, the crew would only feel and hear the bump-and-thump of a normal landing.

It would be the landing gear that would get the worst of the impact forces when they contacted the moon. Once the ship had been maneuvered into the correct orientation, there would be no way to stop its motion other than contact friction with the surface. If the touchdown area was a smooth, prepared surface there would be no problem at all, but this was a rough, uneven surface, pocked with craters and rocks of varying dimensions. The area selected was the best one available under the circumstances. There were no large protruding features or crevices – large being a relative description. Since this would be a three to six larn long traveling landing, the landing gear would be impacting an unknown number of surface imperfections before the ship's momentum was dissipated, and they came to a stop – not the type of landing the gear was designed for.

6

Contact

The ship's main computer communicated with almost all of the systems and sub-systems on the ship by multiple methods, depending on how important the system was considered to be to the safety of the crew, and success of the mission. Modern Systems Control and Communications was a technological wonder, and a challenging career field in itself. Communications channels on the Orysta consisted of highly multiplexed, and highly encrypted, super-high frequency signals that were sent by electromagnetic transmissions, fiber optic cables, induced gravity waves, and even some electrical signals over metal conductors (which even included using parts of the ship's structure). These multiple channels of communications gave redundancy when needed, and encryption gave protection from unexpected interference. All of these systems usually involved some sort of computer processing.

Backup systems, especially those that no one ever expected to use (like the emergency thrusters) had no multichannel redundancy and no sophistication. They were manual operation only, single circuit systems which meant that a crew member had to take complete control of their use. Even the control panel display with which the operator would activate these, was basically just a fancy looking face on a switch that connected two wires together to complete a circuit. There wasn't even any monitoring capability by the main computer, although it could measure the thruster force on the hull and could therefore determine if they were firing or not. By timing the length of the activation, it could calculate the effect on the ship.

The display screens at both pilot stations and the engineering station showed a diagram of the external view of the Orysta. Dark blue dots on the diagram indicated the location of each emergency maneuvering thruster. They could be fired and shut down with a touch of a finger on the screen. Touch one or more dots and those thrusters fired, and the blue dot turned bright red. Touch it again and the thruster would shut down, and the dot turned blue again. It was a simple toggle signal – touch once and it's on, and touch again and it's off. Since these were rarely used backup systems, they were not under the control of the main computer. The signals were routed from the display console to a demultiplexer which then sent them via individual wire signal paths to the associated thruster. All of the thrusters would be tested during the braking maneuver – those not actually needed for the maneuver would be initiated for a very short burst to confirm they were operational. The consumption of the small amount of thruster propellant was a price that had to be paid. Calculations were based on known available thrust, so they had to know if there were any defective units.

Califas would be controlling the thrusters. Munen would act as backup, and Plessa would be keeping an eye on the ship's systems and thruster functionality. The main computer would monitor all sensors and report verbally and visually how the ship was responding. Hull pressure sensors in the vicinity of each thruster would measure the force generated by them, and from that the actual thrust could be calculated.

"Confirm all crew secured in their pods." said Munen.

"*All crew members secure in crash stations,*" said the computer, "*except for the Captain, First Officer, and Chief Engineer.*"

31

Munen noted that the main computer's voice had changed again into the very commanding male voice. This meant the computer had marked this time as the beginning of a dangerous event. It was. Even if everything went as well as was possible, the ship was going to be damaged – and if the ship was damaged, the crew would be in danger. He realized how much more he preferred the computer's female voice.

Their speed was increasing now, even though they were not generating any thrust. The ship was being affected by the combined gravitational pull of the planet and its moon. Both spacial bodies were in line with the ship's path, and their combined gravitational influence was at its maximum – Ilmert's Law. If they were to hit the moon at this speed it would be unsurvivable. It was time to decelerate the ship.

"Attitude stabilization systems." prompted Munen.

"Attitude stabilization set to Auto." came the response from Califas.

"Initiate lateral pitch – ninety arcleesons." commanded Munen.

"Lateral pitch plus ninety arcleesons." replied Califas, as he touched the appropriate indicators on his control panel screen. The lower front and the upper aft thrusters fired.

"Terminate thrusters now." said the computer, and Califas quickly touched the same indicators again, shutting down the thrusters. They had only fired for a fraction of a fracin. The ship rotated around its lateral axis, accelerating briefly and then slowing until it stopped.

"Plus zero nine zero arcleeson rotation." said the computer.

It was a perfect burn. Both pilots looked at each other, surprise and delight showing in their expressions. They had expected it to be close, but not dead on. What they had not realized was that when the ship's main computer calculated the burn time it was taking into account Califas' reaction time, based on his medical records and the continually ongoing physiological monitoring. It had factored in not only his physical state, including level of fatigue, but also the time it took the electrical impulses traveling from his brain to reach his fingers. The computer knew the mass of the ship, and measured its acceleration as it was rotated by the thrusters.

It then calculated the amount of time it would continue to rotate before stopping. From all the information available, it then calculated exactly how long after he had initiated the thrusters to notify Califas to shut them down.

"Fire lower central thrusters on my command – full burn – Actuate!" said Munen.

Califas fired the thrusters. In ten fracins the thrusters had used up their fuel, and died.

"Lower central thrusters expended." stated the computer. *"Total speed reduction seven percent."*

"First phase went well." said Munen. "Let's do it again."

"Ready when you are." said Califas.

"Initiate lateral pitch – plus zero nine zero arcleesons." commanded Munen.

"Lateral pitch plus zero nine zero arcleesons." said Califas, once again firing the lower front and the upper aft thrusters.

"Terminate thrusters now." said the computer again, and again Califas quickly shut them down.

Once again the ship rotated and stopped.

"Plus zero nine zero arcleeson rotation." said the computer.

"What?" asked Califas, confused at this occurring twice.

"I don't… What is going on here?" asked Munen. "Confirm our attitude."

"I don't believe it either," said Plessa, "but it's true. We've just completed two perfect ninety arcleeson rotations. Instruments confirm it."

"Under manual control?" said Munen, in disbelief.

"Yes," said Plessa, with a smile on his face, "under manual control. Looks like we have a super pilot on the bridge."

They both looked at Califas, who had a big grin on his face. Munen shook his head in disbelief. But if the computer and instruments indicated they had done it, then he had to accept it. They continued on with the procedure.

"Fire rear thrusters – full burn – Now!" said Munen.

Califas did so. The thrusters burned until exhausted, then died.

"*Rear thrusters expended.*" stated the computer. "*Total speed reduction forty-seven percent.*"

"One more time." said Munen, looking over at Califas, who nodded. "Whenever you're ready."

"Initiating ninety arcleeson rotation – Now!" said Califas, as he touched the control panel.

"*Terminate thrusters now.*" said the computer once again.

Once again Califas shut down the thrusters, and the ship rotated and stopped.

"*Plus zero nine zero arcleeson rotation.*"

Califas looked at Munen, waiting for the next command. Munen just looked back at him for a few seconds.

"I'm not even going to comment." said Munen in disbelief. "If it's not broke, don't fix it. Fire upper central thrusters when you're ready. Full burn."

"Magic fingers." said Califas, wiggling his fingers and smiling.

Then he tapped the control panel screen. The thrusters fired, then burned out.

"*Upper central thrusters expended.*" stated the computer. "*Total speed reduction fifty-four percent.*"

They repeated the procedure once more. Another perfect ninety arcleeson rotation. Plessa also shook his head in disbelief. Califas then fired the forward thrusters, which burned until exhausted.

"Forwarded thrusters expended." stated the computer. *"Failure on thrusters three, seven, and twelve. Total speed reduction ninety-four percent."*

Ninety-four percent speed reduction using only the emergency thrusters, and not all of them at that. Not bad, but not as good as needed. Ninety-eight percent would have been ideal. Munen wondered if the three thrusters that failed would have given them the extra four percent – Ilmert's law at work. Ninety-eight percent reduction would have left just enough forward speed to allow the landing gear to dissipate the remaining energy by contact friction, as the ship settled against the moon's surface in a relatively short landing run. But that was wishful thinking – they couldn't afford to use the remaining thrusters for further speed reduction.

The thrusters that were still functional were needed to maneuver the ship into the landing attitude. It would be a one shot event – they had to get it right the first time. They didn't have fine enough control of the thrusters to make subtle adjustments as they were touching down. It all had to be calculated, implemented, and fingers crossed – and there was still the unknown factor of possible thruster failure. Any use of thrusters while they were making contact would guarantee an uncontrollable crash. If they touched down with too much vertical velocity they could jam the gear up into the fuselage – not good at all.

7

Fingers Crossed

"Three larns to attitude adjustment point." said the computer.

Munen, Califas, and Plessa were at their stations, securely restrained, with crash systems armed. Califas had his index finger touching the display screen, pointing at the next step of the emergency checklist – it was an important one.

"Two larns to attitude adjustment point."

Munen was intent on the navigational displays, cross-checking the computer's announcements.

"Suspend Command Security protocols." read Califas from the emergency checklist, as he and Plessa looked at Munen.

Munen looked back and nodded. All three placed one hand on the display screen in front of them. Their identities were checked and confirmed by the ship's computer.

"Suspend Command Security Protocols." said Munen.

Each of the other men stated the same thing aloud. The verbal declarations were required for the official ship's log to record their intentions. On their screens, next to the green outline that surrounded their hand, was displayed an alpha-numeric keypad. Each man carefully entered his own security code.

The codes were one of the several security measures used to make sure the ship could not be controlled by an unauthorized person. They were memorized as part of the acceptance procedure of their respective command positions. They were never written down or recorded in any way on the ship, and never shared with any other person. To do so could put the lives of other crew members in jeopardy. Even the main computer did not store the codes as data. Instead, it used a variable algorithm with a derived base that was different for each person, and every ship's computer used a different method to determine the base. Since the base and the method for determining it was different for each ship, and each person, it was considered uncrackable – certainly uncrackable in any practical amount of time.

Even with the computational power of the main computer, it took some time to extract the codes. The main computer had begun the calculations at the beginning of the deceleration procedure. It had completed the calculations just a few fracins ago. Six command security codes had been derived.

Three other crew members also had Command Authorization security codes – and no other crew member knew who they were. It could be the ship's Head Cook, or the Chief Mining Engineer, or one of the maintenance crew. If the bridge staff were incapacitated or lost, one or all of those unknown three could take command of the ship and the main computer would recognize their authority to do so. All of these precautions were necessary because there were a lot of dangers in space travel. Some were physical, and some were criminal.

Suspension of the Command Security Protocols was necessary because as a safety precaution they would be in environmental suits, in case the worst happened and the hull was breached. Once in the suits normal crew recognition procedures could not be carried out by the main computer. Without the suspension of the protocols, and with the computer unable to confirm their identities, they would effectively lose control of the ship – the main computer would not accept their commands. With the protocols suspended anyone could command the ship's computer, and therefore anyone could control the ship. Even abandoned ships maintained their Command Security protocols by requirement of law.

It was something that was rarely done, and required at least three of the highest ranking authorized crew members to concur on the procedure. To authorize this was to invite an official investigation into the reason for doing so. If it all went well, and everyone and the ship returned home safely, there would still be an investigation into their actions. All members of the crew, and the ship itself, would be held inactive until the investigation was completed. This meant no work – and no income – for the crew, and the temporary loss of the use of the ship by the company. A lot of people were going to be unhappy.

"Command Security protocols suspended." stated the computer. *"Authorization Artau-sil-Munen – Grilik of the Orysta. Authorization Intul-sil-Califas – Tahn-grilik of the Orysta. Authorization Benua-sil-Plessa – Chief Engineer of the Orysta."*

It was done. They all knew what they were in for when they made it back home – if they made it home. It was time for the next step.

8

The Final Phase

The environmental suits were a wonder of modern engineering and chemistry. The middle layer was a carbon fiber micro-lattice, that kept the suit very light, allowed it to flex without loss of function, and acted as a superb insulator. The structure was similar to the metallic macro-lattice that formed several layers of the ship's hull. Biometric sensors continually monitored the wearer's physical condition, and transmitted the data to both the ship's main computer and the medical computer. The inner layer contained medicinal infusers of various types which could treat minor physical injuries, physiological stress from migraines to fatigue, or if necessary induce a comatose state. If the person was injured, the medical computer initiated rescue operations while continuing to monitor the wearer and the automated response of the suit.

Depending on the circumstances, if the wearer's life functions ceased the main computer marked the crew member as deceased, or missing:presumed lost, and notified the other crew members. The suit's outer layer contained various electronic devices that allowed tracking, communications, and environmental analysis. And all of that was just the more obvious stuff. There were other functions, like protection from radiation. If the suit was punctured, it could seal itself and reestablish environmental integrity – if the damage wasn't too extensive. But for all its wonder and capability, it was still a space suit – it still hindered movement, still dulled your natural senses, and still made everything slightly more difficult to do. It was like a second skin – but a thick second skin.

"Initiate Tertiary Safety Protocol." commanded Munen.
"Tertiary safety protocol initiated." said the computer.

Technology is a great thing. It allows normal people to do extraordinary things. It extends their senses and capabilities. It allows them to survive in deadly environments. But it can not overcome the laws of physics. Those laws decreed that at the speed they would be moving at the time of contact with the surface, the forces that would be experienced would be so great that no normal person would be able to control the movement of their body, or stop themselves from being violently thrown and becoming a messy splat of smashed bones and crushed organs as their bodies impacted the front of the bridge. The only function they would be able to control was their thoughts. That was why the tertiary safety protocol was necessary.

Under control of the main computer, the seats the three men were sitting in moved like they were alive. They swiveled around and reclined so that the men were supine and facing the rear of the ship. From the sides bloomed contoured extensions that molded to, and secured the head, upper body, upper arms, waist area, and legs, while allowing the lower arms a small amount of movement. The men were effectively trapped in their seats.

Smaller control screens pivoted up until they were in a position that the men could reach with their hands.

This was one of the oldest and least used safety system in this modern era of space travel. It was the most basic system of protection available to crew members. It restrained and cushioned the body from impact forces, but also made it difficult to function because it limited physical motion. But there were times when its use was necessary, and the only practical way to accomplish what was needed. Normally, no crew member would be on the bridge during an emergency landing – they would be in protective crash stations where they would control and monitor systems through the main computer. With so many systems on the ship damaged however, and the main computer limited in its control of the remaining systems, there was no choice. It was a section of the Flight Manual's Emergency Checklist that was rarely used in actual situations – and even though they practiced it in training sessions, like the emergency thrusters, no one ever really expected to have to use it. Now they had to.

Above them, a three dimensional depiction of the view in front of the ship appeared. This would give them a real-time view of what was going on outside the ship. It was actually a better perspective than they would have had looking out of the view port, and it displayed a wider angle of view.

"One larn to attitude adjustment point." said the main computer.
"Here we go." said Munen.
"Engineering ready." said Plessa.
"Ready here." said Califas.
"Grilik has control of the ship." said Califas, reading from the checklist. "Engineer has authority to override on exigent circumstances."
"I've got the ship." confirmed Munen.
"Acknowledged." said Plessa. "Releasing final beacon." He touched his control panel, and the emergency beacon fired, and navigated away from the ship. "Beacon away."

With those words Plessa's level of tension rose greatly. He was now in a dangerously responsible position, but still not as bad a position as Munen. It was Munen who was the ship's Commander, and it was his responsibility if anything went wrong. Plessa would monitor what Munen was doing and the resulting response of the ship. If the response was not as expected, due to system malfunctions or unexpected internal or external influences, he had the authority to negate Munen's control and do what he considered was necessary to save the ship and all their lives. This was necessary so that Munen could give his full attention to the landing. But again, any results – good or bad – due to Plessa's actions would still be the responsibility of Munen, whether his hands were on the controls or not. Plessa's responsibility was to save their lives if something unknown to Munen went wrong – a heavy burden. Munen's responsibility was to take the blame if it then went badly.

The final beacon that was launched carried additional information to that of the previous ones. Besides all the ships logs, system status recordings, Command Authorizations, and navigational information that the other beacons also had, there were personal messages by every member of the crew. If things went wrong – if they didn't survive the landing – if for any reason they were never found or rescued, there would still be a very good chance the beacon would be recovered. The messages would be delivered to family members. They were a last goodbye.

"*Initiate longitudinal rotation now.*" stated the computer.

Califas had been waiting for the instruction, and using both hands, he immediately fired the lower right side and upper left side thrusters. The ship began to rotate around its longitudinal axis.

"*Terminate thrusters now.*" said the computer.

Califas quickly shut them down.

"*Zero nine zero arcleeson longitudinal rotation.*" stated the computer.

"Good job." said Munen.

Now the top of the ship faced in the rotational direction of the moon. All three men relaxed slightly, as they waited for the next step in the procedure.

"Extend landing gear zero point seven zero. Cant plus zero point two five." said the computer.

Plessa slid his finger down one side of his control screen to the proper position, and then to the right at a slight angle. Seventy percent extension would give the ship the best impact absorption for this type of landing. Twenty five percent cant would allow the gear skids to make contact at the rear edge first. As the front of the skids came down, more gordaelate fingers would make contact and begin to dissipate the energy of their momentum. The cant angle also compensated for the changing direction of force as the ship contacted the surface, and its weight settled onto the gear while they were moving forward. It would be a rapid deceleration.

The ship shuddered a little as the gear doors unlatched and opened. Then came the subtle, familiar vibration that indicated the gear were extending. Plessa monitored the graphic indicator that reflected the physical position of the gear. The vibration stopped, and a slight "thunk" was heard as the gear locked in position.

"Landing gear at seven zero percent extension and plus two five percent cant." said Plessa.

"Confirmed. Landing gear zero seven zero percent extension plus zero two five percent cant." replied the computer.

9

Touch Down

"Zero point one larn. Begin flare maneuver. Phase 1. Designated bottom thrusters." stated the main computer.

The time had come to redirect the ship's momentum. There was no atmosphere to take advantage of, so the ship's lifting surfaces would be useless for this. All they had were the thrusters that had been kept in reserve for this maneuver. If it was done successfully, the ship would move in an arcing path that would change from heading directly toward the edge of the moon to traveling in a declining path parallel to the surface.

It was now up to Munen to follow the direction of the ship's computer. It had to be his hand that input the final corrections. Califas was more than capable of handling the landing, but he wanted there to be no doubt as to who's control the ship was under at the time of contact with the surface, so that there would be no doubt as to who's actions were responsible for whatever happened. On his display screen was the diagram showing all the bottom thrusters. The designated ones he was to use were flashing. Munen poked at the display screen with his fingertips, quickly touching the control points, and the lower forward, mid, and aft thruster pairs fired. The force applied by the thrusters on the bottom of the ship acted on its forward motion, and the path changed from a straight line to the desired arc, with the nose of the ship still pointing at the surface. *'Vectors.'* Munen thought to himself, as he felt the ship changing direction. *'It's all in the vectors.'*

Their surface facing point of view was now useless to them. Because of their relative speed and proximity to the surface, and their lateral motion in the same direction the top of the ship was facing, the three dimensional image of the moon's surface became a blur.

"Designated bottom thrusters expended." stated the computer.

There were three main force vectors acting on their path of travel – their initial momentum towards the moon, the reaction to the thrusters just fired, and the pull of gravity from the aligned planet and moon. The second force was now influencing the first and third.

"Initiate phase 2. Rotate pitch thirteen arcleesons nose up surface relative. Designated forward lower and aft upper thrusters." stated the main computer.

Munen touched the control screen again, and the lower front and the upper rear thrusters fired. The ship began moving around its pitch axis. The downward pointing nose began moving up.

"Terminate thrusters now." said the computer.

Munen's fingers moved while the computer was still giving the instructions. The ship rotated through level to the moon's surface, then continued until the nose was slightly high relative to the surface of the moon. The three dimensional depiction now displayed a more normal approach to landing view, and they could better judge the closure rate with the ground as it came closer.

The adjustment took less than three fracins, and the ship stabilized in attitude. That was it. That was all they could do. They couldn't take the chance of firing any thrusters again. Now it was a matter of physics and luck – and waiting – but not for long.

"Plus one three arcleesons surface relative attitude." said the computer. *"Altitude zero point zero eight larn. Descent rate zero point zero zero six larn per fracin."*

'Huh!' thought Munen, surprised at the accuracy of the adjustment. *'I can do*

this as well as Califas.'

It was only a matter of fracins now. Thirteen arcleesons nose up pitch was just what was needed, but the descent rate was a little too fast. Five thousandths of a larn per fracin was the optimum rate, but the crude thruster control, and possibility of thruster failure meant they had to accept the compromise. Three thrusters had already failed during their maneuvers – it would be too much risk to try an adjustment now. The ship should tolerate the hard landing that was coming, and do so without damage – if nothing else went wrong.

"CONTACT IMMINENT." yelled Munen over the comm.

It wasn't necessary. The crew had been monitoring the procedure in their pods. Munen, Califas, and Plessa had their eyes locked on the three dimensional image in front of them, watching the ground get closer. There was nothing else they could do. With no atmosphere, there would be no pitch or roll adjustments they could make. They were just passive observers now.

"Contact in four fracins." said the computer. *"Three fracins... Two fracins... One fracin..."*

Chapter 2

The Beginning

Operation 361

1

August 4, 1981
1500 hours
The White House
Staff office in the West wing

Ransen Ramsdel looked around the office, and did what a man of his training always did – he checked for surveillance equipment. He didn't really expect to find any, but better safe than sorry. This was just an auxiliary office used by many staffers who performed various jobs throughout the White House. It did have one thing going for it that was necessary to this meeting – thick, sound deadening walls and doors. Still, you couldn't be too cautious with something like this – not in the present geopolitical climate. Ramsdel and the other man in the room occupied themselves with smalltalk, while waiting for the third member of the meeting to show up.

Ramsdel had been a member of the SAD for five years. He had

worked his way up the company ladder to Special Agent status and, until recently, had expected to continue rising in the organization. But if anyone looked at his classified employment record, they would see one other item appended to his status of 'Special' – stamped in large red letters at the top of each page were the words 'NON-INDICATED'. Non-indicated meant that he had been assigned a unique and out of the ordinary assignment. No one – not even the Oversight Committees of the Senate or the House of Representatives, could require him to explain what his assignment was. It was in fact a violation of federal law for them to officially inquire. Once designated, and assigned a mission, a Non-Indicated agent didn't even have to report to the CIA hierarchy. The designation of 'Non-Indicated' was only given to an agent who had accepted an assignment that was so dangerous, or so politically volatile that their physical or vocational survival was not likely. Very few people accepted such an assignment. Ramsdel was only aware of three other agents so designated in the whole history of the SAD – their official records no longer accessible to anyone except the President and the Director of the CIA. And now he was number four, which meant that if he failed in his mission he would either be at the end of his career – or the end of his life.

SAD – the Special Activities Division of the CIA – was unknown to the average American citizen, which was partly by design, and mostly by luck. Its existence was well documented public knowledge, but you had to have a reason to look for it to know about it. It wasn't advertised or promoted publicly. It was outside the scope of most people's every day lives, and that put it outside the sphere of their awareness. The SAD was the division of the CIA that handled Covert and "Special" activities. It was a very broad mandate, which allowed a lot of wiggle room in the limits of its authorization. As long as the SAD had a Presidential Finding issued by the President of the United States, it could acquire the financial backing it needed to carry out the mission. A Presidential Finding was what Ramsdel was here to get.

Ramsdel carried a soft, tan colored, leather brief case, in which there were three copies of a seven page typed document, a portable micro-cassette player, a ball point pen and mechanical pencil, and a few personal items – only what was necessary to accomplish the job at hand. This assignment was something he never would have conceived himself. It was completely outside his personal realm of thought. It was conceived by those unknown analysts in the agency, whose job it was to look ahead in time and predict possible world events – to predict economic and political conditions before they happened – to predict the rise and fall of nations, and wars not yet started – and they were very good at their jobs. The few times he was aware of that their opinion had been ignored by political policy makers, had ended in the country being embroiled in military actions that had cost thousands of American lives, and a very large part of the country's wealth. This had also caused some of the best of these analysts to sever their ties with the agency – after all, what good was it to do your best work just to be ignored but then proven correct. That was a formula for great frustration, and most people could only handle that so many times before it began to affect their mental and physical health.

Ramsdel didn't know how many of these analysts the agency had – that was classified of course, as were their identities. He knew something about how they worked though. Each had a field of expertise, and made predictions and observations within that field. Then their reports were gathered and compiled and analyzed by another group of specialists whose job was to find the coincidental threads among them. With enough of these threads, projections of the future could be deduced. Finally, this was condensed into a report that was then supplied to the appropriate decision makers in the intelligence community or the government.

The history of the CIA's success could be mapped by the times these analysts were in and out of favor by the federal bureaucrats. When intelligence organization haters were in power, and funding was cut, these analysts were usually some of the first to go since most were independent contractors. Failures in the agency's effectiveness soon followed. When a strong political leader was in office, funding was restored, and agency manning was rebuilt – with the agency's level of success increasing almost in direct proportion. It was ironic that the U.S. Congress, whose job it was to provide stability and security for the country, often was the cause of putting it at greater risk.

Ramsdel remembered clearly the meeting in his superior's office five months ago. He was handed a single sheet of paper describing the concept and goals of the project, and the risks involved, and asked simply if he wanted the assignment. He had one day to decide. He thought about it for a solid twenty-four hours, unable to sleep that night. It was the strangest thing he had ever heard of. He thought about the usual career pros and cons, and the technological challenges involved. He tried to imagine how he would accomplish it, and realized he didn't have a clue. He knew nothing about this type of thing. Hell, the world knew nothing about this type of thing, give or take a few arcane scientists. But from the moment he began to think about it, it was all he could think about. He also realized that accepting this assignment would also effectively end his present career path, and place him in a completely separate category. He would be creating a new governmental organization in which he only answered to himself, one other person in the CIA, and two people in the military – one of which was in the room with him at that moment. An organization that only four people in the world would be in control of – and two of them were inactive backups, who were there in case of emergency. It was in effect a two man operation. The decisions would be theirs, and good, patriotic Americans could die because of them. He had been on missions where people died – people he knew, and liked. Some had died within a few feet of him, his own life being spared only by a quirk of fate and a badly aimed bullet. But dying on this mission would be the stuff of nightmares – and he would be one of the men deciding to send some very brave people possibly to that nightmarish death.

2

Lt. Col. Robert Farber-Chatwell, USAF, worked for the Defense Intelligence Agency. The DIA's function is to be aware of, and prevent any strategic surprises – in short to know the enemy and what they are up to. The DIA's information, analysis, and conclusions are supplied to military heads, and defense planners. These people then decide where and how far up the command structure to delivery this information. The DIA's job is made a lot harder by departmental political infighting, corrupt politicians, megalomaniac bureaucrats, and constant budget cuts, to name a few of the detrimental factors directly affecting the effectiveness of the organization. But the DIA is not just made up of a bunch of analysts and information pushers hunched over long tables covered with maps and reams of statistics. They deploy to battle zones alongside the military warriors, and work in the field with inter-agency counterparts.

Farber-Chatwell walked with an almost imperceptible limp, caused by a wound he received during his military service in Vietnam. He had taught himself to ignore it, physically and mentally, and never spoke of it – not because of some kind of macho attitude, but because too many of his friends and comrades had suffered much more severe injuries. Many hadn't come back home. Farber-Chatwell considered it selfish and disrespectful – even an insult – to their memories to acknowledge his own minor injury. He knew who the real heroes were – and he didn't consider himself to be one of them.

The Purple Heart had been awarded to him and the other wounded men who had fought alongside him. His presently sat at the bottom of his sock drawer, also intentionally ignored. Farber-Chatwell would have given the medal back, but his now ex-wife threatened him with dire legal action and physical harm if he did. She maintained that the medal was not only a reflection of his bravery and patriotism, but also of what she had put up with as a military wife. She had waited for him to return home safely, and get back on his feet, before she left him. To her, that medal was as much a reflection of her honor as it was his. She told him in the foulest language he had ever heard her use that he would regret it if he ever tried to return it, and then she went to his Base Commander's office and told him that if he ever allowed Farber-Chatwell to return it she would take legal action against him, the base, and the U.S. Government. Before she drove away from Farber-Chatwell and the on-base housing she had lived in for over eleven years, she had made it very clear to every living person there that the medal was awarded to her just as much as it was to him.

When Farber-Chatwell was again fit for unrestricted duty, he accepted an assignment to the Defense Intelligence Agency, and over time had gained a reputation as the Go-to person for impossible jobs. Most intelligence operatives didn't get personal with lead, steel and gun powder, but Farber-Chatwell was a field agent in the truest sense of the phrase. His job was to go on operations behind enemy lines, to gather first hand intelligence. Sometimes he had been very skilled at his job, and other times had just been very lucky – and he knew it. He had a knack for recognizing the unseen possibilities others overlooked. It was the Director of the DIA and the Secretary of Defense who had jointly offered him this assignment. He was in fact the only candidate that they felt was qualified for the job. It was an impossible assignment to begin with, and the odds of success – and survival – were extremely low.

3

When the door to the room opened, both men turned, and stood upright at attention – a reflex action for Farber-Chatwell, but one Ramsdel performed only for people he respected. The last member of their party, Ronald Wilson Reagan, the fortieth president of the United States entered the room.

"Sit down gentlemen," said Reagan, as he went to the biggest and most comfortable chair in the room, "and let's get this done. I've got a lot on my mind right now, and too little time on my hands. I can give you twenty minutes."

"Thank you for agreeing to meet with us, Mr. President." said Farber-Chatwell.

"The only reason I agreed to this meeting was the high recommendation of your bosses. They seem to think very highly of you."

"Won't take any more of your time than necessary." said Ramsdel.

He took a folder marked 'SECRET – MPO' in bold red lettering from his briefcase, and handed it to the President. In the folder was a twenty-seven page brief, with each page titled 'Operation 361'.

"The first ten pages explain everything sir. The rest is just cost analysis and possible logistics details."

They sat silently while the President read the mission outline. The expression on his face changed as he read, from surprise, to astonishment, to anger, and through all of them again. When he was done, President Reagan looked up at the men in front of him, his eyebrows raised in incredulity of what he had read. He also had a little doubt about the sanity of the two men he was looking at.

"Are you SERIOUS?" he asked, with some anger and doubt in his voice. He was beginning to wonder if this was some kind of joke his senior staff had thought up – many of them did have a strange sense of humor.
"Yes sir." said Ramsdel.

The President looked at Farber-Chatwell for confirmation. He nodded his head in the affirmative.

"If I understand this correctly, this is more like a group suicide than a mission." said the President, his voice still angry, and growing louder. "Potentially and VERY LIKELY a suicide mission. Is that correct? This has never been done before, and according to your own report, is beyond the limits of our present capabilities. Who the hell are you going to get to go on this thing? You are effectively asking me to send people to their deaths – as an experiment!"
"We already have personnel, Mr. President," said Farber-Chatwell in a controlled and level voice. "willing to go now. All of them well aware of the mission risk profile. But as I point out in our proposed time-line, the actual mission wouldn't take place for at least another ten years. It will take us that long to prepare, work out the specifics, and take advantage of any

new technology that comes along. Possibly even longer. Choosing the volunteers will be one of the last things we do." He waited for a response from the President, but didn't get one.

"Some of our Top Secret research projects would amaze you, and the people conducting them are the best in their field. These are people whose vision of the future makes me feel like my brain is stuck in idle. It's only after they explain the science behind it that you can get just a basic understanding of what they are doing. These are brilliant minds, Mr. President. If only a fraction of them are fruitful, we should be able to successfully accomplish what is outlined in that brief." He paused again but still didn't get any reaction. He thought – hoped – this was a good sign.

"In the time frame laid out, we expect our capabilities will be far advanced from what we can do today, judging by the rate of advancement we've made in the last twenty years."

Reagan sat back in his chair and looked at the two men. He could tell that they both thought the mission was a good idea. He was still trying to accept the fact that someone would propose such a thing. He knew progress only came when boundaries where pushed beyond their limits, but he couldn't get his mind passed the risk factor. He was sure that anyone going on this mission – even ten years from now – was a dead man. He had always considered himself to be slightly more visionary than normal, but any way he tried to twist it this came out as a suicide mission. He thought about what Farber-Chatwell had said, and considered the advancements made in the last twenty years but concluded that another ten years would not be enough. '*Hell,*' he thought, '*another twenty years won't be enough to make this safely feasible.*' He leaned back in the chair and crossed his arms across his chest.

"I know that in the military you have to sometimes send men out on missions they are not likely to come back from," the President said, looking at Farber-Chatwell, "but doesn't the level of risk here bother you at all? I don't care if they are volunteers. They are investing their faith, and lives, in your assessment of the situation. Are you ready to take that

53

responsibility? Either of you?" he said, now looking at Ramsdel.

"Some things are necessary for the good of the nation." said Farber-Chatwell. "My people all know that. They are all willing to take the risks explained to them. I believe, as outlined in the mission statement, success is possible. If I didn't believe it, I wouldn't be going."

The President's eyebrows raised up in surprise.

"You're going?" he asked Farber-Chatwell.

"Yes sir." he replied. "That's the reason there are two of us." indicating Ramsdel with a nod. "One to handle things here, and one on site."

Reagan stared at Farber-Chatwell for a while, quietly evaluating the man. Then he looked and Ramsdel. After a while, his eyes went back to the document in front of him.

"What about training?" asked the President. "You're going to have to train people for this mission. How are you going to accomplish that and still keep this secret. The only organization in the business to train people for this kind of thing is a very public one. Unless there is another agency for this sort of training that I don't know about – is there?"

"No sir. Page sixteen covers that. No other organization exists for this type of training. But that's not a problem. A lot of people are put through the specialized training required, so that there are available backups in case something happens to the first string. As far as anyone will know, our people will be just some of the backup team and not really expected to ever fly. There is always some promotional good will activities carried out in these organizations. Some high profile congressman will be allowed to go through some of the training as a good will gesture, and of course because it never hurts to develop friendships with the people who control the purse strings. These promotional activities will supply some of the cover for our true purpose. My personal training will just be considered to be inter-organizational good will."

There was no response to what he said. They sat silently while Reagan continued reading.

"Of course," the president said after a few minutes, "this cost estimate is complete bull. It always costs the tax payers a hell of a lot more."

"Actually, we tried to evaluate the cost as accurately as possible." said Ramsdel.

"Your ten year estimate is in the hundreds of millions." said the president. "How are you going to finance this?"

"With your Presidential Finding, we'll be able to fund from the black ops budget. That way, no questions – no exposure." replied Ramsdel.

"But Congress will ask questions. Not of you, but of your bosses. They always do – especially when your expenses exceed the hundred million mark. For some reason they seem to think that's a touchstone figure." Reagan said. "And once money questions start, questions about the operation soon follow."

"That's why we proposed the operation the way we did. They can't ask about the operation. Once it's authorized, even they can't question it."

"Don't be naive." snapped Reagan. They might not be able to question you, but they will ask about the authorization, and then they'll start questioning those people. It only takes one slip. They will find out who authorized, and use every trick they have against them. It won't be long after that you'll read in the papers about some 'unnamed source' giving them information they shouldn't have."

"Circular authorization." interjected Farber-Chatwell.

"What?" responded Reagan.

"Circular authorization. The CIA and DIA have many different offices of operation, each one specializing in a separate field of expertise. The first office authorizes the second to do the mission. The second authorizes the third – the third authorizes the next, and so on, until the last office comes back around and authorizes the first. While they are doing that, each office of the CIA is authorizing the DIA to perform the mission as a contract operation. At the same time the DIA is doing the same thing the CIA did. Any investigation of authorization will just take them in circles – and circles have no end."

Reagan looked back and forth at the two men for a minute. Farber-Chatwell had explained all this with a straight face. Ramsdel was smirking.

Reagan flipped back to the first page, and started asking questions about every aspect of the plan. The question and answer session went on for over an hour, with Farber-Chatwell and Ramsdel each taking turns answering within their field of responsibility. When all his questions had been answered, The President rubbed his eyes, took his pen from his pocket, and signed both copies of the Finding.

"One more thing, Mr. President," said Ramsdel, "if you will. Because of the nature of the mission, and the fact that implementation is so far in the future,…" he said as he removed an ink pad from his attache´, "and that we don't have an official stamp of office here…". He handed the pad to the President. "This isn't SOP," he continued, "but as you said, there will be questions sooner or later. Both thumbs should suffice – just under your signature."

President Reagan took the ink pad from him, and smiled.

"I'm impressed." said Reagan. "There may be questions in the future, but they won't be able to question my signature." He nodded in approval.

The President inked both of his thumbs, and placed an imprint of each under his signature, on both copies. Ramsdel then handed him a small cloth and a plastic bottle of ink remover. Reagan cleaned off as much of the ink as his could.

Both men thanked the President as he handed each one a copy.

"All I did was sign the Finding, gentlemen." said Reagan. "You're the ones who'll have to carry the ball." He paused for a second. "You also helped me make up my mind about a little problem I'm having with Air Traffic Controllers and the union. As you said, some things are necessary for the good of the nation."

He looked at the two men for a while, trying to get a better sense of them.

"My wife is waiting. I told her twenty minutes, and it's been over an hour." He stood up and walked to the door, then paused and turned around. His face was serious, and his eyes lowered in thought. "Good luck."

After the door closed behind the President, Ramsdel signed his copy of the document, imprinted his thumbs below the signature, and handed it to Farber-Chatwell, who did likewise. After both had cleaned the ink from their hands, he offered his hand to the other man who shook it. Neither of them were smiling. The mission was now effectively authorized, and suddenly they both felt the weight of it on their shoulders. Until this moment, it all was just an interesting mental exercise – now it was reality. Both knew how to get in touch with the other. They gathered their belongings, and said brief goodbyes. Shortly after the President had left, Farber-Chatwell walked out of the room and turned right, to the elevator. A few minutes after that Ramsdel walked out and turned left, to take the stairs. No one had paid much attention to them. They were just two more visitors in the White House hallways.

4

President Reagan went to the living quarters in the White House. He knew his wife would be ready for the evening's events, and waiting for him. He found her talking to some staff members about tomorrow's reception. They greeted him as they left, and he walked over and kissed his wife.

"Ready for dinner?" he asked.

"Oh yes. You're late. That must have been an important meeting." she said.

"There was no meeting." he told her. "No meeting ever took place tonight, dear."

Mrs. Reagan looked at him for a while, then said, "I see. No meeting ever took place. I guess that means you were here with me all this time then.", she said smiling at him.

"And that's just one of reasons I love you so much." the President said, as they left their quarters. He smiled at her, and kissed her hand.

Chapter 3

Preparation

December – <u>1999</u>

STS 103

From: OP361MBC

To: OP361EBC

MISSION STATUS UPDATE
31DEC1999

SEASONS GREETINGS – HOPE YOU ARE WELL

BRIEF FOLLOWS -

DECEMBER 1999 – SPACE SHUTTLE DISCOVERY LAUNCHED ON
THE ONE HUNDRED AND THIRD MISSION OF SHUTTLE
PROGRAM – COMMANDED BY CURTIS LEE BROWN AND
PILOTED BY SCOTT JOSEPH KELLY. SHIP CARRIED FIVE OTHER
CREW MEMBERS REPRESENTING AMERICAN AND EUROPEAN
SPACE AGENCIES. MISSION WAS TO SERVICE AND UPGRADE
HUBBLE SPACE TELESCOPE. THROUGHOUT THE YEARS IT HAD
BEEN ORBITING PLANET THE HUBBLE HAD GIVEN SCIENTISTS

OF INTERNATIONAL COMMUNITY VIEWS OF SPACE THAT
CHANGED OR CONFIRMED THEIR BELIEFS AND KNOWLEDGE
OF UNIVERSE. THERE WAS NO REPLACEMENT SYSTEM
PLANNED FOR IN NEAR FUTURE SO KEEPING IT IN WORKING
ORDER WAS VERY IMPORTANT TO SCIENTIFIC COMMUNITY.
WE WERE ABLE TO TAKE ADVANTAGE OF THIS AS FOLLOWS.

PREVIOUS WAS WHAT PUBLIC AND NATIONAL PRESS WERE
TOLD. ALSO WAS WHAT MOST OF SHUTTLE CREW BELIEVED.
REPAIR COMPONENTS AND TOOLS FOR JOB DID NOT COME
CLOSE TO 50000 POUND PAY LOAD CAPACITY OF SHUTTLE SO
IT – OFFICIALLY – WOULD BE FLYING ALMOST EMPTY.

TRUTH WAS THAT STS 103 WOULD ACTUALLY BE LAUNCHING
AT MAXIMUM SAFE PAYLOAD CAPACITY. STORED IN CARGO
BAY – INSIDE OUR SPECIALLY DESIGNED CONTAINER – WERE
TONS OF CARBON FIBER PANELS – AND OTHER STRUCTURAL
COMPONENTS AND FASTENERS. -- NOTE – WE HAVE
DEVELOPED NEW FASTENER COMPONENTS AND TECHNOLOGY
THAT WILL PROVE USEFUL TO COMMERCIAL APPLICATION.
DUMMY COMPANY BEING SET UP TO MAKE THIS TECHNOLOGY
AVAILABLE TO INDUSTRY. -- END NOTE – THE CONTAINER IS
COATED IN BLACK COLORED LIGHT ABSORBING MATERIAL.
TO CONCEAL FACT THAT SHUTTLE WAS LAUNCHING IN
HEAVY CONDITION FLIGHT CONTROLLERS AND SHUTTLE
CREW MEMBERS WERE TOLD THAT A NEW LAUNCH PROFILE
WOULD BE TESTED ON THE MISSION. OF SEVEN MEMBER
CREW ONLY ONE PERSON WAS AWARE OF WHAT WAS
ACTUALLY ON BOARD THE SHIP. IT WAS NECESSARY THAT
ONE OF OUR ASSOCIATES BE ON CREW AND AWARE OF THIS IN
CASE PAYLOAD BECAME A FACTOR IN AN UNFORESEEN
EMERGENCY – SOMEONE HAD TO KNOW WHAT COULD
POSSIBLY MAKE A DANGEROUS SITUATION WORSE AND ACT
TO MITIGATE IT.

BRIEF ENDS -

MISSION REPORT FOLLOWS -

03NOV1999 – MISINFORMATION WAS DISSEMINATED TO THE PRESS AND PUBLIC THAT A PROBLEM HAD BEEN DETECTED AND MAIN ENGINE REPLACEMENT WAS NEEDED TO BE PERFORMED ON SHUTTLE. THIS CREATED PROBLEM OF NASA AND CONTRACTOR SUPPORT PERSONNEL WAITING TO BE CALLED IN TO PERFORM THE MAINTENANCE.

04NOV1999 – NASA AND CONTRACTOR SUPPORT PERSONNEL TOLD THE ENGINE REPLACEMENT WAS DETERMINED TO BE UNNECESSARY. UNKNOWN TO THEM – IN PREVIOUS TWENTY-FOUR HOURS – ADDITIONAL PAYLOAD WAS PLACED IN THE CARGO BAY BY OUR PEOPLE. CARGO NEVER RECORDED IN SHUTTLE LOGS AND NEVER DOCUMENTED IN NASA RECORDS.

05NOV1999 – SHUTTLE DISCOVERY WAS SET TO BE MOVED TO THE LAUNCH PAD. IT WAS NOT. DURING LOADING OF OUR CARGO CONTAINER SOME OF THE SYSTEM WIRING WAS DAMAGED AND MOVE HAD TO BE DELAYED WHILE IT WAS REPAIRED. SPECIAL TEAM OF OUR TECHNICIANS WAS BROUGHT IN TO PERFORM THE REPAIR SINCE IT REQUIRED WORKING IN THE CARGO BAY.

19DEC1999 – AFTER MULTIPLE DELAYS DUE TO MAINTENANCE AND WEATHER DISCOVERY FINALLY LAUNCHED ON MISSION TO REPAIR HUBBLE. UPON REACHING ALTITUDE AND ESTABLISHING STABLE ORBIT THE CARGO BAY DOORS WERE EXERCISED OPEN TO CONFIRM THEY WERE FUNCTIONING CORRECTLY. IT WAS DURING THIS TEST OF DOORS THAT

CARGO CONTAINER WAS EJECTED. CARGO RELEASE TOOK ONLY FEW SECONDS TO COMPLETE WHILE REST OF CREW WERE BUSY GETTING READY FOR THEIR ASSIGNED TASKS. RETAINING CLAMPS WERE SURREPTITIOUSLY RELEASED BY OUR COLLABORATOR AND SMALL CALIBRATED SPRINGS THAT WERE ATTACHED TO BOTTOM OF CARGO CONTAINER PUSHED LOAD GENTLY AWAY FROM SHUTTLE. CLAMPS ARE INTEGRAL TO CONTAINER SO THAT NO UNEXPECTED HARDWARE WOULD BE FOUND IN CARGO BAY. CONTAINER DESIGNED SO THERE WERE NO NOISE GENERATING ROCKETS OR ANY OTHER DETECTABLE PROPULSION SYSTEMS. ALTHOUGH SPRINGS NOT REQUIRED TO BE VERY STRONG IN THE WEIGHTLESS ENVIRONMENT OF SPACE THEY DID HAVE TO BE SPECIFICALLY CALIBRATED FOR LOAD THEY WERE ATTACHED TO. SPRINGS AT REAR OF LOAD WERE SLIGHTLY WEAKER THAN THOSE AT FRONT. SYSTEM OF SPRINGS DESIGNED TO IMPART AN OUTWARD AND SLIGHTLY REARWARD MOTION TO LOAD. CONTAINER HAD TO ACHIEVE ENOUGH SEPARATION DISTANCE FROM THE SHUTTLE TO CLEAR VERTICAL STABILIZER BEFORE MOVING BACK AND AWAY FROM SHIP. REACTION BY THE SHUTTLE WAS SLIGHT – EASILY COMPENSATED FOR BY OUR CREW MEMBER.

AS CONTAINER MOVED BEHIND SHUTTLE NAVIGATION RECEIVER DETECTED AND LOCKED ONTO MODIFIED MILITARY GPS SATELLITES HAVING SECONDARY USE CAPABILITIES. –- NOTE – ALTHOUGH NASA HAD BEEN AGENCY THAT PUT THESE IN ORBIT IT WAS NOT AWARE OF THIS CAPABILITY. EVEN IN MILITARY ESTABLISHMENT THERE ARE ONLY A FEW WHO KNOW ABOUT THIS. EXCEPT FOR THEIR SPECIFIC CONTRIBUTIONS TO PROJECT, THEY KNOW NOTHING ELSE ABOUT HOW IT IS BEING USED. SATELLITES ALREADY BUDGETED AND SCHEDULED TO BE ORBITED WERE MODIFIED WITH THE EXTRA CAPABILITIES TO REDUCE COSTS AND HIDE

EXISTENCE OF THE PROJECT. MODIFIED SATELLITES HAVE MULTIPLE ANTENNA CONFIGURATION THAT ALLOWS THEM TO SIMULTANEOUSLY BE USED BY EXTRATERRESTRIAL VEHICLES I.E. VEHICLES MOVING AWAY FROM THE PLANET. — END NOTE

WHEN ON-BOARD RECEIVER HAD LOCKED ONTO ENOUGH SATELLITES FOR NAVIGATION THE EMBEDDED COMPUTER CALCULATED THRUST AND VECTOR SOLUTIONS. NOZZLES FOR COMPRESSED NITROGEN ROCKETS WERE OPENED AND ANGLED TO PLACE CONTAINER ON COURSE. COMPRESSED NITROGEN JETS USED BECAUSE THEY REQUIRED NO IGNITION SOURCE – GENERATED NO HEAT SIGNATURE – ADDED LITTLE OVERALL WEIGHT. — NOTE – WE ADAPTED TECHNOLOGY THAT HAD BEEN DEVELOPED AND ABANDONED BY NASA IN 1984 FOR THE ASTRONAUT MANNED MANEUVERING UNIT. IT TOOK ONLY A LITTLE WORK TO MODIFY SYSTEM FOR THIS APPLICATION – QUICK AND RELATIVELY CHEAP. — END NOTE

CONTAINER DID NOT REQUIRE A LOT OF THRUST, AS THERE WAS NO NEED FOR RAPID ACCELERATION. MORE IMPORTANT TO BE ON COURSE AND SCHEDULE FOR PERIHELION THAN TO GET THERE QUICKLY. ION THRUSTERS ACTIVATED TO PROPEL IT TOWARDS DESTINATION WHEN CONTAINER REACHED DISTANCE OF FIVE NM FROM SHUTTLE AND HAD BETTER CHANCE OF NOT BEING DETECTED. THERE WAS PLENTY OF TIME AND ONLY 225,623 MILES TO GO. — NOTE – THAT WAS A JOKE. — END NOTE

AS IT TRAVELS THROUGH SPACE COMPUTER CONTINUALLY MAKING COURSE CORRECTIONS – AT FIRST USING GPS AND LATER USING INERTIAL NAVIGATION.

ON-BOARD LOW POWER HF TRANSMITTER PROGRAMMED TO

SEND DATA BACK THROUGH HIGHLY DIRECTIONAL AND STEERABLE ANTENNA. ENCRYPTED AND TIME STAMPED SIGNAL SENT AT IRREGULAR INTERVALS. SIMPLE DATA STREAM TO TELL TRACKING PERSONNEL WHERE CONTAINER WAS AT TIME OF TRANSMISSION – AND POSSIBLY WHERE IT WAS WHEN/IF THE MISSION FAILS.

PACKAGE ON COURSE. WILL NOT ARRIVE FOR CHRISTMAS. HAVE TRIED TO INCLUDE MORE OPERATIONAL DETAILS PER YOUR REQUEST.

MISSION REPORT ENDS -

HOPE YOUR HOLIDAYS ARE MEMORABLE AND ENJOYABLE.

Ransen Ramsdel sipped his coffee as he read the latest update from Farber-Chatwell. *'Hope you have a good holiday as well.'* he thought, as if he could send the words to the other man by telepathy.

The two men had only met face to face a relatively few handfuls of times over the years, for security reasons. Still, he considered Farber-Chatwell to be a friend. How could he not – the two of them shared what was presently the greatest secret in the world. Even the people that worked for them weren't aware of the final goal. But that would change in the next few years. It was all coming together now. They were finally closing in on the point where they would have to pick the operational team, and those people would have to know everything.

It had taken years of work, planning, and recruiting the necessary people – longer than they had hoped. Years of developing or adapting the needed technology. Technology that ranged from secure communications to rocket science – and the recent advances in technology had been amazing.

Years of managing a project that more than once seemed impossible – and unmanageable. Now the proverbial light at the end of the tunnel could be seen. But even at that, the end of the tunnel was still years away. *'But finally – FINALLY!'* he thought, *'It all now seems real and tangible.'*

They were now in the staging phase of the operation – the last phase before mission launch. Only Ramsdel and Farber-Chatwell knew what the goal of all this work was. Some people in 361, those that dealt with multiple parts of the project, had a vague idea of where all of this work was headed – but they still didn't know enough to realize what the conclusion would be. It had gone slowly, but they now had enough of the puzzle pieces located where they needed them. As Ramsdel thought about some of those pieces, he realized how much the technology they had developed had affected the lives of the civilian population of not just this country, but of the world. Everything was getting smaller, faster, and more powerful. The cargo container, in the report he just read, had navigation capabilities that were not thought possible during its original conception. Now an unmanned, auto-guided 'space ship' in effect, because that is really what the container is, was making its way through space and sending back status reports as it traveled. It could detect changes to its desired course, and automatically compensate. It could sense partial failure of its propulsion system and compensate for that also. More than just a container pushed into space, this was a computerized vehicle designed for a specific mission.

They had borrowed a lot of technology from the space program, but unknown to the official bureaucracy was the fact that it was Operation 361 personnel (working as employees of NASA and various private companies) who had developed a lot of it. It was a win – win situation. By giving the technology to the space program, they allowed NASA and its associated contractors to use their budgets to pay for refining and testing it. Then 361 used the matured technology for their own applications.

Ramsdel took another sip of coffee as he thought about the successes and failures of the past several years. One of the most successful concepts they had pursued was to recruit people employed by companies that had the potential to develop technologies that 361 might need – not an easy task when you consider they were winging it most of the time, and didn't always know what they might need. Some of those companies went out of business, and the financial investment was lost. But even with those, any technological developments were theirs to use or bring over to other companies that were more successful. It elevated the status of their people when one of them suggested these partially developed ideas to their new employers, and showed a strong background in the idea. They would soon be placed in a position where they would either have control over the project, or have all the technical data available to them as the project developed. And if it was available to them, it was also available to 361. It all seemed risky at first, but time had proved the concept to be a very good one.

361 associates had their names on thousands of patents as either the sole inventor or in collaboration with others. This usually translated to bigger financial success for their commercial employers. This made the employers very happy, and they showed their gratitude in ways which translated to increased financial, industrial, and social status for the associates. This made everyone very happy all around, and kept these people more than willing to continue their association with 361. This of course meant that 361 always had the latest and greatest – and sometimes experimental – tech available to them.

Ramsdel scanned the report into the project database system, confirmed the integrity of the scan, and clicked on the key marked 'SECURE' on his keyboard. The scanned data was encrypted and sent to off-site storage. He then took the printout to the shredder, which cut it into little pieces, burned them, and broke up the ashes into a powder. It was a little past six in the evening and he was tired. He grabbed his coat and briefcase, and said goodnight to the people he passed as he left the office. Along with the fatigue, he felt a feeling of satisfaction. He would sleep well tonight.

Chapter 4

Milestones

1

FROM: OP361EBC

TO: OP361MBC

MISSION STATUS UPDATE
01JAN2005

HAPPY NEW YEAR – GOOD NEWS

BRIEF FOLLOWS -

JANUARY 2005 – DETAILS OF THIS BRIEF TO BE COVERED AT
NEXT FTF. TWO ITEMS.

1 – AS OF THIS DATE 361 IS NOW FINANCIALLY INDEPENTENT.
FINANCIAL INVESTMENTS NOW GENERATE MORE WORKING
CAPITAL THAN AGENCY AND MILITARY FUNDING COMBINED.
ALTHOUGH 361 WILL CONTINUE TO DISSEMBLE IT CAN NO
LONGER BE TERMINATED. OUR OWNERSHIP OF
INTERNATIONAL BUSINESSES THROUGHOUT THE WORLD, AND
INTEGRATION OF ASSOCIATES IN ESTABLISHED EXTERNAL
ORGANIZATIONS GIVES US THE ABILITY TO DISCRETELY
ACCOMPLISH OUR GOALS. 361 CONTINUES TO GROW AT AN

ACCELERATING RATE. WE ARE FULLY AUTONOMOUS AND CAN NOW GIVE OUR OPERATIVES THE FINANCIAL SUPPORT AND RENUMERATION THEY DESERVE. CONGRATULATIONS – YOU ARE GETTING ONE HELL OF A RAISE AND YOU HAVE EARNED IT. I AM LOOKING FORWARD TO MINE.

- LONG TERM ASSOCIATES WILL GET AN IMMEDIATE TEN PERCENT PAY INCREASE UPON YOUR APPROVAL WITH ANOTHER TEN PERCENT INCREASE AT CHRISTMAS TIME. FULL MEDICAL COVERAGE BENEFITS WITH ZERO DEDUCTIBLE.

- IT IS MY INTENT WITHIN TEN YEARS TO HAVE 361 SUPPLY FULL SALARY DEATH BENEFITS FOR SURVIVING SPOUSE FOR REMAINDER OF THEIR LIFE. PACKAGE TO INCLUDE FULLY PAID COLLEGE TUITION FOR CHILDREN. WE CAN NOW DO GOOD THINGS FOR OUR PEOPLE.

2 – I HAVE REVIEWED YOUR REPORT OF FIRST TEST FLIGHT OF DELTA 4 ROCKET IN HEAVY CONFIGURATION LAUNCHED ON DECEMBER 21 OF LAST YEAR. ROCKET IS INTEGRAL TO OUR MISSION PLANS. PURPOSE WAS TO TEST CONFIGURATION AND DETECT FLAWS. PREMATURE CUTOFF OF COMMON BOOSTER CORES BY SEVERAL SECONDS PLACED THE DEMONSTRATION SATELLITE IN INCORRECT ORBIT. CONSIDERED A PARTIAL FAILURE BY DOD. PROBLEM WAS DETERMINED AND CORRECTED BY BOEING LAUNCH SERVICES. OUR EMBEDDED ASSOCIATES REPORT THAT THEY ARE AN IMPRESSIVELY SHARP GROUP. CONCLUDE THIS DOES NOT DELAY OUR MISSION.

IN RELATION TO THE ABOVE – 361 INFLUENCE WITH THE AIR FORCE RESULTED IN a 16 MILLION DOLLAR CONTRIBUTION TO THE X-37 DEVELOPMENT PROGRAM. THIS RELATIVELY SMALL INFUSION OF FUNDS HELPED THE PROGRAM REACH OPERATIONAL TESTING STATUS AND GAVE AIR FORCE ACCESS TO PROGRAM DATA. THE PROGRAM HAS NOW REACHED AN ADVANCED STAGE OF DEVELOPMENT AND PER YOUR DESIRE

361 OPERATIVES WERE ABLE TO GET THE X-37 PROGRAM TRANSFERRED FROM NASA TO THE DEFENSE ADVANCED RESEARCH PROJECTS AGENCY (DARPA) ON 13SEPT2004. AFTER THE TRANSFER OF THE PROGRAM IT BECAME CLASSIFIED. THIS TRANSFER GAVE 361 GREATER CONTROL OVER DESIGN AND DEVELOPMENT OF THE PROGRAM. ALTHOUGH ORIGINALLY INTENDED TO BE CARRIED IN THE SPACE SHUTTLE CARGO BAY WE HAVE INFLUENCED A DESIGN CHANGE TO HAVE IT LAUNCHED ON A DELTA IV OR SIMILAR ROCKET SO THAT 361 MISSION REQUIREMENTS COULD BE MET.

LOOKING FORWARD TO OUR FTF NEXT MONTH. WE HAVE MUCH TO TALK ABOUT. PLAN ON LONG DAYS.

MISSION REPORT ENDS -

2

Container number MBM0793 was close enough to be affected by the moon's gravity, and its closure rate increased due to its influence. This triggered a sub-routine in the embedded computer's program which opened the valves on the pressurized nitrogen cylinders. The nitrogen inflated the flexible blisters that covered each side of the container, changing its overall shape from cubical to bumpy spherical. The inflated blisters were designed to absorb the landing impact forces when the container made contact with the moon's surface. Its trajectory was designed to skim the surface, bounce on contact, and roll to a stop. This landing method would reduce contact forces compared to what would be sustained by a vertical landing profile.

MBM0793 cleared the raised rim of the crater by ten feet. Its first contact was with a rocky outcropping that stuck upward like a can opener, which penetrated one of the inflated blisters and tore into the side of the container, damaging the equipment inside. Considering the surrounding terrain, it was approximately a one in ten thousand chance occurrence. The integrity of the container was destroyed, and the contents strewn over the surface of the crater. But the on-board computer had limited capabilities and could not detect that the container had been damaged. It could only determine that it had made contact and had stopped moving. With those two criteria having been met, the 'Package Arrived' message began its transmission sequence, which was programmed for the time periods the signal was most likely to be received on earth.

Operation 361 received the transmission, and knew the crate was on the moon and waiting. To the best of their knowledge it had been a successful delivery.

3

September 26, <u>2006</u>

Farber-Chatwell was just one of many military observers looking up at the sky at Edwards Air force Base in California. It was a clear and sunny day. They had watched the composite structure White Knight aircraft carry the X-37 test vehicle aloft. Without binoculars it was barely visible. Everyone listened to the conversation between the ship and the flight controllers being piped to the outdoor speakers. The countdown had started, and everyone strained to try to see the moment the X-37 disconnected from the aircraft.

"… three… two… one…" came the voice from the White Knight. "We have separation!"

It took several seconds before the test vehicle and the White Knight could be seen as individual objects in the sky. Approximately three minutes and twenty-four seconds after separation, the X-37 touched down on the runway and maintained the centerline as it slowed to a stop. The landing was completely automated.

It was the second successful landing, and it was what Farber-Chatwell was waiting for. This was the confirmation he needed to give a green light to 361's ultimate goal. Due to 361's influence during the development of the robot ship, the craft was human-rated. A ship that could fly itself and carry a crew was the last piece of a puzzle that 361 had been assembling for over twenty-four years. It was time to begin the execution stage of the plan – the most dangerous stage.

Chapter 5

Mission Launch

1

February – 2007

Overberg

Robert Farber-Chatwell looked at the wall of monitors inside the launch control room of the Overberg Toetsbaan, as it is called in the Afrikaans language on the coast of South Africa. It was more commonly referred to as the Overberg Test Range or OTB. He looked text book perfect in his impeccably tailored Air Force uniform, except for the slit open pants leg and large cast covering his lower leg. The OTB monitors showed the views from different cameras that pointed at the launch pad where the Delta 4 Heavy rocket sat in preparation for launch. As far as the range technicians were concerned, this was another test launch of the vehicle. The Delta 4 rocket was considered a mature operational system. In the Heavy configuration however, when two additional Common Booster Cores (CBCs) were connected to the main one, the system raised some doubts. No one was asking questions as to why development was being carried out here instead of a facility in the U.S. They all thought about it, but no one asked. Overberg was a commercial operation, and that meant as long as the bill was paid they were happy for the business and they would do the job they were hired for – without question. It had been a logistical nightmare getting the rocket here in secret, but when you control several international shipping companies, as 361 did, it becomes a lot easier getting cargo to where you want it. Easier to move large items away from the public eye. This launch would not be covered by the press, or made public knowledge. All personnel involved knew that today's launch, whether a success or failure, never took place.

Besides secrecy, there were also some very practical reasons for launching from OTB at this time of year. It was February, and back in the States the weather could be unpredictable, being the back end of winter there. But February was the beginning of Autumn in South Africa. It was still warm during the days, and temperatures wouldn't be getting much colder for at least a couple of months. There were many more launch days here at this time of year. But the real and unspoken reason was that the cargo at the top of the rocket would not be questioned by anyone – as long as the bill was paid – and Farber-Chatwell made sure that payment was always made on the morning of the date due.

If Operation 361 had been a commercial venture it would be a multi-billion dollar international operation, and he would be in a category of CEOs with very few peers. But anyone looking into his life would only see a career military man working at an undesignated and classified job. He had had to acquire many new skills, and master many new fields of endeavor, and he was very proud of what he had accomplished. 361 had early on decided to invest in companies and personnel that would enhance its ability to accomplish the mission. It had been so successful that it no longer needed financial backing from its black ops fund. It had to keep taking the money anyway, and even occasionally requested increases in funding, because this in itself was cover for how successful 361 really had become. As long as 361 took the money from the fund, no one in any possible future investigation would be able to imagine how extensive and influential the organization was. Any person or committee, no matter how powerful, seeking cancellation of funding in order to kill the project would have no idea that the loss of their funding could no longer terminate the operation. 361 was a self sufficient organization.

It had taken many years to get to this point in time. It had been an organizational challenge Farber-Chatwell had not imagined when he signed on for the job – a job he was not at that time really qualified for, as he later learned from its demands. In a way he was now, by accepted definition, one of the most powerful men in the world. Intellectually he knew that, but psychologically he didn't feel that way. With all the power and influence at his disposal, he was still no more immune to the every day dangers of life than any other man – which was why he was here, in the control room, instead of sitting up there at the top of the rocket.

It had happened while he was involved in the most dangerous activity of his daily life – driving on a public highway. He had noticed the car in the lane next to him slowly pulling up beside him. The woman driving was in conversation with her male passenger. Her car was next to and slightly ahead of his, when Farber-Chatwell saw her suddenly yank her steering wheel left, and everything was in slow motion from that point on. She never look in his direction. Never checked if the lane was clear. He doesn't know how he was able to steer his car away from the impact, but they never touched. Having been in the inside lane, he quickly went into the grassy center divider and was just about to regain control of his car when the inconveniently placed overpass support came at him. Luckily the support was surrounded by a cable barrier which did prevent his impacting the large concrete structure, but also turned his car to scrap metal and in the process broke his leg. He had been very lucky.

He found out later that the other driver, after realizing what she had done, just kept on driving and got off the highway on the next exit. By that time her actions and license plate number had been reported to the Highway Patrol by other drivers who had witnessed the incident. Whether she was trying to flee the scene or was just dumbfounded by what had happened Farber-Chatwell didn't know. He never bothered to find out if any legal action was taken against that driver, and he was never contacted by the Highway Patrol after the initial interview that day – but as far as he was concerned the timing couldn't have been worse.

So now he was standing in the launch control room watching the beginning of what should have been his mission. '*MY MISSION!*' he thought. '*I was supposed to be in that rocket commanding MY mission.*' But you can't go flying in a rocket with a broken leg and a large cast. Not that he wouldn't have tried if he could, but being partially incapacitated would have put at risk the lives of the five other mission members. Farber-

Chatwell nervously chuckled at the strangeness of that thought. How do you define "put at risk" to six people, packed in a proverbial sardine can, sitting on top of a potential hydrogen-fueled bomb, ready to be shot into outer space with minimal on-hand safety equipment, no backup equipment, limited life support time, and only one shot at getting it right and surviving? That was the mission. In a way, that was what 361 existed for. What he had been planning for and looking forward to since it began. It had taken many years longer than he had foresaw. So here he stood, his eyes rapidly scanning the monitors – feeling helpless and disappointed. He could have sat but standing was more painful, and in some weird way of thinking the pain was his penance for missing the mission.

361 technicians had set up communication stations in the control room and were monitoring data links from the rocket that were not made available to the OTB personnel. Installed in the ship was a specialized communication system, with preprogrammed messages, that were transmitted using encrypted frequency hopping technology. This was nothing out of the ordinary for the OTB. They often hosted very secretive launches for various countries and didn't expect to be included in any classified operational factors. Farber-Chatwell stood behind these stations so he could immediately see all transmissions from the ship.

He studied the view from the camera aimed at the payload capsule. It was cylinder shaped, and about twice the diameter of the center rocket booster. At the base it flared in to mate with the top of the booster, and was topped with a nose cone. For OTB personnel this was just a test of one possible flight configuration of the rocket. What they weren't told, and couldn't see, was that within the payload capsule was a highly modified X37 Orbital Test Vehicle with its own attached booster rocket. Originally designed as an instrument platform only, this one had been modified to carry passengers. Inside this X37 was a crew of six people in customized space suits, and minimal life support. The crew were the last things placed in the vehicle before the payload capsule was sealed. Their bodies were interleaved with each other and their equipment, and they had little to no room to move around in.

Farber-Chatwell thought about the training simulations the mission candidates had to endure – that he also had endured. The simulations confirmed that one of the most difficult challenges to overcome was to remain very still for the planned sixteen to forty eight hours the journey would take. Two days of almost immobile confinement brought most people to their psychological and physical limits. It turns out that for a normal healthy individual, a lack of physical activity can be almost as challenging as too much. There were instruments to monitor, and conversation to be had, but conversation waned after the first six hours and the vehicle was a programmed robot that could fly itself to destination and back without human intervention.

Farber-Chatwell had pushed himself to his limits during the training and evaluation regimes – as had all the volunteers. He could have just reserved a position on the crew for himself, on his authority alone. He was, after all, in charge of everything related to this part of 361's operation. He was the boss. But he knew that the rest of the crew had to know they could rely on him for support in an emergency. All the other candidates were young, strong, and physically at their prime – they had to be for this mission. He had known what would be required physically and mentally to accomplish this mission, and had kept himself in the best physical shape he possibly could at his age. He had to be an asset to the mission, and not a detriment. Psychologically his years had made him more stable and mentally focused than the younger and more aggressive personnel, and his mental attributes had contributed to his ranking near the top of the training class. The requirements of running his section of the 361 operation had kept his mind fast and agile. His overall test results had actually qualified him to be on the mission – no one could dispute that – and he was proud of that accomplishment. As he thought about this he realized that one thing he couldn't be certain about was what he would have done if he hadn't qualified after all of that effort and commitment. Would he have used his command authority to place himself on the crew? His mind refused to come up with the answer to that question.

2

The launch controller counted down the time in Afrikaans. As Farber-Chatwell watched the numbers decrement on all the displays in the room, his muscles stiffened throughout his body. He realized he was clenching his teeth, and consciously relaxed his jaw. His dentist said he showed signs of doing that, probably in his sleep, and it was wearing down the surface of his teeth. His dentist didn't know what Farber-Chatwell's job was – his teeth clenching actually occurred more during the day than while sleeping. Farber-Chatwell stared at the image of the payload capsule on the monitor, as he began to review in his mind the planning, calculations, and conclusions 361's technical planners had arrived at.

The X37 was a first generation test vehicle. A second and more capable version 'B' was already being designed, thanks to 361's influence in the Air Force. By proposing it as a military test vehicle, the Air Force had been convinced to finance the development of the X37B. It would supply them with a space vehicle all their own, for which they already had clandestine missions planned. By interesting the Air Force in financing the program, 361 had relieved itself of the financial burden of developing a more capable space vehicle on their own. Once the plane had been developed, all plans and technical data would be available to 361. And with the right comment in the right ears, the vehicle would also be available to "borrow" for future 361 missions, masked as being for the Air Force itself.

The first generation X37 was the best equipment they had for the job today, but it had limitations. It didn't have enough thrust or fuel capacity to accomplish the mission by itself. That's where its extra booster stage and the Delta 4 Heavy rocket came in. The Delta 4 Heavy had too much thrust and capacity for today's mission. The plan was to use that extra performance to compensate for the lack of it in the X37. Combined together, The rocket and X37 should be able to deliver the crew to destination, in the planned time frame, and still get the space vehicle back in one piece – if everything went as planned. It was a get there fast, and come back slow mission profile. The crew had to be on destination, and then out of the X37 in the twenty hour survival window. Less than eighteen hours would be very good, while anything after that was considered an emergency directly limiting survival probability. The X37 did not carry enough oxygen to keep them alive during the slow return trip.

The remaining fuel on the X37 would get it back to earth, but at a very slow rate. Like most "secret" military missions, word would eventually get out to the news media. The cover story had already been created and was ready to go if needed. Like any good cover story it was very simple – "Top Secret, Classified, had some problems but were able to regain control and successfully bring the ship back, etc., etc."

The Delta 4 rocket was fueled to capacity, and would use all of its extra fuel to continually accelerate until burnout. It was this continual acceleration that would get the X37 to destination in the mission window. The external CBCs would not fall back into the ocean though, as a normal launch might allow. In fact, they would not even separate from each other as they normally should. On this mission, throttle back on the engines would only occur if structural damage was being detected by sensors. The maximum safe operation structural dynamic pressure had to be exceeded if this mission was to succeed, but it would only be pushed to the design safety limits.

Generating close to two million pounds of thrust from its three hydrogen/oxygen fueled main engines, and having a spacious nose cone, the Delta 4 Heavy's characteristics made it the obvious choice for this mission. But on its only previous flight three years ago, the rocket encountered an unexpected fuel line problem causing the engines to shut down sooner than planned. That flight didn't reach its intended orbit. 361 had convinced the Air Force to finance that 2004 test flight to uncover possible unknown flaws in the system before expensive and vital national security payloads were risked. Those flaws had been corrected, and the system was considered to be reliable enough for operational status. So this flight was serving two purposes. It would act as 361's long awaited transport vehicle, while also being a final test flight of the Heavy configuration.

OTB personnel were told that this launch was to be for destruction testing of the rockets limits – which was true in a way. They had no idea that six lives could be ended if anything went wrong – and why should they? Why should they have to suffer the loss of six lives that they didn't even know were at risk. That burden of grief would only be for Farber-Chatwell, and several others back home. The tracking facility was expecting to see the rocket far outside its normal orbit envelope, so no questions would be asked as it moved away from the planet. At T minus three in the countdown, Farber-Chatwell saw flames at the base of the rocket. The engines came to life and the rocket lifted off the launch pad and headed upward. He watched as the tracking cameras followed the rocket through the atmosphere.

3

The long wait there

Anthony Travellor listened to the launch controllers over the audio link to his helmet. The audio was relayed to him and the other members of the mission by the 361 techs in the OTB control room. All the people on the team knew what to expect from their training. The people in the space program who had actually had a rocket strapped to their butts at one time had all explained that its never like you expect. The combination of incredible acceleration, and the roar and vibration of the engines that permeated your body would trigger the primal fight or flight response of your brain. The few seconds it took for your intelligence to assert control over this survival reaction was a persons initiation into space flight in its present state of the art. Travellor was supposed to have been number two in command of this mission, but an injury to the man who not only should have led it but also helped conceive it had put him in the number one slot – and he wasn't so sure that he should be there. He was better as a second in command – it gave him more freedom to act as he thought necessary. But there he was, leading the mission – strapped and bound to the command position.

It wasn't that he doubted his ability to do the job, so much as his being more comfortable in a supporting role where he could stand apart and look at the overall picture with a critical eye. That was his strength, to be able to see the potential faults and hazards of a mission as it progressed. What he was good at was seeing what needed to be done and in what sequence to do it. He had always been able to organize missions in his head, once he had all the information available to him. For this mission he knew where it was to take place, what was done in preparation, what resources were going to be available to him, and what personnel would be with him. There was one other factor to consider that was very important to every mission – the possibility that the expected resources wouldn't be available when and where they were expected.

That's what had built his reputation with the teams he had worked with in the past. This mission didn't require a soldier. There would not be an enemy waiting when they arrived. There would not be any need for weapons or tactics. The mission was predefined and the preparation for it had taken decades. What this mission needed in a leader was an organizer – someone who could quickly organize the tasks and solve any problems that popped up. He was good at that. All of his life he had recognized the problem, then taken existing items and assembled them together to accomplish the solution. He was an experienced tinkerer in all of his fields of interest, and they were many. He was a pilot, a small arms instructor, an electronic technician and amateur astronomer among other things. His curious nature had involved him in many interests, and he was always an active participant. The trait that put him in the leader position today was his demonstrated ability to quickly come up with a makeshift plan when faced by an unexpected problem.

It had started with a change in his military career that put him where he was now. A need for a technical adviser for a covert spec ops mission put his name in the pool of people who might be able to do the job. Knowledge of missile systems, and his personal interest in small arms and outdoor activities had put him at the top of the list. His military career began in the technical field of missile guidance systems development, and he was happy there. His personal interest in weapons and electronics, a lot of which was learned on his own time, soon added to his official dossier and made him a wanted man – wanted by special ops teams who needed a versatile consultant with varied skills. He had taken pride in the fact that people in the covert establishment knew his name, what he had done in the past, and what he was capable of. He wasn't officially a special ops actor, but considered a technical consultant – someone who normally would advise from a safe location back at base camp.

But he wasn't very wanted on that first covert field mission however. A special ops team was to go into Iranian territory and destroy an anti-aircraft missile installation that was just over the Iran-Afghanistan border. The site had to be destroyed before it became active. The destruction of the site was standard fair for the special ops team – the proverbial "Do it in their sleep" operation, and it could even have been taken out by a guided missile or drone strike. But intelligence had indicated that the site had the latest Russian tracking technology that might be able to detect stealth aircraft at a great distance. They needed someone who could evaluate the hardware and bring back any intelligence if possible. The Spec Ops team was not happy to have him along. They didn't want someone who they believed would either end up dead, or have to be literally carried back while endangering their own lives – and they really didn't want someone who had never been in the field.

Travellor surprised them. His goals were simple – to not be a detriment to the team, to get the job done without putting anyone else at risk, and to do it under his own power. He expected that he wouldn't be on the same performance level as the regulars, who probably had been doing this kind of thing throughout their military career. He had always kept himself in fairly good condition, and believed he was in good enough condition where he would not be a hindrance. Before that first mission he had also taken the time to learn as much of their operating procedures as he could, down to the hand signals and field tactics that the short time before the mission allowed. The team was surprised and relieved to find that he was familiar with the manual of arms for all of their weapons, and that he

81

could actually use them, and qualified on them – something that was not in his official record. When he had the time he also learned as much as he could about the use of explosives and explosive devices, and had learned enough that he wouldn't accidentally kill himself with one. That at least reduced the resistance to his going along – a little. But there was more to these missions than knowing and handling a weapon. Time was too short to become proficient with all the tools of the trade, so on the mission he looked to the so much more experienced team members to tell him when, where, and how to move. The insertion point was several miles away from the missile site, over rough terrain. The team was again surprised when he was able to keep pace with them. As they progressed he studied the way they operated in the field, and learned to be part of the team "On the job".

Travellor turned out to be a good choice for this mission – with his expertise in missile systems he had quickly learned everything about the Russian systems that was known at the time. The missile system was not yet operational, and there were only a few guards left on site when they arrived, who were quickly subdued. As he examined the installation, he recognized some of the sub-assemblies, and understood the layout of the controls. There was a lot about this system that was still the same as the older ones he had studied while prepping for this mission. On return from the mission, Travellor had brought back video of the installation, DVDs that surprisingly contained software for the computer tracking system, operating manuals with schematic diagrams, and even training programs for the Iranian operators. He took pictures of the wave guides with a .45 caliber bullet sitting on top as a size reference, which confirmed the operating frequency of the system. Apparently this had been one of the first installations of this type, and the only thing missing were the Russian technicians who had installed it. Someone was going to be in serious trouble for leaving all this operational material unsecured at the site.

What really made a name for him was the fact that Travellor had the foresight to bring back some of the circuit boards he had removed from the system, with several inches of color coded wiring attached. This was more than the intelligence section was hoping for. Knowing the standard color code system the Russians used for wiring allowed them to quickly determine how to hook up the boards for testing. They were so thrilled by this, their accolades to their superiors for the team and the operation were profuse. Travellor got a few pats on the back from his new spec ops buddies, and went back to his regular job thinking that it had been a very interesting one time experience – but his reputation was now made, and passed along throughout the Special Ops community.

What he had thought was a one time thing became a change of career for Travellor. The number of special missions he was requested for grew until he could no longer do his regular job, and he was re-assigned. For the following six years of his military life his file was classified. He was very happy in his new field, and content to continue on in it until it was time to retire. The excitement and danger were exhilarating. The intense fear he felt on the way to each mission, and great relief when he made it back safely, made him appreciate the quieter times with his family and friends when he came back home. He was a happy and satisfied man.

That all crashed down around him on the day when he was informed that his sister and her husband had been killed in an avalanche while vacationing at a ski resort. His niece had not gone with them, and at that moment the only important thing in the world to him was to be with her. They were very close – as close as if she was his daughter. There were very few vacations over the years when he hadn't spent them with her, his sister and his brother in law. His grief over losing his only sister became secondary to that of his young niece who had lost both parents at the same time. He called in some favors and arranged for several months emergency leave to be with her. It was a day by day process, and slowly with his help she started adjusting to her loss. Slowly the daily flood of tears subsided. Slowly smiles appeared again, and eventually even some laughter. Slowly he had helped her little heart mend, as much as it could. Eventually, with the help of friends and relatives, he could see her looking to the future again.

4

Now he was sitting atop a Delta 4 rocket, and he really didn't like it very much. In Travellor's mind a rocket was not a vehicle – it was a propulsion system. A vehicle is something that can be controlled and maneuvered in and out of atmosphere. People shouldn't fly in propulsion systems – they should fly in vehicles. Bolting a seat on top of a propulsion system did not make it a vehicle. Bolting an experimental spacecraft on a propulsion system also did not make it a vehicle. Astronauts like to think of these type of things as vehicles. *'But astronauts are crazy.'*, thought Travellor. He wanted some wings, and a throttle that he could control, and a nice long and wide runway.

He felt a change in the ship. Something very subtle, and tried to understand what the controller was saying. He should have been paying closer attention, but guessed that the sparklers – the radial outward firing ignitors – had been lit. Everyone on the outside would be seeing a steady flow of hot sparks being emitted under the engine nozzles. His muscles tensed at the thought.

"Tien" came the voice from the speakers in Travellor's helmet. He didn't speak Afrikaans but he understood enough to know that the ten second countdown had started.

"Nege" said the voice.

"Here we go gentlemen." said Travellor to his teammates.

"All instruments and systems are normal." said Antonio 'Tonio' Vargas. Tonio was the man in charge of instruments and systems on their "little space car" as he called it.

"Agt" said the voice.

"Is that nine or eight?" asked Little Petey Eallyn.
Little Petey was, of course, the tallest, largest, and strongest member of the crew. He never minded being called Little Petey – rather, he wore the name

as a badge of respect. He was right. Little Petey was a very sharp and capable person. He was one that Travellor would have personally picked for the mission – if he had had any say in the matter.

"Sewe" said the voice.

Travellor looked at the instruments and systems he was responsible for during the journey. All looked normal.

"Ses" said the voice.

"That's six." said Travellor. "Pucker up!"

"I've changed my mind." said Dal Yimka. "I'd like to go home now, please."

There was a collective laugh at his comments. Yimka was the Structural Engineer on the team. Anything that needed to be built or designed was his job.

"Vyf"

"Five!" said "JJ" Jonathan Jennings, with some obvious nervousness in his voice. He was the Electrical Engineer on the crew, with expertise in several fields.

There was a new noise now, but Travellor couldn't identify it – like something was moving, or flowing.

"Count it down for us, JJ." said Travellor.

"Vier" said the voice.

"Four" said JJ.

"Drie"

"Three" said JJ.

"Twee"

"Two" said JJ.

The noise level suddenly shot up, and everything vibrated. The engines had ignited.

"Een" said the now barely audible voice.

"ONE!…" yelled JJ, trying to overcome the sound of the roaring engines, but no one heard him.

Except for the primal fear inducing vibration, the effect on their bodies was not instantaneous, but it came on fast enough to be scary. Starting as a pressure building on their bodies, the G-force from acceleration quickly deprived the crew of the ability to control their head or limbs. They were plastered to their seats, and their skin felt like it was trying to pull off of their bones. They had been trained for this, but when you know the raging thing underneath you is a real Delta 4 rocket pushing out almost inconceivable amounts of force, it changes your psychological outlook a little. A distorted and muffled "OH SHIT!" came over the intercom.

Travellor looked at the speed indicator which was mounted directly in front of him. At the beginning he was able to follow the changing numbers as they increased, but soon they were changing too fast for him to read any but the first two digits. The rate of acceleration was incredible, and with every passing second it seemed to be increasing until he wondered if it would ever stabilize. In his mind he pictured looking at the rocket from the outside and watching it disintegrate from all the forces on it. He forced that thought away, refusing to accept the possibility, and instead thought of coming home to see his niece. Then he wondered if he would ever get the chance to hug her again.

5

Farber-Chatwell listened to the launch controllers and technicians in the OTB. He listened to their calm voices as they monitored the launch, and relayed information to each other. It was a perfect performance by the

Delta 4 rocket. In front of him he saw the telemetry being received by the 361 technicians. Crew life signs were normal for this phase of the flight. They were all breathing rapidly, and physical stress levels were increasing, but this was all normal for the circumstances. Farber-Chatwell realized he was feeling a little exuberant and happy. It was finally happening. After years and years of preparation and planning, the day was finally here. If everything continued to go well, the people in that ship would go down in American history as pioneering heroes. When the world later found out what they had done it would be the greatest international upset in recorded history. But that thought was for later. There was still much to be done.

In a short while the rocket would expend all of its fuel and would continue to travel away from the planet. Telemetry from it would cease, and everyone would consider the launch a success. Data would be compiled and stored, and eventually the OTB would start preparing for its next customer. What the OTB wasn't aware of was that when the X37 fired its engines, and separated from the Delta 4, the equal and opposite push against the rocket would eventually send it back into the earth's atmosphere. If everything went as planned, the rocket would break up and land in the ocean, hopefully unobserved. At the end of the day Farber-Chatwell would be in the South African headquarters of 361, looking at coded transmissions from the X37 as it continued on its way to the destination. There was reason for Farber-Chatwell to feel happy. He thought that he might even pat himself on the back when he was alone.

Chapter 6

Trailblazer

1

From: OP361MBC

To: OP361EBC

MISSION STATUS UPDATE
19FEB2007

Ransen

Hope you are well

Sad news

I am writing this to you directly as it is my position to shoulder the responsibility of this tragedy.

Two days ago, on the morning of 17 February, we successfully launched mission Trailblazer. All equipment functioned as expected. At our operational headquarters in SA we monitored the automated telemetry transmissions, which arrived every fifteen minutes. Boost faze could not have gone better. We were all happy and tired, as we monitored the mission.

Everything went well for the first sixteen hours and twenty minutes of the mission. The ship was fifty three minutes away from destination. It was at that point that we did not receive the next programmed transmission. With all the variables involved we were not overly worried that communication with the ship was not one hundred percent reliable. Ten minutes later we received a partial transmission. The data was incomplete, and we assumed that transmission was being interfered with by some outside influence. It took some time for our team to decode the damaged data. From the information we were able salvage from that partial transmission, we determined the ship had lost atmosphere, and biometric data indicated at least one crewman had abnormal physiological responses. Fifteen minutes later we received another signal which was undecipherable. No other transmissions have been received to date.

I am truly sorry to report that the ship is now considered lost with all souls on board. God help and take them all. They were the bravest of souls. They died trying to protect their country and families.

We are presently analyzing data from all of our monitoring stations in an effort to determine what happened.

A final report will be issued when completed.

I intend to make it my job to inform all of the crew's families in person. I can do no less. I will wait until after the expected return date of the X37 before performing this sorrowful task.

After we close the file on this we will have to confer about our next step. You have this short time to think about it.

Hope you and yours are all safe.

With great sorrow,

Ramsdel's hand dropped to his side, still holding the printout of the mission update. His mouth was dry, and his body felt as if it were made of lead. He was in shock. He wanted to read the report again, just to convince himself it said what he knew it did, but he couldn't seem to raise his hand. His head fell back against the back of the chair, and he had trouble catching his breath.

He had met some of the men on that crew. He considered a couple of them friends. '...*and I was instrumental in their deaths.*' he thought. '*That's stupid,*' he quickly chided himself, '*someone had to go... was going to go. They all knew the risks. WE all knew the risks.*'. It didn't matter how he tried to justify it to himself, no matter how true what he told himself was. He still felt partially responsible. Ramsdel wondered why he was reacting this way. He had known other people who were killed while performing their jobs. He had buried some of them. But he had never felt like this before. He thought about it for some time. Finally he realized this was the first time anyone had died while under his direct command – his and Farber-Chatwell's. He had never been in this position before. Before this he was the one under the command of someone else. He either failed or succeeded, lived or died, but never responsible for sending people on the mission.

Ramsdel didn't know how long he sat like that, in his office. It seemed like hours, but looking at the clock told him it hadn't been. He felt drained of energy. He wanted to talk to someone about it, but there was no one he could confide in. There was a room full of people outside his office, and he couldn't talk to any of them about this.

.

2

Ramsdel had canceled his schedule for the rest of the day, and went home. His house had a big, airy, well lit living room with large windows that let lots of sunlight in. He sat on the couch with a glass of wine. It wouldn't take much – he wasn't a drinker. The occasional beer or glass of wine was all he ever had. His total yearly alcohol consumption was maybe a six pack of beer and a bottle of wine. Some years not even that much, and some years maybe a little more depending on family gatherings and celebrations. The small glass of wine he was drinking would relax him without affecting his thinking, and that's the condition he wanted to be in. He was having an internal battle. He had known the risks of the mission – everybody had. He knew there was a risk of this specific outcome occurring, but like everyone else, as soon as the thought had entered his mind he had unconsciously pushed it away. Now it was reality. Now it had happened. Now, the Trailblazer crew were all dead – even before they had a chance to start their mission. That was the factor that bothered him the most. It was one thing to accept the risk and lose while working toward your goal. It was a waste never to have had the chance to try. It was sad, tragic and unfair – it was life. Life was a lottery that required no ticket. Whether you wanted to or not, you were playing it.

Ramsdel's chest still felt heavy. It seemed to him that he had to put extra effort to pull air into his lungs. He remembered meeting each of the lost men and the one woman. He remembered reading their dossiers. He remembered which ones had a family. His eyes would start to tear and then just dry up, over and over again. He made a mental note to read their files again, and to take a close look at the pictures of their wives – widows – and children. There was one thing that 361 could do – would do. Those families would receive ongoing financial benefits, and schooling for the children would be completely paid for. He would arrange all of that as soon as Farber-Chatwell's investigation was concluded.

As Ramsdel got up to go to the kitchen, another thought entered his mind. Could the bodies be retrieved so that the families could bury them? That would be the first thing he would look into tomorrow. *'Damn, I'm tired.'* he thought. It was still early in the afternoon. It would be useless to go to bed. Suddenly his spine straightened as if someone had strapped a brace around his torso, and a realization entered his mind. Now it would begin again. No matter how great the loss or tragedy, no matter the effect on the families, the mission still exists. It would go on – it would be completed.

3

Erica Aimsler looked at the neon clock that hung on her bedroom wall. It was ten in the evening. She had been working on her school project for over three hours now. It was way beyond the time her uncle, Anthony Travellor, would have normally Skyped her. He had told her that for the next few months he may be out of touch, but also that there was a possibility he might be able to call. She clung to that possibility. It had now been three weeks since she last heard from him, and each week without any contact made her sadder than before. She was being ridiculous and she knew it, but for as long as she could remember in her young life she had been in contact with her uncle at least once a week. Even though he had told her he would not be able to contact her, it still depressed her. It had been just a few weeks since his last call – how was she going to be able to handle a few months – or longer? Her thoughts were interrupted by a knock at her open bedroom door.

"Popcorn and a movie!" said her aunt Jennifer. "The boys got to pick tonight, so I hope you're in the mood for blood and gore."

'*Blood and gore without doubt.*' Erika thought. Her cousins Robert and Ernst ("Call me Earnest") loved any movie that scared and disgusted the viewer, and there was no shortage of those. They were also the ones whose eyes were widest, and who jumped back the farthest at the scary parts. Next week was her turn to choose, and she already knew what she wanted. Her uncle Tony had introduced her to Sherlock Holmes movies with Basil Rathbone in the role. He thought Rathbones' portrayal of the character was one of the best ever done. She had seen a complete works collection at the store, and she was going to buy it. All of those movies were in black and white, which added a stronger air of mystery to the stories. Mostly, the movies reminded Erika of spending time with her uncle. If he hadn't called her by next week, she would be in need of that feeling. She closed her books and got off the bed. That was enough homework for one night.

"Ernst is not going to sleep well again, after another one of those movies." Erika said.

"Did he come to sleep with you last time?" asked aunt Jen, as she put her arm around her niece's shoulders.

"Yep." Erika giggled at the memory.

"You're his hero, you know? He used to come to our room, but now he sees you as his protector."

"I don't mind." said Erika. "The bed is big enough. But his feet are ice cubes!"

"I know." laughed aunt Jen. "Your uncle and I would make him put socks on, if he wanted to sleep with us."

"Why didn't I think of that." Erika said, as she put her arm around her aunt's waist. "At least he brings his own pillow with him – give him credit for that."

They went down the staircase, and to the family room. The great smell of freshly popped corn filled the air.

"Wait 'till you see this one scene!" said Ernst excitedly, to Erika. "This one guy, he's torn apart, and blood goes everywhere! It spurts out his neck and…"

Socks. thought Erika. *Remember socks.*

Chapter 7

Remembering Nevil Maskelyne

"It is an experience common to all men to find that, on any special occasion, such as the production of a magical effect for the first time in public, everything that can go wrong will go wrong..."

1

Anthony Travellor watched the destination timer counting down. It would be less than an hour to landing. *'We made it!'* he thought. *'We're practically there.'* He almost couldn't believe it. He knew the flight was a big risk – Hell, the whole mission was one big risk. But it was the flight phase that bothered him the most. It was because they were practically imprisoned in the ship. They couldn't move around – they could barely get out of their bunks – and that was the factor that bothered him most. He considered the ship to be little more than a sardine can with engines – and they were the sardines. Everything and everyone was packed tightly inside. He had gone over the calculations many times – they all had. The mission envelope was at best marginal. This was just slightly better – very slightly better – than a suicide mission. Everyone knew it. But they all felt that what they could accomplish, if successful, was worth the risk. It was the scariest thing he had ever done.

He felt his jaw relax, and realized how tense he had been. But they were almost there, and this phase of the mission would soon be over. He was breathing easily he realized. That was good. The carbon dioxide scavenging system was working as designed, removing the CO_2 they were exhaling, and adding enough oxygen to the air for all of them to breathe. Once they left the ship they would be breathing from a similar system built into their space suits. It was bulky and heavy, but the weight wouldn't be a problem on the moon. He started breathing deeper – might as well take advantage of the free air. There was no preparation to complete for landing, since the ship was completely automated. They would just lay back and go for the ride – and Travellor hated that! You cant' be in control when you have no control. He was used to having control – at least a little. When you are literally risking your life, you want some control. *'But the risk is almost over.'* he thought. *'Once we're down, I can relax.'* He moved his hand slightly to reach the auxiliary panel within his reach, and pressed the SYSTEM TEST button. He knew everything was operating correctly, but what the hell! The techs had given him a system diagnostic function and he was going to use it. Hell – he was going to punch it every ten minutes until they landed, for no other reason than it would make him feel good to see the series of indicators all turn green.

Travellor pushed the button, and the indicators turned orange to show that the diagnostics were in progress. One by one they turned green until they were all green. He smiled. *'And there you have it!'* he thought. *'All functions operational.'.* He relaxed a little more, and exhaled in relief. He wasn't expecting the sudden, loud bang, and his vision went white for a fraction of a second before his helmet visor slammed itself shut, making him jerk in the bunk as his body reflexively tensed.

The ship had suffered an explosive decompression, and the water vapor in the air immediately condensed to fog just before it was sucked out of the hole in the ship – along with the cabin air. In those few moments he saw papers, a pen, and a candy wrapper fly into the air and out the side of the craft. Another piece of paper almost made it out of the hole, but all of the air had already been drawn out, and it ended up just floating around. With his next breath he could feel the extra effort needed to breathe as his suit pressurized. Then he heard someone scream in pain and surprise! A flashing red indicator brightened on the panel at the end of the cabin, where it had been green before. Then there were red droplets floating around, and small pieces of what Travellor thought looked like raw meat.

"TONIO'S BEEN HIT!" screamed a voice over the

communications system. "I THINK A METEOROID STRUCK THE SHIP."

"SHIT!" yelled Travellor, now realizing it was Little Petey's voice. His brain switched from thinking mode to conditioned mode, and all of his training took over. "JJ – take care of Tonio! Petey – how many holes?"

"Already moving to him." said JJ, over the short whooshing sound of the pressurized air leaving his umbilical as it disconnected from his suit and sealed itself off.

"Two, I think." said Petey. "It was just one rock."

"Who has eyes on the holes?" asked Travellor.

"There's one by Tonio." said JJ. "About three inches wide."

"I have one by me." said Dal, as he looked at the hole that was just inches from his face shield. "Looks a little bigger than four inches."

"You take care of that one, Dal." said Travellor. "Petey – can you work around JJ and patch that one?"

"I think so." said Petey. "I'll give it a…" He was cut off by a pained scream.

'Damn it!' thought Travellor, *'There's barely any friggin room to work in.'*

"I want a point by point report." said Travellor. He wanted to visualize what was happening in his mind, in an attempt to foresee any problems. With each person reporting almost every action they took he could play the scene in his mind even though his vision was very restricted.

"PETEY! – I'll take the hole by Tonio!" yelled Marisa Delgadillo. "I'm smaller. I'll have more room to move around.

Marisa Herrera Delgadillo, known as 'Radio', was the communications specialist on the team. She was good at her job, and dependable when things fell to crap. Her test scores in abnormal situation simulations were in the highest ten percent of all trainees on record. She was physically small, but capable, and Travellor had not wanted her on this team. Every time he heard her voice she made him think of his niece, and that made him feel a little protective towards her – and he was damn glad

96

she was here now.

"Good thinking!" Travellor said. "Let Radio handle it Petey."
"Roger."
"I've got the patch kit." said Dal. "Foaming up now."

Mounted on the side of each bunk was a small pressurized canister of a special high temperature expanding foam, that was an adhesive and a sealant. With the canister were pieces of precut mesh made from carbon fiber and interwoven with steel threads. Together they formed a patch kit that no one had thought would need to be used. The final repair should stand up to temperatures of thirty-five hundred degrees, and the mesh would make the repair strong enough to handle the physical stress of re-entry. The properties of the foam caused it to cling to and flow over anything it came in contact with. As Dal sprayed the foam around the damaged edges of the hole it clung to everything it contacted, working its way inside the fuselage structure and flowing outside onto the skin of the ship. It did the same thing on the inner surface of the vehicle. As it set, Dal built up the material until it plugged the hole. Then he took one of the mesh pieces and pressed it against the foam, over the damaged area. Over that he sprayed another layer of foam.

Radio released her restraints, pulled her weightless body away from her bunk, and slid herself into the more open area of the center of the ship. Then she slowly rotated herself to face down to where Tonio's bunk was.

"Out of my bunk. Heading for Tonio." she said.
"First mesh on." said Dal.
"I'm with Tonio." said JJ, as he quickly assessed his injuries. "He's unconscious. Right leg torn up. Femur's broken completely through. SHIT! He's lost all pressurization, and he's losing most of his air."
"Second mesh applied." said Dal.
"He's losing blood." said JJ, as he watched red droplets floating out of the wound from both sides of the injury. "I'll have to put on a tourniquet."

"SEAL HIS SUIT!" yelled Petey.

"Got the kit." said Radio, as she edged passed JJ and extended her arm with the canister. Drops of Tonio's blood escaped from his leg, froze solid, then hit her face shield and bounced off.

"JJ. Put the tourniquet on so that it seals his suit and stops the bleeding."

"Right."

"Foaming up." said Radio.

JJ applied an elastic tourniquet just above the tear in the suit leg. He looked at the gauge on Tonio's suit. Slowly it rose, indicating internal pressure was increasing.

"Got the first mesh on." said Radio.

"Tonio's suit is pressurizing, but it's leaking at the tourniquet. It'll keep him alive though." said JJ. "Bleeding has stopped from the upper part of his leg, but I've got blood and fluid coming out from below the injury. His tissues are out-gassing."

Radio sprayed more foam over the first piece of mesh, and applied the second piece to it.

"Second Mesh is on."

Travellor started the timer on the panel in front of him.

"I can't do anything more until we get pressurization – and fast! He'll lose his leg if this goes on much longer." said JJ.

"Pressurization shut down automatically when we lost hull integrity." said Petey. "Won't do any good to turn it on until we're sealed again."

JJ pulled a thermal blanket out of its holder above Tonio's bunk.

With the scissors from the medical kit he cut a wide strip. Radio watch his actions as she slid away to give him more room to work.

"What are you doing?" asked Radio.
"Improvising. Stand by with that can of foam."

Taking the strip of the blanket, JJ wrapped it around the injured leg, overlapping the injury by several inches. Then he took the can of sealant from Radio and ran a bead of it around the top and bottom seams, and across the edge of the strip, sealing it above and below Tonio's injury, and across the edge of the strip. This closed the hole in the suit that was letting the pressurized air escape. He counted to thirty out loud, to allow the foam to cure enough to hold together. Then he loosened the tourniquet slightly, and the suit's internal pressure slowly increased.

"Beautiful! Absolutely beautiful" said Radio, as she appreciated his make-shift suit repair.
"It's only temporary." said JJ. "Won't hold for very long. How long before the seals set?"

Travellor glanced at the timer.

"Sixty-two seconds until we can pressurize."
"It's going to be a mess in there, when you unwrap his leg." said Radio, looking at the unconscious Tonio.
"It already is." said JJ. "I don't know if he'll be able to keep his leg. TIME?"
"Fifty seconds more!" said Travellor. "Petey, as soon as I give the word, pressurize the ship!"
"My hand's on the button." said Petey.
"Forty seconds."

Radio pulled her legs in and rotated her body to face the end of the cabin. Hand over hand she pulled herself to the pressurization panel, Where

Little Petey's hand hovered over the ON button. With both legs spread, she braced her feet against the bunks on either side, and held on to a post with her right hand. She held her left hand a few inches behind Petey's. His eyes widened when he saw what she was doing.

"What?" said Petey, "You want to do the whole mission by yourself?"

She gave him a broad, exaggerated smile.

"Just think of me as your backup system." she said.
"Twelve seconds." came Travellor's voice.
"We're ready." replied Radio.

Travellor squirmed around in his bunk so he could look down to the end of the cabin, where he saw both Petey and Radio ready to turn on the system. He looked back at the timer again, and started counting down.

"Five… four… three… two… HIT IT!"

2

'*Only minutes now.*' thought Travellor, as he kept one eye on the timer that counted down to the moment of touchdown. The ship was holding together after the meteoroid damage was patched, and the cabin re-pressurized. They were skimming the edge of the far side of the moon, and approaching the landing site. The ground proximity radar indicator fluctuated as they traveled over the uneven terrain of the moon. The rear sections of the modified rocket engine nozzles had already pivoted and locked into position in preparation to re-direct the rocket thrust from the now idling engines. This would provide the reverse thrust needed to slow and stop the ship after touchdown. The large meteor crater they would land in would provide a relatively flatter surface for their landing. The ship was flying itself, which Travellor hated very, very much. It was another of the risks built into the mission. The ship was a flying robot, already programmed with a flight profile, and only capable of handling a few minor contingencies. If anything went wrong during the landing phase, there was no pilot to take control of the craft. If the forward looking ground scan radar detected any dangerous obstructions the ship could deviate slightly to avoid it, but this would put them farther away from the waiting equipment their survival depended on. No one on the crew was happy about that.

If everything went as planned, they would end up parked within a hundred yards of the equipment containers that had preceded them. Then they would have thirty minutes to get out of the ship, check it for any damage, and close it up for its return trip to earth. It would be a slow flight back. Much slower than the flight getting here. The engines would have only enough fuel left to get the ship off of the moon, and headed back home. If its flight path was correct, it would eventually be captured by earth's gravity, re-enter the atmosphere, and make an unpowered programmed landing at one of several designated secure runways. There it would be surrounded by Air Force personnel and quickly hidden in a secured hangar. Travellor almost smiled at the thought of Farber-Chatwell's expression when he saw the hull patches on both sides of the ship. *'Let's hope he gets to see it.'* he thought.

This modified X37 had two sets of landing gear. The standard tricycle gear, with rubberized tires, were for landing on earth after the return trip. These would remain retracted during the moon landing. The second set of gear had four wheels, like a car. The "tires" were made of interwoven steel bands that were welded to the hubs. The bands formed a skeletal tire that was designed to flex and give in order to absorb the landing forces, while maintaining their shape to support the ship. These gave a harder landing but could better survive contact with an unknown and unprepared surface. They also had a second purpose – they would be detached from the ship after it got off the surface, and later recovered to be used as the wheels for a crude battery powered vehicle whose parts were in one of the waiting crates. It wasn't anything fancy, but it would be transportation. The whole thing snapped together and was secured by steel locking pins – simple but effective.

All of that depended on everything going well with the landing. There was always the possibility of a crash, and then none of it would matter. But the very first thing now was to assemble an environmental chamber so Tonio could be treated. Travellor knew that Tonio would probably lose his leg, but they would do everything they could to save his life. After the ship had re-pressurized, everyone except Tonio had opened their face shields so they could breathe cabin air instead of that from their scrubbers. Tonio's was left closed and ready for this next phase of the flight. Now it was time to close face shields again as a safety precaution during landing. The possibility of damage to the ship and loss of cabin air was relatively high, so you wanted to make sure your suit was sealed and supplying air before touchdown.

"Secure face shields. Verify integrity of your suits." said Travellor into his helmet microphone.

He listened as each person confirmed they were ready. Tonio's voice was the only one missing. He had been checked by JJ a few minutes before. The temporary seal at the leg of his suit should hold.

Upon landing the team would start assembling two structures – the chamber for Tonio, and the habitat for their survival. Afterwards the two would be connected. This was the most important phase of the mission. They could survive in their suits for only a short period. The habitat would provide them with air, warmth, and protection. With the waiting supplies of food and water, this would be their home for some time. It would be a simple thing at first, but with each day they would expand the structure to encompass almost ten thousand square feet of living and working space. Once everything was set up and working, they would have enough supplies on hand to survive for eighteen months.

The equipment that waited for them on the moon's surface would allow secure communications, and covert monitoring of the earth. It would be the most secret military base in existence, as well as the first manned colony on the moon. With planned deliveries of equipment and supplies continuing into the future it would become a permanent base of operations. Eventually they would be able to send personnel back to earth, allowing for regular tours of duty.

"ORANGE LIGHT!" yelled Radio, indicating the pre-touchdown phase of the journey.

The 361 techs loved to keep things simple. Whether this was out of consideration for the people using their equipment, or a lack of respect for the perceived lack of intelligence of those people (Yes, this type of status discrimination went on even in a well run organization like 361), Travellor wasn't sure. There were three horizontal light panels at the top of the front bulkhead, located where everyone could see them. The blue light was lit throughout the flight, indicating the transit phase of the journey. Obviously the blue light didn't care about small rocks punching through the hull and injuring people since it remained illuminated throughout the episode. The orange light indicated there were five minutes until touchdown. This was a warning that if you weren't ready for landing you should get ready now. Travellor had already run the crew through the landing checklist. They were ready. The red light indicated one minute until touchdown. At that time both the orange and red indicators would be lit. At touchdown the orange indicator would go off and the red would stay on until the ship stopped moving. Travellor had wondered if the orange light was turn off by just a timer, or a sensor that indicated contact with the surface – not that it mattered – it was just his curious nature.

"One last time." said Travellor. "Dal and Radio go out first to assemble the medical compartment. Petey and I are out next to assemble the habitat. JJ will stay with Tonio and get him ready to be moved. Once we have medical working and Tonio inside, everyone except JJ and Radio will continue work on the habitat." The red indicator turned on and caught his attention. "One minute to touchdown. Check your straps again. It may be rough."

Everyone tightened their safety straps a little tighter than they were already. Only a few seconds later the sound of the rocket engines firing permeated the cabin. Then came the bumping and shaking as the steel wheels made contact with the moon's surface. Some of the rocks they hit must have been small boulders judging by the way they were tossed against their straps. It wasn't a landing like an aircraft would perform on earth. On earth, with its atmosphere, the forward momentum of the aircraft would be converted to lift by the wings, to slowly bring the plane in contact with the runway. This landing was more of a controlled impact. Here on the moon there was no atmosphere for the X37's stubby wings to grab on to, so there was no level off. Just a reduction in speed as the ship made a straight line flight at a shallow angle until contact was made. The ship moved forward for slightly more than a minute, and finally came to a stop. There was sudden quiet as the engines shut down.

"Cracking it open!" said Radio, as she slid off her bunk before anyone else.

She grabbed the lever by the door, lifted up and twisted, then pulled it away from the wall. The decompression valve opened and the cabin air was vented from the ship. Reaching for the other lever mounted on the center of the door, she lifted up and pulled out, releasing the locking lugs. With just a slight push the door swung down to act as the stairway.

As Radio moved out of the ship she grabbed the black locator box that was mounted above the door. Dal, Petey, and Travellor were right behind her. The ambient light was very dim and the lights on their helmets weren't strong enough to illuminate very far in front of them. They had thirty minutes before the ship's computer ignited the engines and guided the ship back to earth, unless the door was left open. This was safety precaution in case there was a problem getting people or/and equipment out of the ship. The open door would keep the ship on the ground, but if launch was delayed more than two hours the chances of the X37 returning to Earth successfully diminished. There wasn't any time to waste.

"I'll preflight the ship." yelled Petey. "Only take a minute."

"Roger." replied Travellor. "I'll clear the takeoff path. Radio, Dal, find those crates." he said as he scanned the ground in front of the ship for any large obstructions.

It was important that the ship leave as planned. Its arrival back home could be the only way to let them know the team made it, if the communications equipment they had yet to set up didn't work. Radio turned on the locater, and its screen lit up with grid lines marking the relative direction and distance of the crates that were scattered around the area. Each of the crates had a low power radio beacon that sent out a coded ID signal. The locater screen showed the location of each one by displaying its coded ID on the grid. Also shown on the grid was a bright blue spot that indicated the desired location for the habitat.

"Oxygen and scrubbers." said Dal, as he tried to point on the screen with his oversized gloves. "Let's get them first." He started walking in the direction of the crate.

Petey had finished his preflight, and had come over to where Radio was standing. She handed him the locater, and started walking after Dal. He looked at the display and found the location of the medical compartment structure crates. There were only two required for the emergency treatment of Tonio. One contained the floor and its supports and the other contained the walls and ceiling that were specially wired for the medical equipment. He spotted the crate with the floor and supports, but not the other one. *Runway is clear.* came Travellor's voice in his helmet. He looked up to see him walking back.

"We've got a problem. I can't find some of the crates."

Travellor moved beside him and looked over the locater display.

"What's the problem?" came Radio's voice in their helmets.

Radio and Dal were already carrying one of the crates into position. Their movement was slow and clumsy. The bulky space suits that kept them alive also made moving awkward, and the reduced gravity took some getting used to. They could walk almost normally if they moved slowly, but as soon as they tried to move quickly their movement got out of sync. Their brains were expecting their forward foot to be touching down but their bodies were still floating because of the lower gravity. They had to skip or jump to move quickly, giving their brains time to adjust the expectation of contact with the forward foot.

"Can't find some of the crates. Can't find part of the medical bay." replied Travellor.

"Can't find several crates." said Petey.

"It's not that surprising, is it?" said Dal. "We knew some of them might not hit their mark. They're probably somewhere outside the crater."

"What's going on out there?" came JJ's voice over the radio. "What do mean you can't find it?"

"Locater doesn't show some of the crates. We think they might have landed outside the crater."

"SHIT! Listen, I don't care if it's the medical bay or not. I need a room to work on Tonio. He's still losing blood and his vitals are dropping. PUT SOMETHING TOGETHER – NOW!"

Travellor knew he was right. They were running out of time.

"I need help getting Tonio out of the ship." said JJ. "We've got less than fifteen minutes before this thing take off."

"You three assemble a habitat room, big enough for all of us, and get the air working." commanded Travellor. "I'll help JJ move Tonio."

They all turned and moved to their assignments. There was nothing else to be said right now. '*What the fuck else can go wrong?*" thought Travellor as he entered the ship. JJ had removed the side panels of some of

106

the bunks, and used them to make a stretcher.

"Help me move him onto this. I'll handle his legs. Be very slow and gentle."

Travellor did as instructed. In the low gravity of the moon it was fairly easy to lift the unconscious man and lower him to the stretcher. JJ then used some of the safety straps to secure him to it. They lifted him and moved to the door. Their suits made what should have been a simple task a clumsy exercise as they tried to maneuver the stretcher around the cramped cabin.

"We're going to keep his legs elevated as we turn him." said JJ. "Lower his head and we should be able to get him out the door."

Travellor lowered his end as much as his suit would allow him to, while JJ raised his end up. The makeshift stretcher was just a little too wide for the door, so they had to cant it sideways to make it through.

"Hold on." said Travellor when they were outside.

Travellor placed his end of the stretcher on the ground, then went back into ship and entered the cabin. He released the four latches that secured the battery operated backup time display to the front bulkhead, and pulled it out of the receptacle. He then went out and secured the door.

"We've got to move away from the ship." said Travellor. "Can't be too close to the engines when they fire."

He saw JJ nod his head inside his helmet. He wasn't sure how far away was far enough, so they kept walking to where the habitat was being assembled. He thought they were far enough, and then he heard beeping in his helmet. They had five minutes before launch.

"Put him here." said Dal, as he pointed to two oxygen tanks that were laid on their sides.

They lowered the stretcher onto the tanks, which held it off of the ground. It was difficult to be gentle with the injured man because of their suits, and it took a few minutes to make sure he was supported and stable. Then there was one long beep in their helmet speakers – thirty seconds until engine start. Travellor reactively started counting down in his mind.

"She's going." he said, when he had counted down to five.

Everyone stopped what they were doing to look at the ship. They could have kept it there by leaving the door open. The X37's computer would have started a fifteen minute countdown to a new launch time. This would go on continuously until the ship's door was closed and secured. But there was no reason to keep the ship here. They couldn't use it to return home in – no one would survive the much longer return travel time. Their last real connection to Earth was about to leave them.

As various thoughts went through their minds, the engine nozzles lit up with fire, and then the fire formed itself into a cone shape. The ship started to move forward. It was strange that there was no sound – no roar of the engines. They also did not feel any vibrations from the engines. The ship accelerated quickly over the surface, sometimes hitting a bump and jumping up a little. As they watched, it kept rolling closer to the side of the crater, seeming to be getting too close. They knew that the forward looking radar was scanning the terrain, and the computer was calculating the distance to the side. Then they saw was seemed to be four puffs of air from the bottom of the ship, and it sprang off of the landing gear as they were ejected from it by powerful compressed gas charges. The ejected landing gear bounced and tumbled for a while and finally settled to the ground. The ship started rising upward though its attitude stayed level. It looked more like it was levitating than flying, and that description wasn't completely wrong.

The thrust directors on the engine nozzles then pointed downward, and the climb rate accelerated. They watched as the ship neared the top edge of the crater wall. If the computer had done its calculations correctly it would travel over it and continue out to space, and back to Earth. From the teams viewpoint it seemed the ship was too low, and they all took an involuntary inhale at the perceived moment of impact – but it didn't hit the wall. It flew over it as intended and soon disappeared from their sight. They turned their attention back to their work, and that was when they noticed something moving towards them.

Chapter 8

Reality

1

To say the Trailblazer team was stunned by what they saw would be a tremendous understatement. It was closer to shock, as they watched ten golden figures walking towards them, their minds almost refusing to accept what they saw. This mission had been more than twenty-five years in the making, and no one could have beaten them here. It just wasn't possible. Travellor saw that they carried weapons, although nothing that he could recognize – but he knew a weapon when he saw one. They were probably weapons specifically designed for use on the moon. He and his team had none – not even a pistol. No one considered weapons necessary in this early stage of the mission. Everyone knew there was nothing here that could threaten them, and that they would be the first to colonize the moon. Everyone was wrong.

"Who the f…"
"Everyone behind me." commanded Travellor. "No threatening moves."

They all stepped back so that Travellor would be the first one the approaching strangers would reach.

"Look at 'em." said Radio. "They look like they're dressed in tracksuits. Look at how easily they can move. Those helmets are barely helmets. They can't be Russians or Chinese – they don't have that kind of technology. No one does!"

"No one that we know of." said JJ.

"IT'S NOT POSSIBLE!" said Travellor, barking out the words. "I've been working on this mission for years. 361 knows every technology of every nation on Earth. Ours is either equal to or more advanced than anyone else's."

"They're robots!" said Petey. "That would explain why they don't need space suits. They're not alive. Just machines."

"Just machines with guns? Mmmm... no," said Travellor, "I'm very familiar with the state of the art in robotics. Maybe in another fifty years – maybe. Look at 'em. They turn to look at each other. They're talking to each other. They're alive – and their technology is way ahead of ours."

"There's another possibility." said Dal, obviously deep in thought. "361 overlooked someone. Think about it. Someone else had a plan similar to 361's. They were to small to worry about. We didn't look at them. The Russians and the Chinese didn't look at them. No one did. A country not even considered to be interested in space. Just the fact that they were so small kept them hidden from eyes that didn't consider them worth looking at."

"Maybe..., but I would really hate to think 361 didn't have any idea someone else was in the game. We've got fingers in every pie on the planet. Something would have turned up."

The two groups were only about a hundred yards apart. Then a hundred yards became fifty. Then twenty-five.

"Hold your hands up, and your palms forward." instructed Travellor. "If they're going to kill us, there isn't a thing we can do about it."

"I... I don't... want... todie!" came a choked and struggling voice. They all looked down at Tonio. He was holding his arms straight up and his hands open.

The strangers spread out in a semicircle as they got closer. Their features could be clearly seen through their face plates. Their weapons were held at ready position, but not pointed at anyone. The man that seemed to be the leader walked up to Travellor. He opened a container he was carrying. Inside were ten orange and yellow emblems with writing of unknown characters on them. He took one of them out and mimed placing it on the side of his helmet, and then he handed it to Travellor. Cautiously, Travellor took the item from him, and once again the stranger mimed placing it on his helmet with another device.

"What is it?" asked Petey.

"Not sure." answered Travellor. "I think he wants me to attach it to my helmet. Maybe it's a communications device."

"Yeah," said Radio, "or maybe it's an explosive charge and they're a bunch of sickos who want to have a good laugh watching our heads blow off."

"If they wanted us dead, we'd be dead." replied Travellor. He placed the emblem against the side of his helmet and it stuck to it.

"Can you hear me now?" came a voice in Travellor's helmet. He looked at the stranger's face as he talked, and his mouth movements didn't match the words he was hearing.

"Who the hell was that?" asked Dal, as the others heard the voice retransmitted through Travellor's microphone and over to their own helmet radios.

"That was the man in front of me." answered Travellor. "It is a communications device!"

"Have your people place one on their helmets." said the stranger as he handed the box the Travellor.

Travellor took one of the devices out, and handed the container to Petey. He moved over to Tonio and bent over to place the device on his helmet.

"You can lower your arms now Tonio. I think we're alright." he said, as Tonio's arms fell and he went unconscious again.

"Is your man injured?" asked the stranger.

"Yes." answered Travellor. "A meteoroid went through the ship and damage his leg. He's losing blood. We need to build a shelter so we can treat him."

"I do not know that word… 'meter-oid'. The translator does not know it either. You can come with us to the ship. We have medical facilities and a doctor." said the stranger, as he tapped a panel on his sleeve and began to talk. This time they couldn't hear what he was saying. "I have called for the transport to pick us up."

"You have a ship with medical facilities and a doctor, and it's big enough to have a transport and hold all of us?" asked JJ. "Who are you? What country are you from?"

"Yes," said Travellor, "we would all like to know that."

"There will be time for diplomatic intercourse later. That is for my captain to engage in. First we will help your injured crew man. I am Benua-sil-Plessa. Chief engineer of the Orysta."

"That's the name of your ship? The Orysta?"

"Yes." replied Plessa. He turned and looked behind himself. "The transport has almost arrived."

Coming over the edge of the crater was a flying vehicle. In a few seconds it had reached them and landed within fifty feet. Travellor was amazed that very little dust was kicked up by the ship, and that was only by the contact of its gear and the ground.

"That's interesting." He said. "What kind of propulsion system does your transport have?"

No answer came as they watched the door on the transport open. One person exited the ship, and behind came a floating platform.

"Welcome to your moon." came the voice of the new arrival. It was a woman's voice. "I am Mersuul-sil-Vaana, Navigator of the Orysta. We will introduce ourselves later, after your wounded crew man has been given medical attention. Place him on the platform. It will carry him to the ship."

"Let's do it quick." said JJ. "Tonio's not looking very good."

"Grab an end and let's move." said Radio, before JJ had finished speaking.

She had already moved to the injured man's feet. Four of them lifted him up and placed him on the floating platform. It dropped about an inch with the added weight, then automatically adjust its height back up. The navigator of the Orysta, and the platform started moving towards the ship. Radio bent over and looked beneath the floating body to confirm for herself there was nothing touching the ground.

"Neat magic trick." she said. "You'll have to show me how you do that."

Plessa tapped his sleeve again and spoke, but the words did not get transmitted to the Trailblazer team. The Orysta personnel moved to the ship, except for one armed man who stayed with Plessa. They moved with ease and speed, as if they were strolling around on Earth. The Trailblazer team moved more slowly, because of their clumsier suits and lack of familiarity with walking quickly on the moon's surface without bouncing. The weaker gravity would take some getting used to. They were the last to board the transport, which was about five times the physical size of the X37.

Travellor watched as the woman who identified herself as the navigator flew the ship. She touched a graphic on a display screen, which must have controlled the throttle, but there was very little noise or vibration. The ship just slowly lifted up vertically, and then without a change of attitude it accelerated forward. As they neared the edge of the crater, she moved the control again and their altitude increased. The ship easily cleared the edge. The flight instruments had strange markings on them, but the graphic displays were easy to understand. They were very similar to terrain mapping instruments used in aircraft on Earth. Travellor was trying to learn which controls were for which function, but there were gesture sensors that read the movement of the pilot's hands and he couldn't decipher which gesture did what. She was also speaking – giving commands to the ship Travellor believed.

The alien crew had removed their helmets, but the Trailblazer team had not.

"Is it safe for us to breathe the air in your ship?" asked Travellor.

"Yes." answered Plessa. "I believe you will find it refreshing."

One at a time the team opened their visors. When they noticed no ill effect, they started breathing deeply.

"I hate breathing that tanked air." said Petey to no one in particular, as he removed his helmet.

Members of both crews mumbled their agreement.

"Your ship is amazing!" stated Radio. "It's so big – and quiet!" Her eyes were wide as she looked around trying to take in everything she saw. "And this is just your transport? It's bigger than our ship was. You would not believe how little room we had."

"We know." said the Navigator. "We measured your ship as you neared here. Calculating the average height of your people, we estimated there would be two of you. Three at most. We were very surprised when four people came out of that small ship. Then, when two more came out, it was very shocking."

"You measured out ship?" said Travellor. "You knew we were coming?"

"Yes." said Plessa.

"How did you know?"

"When we first discovered your containers, we wondered who they belonged to. As more of them arrived, we realized they were in preparation for the arrival of personnel. This changed our original mission greatly. We did not know when you would come. We monitor all activity outside your planet's atmosphere. When one vehicle acted differently than the others, by continuing to travel into space and on a path to intercept your moon, we knew it was either a satellite or a ship. As you came closer we could tell it was a ship, and knew you were coming here. It was Vaana who followed and documented your preparation and your flight."

115

Mersuul-sil-Vaana had a big smile on her face, as she turned to look at the Trailblazer crew.

"I have many questions. I was amazed that you would attempt this journey with your level of technology." she said. "You are explorers, as we have not seen for over twenty tanrha."

She looked at the quizzical faces of the Earth crew, and thought about what she had just said.

"There is no direct translation for tanrha in your language." she said, as she did some quick mental calculations. "Approximately 300 of your years. You are all very brave to attempt this journey in a ship that is nothing more than an unprotected container." She turned and looked at the Trailblazer crew with very wide eyes. "YOUR SHIP DOES NOT HAVE A DEBRIS SHIELD!" she stated loudly, with an amazed look on her face. "No one would travel in space without a shield." she said. Then suddenly the smile on her face disappeared, replaced by a look of shame as she looked at the injured crewman. "I am sorry." she said, turning around quickly, "We are almost to the ship, and our doctor is very good. She will take care of your friend." Then in a low voice she murmured as she shook her head, "You are all so amazingly brave."

The flight lasted only a few more minutes before the ship slowed down. Mersuul-sil-Vaana touched her sleeve as Plessa had done before, and started talking in her own language. The words she spoke were not being translated. She was answered by another voice over the ships speakers, which also was not being translated.

"The doctor is expecting your injured man. She will be ready for him when we arrive." said Plessa.
"How's Tonio doing, JJ?" asked Travellor in a loud voice.
"He's alive. But he's in bad shape. He's going to need blood.

DAMN IT! I forgot to bring some with us. Radio and you are the same blood type, Commander. We'll have to transfuse."

"I'm ready!" snapped Radio.

"Whatever he needs." said Travellor.

"Blood will not be a problem." said Vaana, now translating her words again. "We have medical blood that is good for everyone, including your people."

"Whoa!" jumped in Petey. "You have blood that can be used for everyone? Are you sure?"

"Yes!" said Vaana. "You would call it artificial blood. It is designed so that anyone's body can use it without any problem."

"Holy shit." said Radio, "…Pardon my French. Do you realize how many lives that could save back on Earth?" she asked, her question directed to Travellor.

"One thing at a time." he said. "First Tonio, then the world. That would be something for 361 to introduce as a discovery by one of its companies."

The transport stopped and hovered as Vanna again spoke in her language to the ship.

"There." said Plessa, pointing out to the window.

In front of them the ground lifted up a few feet and then split in two, the sections moving in opposite directions. Light came from the gaping opening that was made, illuminating the surrounding darkness. Slowly Vaana moved the transport over the opening and lowered it into the hole. The shuttle dropped quickly down a man-made shaft – and kept dropping. Travellor tried to figure out how far they fell, and guessed it was at least five stories down. As the transport's windows dropped below the end of the shaft they could make out the large transport bay, with another ship parked at one end. The bay was huge, with enough room for at least two other transports.

They touched down, and with a few words and a swipe of Vaana's hand all the displays went dead and the transport became completely quite. Seconds later the door opened, and two crewman came in followed by a tall authoritative woman who pointed to Tonio and gave instructions to the others. Before the Trailblazer team had a chance to get out of their seats, they were gone.

"Toisae-sil-Blin," said Plessa. "our doctor. She will take care of your... Tonio? Do not worry. She is very good. You should all get out of your suits. We have more suitable clothing for you. Then I will take you to the doctor."

"JJ, Radio, you two go with Tonio. We'll relieve you as soon as we can." said Travellor. They both moved out before he finished talking. Plessa looked surprised at first, then understood.

"That is not nece..." started Plessa, then realized he would have done the same. "Of course. It will not take long for you to change. I'll show you to the spare rooms."

As Travellor, Petey and Dal followed Plessa, their heads were constantly turning as they scrutinized the ship they were in. As the structural engineer of the team Dal was especially interested. He wondered how big the ship was. How fast could it travel? How many people lived aboard? What kind of engine powered it? How far could it travel without refueling? Lost in his thoughts, he almost tripped as he walked in his clumsy suit.

2

"*Analyzing physical structure.*" said the computerized voice coming from the array of medical equipment in the operating room.

Toisae-sil-Blin had been an accomplished medical practitioner on her home planet – what the strangers called a 'doctor'. She had won the accolades of her colleagues and her profession. Then her chosen lifemate had died at far too young an age. What made it worse was that he died of injuries that were so bad he was dead before the rescue personnel could arrive on the scene. They couldn't do anything for him. With all her knowledge and skill, she couldn't do anything for him. Dead is dead. *'Even with all of our technological capabilities,'* she thought, *'we still cannot overcome death that can take you in an instant.'* That had only been a few decitans ago, and she still felt the pain. A short time after his death she developed a powerful wanderlust, and decided she wanted to see more of the universe that was still unfamiliar to her. Even in these modern times there were still amazing things out there that no one had encountered yet. She took employment with the mining company, because mining companies were the ones who explored the unknown reaches of space in their search for natural resources.

She looked down at her naked patient suspended in the air in front of her, and watched as the medical analysis computer scanned his injury with high frequency sound and radio waves. The energy field around his injured leg made it look like it was wrapped in thick translucent gauze. This field kept the injury sterile, and stopped blood loss from the damaged tissue. She had seen worse injuries, but what amazed her the most was the briefing she received about these Earth people. They had traveled here with technology that was so old it was astounding – except that it wasn't old to them. To them it was the newest available – even if it was only slightly more than a metal can with some insulation on the walls. Her own ancestors had first explored space travel with similar vessels – and many of them had perished doing so.

"Circulatory vessels scanned and mapped." said the instruments voice, as it continued its analysis. *"Connective tissue scanned and mapped."*

Blin prepared herself for the prognosis. There really was nothing to worry about. The man had been stabilized as soon as he arrived, and blood substitute continued flowing into his body. The injury looked terrible to the

119

untrained person, but this kind of damage could easily be repaired, once the computer knew how to put the limb back together again. The man would live. There really was no doubt about it. He was in good physical condition – *'Very nice physical condition.'* she thought, looking at his naked body – and would recover very well.

"Skeletal structure scanned and mapped. Comparing to intact limb."

The computer mapped the intact leg, to use as a design model for the damaged one.

"Analysis complete. Ready to begin reconstruction." said the computerized voice.

"Verify blood, nutrient and mineral flows." commanded Blin.

"All reconstruction materials available in the required quantities." replied the computer.

'Good.' thought Blin, looking at her patient. *'Luckily for you we are not short on medical supplies.'*

"Begin reconstruction." said Blin, noticing for the first time the two members of the Earth crew watching through the viewing panel.

3

Marisa Herrera Delgadillo, known as Radio to her team, closed her eyes and leaned against the wall of the shower stall, as she let herself get lost in the soothing massage of the hot water that pulsed onto her body. It was wonderful – real hot water. She hadn't expected to know another shower for at least a year. On mission launch she had mentally prepared herself for minimal cleanings with chemical wet towels. That was the only thing that would be available to the team as they established the first human colony on the moon – the first secret human colony. For a short while she had thought it would be more correct to consider it the second secret human colony. But after seeing Tonio's leg be rebuilt (regrown?) she started to think that maybe these people were not from Earth.

They still had to build the colony, but until then she was going to enjoy every second of this shower. She found it surprising that so many basic daily needs of an alien people from another planet – from another galaxy she was certain, because scientists on Earth knew enough about our own to be aware of another inhabited solar system (didn't they?) – were so similar to her own human species. Could our scientists have missed that she wondered? Our galaxy was unfathomably big. Perhaps another inhabited solar system did exist without the human race knowing about it. No, she was sure something would have been detected from the activities of a planet of space traveling aliens. If they were from another galaxy, the technology that allowed them to travel such unimaginable distances had to be far ahead of ours. How long did it take them to get here?

What she had seen so far also confirmed that their technology was far in advance of Earth's. She had watched through a window into the operating room of the medical bay, as the tall woman doctor not only stopped Tonio's bleeding, but also regenerated the damaged bone and tissue in his leg – like an unbelievable magic trick. Hell, he had regained consciousness before the procedure was over! He showed no signs of any pain. He was even talking to the doctor as she finished the procedure – was even flirting with her while she worked on him. She had watched as the torn muscles and ligaments came together, and Tonio's skin sealed itself. She was so enthralled with what she was seeing that it wasn't until her throat felt raspy that she realized she had been watching with her mouth gaping open in astonishment.

Some of the ship's crew had helped her and JJ take off their spacesuits as they watched Tonio being treated, and it wasn't until the suit was off that she noticed the odor coming from it – and from her and JJ. The stress, running around, worry, and danger of the mission had caused her body to do what any normal human body does. Doing that in an enclosed spacesuit meant the body odor had no place to go. She had noticed that the ship didn't smell like a locker room though, and she had seen a group of the aliens sweating hard as they manhandled some large equipment. Surely the alien's bodies also required regular hygiene. She was certain there had to be some way to bathe on this ship. She just hadn't dared believe they would have hot showers available. Hot showers also meant that these aliens came from a planet with abundant water. A planet like the Earth perhaps.

It was about thirty minutes after arriving on the alien ship that Mission Commander Travellor, Dal, and Petey joined them, all wearing clothing supplied by the aliens. The garments didn't fit very well on them, but they were probably scrounged up from the ships crew. Beggars can't be choosers. They were all also wearing a black wristband with a graphic display. They brought one for her and JJ, and as soon as it went on her wrist, the communications device proved to also perform as a translator like the ones they had attached to their helmets. These were different than the helmet units. Instead of converting the translated speech to sound, these wrist comms sent the translated speech through a persons nervous system as electrical impulses, and directly to the brain, bypassing the ear completely. This made the translation much faster, and the slight time delay for it all to happen was barely noticeable. With these bracelets the conversations between the Trailblazer team and these strangers was almost natural. She looked at it now, and watched the water dripping off of it. The crewman who showed her to this room had said it was waterproof, so she was determined to test that to see just how good their equipment really was.

After they had all talked to Tonio, who seemed like nothing had happened to him except for the fresh hairless pink section of skin on his leg where he had been injured, she and JJ were relieved of their watch detail by Commander Travellor and had been guided to their quarters to get cleaned up. That was when she first realized that she was walking normally – as in walking like she would have on Earth and not the careful skipping they were doing when they landed on the moon's surface. This ship had its own gravity. The aliens knew how to create gravity! Scientists on Earth barely understood what gravity was. That was a stunning realization, and she wondered what else they were capable of.

Everything had happened so fast. It was less then two hours ago they had landed, thinking that Tonio might be the first victim of the mission. Now she was enjoying the hell out of a hot shower, and Tonio was trying to make time with an alien women from another galaxy. That thought brought to her mind the question of whether human and alien anatomies were alike. She smiled thinking that maybe Tonio could be in for an anatomical shock. But they did look human. They had two eyes, and two ears, and a mouth, and head, and arms and legs, all in the correct places. The women had breasts where breasts should be, and from what she could see of some of the male crew it was obvious the men had their equipment in the right place also. This wasn't turning out like the scifi movies she had grown up with. Weren't they supposed to be green, with a big bulbous head and large eyes that could rotate in opposite directions. '*I know!*' she thought humorously, as she let her imagination wander, '*They're wearing some kind of electronic device that makes them look human but they are really big gelatinous blobs with eyes all over their bodies.*' She laughed at her thoughts, and then admitted to herself that she had seen several very handsome alien men that she wouldn't mind getting to know better.

Her bracelet toned, and the sound broke her mental wanderings. At first she wondered if the waterproofing wasn't as good as advertised and the device had failed. Then Travellor's voice came from it.

"Radio? This is Travellor. Are you there?"

"Water off." she said to no one, and the shower spray stopped at her command. "Yes commander, I'm here."

"I really like these things." he said, obviously referring to the communicators.

"I... wait a minute!" she started to reply, then realized she was naked and wet. "These things don't have video, do they?" she said, aiming the top of her wrist to the wall while looking around for a towel.

"Wish they did. That would be ideal. I think we were given the economy model. Just talk and translate functions. Where are you?"

"Just finishing my shower."

"You are? Are you still wet?"

"Uh, yeah. I am. Where do they keep the towels in these rooms?"

"Oh you're gonna love this! Just stand in the middle of the stall, and say 'Dry' or 'Dry off' or anything like that – AND CLOSE YOUR EYES!"

"O… K…" she said, while looking at the walls for an opening where the towel would be shot out at her. "DRY!" she said loudly.

Immediately, intense jets of warm air came from the walls, starting above her head and traveling downward. She had just remembered to close her eyes when the pressure hit them. She could feel the high pressure air hitting her from every direction, as it moved down over her body, pushing off the water and effectively squeegeeing her dry.

"ALLRIGHT!" she said. "I like that!"

"It's part of the water recovery system. Water is a precious commodity on the ship. It's easier to process for re-use if they can capture it in liquid form. Harder to recover in vapor state."

"OK. But my hair is still damp."

"Now comes the really neat part." said Travellor. "Go sit at the dressing table, and look at the wall."

Marisa did as instructed. There was a small counter against one of the walls, with a chair in front of it. She sat down and faced the wall. It was just a blank wall – and then it wasn't. In front of her, looking back at her, was herself – in three dimensions and full color. Even the room behind her was represented in the image. It was like having an exact mirror image twin looking back at her. When she turned her head, the image also turned, and kept turning until it turned a full three hundred and sixty degrees. She found that even though she was sitting still, she could turn the image in any direction and in any amount just by the movement of her eyes.

"That's amazing." she said, while looking at the scar on the back of her neck – or rather on the back of the image's neck.

"Now tell it what you want." said Travellor.

"Tell what what I want? The image?"

124

"You're actually talking to the computer that controls the image. Say 'hair'."

"Alright..." said Marisa, "... hair!"

"*Style choice.*" came a female voice from nowhere, and she jumped up before realizing it was a computer generated voice.

"Holy...! Style choice? What are my options?" she said, sitting down again.

"Now you're getting the hang of it." said Travellor. "When you're dressed, ask for directions to the dining area. We're having an introductory meeting with the ship's captain."
"OK. Shouldn't be more than fifteen minutes." she replied.

In front of her, her 3D image split into six smaller ones, each with a different hair style appropriate for the short length of her hair. She could turn each one around to see how it looked from all angles.

"I could make a fortune with this back on Earth." she said to herself. "How about it computer? Want to go into business with me?"

There was no reply.

"Ohhh..., holding out for a bigger cut, huh?" she said as she pointed to her choice. "I'd like that one."

The six images disappeared leaving only her face with the still damp hair. She felt something moving from the back of the chair. Behind her image she could see a dozen slender mechanical arms extending upward, each with a shining oval plate on the end. They positioned so that the plates defined the shape of a bowl around her head, and about eight inches away. Then she felt a tugging on her scalp and every strand of her hair stood directly out from her head, each one separate from the others. The oval plates now looked as if electrical worms were crawling over their surface. As she looked at her 3D representation she couldn't help thinking that she looked like a Chia pet. Her hair then separated into two sections, and strands folded themselves into place. A mist was sprayed onto her hair from the plates, and then they dropped back into the chair. Her image now showed her with the hair style she had selected. She touched her hair lightly and wished she had a mirror, not yet trusting the 3D image, which slowly rotated in front of her.

"Is there a mirror in the room?" she queried.

The 3D image disappeared and the wall in front of her became a highly reflective surface.

"Computer," she said, "you are hot stuff."

She turned her head to see her reflection from different angles. She looked exactly like the image she had selected.

On the bed were new under clothing, and a suit similar to the ones the crew of the Orysta wore – their idea of a jumpsuit, although she didn't recognize the material it was made of. Probably some kind of synthetic. It didn't take her long to dress, and she wasn't happy with the fit. It was a little long in the arms and legs, and baggy everywhere. She instinctively looked around for her purse and keys, then smiled at herself when she remembered she had left those in a locker back on Earth. *'Habits.'* she thought.

"How do I get to the dining area?" she asked.

4

Farber-Chatwell walked around the hangared X37, deep in thought. It was the fourth time he had circled the ship, scrutinizing every detail his eyes could discern and alternating between shock and surprise. It had taken two weeks for the ship's return trip – possibly the worst two weeks of his life. Two weeks of wondering if he had sent six people he knew and liked to their deaths. From the blood painted splatter he could tell which hole was the entrance and which was the exit of the projectile. It could only have been caused by a solid object traveling at tremendous velocity. He didn't want to go back inside the ship until the tech team had finished, and it was cleaned up.

He had been the first to enter the ship – against the advice of the safety team – when it had landed and the door was opened. What he had found both amazed him and made him a little sick. There were pieces of dessicated flesh, and bone scattered around the middle of the cabin. One side had been painted with splatters of blood and one of the bunks was covered in it. He knew this had been Vargas' bunk, and wondered if the man had survived.

He surmised that that at least one crew member had been injured severely – hoped that only one had. DNA testing would tell him who it was – he had already ordered a priority on that. He could also tell that the rest of the crew were able to secure the ship and make it to the moon – that was made clear by the fact that no bodies were in the ship. They had landed and disembarked, then closed the ship up for the return flight. The flight profile that had been programmed into the ship's computer was written with plenty of tolerance on the safe side, and the ship took off and made its way back without incident. But it had been two weeks and still there was no communication from the Trailblazer team. That had him worried.

It was a dangerous mission from the start, and each person on the team knew they may not survive to return home. Now the question was were they still alive? If they were, why hadn't they contacted him? On the positive side of the equation, if there was one, Farber-Chatwell could put off family notifications until more was determined. It would be a terrible cruelty to inform a family of a team members death and then have them show up alive a year from now. For now, he had to find out who's blood, flesh and bone were in the ship. He would update Ramsdel as soon as he got back to the office. Ramsdel had wanted to come with him to notify the families – now maybe they wouldn't have to. But where the hell was the crew?

5

Mersuul-sil-Vaana stood in front of the conference room that held all of the Trailblazer crew members. This was mandatory education, as agreed to by Mission Commander Travellor and Grilik Artau-sil-Munen. Travellor wanted this because any information learned from a civilization with technology as advanced as the Ganaphe's would benefit his team and 361. Grilik Munen wanted this because keeping the Trailblazer team alive would benefit his own people. Contact with the people of the inhabited planet Earth – initiated by their own actions – gave Munen the legal right to trade with them, and trade meant fresh supplies and a chance to rest his crew on a habitable planet. Under the IGT this would have been illegal for them to do otherwise. They had been stuck on this moon for too long a period. And also, within the short period of time the two peoples had been together they had found a mutual trust and understanding. They worked well together, the Ganaphe' helping the Trailblazer team construct their surface dwelling, and the humans helping the Ganaphe' with repairs and modifications to the ship.

There was much for the Trailblazer team to learn, including survival in space, familiarity with much of the Ganaphe' technology (which they were now using on a daily basis), use of Ganaphe' equipment, and the part both crews seemed to enjoy most – exposing the Earth crew to Ganaphe' foods. The Ganaphe' were looking forward to trying foods from Earth, and spending time there. With each day, and the nearing completion of the Trailblazer habitat, this goal came nearer. The human's communication equipment and some other items had been damaged during bad landings of some of the crates, and although it would be illegal to allow them to use Ganaphe' communication equipment to contact Earth, it wasn't illegal for the Ganaphe' to assist the humans in repairing theirs. Today, the class was on space travel and navigation and, as the navigator of the Orysta, Vaana was the best qualified person for teaching this lesson.

Hanging in the air behind Vaana was a three dimensional depiction of several galaxies with bright colored lines indicating travel routes. The image was so real it gave the impression of looking through an opening in the ship, out at the universe. It made you want to reach out and grab the planets shown.

"Just as you have designated air travel routes on your planet, inter-galactic travel also requires designated routes for safety and efficiency. Traveling these routes increases your chance of survival if anything happens to your ship." lectured Vaana.

Normally this type of education would be handled by IGT instructors delegated to introducing these subjects to newly contacted peoples, but the unique situation between the crews of the Orysta and mission Trailblazer had made it imperative to quickly raise the knowledge level of the Earth crew to a basic understanding of galactic travel and law. The classes on law (there would have to be many of them) would be the hardest to grasp. Even though the Earth team was not bound by IGT law, the Ganaphe' were. The humans could do some things that the Ganaphe' were legally prohibited from doing. Grilik Munen was planning on taking advantage of these legal anomalies.

"Routes are generally categorized as Local or short navigation routes, Galactic or intermediate navigation routes, Inter-galactic or extended navigation routes, and Explorative or unknown and uncharted routes." said Vaana. "The Local routes are used for travel within a solar system. Your journey from Earth to this moon is considered a local route. When you travel to other planets in your solar system, you will also be using local routes. Although you do not have any formalized routing system established yet, you will discover that when space travel becomes more common for your people, formalized routes will be the safest way to travel." she continued. "When you travel to other solar systems within your galaxy you will be using galactic routes. Both of these types of routes will be designated and controlled by your people. When you begin to travel inter-galactic routes you will find that there is an established system already in place, and controlled by the Interconnected Galaxies Treaty Organization. When your people travel to these far locations outside your own galaxy you will probably use this system. Although you may choose not to use these established routes, you would be giving up the added safety that comes with using them. These routes are regularly patrolled by IGT security ships manned by mixed crews from every signatory galaxy or planet. There are a lot of dangers in inter-galactic travel, including many you have not been made aware of yet, but that subject if not for this lecture."

Tonio listened to the lecture as he sat in his wheelchair. *'Wheelchair?'* he thought, *'Can't exactly call this a wheelchair since it has no wheels, and floats above the ground.'* His attention drifted to thoughts of his medical treatment. Although Ganaphe' medical technology can rebuild bone and soft tissue in real time, those reconstructed parts are as weak as a new born baby's. Physical therapy is then needed to strengthen muscle and increase bone density. Tonio's therapy was going quite well, right up until the time he was sure he could push beyond the programmed therapy. Unfortunately he forgot how effective Ganaphe' pain control was – he was causing damage to himself but wasn't feeling it. He pushed the new muscle beyond its capabilities and now was chair bound (floating seat bound?). To make her point that Tonio is to follow her program EXACTLY as she directs, doctor Toisae-sil-Blin removed his pain control leg band and now Tonio was feeling every jab, twinge, ache, and scream of pain – lesson learned! At the time she seemed angry at him – in a professional, controlled way – for setting his recuperation back. Still, he couldn't be mad at her. Every time he thought about the beautiful doctor he found himself smiling. He thought she was the most beautiful woman he had ever seen – and the fact that she had saved his life didn't hurt his opinion of her at all. He only worried that he had damaged her opinion of him. They had been spending a lot of time together, during and after therapy, and he thought she enjoyed his company. He could only hope he hadn't screwed it up. Maybe he was being too critical of himself – he always had been his own severest critic.

His leg reconstruction procedure had been video recorded, and Tonio had viewed the video. He was shocked to see what his leg had looked like, and how much of it was missing when he was brought into the operating room. Hamburger was the only way he could describe it. Anyone from Earth watching that recording would have thought there was no way to save the leg, or even his life. He knew he had to be the luckiest person alive. If the Ganaphe' hadn't been here he would probably be dead. Slowly his attention drifted back to the lecture. He focused his attention on Vaana, knowing that even this basic level class was an introduction to an unimagined universe – one that was way beyond any previous expectations. Before leaving the Earth he had thought that Operation Trailblazer would open the doorway to the future. Now he knew the future held much, much more.

"Then there is the Explorative routes. These are undocumented and untraveled routes. In your language, these might be called 'Trailblazer' routes." she said smiling as she looked at the Earth crew. "Filing a travel plan with your home authority is the intelligent action to accomplish for all travel outside your own solar system, and is especially important for explorative travel. If something happens to affect your safety, this plan will give rescue teams a good reference for their search. You have something similar on your planet. I believe you call them flight plans. It is the same concept."

"I have a question." said Yimka. "This is all probably good to know as general knowledge, but I don't think our technology will reach the level of yours for fifty to one hundred years – if we are lucky. Your laws don't allow you to teach us what you know concerning the scientific principles involved in faster than light travel. You have ships that can travel safely through meteor storms, and engines powerful enough to exceed the speed of light by many times. Our scientists don't even believe that is possible. So why are we spending time on this subject?"

"I will answer that question!" came Munen's voice from the rear of the room. He walked to stand beside Vaana. "In all histories, of all the peoples of the known universe, the hardest part of achievement is knowing something can be done. Now YOU know that it CAN be done. Your contact with us, by your own actions, initiates the right of trade, of not only materials, but of ideas as well. Under the laws of the IGT, this moon legally belongs to you as of the moment you landed here with the intent to colonize it. Your moon contains a valuable mineral that your people do not know about yet. We came here to mine that mineral on an unoccupied moon, which under our laws it was legal for us to do. Since your arrival it is no longer considered unoccupied. That means we have two options to obtain that mineral – buy it from you or trade for it. If the value of the mineral on this moon is as great as our surveys have indicated, trading for a ship that is capable of inter-galactic travel is not out of the question. Your people could be traveling to other galaxies much sooner than you might think. This is what has been done in the past. Of course some of the crew members on such a ship would have to posses the knowledge to maintain it, so you would have to hire personnel from outside your own solar system. There are also the legal aspects of the Interconnected Galaxies Treaty that must be learned about before you will be allowed to freely travel to other occupied galaxies. Learning and understanding those laws will be more difficult than traveling through the universe."

The noise level in room increased slightly as the Trailblazer team tried to comprehend what Munen had just said. There eyes were wide, and more than a few expressions of surprise escaped their mouths.

"So you're saying that we can buy technology from you, even though you can't teach us about it – is that correct?"

"Yes."

"You can teach us how to use it, but you can't teach us how it works?"

"Correct."

"Sounds a little dangerous to me." said JJ.

"On your planet, you have many vehicles for transportation." said Munen. "Yet few of the people who use those vehicles know how they work. Most don't want to know what makes them work. They just know how to use them. It would be the same thing. Of course, space travel is much more dangerous, which is why you will have crew members who do know how they work. These crewmen will come from other planets."

"YES – YES – YES!" said Radio loudly from excitement.

132

"Oops…," she said, lowering her voice, "I didn't mean to be that loud. BUT THAT IS DAMN EXCITING! We were only thinking about making it to the moon a few months ago." she said, looking around at her crew mates. "Now we may be able to go to the stars!"

"Not only that," said Munen, "it is usual for new signatory peoples to send ambassadors to live on other planets to learn about their cultures and laws. If you learn scientific principles on another planet during your journey, and bring them back to your home planet, that is not illegal. Of course, no one will intentionally teach you these things, but when you have access to schools, libraries, and people, it would be hard not to learn some things."

The questions on trade and legality continued on with growing excitement, putting an end to the scheduled class. This was a doorway the Trailblazer personnel had not seen in front of them. Once it was open, it was easy to imagine all the good aspects without thinking of any of the bad. For that part of their day, they forgot that they were on a crippled alien ship that was unable to lift off from the moon – which was exactly one of the dangers Munen and Vaana had been talking about. Travellor was thinking thinking about the mineral Munen had mentioned, and wondered just how much of it was on the moon – and how much was it worth.

Chapter 9

Contact

1

March – 2007

Tonio looked up at the stars that shone overhead. It was an amazing sight. The crater was presently in the shadow of the moon and there was no ambient light to affect his view. As he lay on top of the crate he could see what must have been millions of stars, and each one distinct and bright. Were they different colors, or was his imagination affecting his vision? Or maybe it had something to do with the Ganaphe' helmet he was looking through. Every astronomer on Earth would love to be here and see what he was seeing. But now it was time to get back to work, and he rolled off the crate and back onto his feet. He was almost done. The freedom the Ganaphe' space suit gave him made it feel like he was just out for a nightly stroll. This was part of his physical therapy. He was out here gathering the bits and pieces of the shipping crates that had suffered a less than successful landing. None of it was very heavy here on the moon. It was Toisae's recommendation to Commander Travellor that Tonio be assigned this task as the bending and lifting would help strengthen his body. The Commander took the doctor's recommendations very seriously. As he had said to Tonio, '*The doctor saved your life. We could not have. As far as I'm concerned, until she gives you a clean bill of health, she owns you.*' He didn't mean it literally of course, but if she said something was part of the treatment for Tonio's recovery, it carried the same weight as an order from Travellor.

Tonio didn't mind. He knew Toisae had his best interests in mind.

After five days of this he had found almost all of the scattered materials, including loose hardware, tools, and pieces of damaged electronic equipment, which he placed on the floating platform that followed him around. Some items could still be used, and some could be repaired. Both the primary and the backup communications systems had been damaged, but JJ had said he could scavenge pieces from both to make one working system. He had almost finished that, and everyone was hopeful they could call home soon. The Ganaphe' had said that it would be a violation one of their laws to allow Trailblazer personnel to use their communications systems for contact with Earth. They had a lot of laws concerning contact with a new species, but who would know if they did? Tonio hadn't made up his mind if the Ganaphe' were law abiding because of respect for the law, or fear of the consequences. Maybe both.

Some of the water containers had been damaged, and the water from them had disappeared. He thought this was strange as he had expected to find it frozen, on the ground close by, but it was gone. '*One small mystery for mankind.*' he thought. The physical work did make him feel better. His various pains and aches had diminished to the point where he no longer paid attention to them and, except for lifting heavy loads, he felt fairly normal. He wasn't going to worry about it. The water containers that had survived would supply the Trailblazer base station that was being built, and they wouldn't have to ask the Ganaphe' to share their supply. But until reliable communication was established with Earth, all water related activities would take place on the Orysta so that the water could be recovered and re-used.

2

"Earth base, this is Trailblazer. Do you copy? Over."

Jibble Delfin choked on the bite of bagel that suddenly was trying to go down the wrong part of his throat. His eyes went wide open, not because he was choking on his breakfast but because for over a month his assignment had been to monitor this radio in the hope of hearing from people that everyone knew were probably dead. Farber-Chatwell himself had put Jibble on this assignment, no doubt as a punishment for something Jibble had never been able to determine. His muscular and slightly overweight body convulsed with his choking as he tried to regain control of his breathing to answer the call, but when he tried to speak his coughing overrode his voice. For over four weeks he had spent twelve hours a day here, going home only to sleep and take care of necessities. That gave him a lot of time to try to figure out what he had done wrong, and still he couldn't.

"Earth base, this is Trailblazer. Do you copy? Over."

Jibble quickly took a swallow of coffee. It helped.

"Trailbl… cough, cough, cough. Trailb… cough, cough, cough." was the best Jibble could do. He took another swallow of coffee, calmed himself, and took a deep breath. Then he tried again. "Trailblazer! …, Trailblazer! …," he got out in staccato, "Earth base responding. Over. Is that you? Is it really you? Jibble looked around at the walls of the room, where sixteen by twenty inch photos of each member of the Trailblazer team had been hung.

There was a pause of several seconds, and Delfin began to wonder if he had lost the signal. Then Jibble heard a group of cheering voices over the radio.

"Earth base, this is Trailblazer. Yes it's us. Who is this? Who am I talking to? Over."
"This is communications specialist Delfin. Over… OH MY GOD – YOU'RE ALIVE!… uuuh, over… again."

There was silence again, which confused Jibble.

"Delfin, did you say? I think I've met you. This is mission commander Anthony Travellor. Listen closely Delfin. We're working on a patched up rig, so I'm not sure how long it's going to remain operational. Get this to Farber-Chatwell. All team members are alive and well. Ran into unexpected welcoming committee on arrival. Details for your ears only. Did you get that, Delfin? Over."

"Yes Commander. All team members alive and well. Unexpected welcoming committee. Your ears only. Over."

The large bright red flashing light on the ceiling immediately caught Delfin's attention. The radio remained quiet, and Jibble thought again that he lost Trailblazer's signal.

"What time is it there Delfin?"

Delfin quickly checked the clock.

"Zero four thirty-seven Commander."

Again silence. He was just about to repeat himself when he heard Travellor talking.

"Ah – good. This clock I took from the ship is working correctly. Sort of lost track of time for a while. Going to sign off now. Have a cup of coffee for me Delfin. Can't tell you how much we'd like one up here. Over."

"SIR! – Before you go. I believe the Commander is on his way here! Don't you want to talk to him?"

Silence again. '*There must be transmission delay from the moon. That's it!*' Jibble remembered. '*How long was that supposed to be?*'.

"Ears only Delfin. When he has that set up, tell him to transmit on our scheduled comm periods. We'll be waiting to hear from him. Travellor out."

3

Farber-Chatwell's eyes popped open, and he didn't know why. He heard voices that shouldn't be there – he was the only one in the house. Then he recognized Anthony Travellor's voice and knew he was still asleep – except he wasn't! *'The receiver.'* he thought, the concept solidifying in his thoughts. *'It's coming from the linked receiver.'* He looked at the clock on his night table – it was four thirty-three in the morning. His body jumped upright of its own volition.

The linked receiver picked up encoded transmissions from the Trailblazer communication control room. There was only two of them – one in his bedroom beside his bed, and one downstairs in his home office – and they only worked when his ID badge was within four feet of them. He had ordered them built so he would have a better chance of knowing if Trailblazer made contact. He was fully awake now. It was Travellor's voice and he was talking to Delfin. He knew he had picked the right people to man that control room. Delfin and Sawyers had both met the Trailblazer team several times while the team was training for the mission. He had wanted radio operators who had a personal connection to Trailblazer and could put faces to the missing people. He believed this would give the men more incentive to do the job, and both men had not disappointed him. For weeks they had worked twelve hour shifts, seven days a week. They had given up their normal lives to accomplish this job – everyone assigned to mission Trailblazer had.

Farber-Chatwell turned up the volume on the receiver, then slapped the large button on top of it, which began to flash red. The button initiated a signal back to the control room causing a red light located there to flash, to indicate to the man on duty that Farber-Chatwell was monitoring the communication. He quickly headed for the bathroom to begin dressing. He had to get there – had to BE there! No time for formal attire. No time for socks. Sweats and sneakers would be the quickest way to dress. *'What the hell? Did he say welcoming committee?'* he thought. That phrase made him stop for a second. *'That's not good.'* He pulled a sweat top over his head, jumped into the pants, slid his feet into the shoes, shoved socks and underwear in his pocket, and headed downstairs. The minutes were ticking by.

4

It was high-fives and cheers all around the Trailblazer team, as Travellor terminated communications with their base on Earth. Vaana and Munen stood further back in the room, each smiling at their friends' success. A lot had been done in the short time the two peoples had been together, but this marked the beginning of the future for both groups. By law, Munen was not allowed to contact the base on Earth. Now that the humans had made the contact he would be allowed to communicate to their commander and attempt to form an understanding that would allow the exchange of supplies, as well as having the Orysta crew travel to the planet. This would allow the Ganaphe' to leave this isolation they had been trapped in for too long. He would create a leave schedule before ending his day, so that it would be ready to be implemented. Before the humans showed up, the isolation was becoming a mental health issue,. Now that they were here everyone hoped it might mean they could soon leave this barren moon, even if just for a short time. To be able to walk on a planet again, where a sun provided light and warmth, and air could be freely breathed, would put a positive attitude back into his crew. The humans would benefit also, as the Ganaphe' could give them the means for real-time travel to and from the planet with much greater safety and speed than would have been possible with their own vehicles.

There was a lot going on, and things were moving quickly. Contact with the Earth would not only affect the physical and mental well being of his crew, but may possibly make available the means to begin the long journey back home – something that was lacking now. The Orysta was stuck, and the equipment and supplies they had on hand could not free it. Munen knew his crew would realize this, and it would energize them. Every mirlot saved would be one mirlot less before they could see their families again.

5

Farber-Chatwell stepped down from the shuttle, and tried to take in what was in front of him. It was less than an hour ago an invisible ship appeared in his own back yard, carrying Anthony Travellor, Dal Yimka, and two strangers that were introduced as Tahn-grilik Intul-sil-Califas and Lead Technician Mengu-sil-Valian. '*What the hell is a Tahn-grilik?*' he remembered thinking. Travellor had placed a bracelet on his wrist, and the foreign language the two strangers were speaking was translated through it, attenuating the sound from his ears and sending signals directly to his brain. It took him a while to learn to ignore the diminished sound his ears heard, and listen to the second louder translated voice. He had been told they would only stay long enough to pick him up and depart, but Travellor did take the time to go into his kitchen and grab a bottle of Irish Whiskey and two pounds of coffee beans, which he claimed were mission critical supplies. He was still trying to believe what his eyes were seeing when they left Earth's atmosphere and made the trip to the moon at what was described to him as minimal cruise speed.

Now he was on the moon, inside the landing bay of the inter-galactic mining ship Orysta – and it was unbelievably large. He had been on container ships that he thought were huge at the time, but some of them were smaller than this. In front of him, standing in a line and facing him were the rest of the Trailblazer team. Opposite them and standing in a similar manner were the crew of the Orysta. That was when he noticed the name tags. Both human and Ganaphe' wore them, with a slight difference. On the Trailblazer team their names were written in English on top, and below that an unfamiliar script. On the Ganaphe' the names were in that script on top, and below they were written in English.

Farber-Chatwell looked back at the four men behind him and noticed for the first time that they were wearing similar name tags. All eyes were on him. The man at the front of the Orysta crew stepped towards him.

"I am Artau-sil-Munen, Grilik of the Orysta. Welcome to my ship."

"Thank you." said Farber-Chatwell. "I am Robert Farber-Chatwell. Commander in charge of the Trailblazer mission. Thank you for taking care of my people. I am very grateful."

Munen introduced each of his crew members, and greetings were exchanged, formally and a bit stiffly. Farber-Chatwell was a stranger to these people, and they were not yet as comfortable with each other as the Trailblazer team and the Orysta crew were.

6

The sharing of a meal is a universal gesture of good will. Farber-Chatwell was introduced to some good but basic Ganaphe' food. But it takes time and familiarity for two peoples from different galaxies to be at ease with each other. The Ganaphe' and the Trailblazer team had reached that point, but for Farber-Chatwell this was all new and strange. The thought that just outside the structure of the ship was the cold and airless environment of the moon kept popping into his mind. The meal consisted of a combination of Ganaphe' foods and re-hydrated Earth foods. At the end of the meal, when everyone was full and relaxed, Travellor brought out from the kitchen several containers of hot black coffee. Now the Ganaphe' would try something they had heard Trailblazer members often mention. The Ganaphe' had several beverages made with various plants from their home world, but nothing had come close to coffee for the Trailblazer team. Everyone in the room was poured a cup. Some sniffed it to see if they could determine if the beverage would be palatable by its smell.

"For our extra-terrestrial neighbors," started Travellor, "I suggest that first you take a sip before adding sweetener or creamer, to get a taste of coffee itself. Be careful – it's hot."

They all did as instructed. Some liked the taste of the coffee, and others thought it was too bitter.

"Now try it with some sweetener. Start with a little and increase the amount to your taste. On Earth some people drink it with a large variety of flavorings, but if it's good coffee you will only need sweetener. I like it with just sugar, and sometimes a touch of cream. After you find the right amount of sweetener, try it with creamer. I'm looking forward to trying it with bliml."

"Blimal?" queried Farber-Chatwell.

"You would consider it a combined creamer and sweetener." replied Munen. "It comes from a plant that grows on our home planet. Commander Travellor has said that it should go well with your coffee."

The Ganaphe' did as suggested, and most of them liked the beverage. Others thought their own beverages were much better. The tasting was as much entertainment as it was a sharing, and the mood grew more relaxed. But there lingered a tension in the room, brought on by Farber-Chatwell's presence. The Ganaphe' hadn't had time to get to know him yet, and vice versa. Travellor had explained to Munen and his crew that Farber-Chatwell had both the capability and the resources to get the things they desired. He made it clear to them that this was a man whose influence should not be underestimated.

Since Farber-Chatwell normally added cream and sugar to his coffee, he decided to give the bliml a try, and a very pleased expression appeared on his face. He took a few more sips of his coffee with bliml.

"This is VERY good!" he said out loud, and then turned to Munen. "May I have some to take back with me?"

"Yes. The Commander has already made up a list of things he thought you would like to try. Our cook will gather together a package for you. Your Commander is a thorough man. I have grown to like him in the time we have spent together."

Farber-Chatwell looked at Travellor, who was going around the room checking that everyone tried the coffee.

"He's a good man." said Farber-Chatwell as he watched him. "I was supposed to lead the Trailblazer mission myself," he said leaning closer to Munen, "but an accident made that impossible. There were three men I considered suitable to lead this mission in my place. I chose him because he had a history of handling unexpected situations. Of course, at the time, I had no idea of how unexpected everything would turn out."

"My people like him." replied Munen. "Our people get along well together. I believe they share something in common. They find themselves under very challenging conditions. Trailblazer came to establish a community in a hostile environment, risking their lives to do so. My crew is stuck in the same environment with a crippled ship, unable to know when or if they will ever make the trip back home. That is why they work so well together."

"Still," said Farber-Chatwell, "you could easily take your shuttles to Earth if all else failed."

"No." said Munen with a sad expression on his face. "That was never an option, until Trailblazer showed up. Our laws forbid contact with any peoples that have not first invited us to do so. The IGT strictly defines this. To violate the law under any but uncontrolled circumstances would mean financial ruin or imprisonment – or both. There is no – wiggle room? I believe that is what your people call it. It was only when your team made contact with you and then invited me to speak to you that it became legal for me to do so. For a while I was worried that was not going to happen. I could not legally allow them to use our equipment to do it. When we located your radios and found both units had been destroyed, we were very depressed. That was when I realized how much alike the two crews were. Your team immediately came up with a plan to make what was available perform the job required. My crew is often in situations like that, and they respond in the same way."

"And if your situation became dire? A matter of your crews survival. Would you still not have gone to Earth on your own?"

"If the lives of my people were in jeopardy," Munen said with a wry smile, "I would have arranged for them to go to your planet in a manner that would make me the only one who had broken the law."

Their conversation continued haltingly, as each man thought about what the other had said. One thing they could understand was expression and tone of voice of the other person. Farber-Chatwell asked if he could have a copy of the IGT laws, but was not surprised when Munen told him it was already one of the items Travellor had requested for his gift package.

"There is also an introductory file called IGT Esploreesum, that Travellor said would be very useful. He calls it 'IGT For Dummies'. He has spent many hours studying it. We have translated everything and stored it in a format your computers can use. There are some words and phrases that do not translate to your language. I or someone on my crew will be happy to explain anything that is not clear."

7

It had been a long day for Farber-Chatwell. His watch told him it was after eleven in the evening – on Earth. He felt worn out as he stood in the shower stall. He could have asked to be taken back home, but he wanted to get a better idea of what the lives of his people were like here. His room was small, but had all the basic comforts. He had asked for a blanket when he saw none in the room, and it was explained to him that the ships environmental system didn't just control the temperature of the room, but individualized that control over the different parts of your body. The temperature that was most comfortable for your torso was slightly different than what was best for your thighs, and your feet, and arms, and hands. The system was so sophisticated that it monitored and adjusted nine different

144

body zones, analyzing your body's reaction and the quality of your sleep by measuring body part temperature and brain wave patterns. Blankets were only used when the system malfunctioned. But Farber-Chatwell wanted a blanket easily available anyway.

"Deluge." he stated, standing in the middle of the shower stall. He figured this command would give him the strongest spray.

It was a lesson in not underestimating the Ganaphe' technology. The water that hit his body from all directions felt like a wave that was going to pick him up bodily, and carry him downstream. Water rushed into his nose and ears and eyes, and he stopped himself from inhaling just in time.

"STO-O-O-P !" he yelled, and the water flow turned off immediately.

He stood there, completely soaked and dripping, with his arms up in defensive manner. He coughed, spit and blew the water out of his nose and mouth. Then he started to laugh. He was standing naked and dripping wet, in an alien spaceship, thinking he was going to drown, and it all struck him as unbelievably ridiculous. He laughed a little harder.

"Medium spray." he said, and the water came out at just the right strength. "Pulsing jets at my back." he said. The spray at his back hit him in pulsing waves, like a massage that went up and down his body. When it hit his neck he relaxed the muscles there and began to enjoy the sensation. "Increase water temperature by five degrees."

The temperature rise brought the water to just below being uncomfortable. It was just what he wanted. He let the heat soak deeper into his body.

All of this was still very hard for Farber-Chatwell to take in. He never had believed in space aliens. '*Space aliens! C'mon. Really? People with a more advanced technology, traveling through the galaxies. Who the hell is going to believe that?*' he thought. For one thing, galaxies were just too far apart – even at the speed of light! Nobody could travel those vast distances in a reasonable amount of time. Yet from what he understood from the Ganaphe', they were not the only ones. There were many galaxies with many inhabited worlds with many different species of beings, all capable of such travel. Some even having already traveled to this galaxy!

From what the Ganaphe' captain had told him, it was the binding legal agreements between species and the accompanying uncompromising penalties for breaking these laws that was likely responsible for the Earth not having been a sci-fi movie like victim of an invasion by an alien species. Even those species that had elected not to sign on to the IGT clearly understood that violation of certain IGT laws would make them susceptible to retribution by its signatories. For someone like him, it was very hard to believe. Yet here it was for his eyes to see. Here it was for his hands to touch, and his body to feel, and impossible to be denied. In a way, it all proved that his mission, his planning, and his life had been mistaken if not false. '*No! Not false.*' he thought, '*Mistaken at worse. Lacking in foresight.*' If anything this proved the basic concept to be correct. In all of the years of his life since the mission began he believed 361 had been ahead of all others in planning and technology, and would be capable of creating something that would protect his country and its people. Now he had to accept that the enemy he feared was small compared to the possible enemy from without. He cursed himself for this lack of vision. But how do you defend from an enemy that you don't even know – don't even BELIEVE – exists. From a time before he was born, this planet had been susceptible to an attack that perhaps – probably – they could not have repelled.

As he continued to let the heat soak into him, his military mind imagined ships orbiting the Earth, capable of firing on any target on the planet, with little to no risk of being struck back. The images swelled in his imagination. The mission of Operation 361 was no longer the same. It now had to expand beyond its original purpose. If these Ganaphe' were indeed friends as they expressed they were, they would be the key to expanding the knowledge of what lay outside the Milky Way. Their misfortune of crashing on the moon would be to the Earth's advantage. '*361's and the Earth's advantage.*' thought Farber-Chatwell.

146

"Off." he said, and the water stopped. "Dry."

Standing still as the air jets squeegeed the water from him, Farber-Chatwell decided that the first thing he wanted to accomplish tomorrow was to take a walk on the moon's surface. Just a small personal desire. He wanted to take that walk on the Earth side of the moon, and gaze at the Earth. From what Travellor had told him about Ganaphe' space suits, it would be a very enjoyable experience. He couldn't remember seeing any surface vehicles on the ship. Were all their vehicles airborne? Maybe the Ganaphe' didn't ride on wheels anymore.

8

Farber-Chatwell sat on the edge of the bed in the dark room, ready for sleep, when a thought entered his mind.

"Computer?"

There was no response.

"Is there a computer listening to my words?"

Still no response.

"LIGHTS!" he said loudly.

The room lights came on full bright. He reflexively squinted, and put his hand in front of his eyes.

"State the name, or the identification designation of the device that is controlling the functions of this room according to my requests."

"LNTGAD475341627144.73.5.3. I have also been given the designation 'ORYSTA'."

Farber-Chatwell was surprised. He hadn't expected an answer to his question.

"Orysta! That's also the name of this ship." he said.
"Correct."
"So you have the same name as the ship?"
"Yes."
"Are you the ship's main computer, or some other processing device?"
"Ship's central data processing computer."
"So the Ganaphe' give the ship's main computer the same name as that of the ship."
"Correct."
"What about the other processors, calculators, controllers and sensors on this ship? Do those all have names?"
"No."
"Why don't the other devices have names?"
"Operational protocol. The ship and the ship's main computer must operate as one unit. It is easier for the crew to refer to both as one unit. All other devices are designated by their function."
"So if I addressed you as 'Orysta', you would know that I am communicating with you?"
"Yes."

Farber-Chatwell had so far found this conversation entertaining, but he wasn't sure he had learned anything important.

"How powerful are you?"
"Inquiry not understood."
"How much... processing capability do you have, Orysta?"
"I have the capability of zero point four seven dedicated brain

148

power."

He had to think about that for while.

"Are you saying that you have point four seven times as much processing capability as the human brain?"

"Point four seven times as much processing capability as a Ganaphe' brain dedicated to a single function. Not enough information available about the human brain to calculate an equivalent."

Farber-Chatwell thought about that. No processor on Earth could come close to the brain's processing power. If you could dedicate all that capability to a single function it would be the same as multiplying that capability by an unknown number of times. And no one on Earth could accurately calculate brain power. It was always underestimated.

"Do the Ganaphe' have more powerful processors than you?"

"Yes."

"How powerful? Is there some way you can explain this to me in something other than fractions of brain power?"

"Will a comparison satisfy your requirements?"

"I don't know. Go ahead, give it a try."

"Orysta is classified as a category thirty-four processor. The portable computer that you have would be classified as a category that is below a zero point zero zero zero zero zero one processor. Its capabilities are very limited."

"This laptop," Farber-Chatwell interrupted, "has the highest end processor on the planet. I hasn't even been released to the military yet."

He got no reaction to his statement.

"Please continue."

"Categories of processors presently go up to two hundred and thirty-one. This will change as more capable processors are developed."

Farber-Chatwell's eyes went wide. '*One hundred and ninety-seven levels higher than you.*' he thought, stunned by the idea.

"Let's talk about something else." he said. "Were you given any instructions concerning my presence or activities on this ship?"

"*Yes.*"

"What were those instructions?"

"*Grilik Munen has instructed that you be placed under a maximum security protocol as an ambassador of another species.*"

Now this was something he found interesting. Could he gain some real insight into Ganaphe' thinking here?

"What exactly does maximum security protocol mean? Am I free to leave the room? Am I free to wander around the ship?"

"*You have access to all of the ship except for three restricted areas. There are no time constraints.*"

"What areas are restricted to me?"

"*The bridge, the engine room, and the food stores.*"

Farber-Chatwell couldn't find any fault with that. He would have done the same thing if the Orysta was his ship. He was feeling very tired now. Sleep was taking over his mind, and any nervousness he felt before seemed to be gone. As he lay on the bed he noticed how perfect the temperature of the mattress and pillow felt.

"Lights off. Thanks for the conversation Orysta."

There was no reply.

Chapter 10

Homesteading

1

July – 2008

Jibble Delfin looked out of the clear dome, in awe. The Earth floating just above the monochrome surface of the moon was a beautiful and inviting sight. Looking at it gave him a sense of warmth and comfort. He wondered if it engendered the same feelings in everyone who saw it from here. HERE! Here he was – on the moon, and the stationing was Farber-Chatwell's way of showing his appreciation for his dedication to the job – and he had thought Farber-Chatwell disliked him! Now he was the Chief Communications Specialist on Moon-base Trailblazer, was given an increase in pay, and had two other people working under him.

He was told he was completely safe from space radiation in here. The dome was a present from the Ganaphe', manufactured in their on-board foundry, and it was made of the crystalline material they had come to mine. They called it Crystal-flow – or that was what the name translated as from their language to ours. It is found throughout the universe, but in concentrations so diluted by other materials that for most of their history they hadn't known it existed. It is most often found in concentrations of 1 part in a trillion or more, which is why it took so long to be discovered. Most geologists studying minerals would see it as a minor contamination of their sample instead of a mineral worth looking at in itself. But like gold or other precious materials, there are places where the concentrations are high enough to make it worth mining. 'High enough' is a relative term though. Here on the moon it is found in the amount of 1 part per one hundred thousand. That means that for every one hundred thousand grains of sand the Ganaphe' process, only one grain will be crystal-flow. That's considered a high concentration, making it commercially viable with Ganaphe' mining techniques. Of course it isn't always so dispersed in surrounding materials. Sometimes it is found in nuggets. A nugget the size of a pinky finger nail is worth a small fortune.

The discovery and commercialization of crystal-flow had changed space travel for every species with the ability to leave their planet of origin. Before its properties were known space ships were more like flying coffins, in the sense that any view of the outside was seen through video links, sensors, or small view ports. The technological links to the outside of the ship were prone to failing, requiring either dangerous extra-vehicular repairs or just flying by instruments. The view ports were often facing the wrong way when an incident occurred. Something as simple as not being able to see outside a space ship, that would be traveling many weeks or months to reach its destination, can lead to cabin fever, depression, and other changes in personality, and greatly affect the mental health of the travelers. The simplest treatment for this was just being able to see outside the coffin.

Before the discovery of crystal-flow, short careers in long distance space travel was the rule. What makes crystal-flow so valuable is that it can be formed into windows as clear as glass, with many times the strength, and most importantly the ability to stop radiation from passing through it. Damaging and potentially deadly high energy particles are blocked and bound by its crystalline structure. On a planet, people are protected from these particles by the planet's atmosphere and magnetic field, but when traveling through space it is the ship's structure that protects the occupants.

Crystal-flow also has an extremely high magnetic permeability. This makes it a very good shielding material from magnetic flux and electro-magnetic radiation – useful in keeping out electrical interference in electronic equipment – especially in medical electronics. This characteristic also allows magnetic flux fields to be used in the manufacturing process, to physically manipulate the shape and thickness of the final crystal-flow product, with unlimited continuous variations. It seems to pull the magnetic field into it, and when in a fluid state it follows the shape of the field.

A dome the same thickness as the one Jibble was looking through is capable of protecting a person standing on the surface of the planet Mercury from the radiation of the powerful solar flares and coronal mass ejections emitted by the Earth's sun. No presently known galaxy hopping species builds ships without crystal-flow ports and domes anymore. It is a rare mineral that is in high demand, and that makes it extremely valuable. There is even a large salvage industry built around recovering the material from damaged or decommissioned ships. Crystal-flow is recyclable, and loses none of its properties in the process.

In the year he had been here the basic structure of the building had changed from the simple single story box concept originally designed for the mission to a multi-level dual wagon wheel shaped building that, thanks to the expertise and equipment gifted by the Ganaphe', was capable of protecting its occupants from almost all of the potential dangers the moon's surface was exposed to. Jibble had even given a hand in the assembly when he first arrived here, since there was little to do on the communications end then. Probably the only real threat they were not protected from was a strike by a large meteor – but even that was mitigated by the advanced sensors on the Ganaphe' ship, which worked fairly well even buried underground as it was. Jibble suspected that they also had the capability of doing something about such a meteor, even though they had never directly stated so. The whole thing was years ahead of the original 361 mission plan, and far more sophisticated.

And these Ganaphe' were miners – very well equipped and experienced miners, which was not overlooked by Farber-Chatwell. Yes, the surface structure of Moon Base Trailblazer was very impressive, but not as impressive as the underground structure it sat on top of. Farber-Chatwell had hired the Ganaphe' to put their mining skills to work, and the result was a ten story underground structure that planned for the future. It was a huge. Most of it was empty right now, but when things went as 361 foresaw the building would house personnel and equipment that would pave the way for mankind's indoctrination into practical space travel. Priority had been given to the shuttle bay, which was on the ground floor. It was completed first and Ganaphe' shuttles were now using it instead of the ship's bay, as an operational test of the facility. With the use of the Ganaphe' shuttles, stronger and better materials had been brought up here for the construction. Several of the floors below the surface were also completed and operational, with the remaining floors not yet habitable.

This expanded construction of the base had the added benefit of giving the Ganaphe' some side work to occupy themselves with while they were looking for the next crystal-flow concentration to mine. Between mining and building they were busy again, and feeling useful, even if it wasn't in the way they originally planned. There was even an excitement about helping with building the Earth's first inter-stellar space port. They knew they would be recorded in Earth's historical record for this, not only as having helped build the base, but also as the first alien species to contact the human race. Commander Farber-Chatwell had a plaque fabricated with their names and the name of their ship, and had it mounted at the entrance of the base reception area for all to see. With their mining engineers mining, their flight engineers working on repairing their ship, and their command crew negotiating with 361 administrators, Ganaphe' morale was high again. 361 paid the Ganaphe' in several ways – cash (used during their recreation time on Earth), supplies, and crystal-flow mining rights.

In the center of the surface part of the base structure was a Ganaphe' device that generated a focused magnetic field around the building, and encompassing the entire area inside the crater. The field protected the people inside it from space radiation, by redirecting the course of high energy particles away from the base. The device was part of the trade agreement that was still being worked out by the Ganaphe' and Farber-Chatwell's legal experts, in exchange for crystal-flow mining rights on the moon. As Jibble understood it, 361's experts were learning IGT law as they went along, and the Ganaphe' were restricted in what they could offer by that same law. IGT penalties could be grave, so both groups were moving carefully as to not jeopardize the Orysta's crew. This type of agreement wasn't usually conducted by a ship's captain and the representative of a covert organization.

As the agreements and trade between the aliens and 361 were

sorted out, and travel to and from Earth increased, communications between the planet and the moon base became a twenty-four by seven job. Personnel rotations, material supply, and the very important OP (On Planet) time had turned the moon base into the first human off world interplanetary space port – and it all had to be done without being detected by outsiders on Earth. Outsiders being anyone not in the 361 organization with a need to know.

Moon base Trailblazer had also been relocated to be closer to the Ganaphe' ship. This was a decision by Farber-Chatwell, and Jibble thought it was a good one. The moon base was now connected to the ship by a short underground passage, with a habitable environment maintained. Apparently, even in its damaged condition, the ship's engine could generate more than enough power for both habitats, with a huge reserve capability left over. With the Ganaphe' camouflage in operation, someone looking directly at the base from overhead would not be able to see it.

Jibble always found a smile on his face when he walked through the passage, a reaction to the ducifels growing out of the walls and ceiling. These multi-colored petal flowers from the Ganaphe' home world are usually found growing at the entrances of caves and tunnels, and they have two useful characteristics. One is the ability to grow downward or sideways without consideration for sunlight or gravity – great when used as a decoration. The other is that they are very sensitive to oxygen levels. Oxygen levels of eighteen percent or less caused the petals to immediately turn white. This last characteristic allowed them to be used like a canary in a mine, giving people a very obvious warning that the air is bad. That's why they were placed in the passage way. But mainly Jibble liked them because they were so colorful. He thought the petals looked like Chiclets gum.

Jibble now also had a better understanding for the rigorous preemployment testing he had to go through when he was first being considered for a job with 361. At the time he hadn't even known it was 361 that was hiring him. He had thought he was applying for a position with an international shipping company, and the psychological tests he had to take just didn't make sense for that type of job. He now understood why they needed someone who was psychologically flexible and loyal. He had gone from handling communications on a secret manned mission to the moon, to handling communications on a secret base located ON the moon. *'And in cooperation with little green men!'* He chuckled at the thought. They were neither little nor green, nor were they easily discernible from any other person – except for the hair of the women – it was almost luminescent. At first Jibble had thought it was a Ganaphe' fashion thing – it wasn't! Ganaphe' females capable of reproduction had that luminescent quality to their hair. Those that hadn't reached maturity and those that had reached an age where they were no longer fertile had hair that looked more like a human female's of similar age. It was just one more thing that was new in his life. If the cosmetic industry on Earth found out about this, it would no doubt start a new fashion trend. Human women all over the globe would want their hair looking like that also. Psychological flexibility – now he understood why it was important to 361 to have people with that characteristic. Now he understood the reason for all the testing he went through. In a very short period of time, all of these new aspects of life had become normal to him.

2

    '12 December 2008. It's been one hell of a year!' wrote Radio Delgadillo in her log. Keeping a log was now required of all the command staff on Trailblazer base. No one had said it out loud, but everyone knew the logs were used back on Earth for psychological evaluation and not just as mission reports. Since she had to keep one anyway, Radio had decided to make it a diary of her thoughts as well. *'The number of 361 personnel had increased to thirty-seven, matching the number of Ganaphe'.'* she continued. *'By mutual agreement the number will not be exceeded without the consent of the Ganaphe', and since they are supplying many necessary resources such as electrical power, as well as desirable creature comforts and advanced safety and life support technology, their opinion carries a lot of weight. Every one of the original Trailblazer crew were given an increase*

in rank and salary, and were assigned specific duties with personnel under their direct command. Flight commander Anthony Travellor was promoted to Moon Base Commander. I don't think he is very happy about that, since he is used to being a hands on person and not one that tells others what to do. In my opinion he was the obvious right choice for the job. His ability to make the Ganaphe' feel that they are our friends as well as allies is the cornerstone of what we have built here. They have in fact become our friends and are our allies. Life on the base at present is as physically comfortable as if we were back on Earth, if you disregard the lack of sunshine and a walk outside being potentially deadly. Still, nothing up here will ever match a warm, sunny day, with blue skies and fluffy white clouds. The original time line for mission Trailblazer would have had us living more like explorers camping in a desolate area at this point in time. Our success is due to our relationship with the Ganaphe', originally forged by us under Commander Travellor's leadership. The newcomers may only know him as the base commander, but all on the original crew know better. The Ganaphe' both like and respect him.'

'Christmas is almost upon us and the Ganaphe' are looking forward to it as much as we are. They are excited about taking part in an Earth custom. They are a little overwhelmed by all of our religions and customs, and are documenting as much as they can. Apparently this will be important information for the sociologists of the IGT planets, since there hasn't been a new species contact in a long time. If and when the Ganaphe' get back home, this will cause a lot of excitement in their intellectual circles. They will probably be invited to go on a lecture tour throughout the known galaxies – known to them, that is. I still have a hard time grasping the number of inhabited planets out there, with almost each one having a distinct species. We hold weekly classes where the Ganaphe' are trying to teach us about all of these peoples, their cultures, and their home worlds. It's a lot to learn, and is a mandatory attendance item for all 361 personnel. Mersuul Vaana is an excellent teacher. She is the Orysta's navigator, but those skills aren't being used very much at present. She is also the defacto Ganaphe' good will ambassador to Earth, as Grilik Munen is busy with negotiations with 361.'

'WE WILL ACTUALLY BE HAVING A LIVE TREE HERE ON THE MOON !!!! Unbelievable! I can barely wait for it to arrive. Both the ship and the base have already been decorated with lights and hangings, and this has created a more festive mood in everyone. The celebration is a needed break, as both groups have been working full schedules for months. It's funny to see the shuttles which have even been fitted with artificial Christmas wreaths hung on the front, to emulate the way cars are decorated on Earth. The Ganaphe' celebrate only two major holidays on their home planet, which are based on the seasonal shifts in the amount of daylight. The land mass on their planet is localized around the equator, instead of being dispersed in all latitudes as on Earth. Apparently their planet looks more like a squashed ball than a round one as Earth does. They only have two major seasons, with minor alterations, and rarely get drastic shifts in weather. I'm told this is not the norm throughout the IGT. Some member planets have drastic weather shifts in relatively short periods of time. They are amazed by our seasonal changes. The turning of the leaves in fall is a very big thing for them, and 361 personnel have had to fill in at light duty stations on their ship so that every one of them gets to see it first hand. This was a major vote of trust by the Ganaphe', to have us stationed on their ship, even if it was not for anything critical. Again I will state that this is due to their trust in Commander Travellor. It is interesting and important to note that the Orysta has automated internal defenses that can kill, and we have been intensely instructed on which areas to stay away from.'

'The Operation Trailblazer team have come to know all of the Ganaphe' crew personally. Half of the Ganaphe' personnel will be spending the holiday on Earth by invitation from host families. Classes about culture and social behavior are held every night on the ship, and it's always a full room. We're not sugar coating anything for them. With the good, they are taught about the bad they may encounter, such as crime, anti-social behavior, drugs, bureaucrats, etc. The exchange of information between us is hot and heavy during the Q&A after each class. Their home world has or had many of the same problems as ours. The most interesting thing I have learned about is their political system. In order for the IGT to *function, the combined legal systems of all IGT member species had to make drastic changes. Some laws are considered inviolate (a requirement for inter-species interaction learned from many sad and terrible conflicts among them), with summary execution being a potential outcome. Politicians are held accountable for all actions, with no immunity from the consequences. Apparently this leads to very good laws being made.'*

'Unfortunately I will be on station for Christmas. There will only be a skeleton 361 crew here, but someone has to do it and I'm one of the someones. It won't be bad though. 361 is shipping in a big holiday meal with all the trimmings (so no one here will have to cook), which the remaining Ganaphe' are also looking forward to. They haven't yet tasted turkey or pumpkin pie. I'll be able to video link with my family, which is done by a signal from moon base to an Earth orbiting communications satellite, down to the surface, and hooked into the internet so that it looks like a regular Skype connection. Since we will be using our own comm equipment instead of the Ganaphe's there will be a delay in the signal, but I've already explained by email that this is because of the poor signal quality in my location (not exactly a lie). I can't wait to see everyone gathered together, even if it will only be on a computer screen. We haven't figured out how the Ganaphe' signals can travel so much faster than ours, and IGT law forbids them from telling us how it is done.'

'Information is one of the main items being exchanged between the Ganaphe' and 361. We now have medical personnel being trained to use the Ganaphe' surgical equipment, while they in turn are teaching Doctor Blin and her assistant about Earth surgical procedures – which are blowing their minds. She is appreciative of not having to be on duty around the clock (being the only doctor on the moon) anymore. The hands-on type of surgery we do on Earth belongs to the Ganaphe' past, and very few of their surgeons actually place their hands inside someone's body to repair them these days. And the time it takes for a patient to heal from a procedure on Earth is driving her nuts. She just mumbles in disbelief at the case histories she has learned about. Anatomy seems to be the easiest thing for both sides to learn since our bodies and organs are very similar. Dr. Blin has requested that she be allowed to assist in surgical procedures back

on Earth. She feels that the experience of medical practice without Ganaphe' technology could be very useful if she ever finds herself in extremely primitive conditions (I think that means us). I can understand her thoughts on this. If the Orysta can be damaged in a crash landing, her medical equipment also can be. She could someday find herself with only her hands and a sharp blade available to save someone's life with.'

'Our technicians are learning the use of Ganaphe' equipment, and our engineers have come up with Earth substitutes for some of the Ganaphe' supplies that are getting low. We've been able to recharge their emergency boosters with a combustible synthetic that generates a very similar reaction to the original material used. Grilik Munen has expressed his gratitude for this accomplishment. He said that in the past he had considered the boosters as superfluous, but that they were an important factor in saving the lives of his crew and the ship. In his mind these low tech boosters have now become GO/NO-GO equipment for him in any future travels. He has even modified his ship's mandatory equipment list to reflect this. At first I had thought he was just being gracious, and making small talk, until he authorized me to listen to the ship's log file concerning their landing here. He wasn't joking. Those boosters – old technology to them as they are – saved the ship and the crew from a lot of pain and damage. Sometimes simple brute force is the right tool for the job.'

'On a personal note: The Ganaphe' can teach us how to use their equipment, but under IGT law they cannot explain to us the principles that make them operate. Although much of their equipment can be classified as 'electronic', the principles of physics that make them work are different than what our technology uses. This is only a guess, and a feeling I get, as I spend more time working with them. This bothers me very much. They can do things easily that our science and technology has yet to understand. The most obvious, and possibly greatest example of this is the artificial gravity they can generate and control. It is almost as if they are able to amplify the moons own gravity and control its strength. All of this is speculation on my part. I have not asked them about this. I doubt they would tell me. The engineering and power plant sections of the ship are off limits to all 361 personnel. I think that is because the answers would become clear if we *knew what went on there. I do not plan on violating their rules. I have talked about this with Commander Travellor and Mission Commander Farber-Chatwell, and they do not plan on violating the Ganaphe' directives either. Curiosity cannot be quenched by only holding the cup of knowledge – you have to drink (Where did I read that from?).'*

Chapter 11

Research and Development

1

January – 2009

The unexpected vibrations were felt through the moon base floors, as audible and visible alarms were going off throughout the Orysta and the base. Bright lights flashed in the eyes like visual explosions. The sirens were loud, annoying, and no one could ignore them. That's what they were designed to do – get your attention. Hatches and section entrance way doors quickly and automatically closed as soon as sensors detected they were clear of personnel. It took less than ten seconds for most sections of the ship and Trailblazer base to be isolated from every other. It only took a few more for doors that were obstructed to be cleared by personnel and sealed. The isolation protocol wasn't that much of a surprise to anyone on the base, after they had felt the structure shake and heard the loud boom that caused the vibration. Even on the moon with its lower gravity this was a heavy building. It would take a powerful force to shake the whole thing, and everyone knew it. Something had gone very wrong, and in the vacuum of space – which was what the surface of the moon was – it was very dangerous.

"WHAT THE HELL HAPPENED ?" came a loud voice over the base wide intercom. Everyone recognized Travellor's voice.

It was a few seconds before Joshua Kibbee was able to respond. Kibbee was one of four ex-Navy Seals and Army Rangers that provided security

162

for the base. They had all been vetted very thoroughly for this assignment, and had only been on station for a few months. The three others reported to him.

"BREACH IN THE METAL FABRICATION SECTION!" Kibbee yelled back. "WE'VE HAD AN EXPLOSION THAT TOOK OUT ONE OF THE HANGAR BAY DOORS."

'*DAMN IT !*' thought Travellor. This was a worse case situation. One he always knew could happen, and always prayed it wouldn't.

"WAS ANYONE HURT ?"
"No assessment yet, sir. Working on that now." said Kibbee.
"Medical team to the metal fabrication area. All available personnel to assist." came the words from Travellor's mouth without thinking. He wasn't yelling anymore. His training and experience was taking over. "Orysta, moon base requesting your assistance. We've had a structural failure in the metal fabrication area." Travellor knew the words were just a formality. The Orysta crew would have already been on their way to help. '*Thank God for friends you can depend on.*' he thought.

"*All members of Orysta crew accounted for. Moon base Trailblazer missing one personnel.*" came the voice over the comm.

Travellor recognized the Orysta's main computer's voice. It had automatically been assessing the damage as the situation unfolded. Everyone on the moon wore either comm badges, wrist devices, or helmets – on or off duty. It was required. Orysta knew who was missing, but didn't specify.

"Orysta – is doctor Blin on station?" asked Travellor.
"*Doctor Blin is on the planet.*" came the computer's reply.

'*And there it is.*' thought Travellor. He knew it might happen sooner or later. They had been working in a hostile environment for years, without a single serious incident. When you handle that much heavy and dangerous materials, in an environment that can kill you instantly, you're playing an odds game. 361's doctors had been training with Blin for months now, and supposedly they were capable enough with the Ganaphe' medical equipment to take over her duties while she was gone. He wondered who was in charge of medical right now. Somehow he found his jacket in his hand and the office door opening as he walked through on his way to the accident area. He tapped his comm badge and it beeped twice to indicate it was online and working. He had just entered the stairwell when Kibbee's voice came from the badge.

"Commander, this is Kibbee. Initial review indicates an acetylene gas leak caused the explosion. I don't know how it happened sir, but we've got five ruptured fuel tanks that were stored in the area. The damage is massive. Outside walls of this section was bowed out by the forced. The blast was strong enough to tear through the structure. One access door is completely missing."

"What about interior walls?" asked Travellor.

"Interior walls are sound, sir. Looks like most of the force in that direction had been absorbed by interior components. The combined resistance of all the crap in the room was able to reflect most of the force outward."

Kibbee had just finished his report when Travellor reached the door to the fabrication area, and looked through one of the observation windows. He could see several men in spacesuits checking the room. It was a charred and blackened mess. The exterior walls of the room had been blown out and torn like pieces of thick cardboard. The explosive force must have been tremendous. Crumpled work benches, cabinets, and other furnishings had been blown back against the interior walls, their contents spilled over the floor. Pieces of their steel legs, which had been bolted to the floor, were still attached and sticking up with sharp points, waiting to skewer a body – but there were no bodies. There was no blood anywhere either. It was strange, but a good sign. However the accident happened, the people working in the section had had enough warning of the pending disaster to evacuate the room. So who was missing?

2

Dolores del Rio opened her eyes to the darkest and most sparkling night sky she had ever seen. Her back ached, and the bed felt as hard as steel. She tried to get up but her body wouldn't respond. She felt warm all over, and oddly cold at the same time. She turned her head left and then right, and notice her arms were spread out in crucifixion style. She knew she was still in her clothes, but didn't recognize the outfit. Her mind was foggy and she couldn't think straight. She must have slept wrong and cut off the circulation to her arms. The night was so beautiful. She thought she could reach up and touch every one of those stars, but her arms wouldn't move. And she noticed there was a strange haze over her eyes, like she was looking through a filter of some sort. But she was warm and relatively comfortable, except for that achy back and the intense itch right at the bottom of her spine. It was beginning to drive her crazy, and she wanted to scratch it in the worst way. But her arms wouldn't move. Worse, the itch was increasing. It was getting painful now.

She tried to remember what she had done last night, that put her in this position. Nothing came to mind. Her memory was blank. She knew she hadn't gone out with her friends. She knew she hadn't over indulged in drinking – she never did that anymore, and hadn't done since her early twenties when she spent one memorable evening laying on the bathroom floor, thinking how wonderful and cool the floor and the base of the toilet felt. '*OW !*' she thought. The itch was getting really, really painful. It was spreading, and now hurt all over her lower back. What the hell had she done to herself, she wondered. The pain was getting very bad now. A groan escaped from her throat.

The pain was spreading. It wasn't just her lower back that hurt, it

165

was the whole back of her body. More sounds made their way from her throat. She couldn't stop them now. Her head was the only thing that seemed to work. She looked to each side, over and over. Why did her bed have bumps sticking out of it? Who picked those sheets? They were ugly and dull. But her mind seemed to be clearing. She was beginning to remember. She could feel more of her body now also. At first she thought that was a good thing. Then the pain hit with so much ferocity that she screamed until she thought her lungs would come out of her throat. Then she choked, and coughed and her vision turned red directly in front of her. And the red spread across the face shield, and she went unconscious.

3

"Specialist del Rio was outside doing an external survey of the structure when the explosion occurred." said Kibbee. "We haven't found her or the missing access door."

"We have shuttles out looking?" asked Travellor.

"Yes sir. We've covered every square foot of the surface within twenty miles. We've found nothing."

"Your conclusion is that the force of blast was strong enough to propel her out of the gravitational pull of the moon?"

"It's the only possible explanation. We just don't know how far or in exactly what direction. Orysta is trying to track her suits transmissions, but the transmitter may have been damaged. Her bio-data stream ended shortly after the blast occurred. Grilik Munen has Orysta's shuttles ready to launch for a search. He is just waiting for your request."

"And our ships? Are they capable of helping?"

"They're operational, and functional within a hundred nautical miles. They can help with the search. If they find her they will have to call one of the Ganaphe' ships to perform the retrieval."

"What kind of suit was del Rio wearing?"

"A hybrid, sir. Ganaphe' suit with our helmet."

Travellor thought about that. The Ganaphe' had brought many spare suits with them, because of the damage they often incurred during mining operations. Helmets were very limited in quantity though – they didn't get as much abuse as the suits. 361 had purchased as many of the Ganaphe' suits as Munen was willing to sell, but had to design and manufacture its own helmet to mate with the suit. 361's helmets weren't as good as the Ganaphe' design, but were decades ahead of what NASA was using. If the Ganaphe' suit was damaged, could the 361 helmet have remained intact?

"Then go – now! All ships are to maintain a comm link signal throughout the search. Nobody continues on their path if the link is broken. Put one of your men on each of our ships."

Kibbee snapped to attention and saluted, more out of habit then requirement. 361 was not a military organization, although it was modeled after one. He turned and left to begin the search. Travellor thought about del Rio, as he watched Kibbee leave. She was young, and had a lot of living left to do. Then he thought about his niece. He felt helpless. They didn't know if del Rio was still alive, let alone where she was. Could the human body survive a blast so powerful it would launch it into space from the moon? How do you search space with only four ships. 361's shuttles were very limited, and only good for observational purposes. They weren't as fast or capable as the Ganaphe' ships – but they were capable of space flight from the moon. They had communications gear, radar, and crystal-flow domes for visual observation.
Travellor thought of his niece once again, then left his office and headed for the communications center. The search would be coordinated from there. He also had to make a call to Earth.

4

Major General Robert Farber-Chatwell stood away from the crowd in the Magic Kingdom Park. Goofy and Mickey were in his peripheral vision, posing for pictures with happy faced children, and some adults as well. He had two stars on his shoulders now – how could he not. The Air Force upper echelon knew that when they had a technological challenge blocking their progress, Farber-Chatwell was the go-to man that got it done. Over the years he had overseen advancements in Space technology, aircraft instrumentation, and computer use in the military. He was one of the men most responsible for changing the face of modern day warfare, yet very few outside the military actually knew this or his name. No one really knew how he got the job done, and they didn't question it too strongly. It was his job, so it was expected of him. He was expected to get it done – and he did! Every one in the know knew that Farber-Chatwell had an unusually influential way of dealing with technology companies.

This was the first vacation time he could remember taking in years. He had taken some down time now and then, when he didn't feel well or when he was just exhausted, but no real vacation time when he put the job out of his mind and just tried to have a good time. He had been having a good time too. Toisae was excellent company. She was intelligent, confident, very attractive, and surprisingly had a good sense of humor – at least he thought she did. The work part of his mind almost completely shut down when she was near him, and he enjoyed every second of it. He should have known it wouldn't last.

"Is it possible she's still alive?" he asked, trying to keep his voice low so he wouldn't be overheard.

"We're not sure." came Travellor's voice over the earpiece. "We believe the suit's support systems are still functioning, but she had on one of our helmets. We haven't really tested those to limits yet."

"You said her bio-data stream stopped."

"Yes, but the signal is missing. That doesn't tell us if she is still alive or not, just that the transmitter has been damaged or the signal is being blocked. That occurred almost immediately after the explosion."

He thought about that for a minute. The Ganapahe' suits were extremely durable. If the blast was powerful enough to damage the suit, could the person inside it survive? As he pondered it, Toisae Blin approached with an ice cream bar in each hand. She would know better than anyone the answer to that question.

"Stand By." said Farber-Chatwell.

"What has happened?" asked Toisae, reading the expression on his face. Her smile disappeared as she handed one of the treats to him.

"There's been an explosion on base. One of our people is missing, and they think she's been blown out into space."

Shock immediately registered on her face, as she realized the amount of force required to do such a thing.

"Are they sending a shuttle for us. I should be there to help."

"No. All shuttles are being used in the search. The suits telemetry signal has stopped, and there is no way to pinpoint her location. Is it possible for someone to survive a blast that has damaged one of your suits?"

She thought about it before answering.

"Our suits are made out of a material that is soft and pliable under normal wear, but turns into a rigid shell when affected by a fast impulse, high intensity force. The normally free floating molecular structure interlocks together to form a lattice structure. The concept is that the rigid lattice structure will collapse under the force, to dissipate the energy. It can offer tremendous protection to the user that way. But if the material was sheared, then life support would be lost. Without more information I cannot say what the result would be."

Almost in unison, they each took a bite of their ice cream, lost in thought. They were stuck on the planet until the shuttles returned. The Magic Kingdom was not the place they wanted to be right now. Farber-Chatwell touched the earpiece.

"Travellor, Toisae says the suit may have protected del Rio, but there's no way to be sure with the information we have. We're heading to the comm center. I want a continuous feed of all communications sent there."

"Ask him who is on duty in the medical bay." said Toisae to Farber-Chatwell.

"Toisae wants to know who is on duty in medical."

Travellor touched the computer's screen until he found the duty roster for the day.

"Dr. Sylvia Krather is on duty. She's our most senior physician."

Farber-Chatwell turned to Toisae to relay the information.

"He says Sylvia Krather is on duty."

"Very good." said Toisae, breathing a sigh of relief. "She is excellent. She is the person I would want to take care of me."

5

John Smith (jokingly referred to by his friends as "THE John Smith" to distinguish him from all the other John Smiths in the world) piloted one of only two X-1 "Hornet" space craft in existence. The name "Hornet" was indicative of the shape of the craft. It looked like a stretched and bent water drop – one end being large and rounded, and the other tapering and curving around to almost a point. The shape reminded a lot of people of a hornet with its stinger extended. The dome on the large end housed the microwave antennae array for the long range radar. Stinger was an apropos description of the more pointed section of the ship, where the thirty millimeter GAU-8/A Gatling gun, modified with a liquid cooling collar, was mounted. The weapon addition to the ship was a Ganaphe' suggestion. On top, covering the cockpit, was a crystal-flow dome that allowed the occupants to see outside. Inside the cockpit was a combination of Earth and Ganaphe' technology. The Ganaphe' instruments were on loan until human engineers could design and build equipment that performed the same functions. Flying a ship in open space required a completely new paradigm in instrumentation design, and there was a steep learning curve to be overcome.

These were the first operational human designed space craft capable of practical inter-planetary travel – at least that's what the design engineers claimed. Neither ship had yet made a test run to another planet – they still hadn't gotten the engine design right. That journey was scheduled for the near future. Hence the X designation for eXperimental. They had made many short test hops within a one hundred mile radius of the moon, and were capable of performing this search operation to find the missing woman. *'Blown out into space! We're not looking for a person,'* thought Smith, *'we're looking for a body.'*

As they flew in a spiral pattern to search their section of space, Smith and his copilot George Washington kept eyes wide open, radar at maximum range, and an understanding that even if the lost specialist was dead, bringing home the body would give her family closure and a chance to say their goodbyes. It was something they would want done for their own families under the same circumstances. As he looked out at the open darkness in front of him, he felt that perhaps their efforts were futile. It had only been thirty-seven minutes since they launched, but even at the speed they were traveling at there was still a hell of a lot of space before them. He

171

was beginning to feel despondent when the intermittent noise started coming over the speaker in his helmet. Since they had audio from all instruments feeding into the comm he didn't immediately recognize what it was. It was just an occasional burst of sound that lasted only seconds, and then it was gone.

"What was that?" asked Washington.

Smith looked over at this copilot and shook his head.

"I don't know."
"It almost sounded like telemetry, but it could have just been noise." said Washington. "It's gone now."
"BACK IT UP!" said Smith, excitedly. "Half speed. Retrace our steps exactly. If it was a signal we should be able to catch it again."

While Smith played with the receiver, Washington brought the Hornet to a stop. He programmed the flight computer to reverse their previous course. The ship pivoted around and began to accelerate.

"Should I notify moon base?" asked Washington.
"Not yet." replied Smith. "Not until we're sure…" He stopped speaking when the comm became alive again.

Washington again brought the ship to a stop. The audio remained active.

"Can we trian…"
"Already doing it." said Washington, cutting off the other man. "That is telemetry. Hold on. I want to try to – YES! Bio-data stream from a Ganaphe suit. ITS HER'S! She's alive!"
"What the hell?" shot back Smith.
"What?"
"I'm getting a radar return. There's something larger than a body out there. It's as big as a bus."

"What have you got?" came the voice over the comm link. "This is Commander Travellor. Report."

"This is Search-two. We've got her, sir. We found del Rio! We've got radar and telemetry, but the radar signal is strangely big. Transmitting our coordinates to the other search crews now. Heading towards the signal."

Washington had already maneuvered the ship, and began moving to the radar return. That's when the telemetry stopped.

"Search-two. We are no longer receiving telemetry relay." said Travellor.

Smith looked down at his comm receivers. The signal was gone. He thumped the panel with his fist, but nothing happened. The radar return remained on the screen.

"Moon base, Search-two. Telemetry has stopped, but we still have a radar return."

"Proceed with caution." said Travellor. "If she's floating around out there she has no protection. Without her telemetry you won't know where she is."

"Understood." said Smith. "Are the Ganaphe' shuttles on their way? Wait a minute… We've got telemetry again!"

"GOT 'ER!" yelled Washington. "Programming flight computer for her location."

"Search-two, this is Search-four. Heading to your location." came a voice over the comm.

"Search-one also on the way."

"Search-three heading to your location."

"Search-one, three, and four. Do not overtake Search-two. Stay behind her until we have visual contact." instructed Travellor. Now that they had found del Rio, he didn't want one of the ships accidentally running into her.

"Commander Travellor, this is Doctor Krather. Del Rio's bio-data indicates serious multiple injuries. Med bay is ready to receive her. You have to get her here as fast as possible."

"Understood Doctor Krather. Search teams, did you copy the doctor?"

"Affirmative."

"Copied."

"Understood."

"Commander Travellor, this is Search-four. We have visual contact with Search-two. We can retrieve Specialist del Rio when Search-two finds her."

"Search-two copies Search-four. Glad your with us."

"Search-one has a visual on two and four."

"This is Search-three. We have visual contact with the other ships."

"Lost telemetry again." said Washington.

"Radar return is solid." said Smith. "We're getting close. Reducing speed."

"Search-two, Travellor. Can you see anything yet?"

"Not yet sir, but we should be seeing something soon. Whatever the radar is picking up is not small. Definitely larger than a person."

"We've got telemetry again. What the hell? All search teams, I show telemetry and radar return coming from same location." said Washington.

"This is Search-four. We have visual on object ahead of us. Sending coordinates. Object appears to be rectangular and relatively flat. It is rotating."

"This is Travellor. Search-four take lead on search. Search-two, fall behind Search-four."

"Search-two falling back. Ready to assist."

"Commander Travellor, this is Search-four. We have visual contact on Specialist del Rio. She appears to be attached to the rotating object. We are accelerating towards her. Transmitting video link now."

In the communications center one of the monitors on the wall came on showing video from the front mounted camera of the Ganaphe' shuttle.

"Search-two sending secondary video." came the voice over the speakers.

A second monitor came alive, showing the viewpoint of the ship behind the Ganaphe' shuttle. The room was crowded now. Travellor saw that Doctor Krather was in the room, as was Grilik Munen, Mersuul, Benua Plessa, and various other personnel from both the Ganaphe' crew, and his own people. Their eyes locked onto the monitors. A third monitor came on as another of the search teams arrived on the scene and began transmitting video.
The first monitor showed a close view of the lost access door that had been blown off. It was slowly rotating as it traveled away from the moon. Flattened against it was the form of Technical Specialist Dolores del Rio. She wasn't moving. Travellor thought he could see an indented outline of her body on the door, and he wondered how she could still be alive.

"Medical bay, this is Krather. Are you still receiving telemetry from del Rio?" asked Krather, speaking into her comm badge in a low voice.
"Affirmative, doctor."
"Send the instrument readouts to the communications center, please."
"Will do."

A few seconds later the medical instrument readouts were being displayed on another monitor in the room. Travellor motioned for the doctor to move over to him, and she worked her way through the crowd.

"I can tell she has a pulse, and it seems regular, but I don't understand the other readings." said Travellor.
"Her blood pressure is dangerously low, and her pulse is slow. Her heart is struggling to pump blood. She's in bad shape. We need to get her back here ASAP."

"Will she live?"

"You get her to me in time, and I'll keep her alive. HURRY!" she said, and then tapped on her comm badge again. "Surgical team to the operating room. Report any no-shows. Brenda – go wake up doctors Gamala and Dierker. I'll need their help."

"On my way." replied a female voice.

"How quickly can you get her here?" Krather asked Travellor, as they watched the door of the Ganaphe' shuttle open to space.

"No more than ten minutes after they get her aboard the shuttle. Stick around doctor. There are no medical personnel on any of those ships. You may need to make an assessment for them."

"I already have." she said, as she leaned towards Jibble Delfin. "Can you patch my comm badge to the ships?"

"Yes ma'am." he said as he began throwing switches and touching the screen of his console. "You're connected."

"Search team four, this is Doctor Krather."

"Doctor Krather, this is Intul Califas piloting search-four."

Krather pictured Califas in her mind. She had treated him a few days ago for broken bones in his hand. He was second in command of the Orysta, but he had a habit of getting involved with the work of the mining engineers – which meant he got injured like the mining engineers. As thanks for treating him, he shared his last bottle of Ganaphe' wine with her at dinner. Ganaphe' beverages were very rare on the Orysta these days – it was a very nice gesture.

"Intul, I need you to put specialist del Rio in a medical straight jacket before moving her. Then I need to get her back to the Orysta as fast as possible."

"We will do as you say, doctor. Is there anything else?"

"Nothing for now. I'll be waiting for her in medical."

"Straight jacket?" asked Travellor.

"It's a device that encapsulates a person in a rigid energy field, and completely immobilizes them. We gave it that name, not the Ganaphe'.

Intul knows what I mean. It will protect del Rio from further injury while being moved. God, I wish we had them on Earth. I wish we had all the Ganaphe' technology on Earth!" she said.

"We're working on it, doctor." mumbled Travellor. "We're working on it."

"That probably saved her life," Krather said, "being plastered to the door. It kept her body from moving and causing more damage."

They watched as two men left the Ganaphe' shuttle. One of them had a long, flat metallic object in hand. As the men moved from the open shuttle door to the motionless form, Travellor couldn't help but notice that there was no obvious form of propulsion moving the men through space. This was one of the technological details the Ganaphe' were not allowed to explain. Travellor had his suspicions, and had talked to 361 physicists on Earth about it. They couldn't come up with any explanations, but Travellor suspected that it was connected to some of their other capabilities – the same capabilities he could feel on the bottom of his feet as he stood there.

It didn't take long for them to reach del Rio. The metallic board was placed lengthwise on her, and then they moved away slightly. Del Rio's form shimmered for a second, and then the men picked her up, one on each side. Her body didn't change position at all, like she was frozen stiff. They moved towards the shuttle.

"We have del Rio. We will proceed to the base at maximum speed." came a voice over the comm.

"That's my cue." said Krather to Travellor. She tapped her comm badge. "Med bay, this is Krather. Our patient is on the way. I'm heading to you now." she said as she walked away.

"Prepared and ready." came the reply.

Travellor watched as the rescue team entered Search-four, and the door closed. The video on the first screen went blank. The video feed from Search-two showed the Ganaphe' shuttle pivoting in place, and accelerating out of view. It would only take them a few minutes to get back and land in

Orysta's shuttle bay.

"Search-two – Travellor. Can you tie a rope onto the door and drag it back here? We might be able to learn something from it."

"Affirmative, Commander. A magnetic grapple should hold onto it."

"Good. See you when you get back. Very good work, all of you. Travellor out."

As he turned to leave the room he caught his reflection in the window, and noticed that he seemed to have a lot more gray hairs.

"Good work, Jibble." he said to Delfin, putting a hand on his shoulder as he went by.

"Thank you Commander."

6

Farber-Chatwell and Doctor Toisae Blin listened to the images of Doctor Krather and Anthony Travellor on the video screen in front of them.

"She had a fractured skull with swelling of the brain, seventy-six broken bones, injury to her spleen, kidneys, and liver. Fluid had built up in her lungs, and she had an uncountable amount of ruptured blood vessels. She almost bled to death internally. The list goes on but that gives you an overall picture of her condition." came the voice of Doctor Krather over the video link. "If it wasn't for the Ganaphe's medical technology she would be dead. Instead she is on the way to healing. Her prognosis is good. She may come out of this with a few minor external scars at most. There may be a long rehabilitation period to overcome some brain damage, but she probably will not lose any mental or physical functionality."

"When can she be brought back to Earth?" asked Farber-Chatwell.

"We won't be sending her back until after she regains consciousness." said Travellor, as he watched doctor Blin nod in agreement. "Doctor Blin can explain the details to you sir, but it turns out that by keeping del Rio in a zero gravity room it helps the brain heal faster, and for the relatively short period expected it will have no detrimental effect on her physically."

"That's excellent news." said Farber-Chatwell. "Have we determined what caused the explosion?"

"Right now it looks like we had a build up of volatile gas from a leaky compressed gas tank cylinder valve. The gas was lighter than air, so it accumulated at the ceiling above everyone's heads. That section of the base was still under construction so there were no sensors in the area. No one smelled anything until just before the explosion. Should have a final report in a few days."

"That was excellent work Doctor Krather." said Blin to her colleague. "No equipment or technology could have saved that girl without your expertise to make use of it."

"Thank you Doctor Blin." replied Krather.

"I second that." said Farber-Chatwell. "Excellent work doctor."

"Thank you Sir."

"I'd like you and the Commander to catch the next shuttle to the planet so that I can thank you both personally."

Travellor started to object but was cut off by Farber-Chatwell.

"No, Commander. No. I know you're busy, and you feel like you have to be on location at this time, but I want you down here. I want you to meet a very important person. He's my counterpart in 361. If anything happened to me he would be the person taking over the operation. He's read every report that's come from moon base, and knows the details of the operation intimately. It's time you both met... and frankly Tony, you look like crap! I'm ordering you to take the next forty-eight hours off duty. Put someone you trust in command there. You and Doctor Krather will be having dinner with myself and Doctor Blin tomorrow night. Doctor Blin is worried you've been overworking yourself, and she wants to have a look at you."

The last part of his statement was an obvious pretext. They all knew it was. Travellor and Doctor Krather saw Blin's eyes widen in surprise when she heard Farber-Chatwell say it, but she didn't remark on it.

"That forty-eight starts at this moment, Commander. When we finish our conversation, your next action will be to put your second in command of the base, and then go find a good book or something. Doctor Krather, it will be your responsibility to see that he does so."

"Yes sir." said Krather, looking a little nervous about possibly telling the base commander how to spend his time.

"Alright." said Travellor. "I'll take some down time. I look forward to having dinner with you and Toisae. There are some B movies on the Sci-Fi channel I've been meaning to watch. I love old sci-fi movies. I'm sure I can find one about space aliens taking over Earth's moon." he said smiling.

"What is a bee movie?" Blin asked Farber-Chatwell, who chuckled at her question.

"It's a cheaply or badly made movie. Some of them can be very funny if you have the right sense of humor."

"But we have many good movies on the base. Why would you watch one that is not good?" she asked, looking at Travellor.

"It's a cultural thing." replied Travellor, with a smile. "An acquired taste. I'll try to explain it to you at dinner."

"Clock's ticking Commander, and you're off it for the next forty-eight." said Farber-Chatwell.

Travellor sighed. He actually could use a short break, and he had several people who could handle the command position while he was away. Two days. He could give two different people a taste of the job, one day each. Their names came right to mind – Delgadillo and Vargas. He could – no – he WOULD take the time to visit his niece. He missed her, and Skyping wasn't a substitute for giving her a long hug. He had time coming.

Maybe he'd take four or five days off and give Delgadillo and Vargas a real taste of the job. *'The hell with it.'* he thought. He was going to take a full week. Delgadillo hated paper work, and the base commander's job had a lot of it. Travellor chuckled at the thought of her reaction. She wasn't going to be happy.

7

"Aiiieeeeeee!"

The seven hundred and sixty-seven mile per hour, ear piercing sound hit Travellor's eardrums, making them feel close to bursting. In another few seconds, he was wrapped in arms and legs, and he couldn't keep from laughing.

"YOU'RE HERE – YOU'RE HERE – YOU'RE HERE!"

He responded to his niece's full body hug by wrapping his arms around her, and kissing her on the cheek. She was growing so fast, but he didn't have any problem carrying her. This was so much better than just seeing her face on a video link.

"Yes I am, sweetie. I've taken three weeks off, and I'm going to spend it all with you."

The timing couldn't have been better. School was out for the summer, and there were no demands on anyone's time. Erika was nineteen now, and no longer a child. Her college years would go by fast, and then she would be a young women who would be making her own way in life, with less time for her uncle. Travellor knew he had better take advantage of being with her as much as possible. All of his built up PTO would get used up with every opportunity to visit her.

"Hello Anthony." came the voice of Phillip Aimsler, Erika's uncle on her father's side.

Travellor and Aimsler had always gotten along. He respected the man for many reasons, and appreciated that Erika had been welcomed into their family as a daughter. He relaxed his right arm and extended it to shake Aimsler's hand.

"Hello Phil. Thanks for letting me stay with you. Hi Jen. How are you?"

Jennifer Aimsler stood next to her husband, with a welcoming smile on her face.

"Erika! A young woman doesn't go around jumping on people." she said, laughing. "Unwrap yourself from your uncle."

Travellor had watched the relationship between Erika and the Aimslers since she came to live with them after her parents deaths. They saw her as the daughter they never had.

"NO, NO, NO! He's mine, and I'm not letting go." Erika replied, and she kissed Travellor on the cheek. She slowly unwound herself from him, and then held onto his hand.

"Where are the boys?" asked Travellor.
"Helping our neighbor cut up a fallen tree." said Jen. "They'll be back in a few hours."
"Let's go inside." said Aimsler. "Bags in the car?"
"Yes."
"I can help." said Erika.

Travellor handed one of his bags to her. He and Aimsler picked up the others, and followed Erika to the house.

8

Antonio Vargas inspected the repaired fabrication area closely. It had taken over four days to replace sections of the outside wall and fit a new access door. The section had passed the pressurization testing, and was now safe for personnel to occupy without spacesuits. The 361 electronics geniuses had fabricated a sensor tree that was now standing in the middle of the room, going from floor to ceiling. Vargas considered the tree to be an excellent device. The geniuses that built it thought it was a very simple exercise more suited to the talents of a thirteen year old – they felt their skills were being under-utilized. Vargas didn't care what they thought. He recognized a useful piece of equipment that could save lives when he saw one, and the tree was such a device.

Relatively speaking the tree was a simple device. It was an array of temperature, pressure, and gas sensors that would alert people around it to any dangerous condition it detected. Vargas liked that idea, and as acting base commander he issued a directive that no area under maintenance would be without one. Of course, his directive would only be valid until Commander Travellor returned, but he knew Travellor well enough to believe he would keep it as a permanent edict. He turned to Chief Astronautics engineer William Good, and nodded his approval.

"Good." said Good. "Now we can get to work."

"How long before the room is completely wired and set up with work stations?" asked Vargas.

"Two days at most. That leaves us about two weeks to get the shuttle modifications done before Commander Travellor gets back."

"Which shuttle are you modifying?"

"Both of them."

"BOTH !" said Vargas in surprise. "That leaves us without any working shuttle."

"Grilik Munen is aware of this. He said his shuttles can handle the extra work load, if needed. Damn good people, those Ganaphe'. They work hard, and they're there when you need them."

"Yes, they are. What are we doing to them?"

"One gets fitted with a new engine designed by Eckelberry Cove. He has a new theory on using resonant energy flow as a propulsion stream. That boy's a genius. Wouldn't surprise me if he's the one who gets us to the outer planets some day. The other one gets new armament."

Vargas had seen the name Eckelberry Cove on some of the engine design schematics. Even heard the name talked about among the engineering staff. Some were awed by his theories, and so far he had proven every one of them. Some scientists were theorists, and some were experimenters who applied another person's theories. Cove was reputed to do both, not being happy until his theories became tangible. He not only designed propulsion systems, he also designed the ships that would use them. Vargas would have to read up on him when he got back to the office. It was 361's policy that all technical papers be accompanied by the same information written in 'plain English' to help non-technical personnel understand at least the basics of what was going on. Vargas' technical expertise was in the practical realm. When it came to theoretical physics he was completely lost. It was the plain English translations that helped him stay current on scientific developments – and in 361 there were a lot of scientific developments – daily. Sometimes it seemed hourly.

"What new armament?" asked Vargas.

"The guns have an improved temperature control system, and they fire a new type of munition. The problem with metal bullets in space is that if they don't hit anything they just keep going until they do. You could end up shooting yourself under the right circumstances. The new ones are ceramic. They still hit hard, but they also have a small explosive charge inside and a timer. If they don't hit a target in seven seconds, the timer triggers the charge and blows the bullet into dust."

"Still…," commented Vargas with a disappointed look on his face, "not as high-tech as the Ganaphe' weapons."

"Nope. Not even in the same ballpark."

"And it's going to take you two weeks to modify them?"

"A few days for the new gun. That's mostly just a system swap out. The new engine installation is a lot more complicated. Has a lot of sub-systems and testing involved. I'll be very happy if we get it done in two weeks."

"I'll get out of your way then. Happy modifying. Let me know if you need any help." said Vargas, as he walked out of the fabrication bay.

9

"We're going deer hunting – really?" asked Ernst Aimsler.

"Yep. We'll be camping for five days. Bring your warm clothes." answered Travellor. "Your parents deserve a few days to themselves."

"Excellent!" said Robert Aimsler. "I've been wanting to try my new broadhead arrows."

"Where are you going to be while we're camping?" asked Ernst, looking at his parents.

"We…" said Phillip Aimsler, taking hold of his wife's hand, "will be enjoying the clear blue waters and warm beaches of the Caribbean. Maybe do a little lobster diving. And if we're having a really good time, we might stay longer. You can keep your uncle entertained until we get back."

"There are some new movies I want to see," said Erika, "and I haven't been to the gun range in a while. OH! – and there's the new ice cream store that opened up. We haven't checked that out yet."

They all talked excitedly about the days to come, as dinner was brought in by the servants. The Aimslers were wealthy people, but as Travellor studied the three younger people at the table he could see no sign of them being spoiled. They had no sense of entitlement. Travellor drifted away in his own thoughts. There was no doubt they would be financially well off as they made their way in life, but both Phillip and Jennifer Aimsler expected their sons and their niece to do just that – make their own way in life. That was one of the reasons Travellor thought so highly of these people. Why he trusted them to take care of the one person he loved most. Yes, they were all lucky kids, growing up without having to worry about food, clothing or shelter. Still, Travellor could see it in the face of the youngest, Ernst, that he knew his parents expected him to become an independent individual. There would be no mamma's boys in this family. Jennifer Aimsler's voice brought him back from his thoughts.

"If you happen to lose one of the boys on your camping trip, just notify the authorities and they will search for him. That's why I had two, so I'd have a spare."

Everyone broke into laughter at her joke.

"But don't you dare come back without my girl!" she continued, reaching over and hugging Erika. "I'm giving her to you in perfect condition, and that's the way I want her back."

As the laughter continued, the boys demanded that their father stand up for them. He made a minor attempt at it, indicating that he had no authority to overrule his wife. The boys proclaimed the unfairness of it all, and the laughter and conversation continued throughout the evening.

10

June – 2009

Launch Complex 41

Farber-Chatwell watched from the observation area, as the Atlas V rocket burned its way through the sky. On top of it was the LRO – the Lunar Reconnaissance Orbiter, on its way to map and measure the moon's surface with high resolution color imaging, UV and other instruments. The project had been conceived and executed by a team that did not include a 361 associate. The general project guidelines were known, and these had him worried.

Grilik Munen had assured him that their camouflage technology would be able to hide the location of the base from the satellite, but Farber-Chatwell would have been less worried if they had been able to put some safeguards into the satellites operating software. The ingenuity of space explorers, be they hardware or software oriented, was not to be underestimated. They were a dedicated group of people always coming up with new ways to do things – find things – see things. The only thing they could do now was refrain from any flight activity during the period the satellite was overhead, and then intercept the data stream to find out if the base had been detected. He knew he had some sleepless nights coming in the near future. He really hated not being in control of the situation.

Making the problem even worse was the fact that this would be a long term satellite mission – years long, which meant that from the time it arrived at the moon the satellite would have to be tracked continuously so that flight activity could be curtailed when it posed a danger of exposure. The only other option was to disable or destroy it, but Farber-Chatwell was not the type to interfere with the achievements of others. 361 and the Ganaphe' would just have to live with the inconvenience.

That wasn't the only thing that worried him. He knew there would be more satellites, and more exploration in the future. A dedicated tracking center might have to be set up on moon base.

Chapter 12

GRAIL

1

December – 2011

Ransen Ramsdel glanced over at the printer that resided by the window of his office. It had come out of stand-by mode, and was warming up. He hadn't tried to print anything. Since he was the only person in the suite who used this printer it could only mean one thing – a communication from Base Command. That printer had started out as a standard WIFI capable type that anyone could buy from any retail outlet – but that was the end of any similarity. 361 technical personnel had added a couple of security enhancements to it. They had added an additional processor board of their own design, which bypassed the basic WiFi circuitry with a much more secure system so that the printer operated only when defined circumstances were met. The first requirement for the printer to work was that Ramsdel was within ten feet of the unit, or more specifically Ramsdel's ring was.

The ring on his hand looked like any other piece of jewelry a man might wear, but although it looked like metal it was made of a special high strength ceramic. Underneath the birthstone was a SOC – a System On a Chip – that was a complete receiver, transmitter, and encoder, all built on a single tiny substrate. It only required a small amount of power to operate, and that was supplied by the magnetic induction generator built into the ring. As Ramsdel moved his hands in his every day activities, a very minute amount of power was generated and stored in a tiny supercapacitor on the ring's flexible circuit board. Supercapacitors were just coming into

189

widespread commercial and industrial use, but 361 technicians quickly recognized the potential uses for them. They have the ability to store relatively large amounts of energy compared to physically similar standard capacitors and even batteries. The one in Ramsdel's ring was small, but when fully charged it stored enough power to keep the ring active for almost forty-eight hours. The 361 engineers on the ring project were very proud of what they had accomplished. The rings were now used for many purposes, including identifying a person as a 361 agent when accompanied with other verification. The existence of the rings was considered to be on a need to know basis.

When the printer received a request to print, it would transmit a radio signal from its internal omni-directional antenna. If a properly encrypted response signal – from Ramsdel's ring – was not received, nothing happened. The printer remained in standby mode, and the print job discarded. If the response signal was received, the print request would be honored and the printer did what it was built to do – print the document, unless Ramsdel pressed the orange 'Store' button. If the orange button was pressed, the print job was stored in the internal buffer until Ramsdel was ready to print it out. This ensured that Ramsdel was the only person to get the printout. This printer in Ramsdel's office recognized only his ring. If another 361 member who had a similar ring came into Ramsdel's office, the printer would not respond to its code.

The second requirement for the printer to work was that the print job had to have the correct encryption protocol. All print jobs processed by the printer had to be in the correct encryption format, and it was not a standard or commercially available encryption type. The print job was taken into the printer's buffer memory, and decrypted. The decrypted job had to have a header section which included an acceptable identification code. If that code was there, the print job was 'washed', which consisted of the processor removing a cover code that hid the actual document. This cover code was interlaced with the actual document code in such a manner that if the transmitted signal was intercepted, and printed on a regular printer, the output would be a highly detailed but normal looking picture of some random insipid subject matter.

The third requirement for the printer to work was that the MAC address of the sending device had to match one of those stored in the printer. This last requirement, which is one used by many standard home WIFI networks for security, was just thrown in by the 361 techs because, as they put it, "It's already there. It's easy. So we did it." This limited the devices that would work to Ramsdel's computer, his smart phone, and three other devices that were in the possession of other 361 personnel. These other personnel were unknown to Ramsdel.

Ramsdel jumped up from his seat and quickly moved to the window. This had become a game for him, to try and spot the vehicle or person sending the signal. He found it a great way to break up the day. The identity of the messenger actually wasn't a big secret. In fact, Ramsdel had been offered the opportunity to meet the person handling that job, but at the time he was very busy with several projects and declined. Now this game had become a mental break from his work – better than a quick nap. He looked over the area in front of the building, checking cars for occupants or antenna, or people using a computer.

The problem with cars was that these days a lot of them had various antenna on them anyway. There were broadcast antenna, GPS antenna, Ham radio antenna, TV antenna, and even some vehicles with small dish antenna. Try to spot the right vehicle by the antenna it had was almost useless, but Ramsdel kept thinking that if an antenna that was peculiar in some way was being used he might spot it. It had to be a directional antenna since he didn't think sending the signal over a wide area would be good security practice – and 361 had become an organization that was very good when it came to signal security. He didn't spot anything that stood out on any of the cars or trucks he could see.

Ramsdel then began to check out the people in the street. There were several people with smart phones, but only one working on an open laptop. She was sitting at a concrete table in the small park across the street, facing in his direction. '*Ah hah!*', Ramsdel thought, '*You must be the one.*' He was very excited now. He had never been able to spot a likely suspect before, playing this game of his. The only problem with his theory was that there was nothing that looked like an antenna, and there had to be one.

Then he spotted the purse on the ground, by the woman's foot. If he could see the purse, then it had a clear line of sight to the office – something the directional antenna needed to have for the message to get delivered.

Ramsdel pushed the 'Store' button on the printer, grabbed his jacket, and jogged out of the office. The childish grin on his face made several of his office personnel wonder what was going on. The plan of attack came to him as he went through the office door. He ran down the back stairwell, taking four or five steps at a time. If the print job was long enough he would have enough time to circle around the neighboring building, sneak across the street at the corner, and come up behind his prey. His grin kept getting bigger. It was just a game after all, but it still had some of the excitement of being in the field again.

He got to the park, and then tree by tree he made his way toward the table, eager to surprise the messenger. He came up behind what he believed to be the tree that was behind and to the side of the table, and carefully looked around it – and she was looking right at him. She was expecting him! How could she know he was there he wondered. She smiled, and wiggled her finger indicating he should come over. His smile disappeared, and confusion broke his train of thought.

"How did you know I…" he started to say, as she turned to the computer and pointed to the screen. On a map of the local area was a blinking dot indicating the location where they – no, where HE was.

"Your ring." she said.

Ramsdel looked at the ring on his finger.

"That's how I knew when to send the reports. How else could I be sure you were in the office to receive them. I would have explained it all to you, but you always refused to meet with me for a briefing. I was very surprised to see your signal moving towards me today!"

"But I thought this was only good for a few feet." he said, looking at the ring, confused.

"Well, yes, a few feet, unless you use a highly directional antenna.

I can pick up the signal of a ring from a few hundred feet with one. Hi," she said, standing up and extending her hand, "I'm Lorraine Lewis".

"Ransen Ramsdel." he replied, as he shook her hand and then froze.

Ramsdel stared at the most beautiful face he had ever seen, and random thoughts flooded his mind. '*How old am I? What have I done with my life? What have I accomplished?*', and other such thoughts that come to a fifty-something year old man who is suddenly questioning his existence. Other questions and doubts followed, and repeated. All of it brought about by one look at one face. She was in her late thirties, no taller than five foot and a couple of inches, with curly chestnut hair. The freckles and facial features indicated an Irish background. Ramsdel stared at her lips – and they were absolutely perfect. She wore an absolutely perfect blue beret, that was tilted at an absolutely perfect angle. Her hand fit absolutely perfectly in his.

"Are you alright?" asked Lorraine, looking a little worried. "Your mouth is open… and you're still holding my hand."

Ramsdel looked down and saw that he was still holding her hand. He didn't want to let go, but thought that maybe he should.

"Uh, yes, I'm OK. Just something that popped into my mind. Didn't want to lose the thought."

Ramsdel suddenly felt like there was a big hole in his life – No, not a hole – a cave, a massive, empty cave. Something very important was missing in it, and that realization hit him like the proverbial wall. The last 30 or so years of his life suddenly compressed together and gave him a mental body slam. She looked into his eyes, with a slight worried expression on her face.

"What's the matter?", Ramsdel asked her.
"I'm just wondering if you're having one of those mini-strokes you hear about on the news."

193

Ramsdel let out a short laugh.

"No," he said, "God has more important things to do than bother with giving me one of those."

He paused to give her what he thought was a reassuring smile.

"I just realized that I've been spending all my time overcoming the obstacles of this job without taking any time to live my life. After all these years, I've just realized why they had to have a volunteer to do this job. Only a volunteer would follow through with it. If it had been assigned to any sane person, they would have quit a long time ago."

"You realized that just now – just this second?", she asked, puzzled. "What brought that on?"

Ramsdel's expression changed and he suddenly felt like an embarrassed teenager talking to a pretty girl.

"I didn't do anything stupid, like blow your cover or anything like that, did I? I mean, being here with me, out in the open, didn't break any rules you had to follow, or anything like that?"

Lorraine smiled at his sudden thoughtfulness. *'A little too late,'* she thought, *'but nice that you're worried about it.'*

"No." she answered. "It probably doesn't matter anyway, since this is my last day. I go back to school next week. Finally going to finish that degree I've been putting off. For the next two years I'm going to be a college student again."

"*Message receipt confirmed!*" said the computer.

They both looked at the laptop.

"I assume you stored the message?" Lorraine said.

"Yes."

She held three keys down with her left hand, and pressed four others in sequence with her right.

"Battery power sufficient. Beginning Hard Wipe in three… two… – Goodbye." said the computer, in a cheerful sounding voice.

"What's a Hard Wipe?" asked Ramsdel.

"That's one of the other things I would have explained to you at the briefing we never had." she replied, with a mocking grin.

The laptop's screen went dark, but the hard drive light remained lit indicating that it was continuing to be accessed. Lorraine closed the lid and placed the laptop in her bag.

"Would you like to get some coffee?" Ramsdel asked. "You could give me that briefing I missed. Oh, wait – do have time? Are you supposed to do something else after this delivery? Maybe you can call your boss and see if you can take time for my briefing. Wait a minute – technically speaking, I'm your boss! – or at least one of them. So technically I can say it's OK to take the time. OK – good – as one of your bosses I authorize you to take the time to brief me."

She chuckled. "You're rambling." she said. "Do you do that often."

"Uh… No," he said as he took the bag from her, "but I seem to be making up for it today. My car is in the garage." he said, pointing to the office building.

"Mine's right here." she said, walking over to the blue compact parked on the street.

Lorraine opened the trunk, took the bag from Ramsdel and placed it inside.

"You know," said Ramsdel, "I've been trying to spot the person delivering these messages since just after we started using the secure printer.

195

I know I've never seen you before, and certainly not sitting at this table."

"I usually transmit from my car. That is, the car I'm driving that day. It's a motor pool vehicle. Get a different one every time. But, since this was my last day, and the sun was shining, and it was a nice day, I decided to sit at the table." she said, as she pressed the button on the key fob to unlock the doors.

Ramsdel got in on the passenger side, and buckled his seat belt. As they drove, he realized that it really was a nice day. Why hadn't he noticed that before, he wondered.

2

It was two hours later, when Ramsdel pressed the PRINT button on the printer. As he waited for the printout he thought about the time at the coffee shop. Lorraine liked the sweet, fancier drinks the coffee shop sold, and she liked to chew on the stir stick as they talked. It was very easy to talk to her, and after the official briefing, which took about twenty minutes, they spent the rest of the time getting to know each other. He was especially happy that she gave him her number and said that she would like to go out with him.

The printer beeped loudly to indicate it had finished printing, and Ramsdel picked up the papers and read them.

From: OP361MBC

To: OP361EBC

Mission Status Update
11Sep2011

Brief Follows -

On 10Sep2011 (yesterday) the NASA Gravity Recovery and Interior Laboratory (GRAIL) mission launched successfully. We were unable to affect the mission in any manner as we had no personnel on the mission team. GRAIL's main mission consists of two satellites that will orbit the moon, mapping its gravity field strength. Although we generate our own gravity field, we believe it is too localized, and not strong enough to be detected by GRAIL. We will take precautions by intercepting the data streams from the satellites, and analyzing for exposure of the base. Since G have their own interest in remaining undetected, they have committed to take lead on this and will be using their instrumentation, which is faster and more capable than ours.

Although we don't expect to be detected by gravity field measurements, GRAILS secondary mission (MoonKam) poses a more direct threat of exposure. The MoonKam phase of the mission will take detailed images of the moon's surface. The O is unlikely to be detected on these images as it is situated in a rille, covered with rocks and soil. Camouflage should protect surface structures from detection. However, while these images are in progress, transport to and from the base will have to be either suspended or curtailed. Depending on moon's rotation and position of satellites, this may mean several days of no transport activity each month. GRAIL mission is expected to last approx 2.5 months, with possible extension to 9 months. Normally, curtailing flight activity would pose no problem, but in case of an emergency there may be a risk of exposure. We are presently exploring ways to disable GRAIL without creating suspicion but having two separate satellites cease operation at the same time may draw too much attention. A possibility exists that we may be able to deceive the satellites with false images instead, but the G say this tampering might be detected under close examination.

It is recommended that we look into ways to influence future exploration missions away from the moon – perhaps to Mars.

Brief Ends -

Ramsdel thought about what he had just read. With possible operational restrictions for the next two to nine months, supply deliveries to the base could become intermittent. He would institute a three-fold increase of on hand supplies at the base, so that they would not have to take any exposure risk because of the lack of necessities. Moon base would have to designate an unused section as a secondary storage facility for the extra supplies. *'Time to feed the dragon.'* he thought, and he fed the papers into the shredder/incinerator/ash destroyer. 361 had used this type of device for years now, and it was still the best way to destroy hard copies of documents. Once the process was complete there was nothing left but powdered ash.

Ramsdel scheduled a video conference with moon base for the next day, to work out the details of the new supply schedule. 361 had ships at its disposal that could travel much fast than the GRAIL satellites were moving, so there was plenty of time to get everything operational and in place. Now he was tired, and ready to go home. As he walked out of the office, wishing everyone a good night as he passed them, he thought of Lorraine Lewis. He didn't realize he had a big smile on his face. She had said to call after seven, and she would be home. He checked his watch. It was six-thirty. Seven seemed like such a long time away.

Chapter 13

Eckelberry Cove

1

February – 2012

"You named the test site 'Eckelberry Cove'?" asked Farber-Chatwell, over the video link.

"I didn't name it. Our people did. Or to be more precise, it just more or less happened." replied Travellor. "The man is a legend up here. It's Eckelberry Cove did this, or Eckelberry Cove designed that, Or Eckelberry Cove said this is possible. He is like a rock star here. People don't just read his papers, they study them, and talk about them. They even have pictures of him at the test site. Even the Ganaphe' find his work impressive. It was a natural play on words to name the test area Eckelberry Cove."

Farber-Chatwell started laughing, and Travellor soon followed.

"That is too much." said Farber-Chatwell. "But it's very understandable. He's a living legend here also. I could sell tickets to his next lecture, and it would be standing room only. Down here the saying is 'When Eckelberry speaks, everyone listens.' It's even stranger to watch his reaction to all of this attention. He just doesn't get it."

"Well don't be surprised if you get a request from the Ganaphe' to be introduced to him, next time they're on planet. They have us all under their lens. They believe they are observing Earth history being made. And there's something about his latest engine design that made them do a double-take. Munen and his Chief Engineer Plessa were suppressing smiles when they reviewed the diagrams, like it was something they recognized."

"Which diagrams?"

"The Resonant Oscillation engine diagrams." said Travellor.

"Oh,… THAT!" said Farber-Chatwell, with a distasteful expression on his face. "I've had Cove explain that one to me three times already, and I still don't understand it. I hate feeling stupid."

"Join the club. I know it's not my field of expertise, but I just don't get the underlying physics involved. Three times? How did you get him to stand still that long. Whenever I have a question about one of his projects I have to put in a request and hope he calls me back."

"Privilege of rank. The man works for me, Commander. When I call, he answers. That always makes me feel a little better, when I'm feeling stupid."

They both laughed at the comment.

"It's strange," continued Farber-Chatwell, "but he and Ramsdel get along like brothers. I can't figure out what an engineering physicist and the man who runs 361's daily business operations can have in common so much. One talks science and the other finance, and they both seem to understand each other perfectly."

"It's the details." replied Travellor. "They both deal in minute details that affect larger systems. Our brains aren't wired like that. We deal in the bigger picture of things."

"You might be right. I just don't like feeling that I need to go back to school, every time I talk to the man. By the way, being the generous person that I am, I'm going to share that feeling of stupidity with you. Cove will be on base for the testing of that engine. When your people are ready to go with the new ship, he wants to be there. Even as his boss, I can't deny him that. Keep it confidential until we're ready for the test."

"PHhhhh…" exhaled Travellor. "He's coming here? Oh boy. Well…, you can expect your efficiency report for that period to take a nose dive. Everybody is going to want some face time with him. Guess I should

200

make it a formal event."

"That sounds like a plan, Commander. Alright – I've taken too much of your time. Sorry to disturb you in your quarters, but I thought you should know. I'll keep you informed when I have the details. Signing off."

The screen went blank. Travellor leaned back in his chair, closed his eyes and rubbed his face with both hands.

"ECKELBERRY COVE IS COMING HERE!"

Travellor jumped in his chair at the loud and excited voice, and turned to face Mersuul. Her eyes were wide, as was her smile, in excitement.

"You were not supposed to hear that." he said. "You heard Farber-Chatwell. It's confidential. You will have to keep it a secret."

"He is coming here!" she reiterated, acting as if she hadn't heard him. "One of the most brilliant humans of your time is coming here – AND I WILL GET TO MEET HIM!"

"Oh my God!" said Travellor, looking at the ecstatic expression on her face. "You remind me of the teenage girls, at my high school, when the Beatles came to the U.S. They lost their sanity too."

Mersuul walked over and sat on his lap, wrapping her arms around his neck.

"You do not understand." she said. "This is the making of history for your planet. This period in time is the beginning of your planet's introduction to the universe. On my world, the early space travel period can only be learned about in school or read about in historical records. Now is an important time for Earth. Eckelberry Cove is very likely to be the person who develops your space travel technology, and I will meet him. I was not alive to witness that time in Ganaphe' history, but I am able to witness it in yours. When I get back to my home I will be famous in scientific circles. Every cultural anthropologist who is interested in your planet will want to talk with me. Your planet will be big news for a long time, and I will be one of only a handful of Ganaphe' to witness it."

"And that would make you happy?" asked Travellor, smiling at her.

"What is that expression you use – It won't stink!"

Travellor chuckled. He always found it funny when she used colloquialisms. They never quite sounded right coming from her, and he enjoyed every time she did it. He slipped his arm under her legs and picked her up, carrying her to the bed where he slowly lowered her on to it.

"Confidential!" he said, quietly.

"Confidential." she replied, then pulled him closer and kissed him.

2

March 24, 2012

"Bad news, Commander." said Farber-Chatwell on the video link. "GRAIL mission has been extended. To make it worse, the orbits of both satellites will be dropped closer to the surface. At some points they'll be as close as 4.3 miles AGL. Looks like our monitoring of the mission will have to take on greater importance. Maybe we'll get lucky and they'll crash – I guess I shouldn't say that. I don't really wish ill on the GRAIL team. Until we find out what the new mission profile is we'll have to stop transport flights immediately. That will mean more work for you, Delfin. If you need more help for it, let the Commander know."

"Yes, sir." said Jibble Delfin, as he monitored the equipment in the Communications Center.

Travellor and Delfin were the only people in the room. Farber-Chatwell had requested a confidential communication with Travellor, and by regulation there had to be at least one communication specialist in the comm room, twenty-four-seven.

"Uh oh. This is bad!" said Travellor, shaking his head. "Everyone knows the big dinner tomorrow is for Cove, and they're not going to like this. You have never seen the base look so clean and organized. The Ganaphe' have even polished the walls of the Orysta. Everyone has put in overtime so that they could be ahead of their work schedules."

Travellor looked at Jibble, who gave him a pitying look.

"Sorry about that, Travellor. At least you can still have the feast. That should keep the natives from getting too restless – just no guest of honor. "

"Excuse me for being blunt, sir, but you are down there – safe. I'm the one who's up here – surrounded by those restless natives."

"I'm really sorry." said Farber-Chatwell, unable to suppress a laugh.

"I'm glad you find this funny, sir. I will get you back for this."

"Now hold on." he replied, laughing harder. "It's not like I have any control over this. It's not my fault."

Travellor thought about that for a second.

"No…," he finally said, "no, I have no problem with blaming you anyway. If that's all sir, I have to go make sure my body armor still fits."

"I really am sorry." said Farber-Chatwell, laughing even harder. "Signing off."

The laughter continued from the speaker for a few more seconds, then it went silent. Travellor just shook his head for a while, feeling a little sorry for himself.

"Would you like me open a base wide link, sir, so you can tell everyone the bad news?" asked Delfin.

"No." replied Travellor, taking a deep breath. "No. Why ruin the atmosphere for everyone. They're all happy and excited, and looking forward to the celebration. I'll tell them tomorrow, at the dinner – AFTER they've had a few drinks. I will have to inform Grilik Munen, though. Might as well do that now. He's going to be very disappointed."

He stood up and headed towards the door. He wasn't sure if he was feeling sorry for himself, or everyone else – or both.

"This is going to be a long day. Thank you, Jibble. Good job. Classify communication as Confidential."

3

"They are not going to be happy about this." said Califas.

In the room with him was Grilik Munen, Mersuul, and Plessa.

"The Humans are always overly cautious." said Munen. "We can accomplish this without any risk of exposure. But you are correct – they will not like this. As an added precaution we will launch when night covers the continent. Is everyone clear on the time table for the mission?"

They all nodded.

"Everyone has their assignment. Remember – stealth and deception are our most important tools."

4

Travellor was still drying off from his shower when he heard the door chime. It had been a day full of disappointed faces and the many times unspoken 'Can't YOU do something about this?', and he wasn't in the mood for having visitors. He tapped the intercom button and the video screen lit up with Mersuul's face.

"This is nice and unexpected." he said. "I thought you were on duty tonight."

He tapped on the sensor that opened the door to his chambers, and walked out of the bathroom with the towel wrapped around his waist. Mersuul came into the room with a bottle of wine in one hand, and a DVD and microwave popcorn in the other.

"Grilik Munen changed the schedule." she said. "I left the ship before he could change his mind again."

She walked up until she was pressed against him, and kissed him lightly on the lips.

"Don't bother getting dressed for me." she added with a smile, as she loosened his towel until it fell off. She placed what she was carrying on the small entranceway table, and began to take her clothes off as she walked towards the bathroom. "I need a quick shower. Want to join me?" she asked, then came back and took Travellor's hand. She pulled him with her.

"I just took a shower. If I had known you were coming I..."
"Then you can keep me company while I do."

5

The formal dining room looked amazing, and to call it extravagant would be an understatement. It was the first formal dinner on the Moon Base. Everything before this had been held on the Orysta. The two rotating glass chandeliers cast flying beams of light in every corner of the room. The tables and chairs were made of dark hard wood with decorative hand carvings, and the table clothes were especially designed so that the carvings were visible while still covering the area of the place settings. The dishes, silverware and crystal goblets were very expensive custom made items. The side tables displayed fresh whole and cut fruit, and pastries brought in from around the world. The side walls were covered in etched glass mirrors. There were two full bars, with a beverage selection from every continent on the planet. It was all definitely not like what Travellor was used to from his military days. The whole thing was at the insistence of Ransen Ramsdel, who stated that the men and women risking their lives for 361 should be given nothing less when celebrating special occasions. This room was the only part of the base design that he had given input on. Farber-Chatwell had told Travellor that Ramsdel never fully got over the time when they had thought the original Trailblazer crew had been lost, and this was his way of expressing his thanks.

The room was full of people wearing clothes purchased for just for this occasion, and those in uniform had them starched and ironed, the brass and silver polished to mirror shines. It was the first time Travellor had ever seen some of the female personnel in dresses, and the males in suits. On his way here he had noticed that even the skeleton crew remaining on duty were also wearing creased uniforms that looked like they were new. He looked at Mersuul, who was walking towards him. She was in a dress that came over one shoulder, and was made of soft, flowing material. He knew nothing about women's clothing, and could only describe it as tropical and 'islandish'. Whatever it was, she looked absolutely beautiful in it. Her smile grew wider as she got closer.

"Time for you to announce the guest of honor." she said, in a quiet voice.

"That is not funny." he replied. "Everyone knows Cove will not be here – but I guess I should officially announce that."

"If you do, you will be telling a lie."

He looked at her questioningly, wondering what she was talking about. Mersuul just smiled and pointed to the main entrance doors. Travellor turned to looked where she indicated, and saw Grilik Munen and several of the Orysta crew accompanying a very recognizable Eckelberry Cove. His eyes went wide with surprise. Others in the room also turned to watch the group coming in, and in few seconds spontaneous applause erupted as the man everyone was waiting to see was escorted to the VIP table.

"What did you do?" he asked, joining in the applause.

"I did not do anything. I spent the night with the man I have great affection for."

Travellor's eye got even wider, as he now turned to look at Mersuul.

"Grilik Munen told you to seduce me? To keep me out of the way while he launched a ship, against Farber-Chatwell's orders?"

"No," she said, grinning, "He ordered me to keep you 'distracted' while he launched a ship, against Farber-Chatwell's orders. The seduction was my idea. The Grilik doesn't work for Farber-Chatwell. He doesn't have to follow his orders. I enjoyed it very much."

"You enjoyed what very much?"

"Distracting you."

Travellor shook his head in disbelief.

"You little Mata Hari!"

"Mata Hari?" she asked, confused.

"I'll tell you later." he said, looking back at the group making their way closer.

Travellor's eyes went wide again in surprise. Walking behind Munen's group came Farber-Chatwell in a suit that cost more than Travellor's pickup truck on Earth. On his arm was Doctor Blin, looking stunningly beautiful.

"You kidnapped Farber-Chatwell and brought him also?"

"We didn't know where Doctor Cove was located. We had to

contact your Commander to find out. Since he could not stop us from using our shuttle, he decided to come along. It made Doctor Blin very happy when she saw him."

"This is the first time I've ever seen him out of uniform. He looks strange."

"I would place a bet that Toisae has seen him out of uniform." she said, broadly grinning.

"This isn't over, Mata. You and I are going to talk about this later."

Mersuul just smiled at him, and then turned her attention to the approaching group. As Cove, Munen, and the rest of the group made their way to the table, the applause reached a crescendo. Even the people who had accompanied Cove to the dining hall were now applauding. Eckelberry Cove looked stiffly around, not knowing how to react to his admirers. He was a scientist, not a rock star. This was slightly uncomfortable for him so he did the only thing he could think of – he said Thank You, and took his seat. The applause died down as everyone followed his example. The serving staff took their cue from this. As Travellor sat down, he avoided looking at Farber-Chatwell. He expected his superior would have a few words to say about today's events. But that would be for tomorrow. Tonight he was going to enjoy a great meal, the company of his own Mata Hari, and he was going to pull rank if necessary and get to talk to Eckelberry Cove. Like everyone else, Travellor also recognized that Cove was fated to go into Earth's history books. Ironically, the world at large knew nothing about him.

6

"What time is it?"

"Time for me to go on to duty." said Mersuul, leaning over and kissing Travellor on the cheek. "You have another hour for sleep."

"Sure," said Travellor, with closed eyes and slurred words, "you just walk away and leave me to face Farber-Chatwell by myself. I smell coffee."

"Yes, and it is very good." she said, taking a sip from her cup. "I reset the pot to brew fresh when you wake up."

Travellor turned onto his back and looked in the direction of Mersuul's voice, only catching a glimpse of her as she left the bedroom. It only took a couple of minutes for his mind to fill with things he had to get done today. He knew he wasn't going to be able to get back to sleep. Stretching his body seemed more difficult than normal, as he got out of the bed and into bathroom. He would have a little time to get some things done before his meeting with Farber-Chatwell. He had a feeling he was going to be reprimanded for letting the Ganaphe' shuttle leave the moon without his knowing. Then he thought about Mersuul, and remembered last night, and had no doubt it was worth it.

7

"I know you're probably upset about me telling you to stop all travel to Earth, and then taking the Ganaphe' to Cove, and accompanying him to the party." said Farber-Chatwell.

Travellor's eyes began to get bigger, but he forced them to stop so as not to show his surprise. His instincts told him to just sit quietly and let things play out.

"I was a little angry with them when they showed up unexpected," continued Farber-Chatwell, "but Munen assured me they took all necessary precautions and weren't detected, and they were already there. I couldn't just say no to them. We get along well, but there is a lot riding on the continued development of our relationship. When Cove received their personal invitation he immediately said Yes, and there really wasn't anything for me to do but accompany him."

Travellor continued to keep his mouth shut. He had thought he was going to be chastised, but instead Farber-Chatwell was apologizing to him. Sometimes the wisest course of action was to just shut up. Finally Farber-Chatwell stopped talking.

"Sir, the whole thing was completely beyond your control." said Travellor. "The Ganaphe' don't take orders from us, and although they are normally very cooperative, we can't stop them from doing what they want to."

Farber-Chatwell looked relieved. Travellor was pleased with himself for taking the right tact by keeping his mouth closed and acting graciously.

"It seems that even people from other planets can get celebrity fever also." continued Travellor.

"That's not so surprising to me. I've had a little of that fever myself, and I never thought I was prone to it. But knowing Cove is a little like it must have been to know Einstein. The man seems to come up with these concepts out of thin air, each one multiple leaps beyond the previous. Anyone with half a functional brain would have to be impressed."

"I understand completely." replied Travellor. "You may not know it but here on the base, reading and discussing his papers has become the pastime of choice. No exceptions. People with absolutely no interest in science are captivated by the possibilities his theories promise, once it's explained to them. The latest popular activity here is the Thursday night lecture, where Cove's theories and designs are explained and discussed by base personnel who understand it – mostly understand it anyway. Everyone feels like we're living in a sci-fi novel. They felt that way when they first got here, but it's just another duty assignment after a while. With the Cove influence affecting them it's like a new exciting episode every week. Everyone is holding their breath waiting to find out what his new engine design can do."

"Where are we with that?"

"I'm told we should be ready for flight testing in three weeks or less. The Ganaphe' have loaned us some instruments which will give much more accurate measurements of everything from frame loading to maximum speed and thrust achieved. Their nav equipment will allow very accurate course plotting and recording. We'll also be running our own equipment alongside for comparison."

"And the crew? Who did you choose?"

"THE John Smith will be test pilot in command. George Washington will copilot. They've been a crew since coming here, and work together well. Tahn-grilik Califas will act as ship's engineer."

"What?" said Farber-Chatwell, surprised. "You're putting a Ganaphe' on the ship. Why?"

"No choice, if we want that Ganaphe' equipment on board. Munen says he can loan it to us as long as he can document that no unauthorized personnel had access to the guts of the instruments. Plus, it saves having to train one of our guys on its use."

"So a crew of three on the test flight."

"Yes. The Grilik strongly suggests that the fire control system on the ship be operational."

"Why do they want weapons on a test flight?"

"Munen said that it is SOP for the Ganaphe' to arm all of their ships – commercial and military."

Farber-Chatwell quietly looked at Travellor for a while.

"Do you get the feeling we're not being told everything."

"Often." replied Travellor.

8

"In one more Earth week you will be testing the new Cove engine. If it is successful, as everyone believes it will be, all of your ships will be fitted with one." said Grilik Munen, addressing the small assembly of people in front of him.

They were in the relatively small conference room on the Orysta. Although the meeting between Ganaphe' and Moon base personnel was restricted to the number of people presently in the room, the audio was being broadcast on a common channel that anyone who was interested could tune in to.

"What we need for our attempt at freeing the Orysta from the crevice is power – a great amount of power. In particular we need maximum thrust energy. The engines presently on your shuttles can generate a greater Sudden Impulse Thrust than the new engine, which is designed to slowly increase output to the maximum thrust level. According to Mr. Cove's specifications, the present engines can generate four hundred and thirty-seven percent of their continuous duty thrust rating, for a short period of time." he continued. Our past attempts at freeing the Orysta from the crevice that it is wedged into were unsuccessful because we didn't have enough power to overcome all the resistance involved."

He gestured to the center of the table they sat around, and a three dimensional and highly detailed image of the Orysta appeared, situated more than sixty feet below the moon's surface level. The image was complete with the huge rocks that pressed into the ships sides and the tons of ground material that wrapped around it, completing a gap-less embrace by the Moon.

"As you can see from this representation, the ship is securely held by the material in contact with the hull. Besides the larger rocks pressing against the sides, loose soil and smaller rocks have sifted down to fill all possible gaps. If our engine was fully functional, getting the ship out of this situation would not be a problem. If one of our salvage ships were here it would have no trouble lifting out the Orysta. The material in the crevice is very fluid, and our previous attempts to remove rocks and sand on top of us only resulted in more material falling in to fill the area that was cleared."

"But your engine, even in its damaged condition, still generates a tremendous amount of energy." said Farber-Chatwell. "That will surely give us an advantage in moving the ship – won't it?"

Munen showed a disheartened look on his face.

"Unfortunately it will not. All the energy we can generate will not be of any assistance in moving the ship. Our engines work on a different principle than yours do. We generate maximum power in a mixing chamber, and then control the amount of power that is released to effect acceleration and deceleration of the ship. The energy can be directed in all vectors to direct the path of the ship. At all times the power level in the mixing chamber is held at a level of ninety percent which is the Design Maximum Safe Continuous Power level, making it readily available. This energy is then routed to a Force Conversion Chamber, the output level of which can be controlled and directed. By using this two step process, we always have a high power level available to be used not only to propel the ship, but in all of the ships systems and external mining operations. That is where our problem is. We can still generate maximum power, but the Conversion Chamber is damaged beyond our ability to repair it. To make our situation worse, we are unable to accept your help in building a new conversion chamber because we would have to give you access to our technology to do so. That would violate the IGT."

"Even in a survival situation?" asked Travellor.

"We are not in a survival situation." replied Munen. "Thanks to our good fortune in making contact with the Trailblazer crew my people are all healthy, and except for not being able to contact their families in a very long time they are also relatively happy."

"Now the situation has changed." said Benua-sil-Plessa, the Orysta's Chief Engineer. "With the Moon Base fleet presently at four ships, we may be able to pull the Orysta out of the crevice with the force of their combined thrust and that of our two shuttles. I've calculated that the combined force generated by all of the ships would be equal to the holding force being exerted on the hull."

"But that's just a stalemate." said Dal Yimka.

"Yes." said Plessa. "A stalemate. That is why to win this game of chess we will place directional explosives around the periphery of the ship, to break the contact of some of the detritus. That may give us just enough advantage to pull the ship free."

"Isn't there a chance the explosives might damage the hull?"

"There is a risk, but Orysta has calculated the shape and formulation of each explosive charge and it is an acceptable risk."

"Who decides what is acceptable?" asked Travellor.

"I do," replied Munen, "as Grilik of the Orysta, and my Tahn-grilik agrees with me. I have also informed all of my crew. They also agree it is a risk worth taking."

"Phewwwwww…" Travellor blew out a long breath, shaking his head. "It's your ship – and your decision. But I've been in situations that required decisions like this, and as often as not they don't work out well. You view the Orysta as a damaged ship. I see it as a machine system more capable than anything else we have available to us on Earth. It's a risk you're taking – maybe a big one. I don't have a problem with trying to yank her out of the ground, but the explosives up against her hull bothers me very much."

"Yes." said Munen. "It bothers all of us very much also. Since there is a possibility of causing damage to outer hull, we would like have all Ganaphe' and Moon Base maintenance personnel on standby. Only myself, Califas, Plessa, and Valian will be aboard the ship during the attempt. All other Orysta crew members will be at the Moon Base as a precaution."

"We can do that." said Travellor. "I need one point cleared up, though. You said our present shuttle engines can generate four hundred and thirty-seven percent of their regular thrust for a short period. Isn't that like using the family car for drag racing?"

Munen looked confused at Travellor's unfamiliar cultural reference.

"If you're asking if that will blow out the engines," said Farber-

214

Chatwell, "yes, it will. But we have replacement engines on site. And with the new engine design being tested in a week, and assuming it will be a successful test and they go into service in a couple of months – we are talking about a Cove engine design after all – I've made the decision to sacrifice the engines for this purpose. They've already reached half their operational life so it's not really much of a sacrifice. Our ships will only be down for the time it takes to swap in the replacement engines, and the Orysta's shuttles will be operational during that time."

"Very well Commander." said Travellor. "Just wanted to make sure that was clear to everyone."

9

The Best we can do right now

"Cable systems?" prompted Munen, over the comm.

"Shuttle 1 connected and ready…" the replies came back from each pilot of the six shuttles.

"…Shuttle 2 connected and ready…, Moonbase 1 connected and ready…, Moonbase 2 connected and ready…, Moonbase 3 connected and ready…, Moonbase 4 connected and ready…" came the other replies.

Munen recognized each voice. Over the years Orysta and Trailblazer personnel had come to know each other very well by working together in combined operations. There weren't that many people on the moon in total, so it wasn't hard to know everyone else. Everyone on station knew everyone else, their job functions, and even had knowledge of their families back home. Personnel changeover didn't occur very much – in fact it was rare.

The exchange of information between the two groups was unprecedented in modern history, as far as Munen knew. Medical personnel of both species had no problem treating either group since their physiology was so close. There were only minor differences, no doubt caused by evolution on slightly different planets. Ganaphe' technology was more advanced than Human technology because they had been developing it for a longer period of time – about one hundred Earth years or so longer. Now that Humans were shown that certain principles of physics were not as limited as they had believed, their imaginations would be released from their present scientific dogma. The same had happened in other galaxies and the accelerated development was without exception.

"Flight Commander Balfour, this is Grilik Munen. I am Turning control of the mission over to you."

There were a few seconds of silence, then a female voice came over the comm.

"Confirmed, Grilik Munen. All ships and flight personnel, this is Flight Commander Balfour taking control of Operation Best Shot. Operation Best Shot is now in effect. Stand by for further instructions." said Brighde Balfour, with the authority of experience and knowledge in her voice, and a slight Scottish accent.

Brighde Balfour was relatively new to Trailblazer Moon Base. In her early forties, she took early retirement from the RAF, after she was enticed into her new position by Farber-Chatwell. Recruiting the top people in their field was what he did, and he did it well. It had taken some time to convince her to accept a position with an unknown organization that promised travel to places she had never been to, and she had no idea that Farber-Chatwell was one of the top people in this unknown agency. They had asked almost too much of her. There were background checks she had to authorize, and intense interviews she tolerated, not to mention the psychological testing she almost screamed about in frustration because she couldn't see the sense of it all. But she had known Farber-Chatwell for many years, and trusted his judgment – and she just couldn't overcome the allure of the promised pay scale. She could spend her whole life in the RAF and still couldn't come close to that kind of money. Even private industry couldn't come close.

It was that first evening one month ago, when she was waiting at the small airport outside of town for the transport that was to take her to her new job, that she learned that none of the promises were exaggerated. Expecting a small private aircraft to arrive and pick her up, she was surprised almost into shock when a strange looking vehicle appeared in front of her from nowhere, and Farber-Chatwell came out of it to help with her bags. She remembered how her heart pounded in her chest as she realized they were actually leaving the Earth's atmosphere at an unbelievable speed and heading into space – and she was wearing her new business suit with appropriate three inch heels. She also remembered how the shock turned to excitement as they approached their destination and she realized they were going to land on the moon! The shuttle doors opened up inside the Orysta, and she was welcomed by a contingent of 361 and Ganaphe' personnel – and she had absolutely no desire to look back. She knew without question that she was where she wanted to be.

Since then she had taken over the position of Flight Commander, and no one had any doubt about her competency. She had learned the best operational procedures of both the Orysta and Trailblazer flight crews and equipment, and combined them into a new encompassing Flight Procedures Manual. It was one of the reasons she was hired for the job, and she did it in less than three weeks – far less time than was expected of her. All personnel operated by those procedures now. When the manual was reviewed by command personnel of both groups, they agreed that it defined the best operating procedures for Earth to Moon flight. Grilik Munen had had to agree to an increase in the number of Trailblazer personnel to permit her to be here, and after seeing her work product he didn't regret it. The total number of ships operating from the base was six, and two more were scheduled to be added to the Trailblazer fleet within the next two months. Flight operations had reached the point where there had to be a single control authority. Balfour was now accepted by both groups as that authority.

217

"Best Shot flight, this is Balfour. Obtain your hovering positions, and maintain cable tension. Report in sequence when ready."

All six shuttles slowly rose above the moon's surface until the cables attached between each ship and the Orysta became tight. They hovered in pattern with a Ganaphe' shuttle at the middle of each end of the the mining ship. Two moon base shuttles were equally spaced at each side of the ship. The shuttles were attached to re-enforced points on the mining ship's hull. This configuration was selected to give a more uniform distribution of lifting force on the Orysta.

"Best Shot 1 in position and standing by…" came the first reply using the mission designation. "Best Shot 2 in position and standing by…, Best Shot 3 in position and standing by…, Best Shot 4 in position and standing by…, Best Shot 5 in position and standing by…, Best Shot 6 in position and standing by."

"Roger, Best Shot flight. Sync flight computers now please."

Each shuttle commander placed their flight computer in synchronous mode. On the screen in front of Balfour, a diagram depicting the shuttles in their positions above the Orysta showed blue connecting lines between the ships, indicating the flight computers were now communicating with each other and working as a single control system. This was necessary so that the lifting force of each ship could be equalized in real time, since the Ganaphe' and 361 shuttles had different power capabilities. As the flight computers linked together, subtle initial adjustments in thrust were made so that each ship applied the same amount of tension on their cable. The amount of tension had to be equal at all six connecting points or damage to Orysta's hull could occur.

Inside the Orysta came a low groan and screeching caused by the rocks scraping the outside of the hull as the ship moved just slightly under the tension of the cables. Then a thicker, flashing blue line appeared on Balfour's screen showing that the Orysta's main computer had achieved control of the linked flight computers.

"Orysta, this is Best Shot control. Shuttles are in position, and I show that your main computer has linked up. Please confirm."

On Benua-sil-Plessa's display was a diagram indicating the Orysta's computer was linked and in control of the shuttle craft flight systems. A diagram of the Orysta was also depicted with the six points where the cables were attached. Next to each point was a digital readout of the amount of tension applied to those points. Also shown on the diagram, in red, was the location of each of the shaped charges that had been placed near the ship's hull. It had taken days of around the clock work to penetrate the surrounding soil and place the explosives in position.

"All systems are functional and ready, Grilik." said Plessa.
"Best Shot control this is Orysta." said Munen. "We show all systems are ready to execute."
"Roger Orysta. Maintenance team, report status." said Balfour, as she read down her checklist.
"Control this is Maintenance team. Ready to disconnect umbilical on your order."

Balfour took a deep breath as she reviewed the rest of the check list. The umbilical supplied the base with an enormous amount of power. Disconnecting the moon base from the Orysta power line was the point of no return item. From that moment on they would be committed to completing the extraction attempt. During the extraction the Ganaphe' camouflage system would be shut down. Anyone with a line of sight view would be able to see the base. The structure was large enough that an amateur astronomer on Earth could spot it with a decent quality telescope. Also, the base would be strictly on its own power generators.

"Stand by Maintenance team. Security, this is Best Shot control. How long before satellites?" asked Balfour, as her eyes scanned the sky around the base while waiting for the reply.

"Control – Security. We have one hour and thirteen minutes until we will be in the peripheral view of GRAIL-B and three hours and seven minutes before the LRO is a factor."

'One hour and thirteen minutes.' thought Balfour. *'That should give us plenty of time.'* It was her decision to make.

"All Best Shot personnel, this is Control. We have slightly more than one hour and ten minutes to complete our job. If all goes according to mission profile, that should be more than enough time. Moon Base – prepare for disconnect from the Orysta. Maintenance Team – disconnect the umbilical and separate the passageway. Report when completed."
"This is Maintenance – will do!"

10

Travellor sat in his office, monitoring the communications of Operation Best Shot, like everyone else on the base was doing. He felt agitated at not being in control of the mission. But it was not his job, and he knew it. He had never considered himself a control freak, but wondered if he was developing into one. No, he assured himself, it was just the anxiety of knowing what was at stake. The only way for the base to continue to exist in safety was for the Ganaphe' camouflage system to be put back into operation as soon as possible. That meant that whether this attempt was a success or failure, they had to get the power connected back from the Orysta on a priority basis. If a secret moon base suddenly appeared in telescopes around the world, there were plenty of countries that would immediately consider it a threat. Trailblazer Moon Base would be targeted by someone. He knew Balfour was aware of this – she had clearly outlined it in her mission plan. It was a very thorough plan, and he was amazed by her competence – especially for someone who had been on station for such a short time. She had immersed herself in learning everything there was to know about the base and the Orysta, and did so far faster than he ever could have.

The lights in the room flickered for just a fraction of a second, and he knew they had disconnected power from the Orysta. The base was exposed now. The one very important thing he hadn't even considered until now was the Ganaphe' – and the Orysta – not being there. He had grown to consider the people and ship as part of Trailblazer Moon Base. That's what happens when you live and work so closely together for a long time. But they weren't part of it. They were far from their home and families, and if the opportunity to go back there presented itself they would. The problem was he hadn't been thinking far enough into the future. Nothing remains the same forever.

So now he had some new priorities to consider, among them being the increase of power generation capacity on the base. Second would be the development of a shuttle that could travel to Earth and back in practical time. He didn't expect they would match the speed capability of the Ganaphe' shuttles – not for a while anyway – but they had to be able to operate in and out of the Earth's atmosphere. They had to develop these now, while the Ganaphe' were still here. *'To hell with going to another galaxy.'* he thought. *'Lets just be able to go to Earth and back.'*

11

"Control, this is Maintenance Team. The umbilical has been disconnected and the passageway separated. We are moving back to the base."

"Roger Maintenance Team." replied Balfour. "Report when you are in a safe and secure position."

"Will do."

The base was unusually quiet. The operation was being broadcast over the base's paging system, and everyone was intent on what they were hearing. Some listened while sitting in the lounge area, where outside cameras showed the shuttles hovering over the location of the Orysta. Those on duty listened in over the comm system, but Balfour now went over the base alert system, so that no one anywhere would miss her next words. The alert system accessed every corner of the base and the Orysta. It went into the living quarters, labs, recreational facilities, and also to any personnel outside on the moon's surface.

"ATTENTION!... ATTENTION ALL PERSONNEL! If you haven't done so already, move now to a safe location. Operation Best Shot is about to execute. Anyone who is not already in a safe location should immediately report their status."

Balfour waited for the next expected status report before continuing. It was only a few minutes before she heard it.

"Best Shot control, this is Maintenance team. We are in the base. Access door is closed and secured."

Balfour checked off one more item on her list.

"Roger Maintenance team. Attention all personnel. This is Best Shot control. All teams are reporting in position and ready to execute. If anyone has a different status report it now."

She waited a few minutes for any replies. Everyone who was not part of the operation turned their attention to the monitors or ports that showed them the view outside the base.

12

John Smith looked around at the other five ships in his view. The

Ganaphe' shuttles were parallel to the moon's surface because they were able to direct thrust downward from the bottom of their ships. The cables were attached at the reinforced center of their underbellies. The four Trailblazer shuttles only had the relatively weak maneuvering thrusters that could be directed downward, so they sat on their tails pointing away from the surface. Their cables were attached to the lower trailing edge of their airframes.

This was going to be one of those simple, easy jobs. All they had to do was pull on the attached cable with all the force the ships could generate – straight up – that's all. Simple and easy. No problem. But Smith recognized the inherent potential hazards. The plan was basically to push their engines as far as they could go just short of breaking them. But these were machines. Machines which had different types and amounts of wear and tear on each of them. Smith knew that that meant they wouldn't break at the same time or in the same way. It had all been calculated based on design specs, and maybe that would have been good enough when the shuttles were new. These ships had been used for both every day chores and experimental flights. Some had more hours on them than the others.

He tried to figure out what the potential dangers were. A cable could snap sending the attached shuttle shooting into space and putting an unbalanced load on the Orysta's hull – but not likely – the Ganaphe' had guaranteed they were capable of holding much greater forces than the ships could generate. One of the engines could fail unexpectedly causing the ship to swing into another as it responded to the forces around it – but they had all been checked over for weak or failing systems. And then there was the elephant in the room – a catastrophic failure of an engine exploding and sending pieces of shrapnel into the surrounding ships. Whenever systems were pushed to the limits as they were going to push these engines, that was a real world possibility.

He sighed, and dismissed all of those thoughts, as he realized what the real elephant in the room was – that this was going to be just a boring, as planned mission going off without a problem. This exploring outer space thing just wasn't as exciting as all the movies and TV shows made it out to be. Except for the great view from the cockpit, he might as well be sitting at a desk in an office. Then another thought came into his head. "*Hot dogs! I want hot dogs for dinner.*" He looked around to the far reaches of his vision and realized that, except for the barren moonscape, it looked pretty much like a starlit night at home.

13

Travellor had just made his way to the Communications Center, when he heard Balfour's last instruction over the Comm. She was controlling the mission from the Control Tower where she could visually monitor everything. He could have gone there instead, but figured that Balfour didn't need to feel the brass was looking over her shoulder – he wouldn't have liked that if he was running the operation. Besides, the Communications center monitors were the next best thing to having eyes on. It was a three-hundred-sixty degree display that was like looking out of the Control Tower itself.

He looked at his tablet computer, which displayed the mission checklist that Balfour was following. Any item not yet accomplished was in bold red letters. Items that were completed changed to a standard green font. His tablet was linked to Balfour's computer and automatically followed along with any changes she made. The Orysta crew could also follow the list on their displays, as could any team directly involved in the mission. It had been quiet for a few minutes before he heard Balfour's voice again.

"Orysta, this is Flight Commander Balfour! Do you hear and understand me?"

Travellor knew she wasn't talking to the ship's crew now.

"*Flight Commander Balfour, this is Orysta. You are being received clearly.*" came the voice of the ship's main computer.
"Orysta, stand by to initiate Operation Best Shot."
"*Ready to initiate.*"

"All flight crews and team members – Operation Best Shot is ready to commence. Pilots prepare to take manual control of your ship in unexpected circumstance. Grilik Munen, operation will commence on my mark. All stations stand by."

Travellor moved his eyes down to a smaller display at table top level. It showed a depiction of the Orysta being overflown by the shuttles, It also showed two side views of the ship with red dots indicating each of the explosive charges next to the hull. Each charge was half encased in an impact absorbing material that was designed to lesson the force against the hull. The open end of the case faced outward, directing as much of the explosion to the surrounding rocks and soil.

"Orysta, this is Balfour. Spool engines to stage one thrust level."

The engines on each shuttle began to increase thrust output, monitored and controlled by the Orysta's computer. Even though the Trailblazer and Orysta shuttles had different size engines, the power levels were controlled by the computer based on thrust output only. This way all the shuttles applied the same amount of tension to the ship. The crew of the Orysta felt a slight jerk upwards before suddenly being again held by the surrounding rocks and detritus. The shuttle crews checked their instruments which all read within normal operating parameters. Not surprising since they were still at a low power output level.

"All shuttle thrust levels at stage one." said the computer.

Balfour's eyes were dancing over her display screens, verifying the numbers looked correct. She took one other look at the shuttles being held in position, then looked down at the ground. She thought she could see an outline of the Orysta on the surface, but knew it was just her imagination.

"Orysta, on initiation of explosive charges bring Trailblazer shuttle engines to maximum SIT and match Orysta shuttles to that level. Confirm instructions."

"Trailblazer shuttle engines to maximum Sudden Impulse Thrust and Orysta shuttles engines to matching thrust. Initiate on activation of explosive sequence."

"Grilik Munen. She's your ship. I'll let you have the honor."

"Thank you Commander." replied Munen. "Count down from five... four... three... two... one."

Munen touched his control screen and the red dots on the three dimensional depiction of the ship started going dark indicating that particular charge had been triggered. They were programmed to explode in a pattern that kept the soil in their immediate vicinity in motion. The Orysta crew could hear and feel the charges going off on both sides of the hull. It was like continuous thunder that caused the ship to vibrate. Shortly afterwards the screeching sound of rocks trying to tear through the outer hull began to get louder, and the ship began to moved in small jerks and jumps.

14

The material the Ganaphe' cables were made from didn't stretch much, but they did a little. John Smith had seen his engine instruments suddenly jump into the red zone when the Orysta computer adjusted the engines for maximum thrust. He felt the shuttle move just a little after the cable went tight. He could almost swear they were moving upward – in millimeters maybe, but still they were moving. He checked the other shuttles and could see the crews monitoring their engines. It was when he looked down at the ground that he was surprised. The explosive charges were causing random sections of soil to bounce into the air. The surface below them began to bulge in spots. Just as he was thinking that this might work, the engines suddenly decreased output to hovering thrust. A faint outline of the ship was definitely there, but the Orysta was still underground. The mission had failed. How much had they pulled her up – half an inch – one inch – two?

"Trailblazer shuttle engines output reduced to hovering thrust before catastrophic failure." said the voice of the Orysta over the speaker.

It was over. Just as Smith had thought, no elephants came to roost. *'Or is that mixing metaphors?'* he wondered. He could see everyone in the other shuttles looking around at the other ships.

"All shuttles and engines operational. No risks to personnel safety at present." said Orysta.

There was a loud exhalation over a live mic, and then Balfour's voice came over the air.

"Grilik Munen, report your status." commanded Balfour.
"No injuries to crew. Ship is intact." replied Munen. "... As far as we can determine."
"Best Shot flight, release cables and dock shuttles in sequence. Use standard arrival procedures."

There was disappointment in Balfour's voice now. There was disappointment in everyone's voices. Each of the shuttle crews acknowledged the command.

"Maintenance Team, you are a GO." said Balfour.
"Maintenance Team – Roger. We are moving. We'll have the tunnel re-established in ten minutes or less. Umbilical reconnected in fifteen."
"Roger Maintenance Team. Report when done."

Balfour checked the time. They had another twenty-two minutes before GRAIL-B flew into a position that could detect the base. She knew it wouldn't be a problem. The Ganaphe' were professional miners, and they had brought their equipment with them when they disconnected the passageway. If they had to create a whole new tunnel from the base to the ship they could do it and still have time left over. Their mining equipment went through rock and soil like the proverbial hot knife through butter, melting the material into a hard supporting wall.

"All Operation Best Shot personnel, this is Balfour. Debriefing in two hours in the mission planning room. Thank you all for a great effort."

15

A few days later

"Power from the Orysta was restored in less than ten minutes. They had the tunnel fixed a short time after that." said Travellor.

"Good to hear." said Farber-Chatwell. "So the camouflage was working before any chance of detection by the satellite?"

"Yes Sir. Of course, we had an outline of the Orysta bulging up on the surface. I sent out a crew to work that over to make it look more natural – more pre-bulge."

"So the Ganaphe' are all feeling a little down now? A little depressed?"

"Yep. I would be too, if I were them. But it's nothing serious. It's only been a few days. They'll feel better in time. They've submerged themselves in their mining, which is probably not bad therapy. They've already got a very impressive load of crystal-flow in their cargo bay, which is a pity since it doesn't look like they'll be going home soon. They keep mining it though. I guess they're hoping they'll be rescued. They mentioned that they were very surprised that rescue ships hadn't come looking for them already. The emergency beacons they had released should have brought someone here like a trail of bread crumbs."

"Hmmm. Well we all know how that worked out for Hansel and Gretel."

"Well, the mining keeps them busy anyway."

"Oh it's more than that." commented Farber-Chatwell. "Munen is a very smart man, and he has business savvy. Look at it this way – they have the knowledge and technology to mine crystal-flow and we don't. They know how to process it – we don't! We have a need for it, and they're the only ones who can supply it to us. That crystal-flow in their cargo bay is just like a bank account. It's ready cash. If they are going to be stuck here for a while, they'll be able to do so in a lot of comfort."

"Good point."

"I've brought samples down for our people to work with. It's so dispersed in the media we have trouble finding it, let alone detecting it from everything else in the soil. It's a miracle crystal-flow was ever discovered – or an accident! I'll have to ask Munen about that."

"I'll mention you're curious about it. Well, that's all I've got for now. I'll write up an official report and have it transmitted."

"Alright. But keep an eye on our friends. If they don't seem to be coming out of their funk we'll have to do something to cheer them up."

"Will do. Out."

Travellor hit the keyboard on his computer and terminated the communication to Earth. The smell of coffee hit his nose, and he picked up his cup and walked to the outer office. Their was intentionally no machine in his office, forcing him to get up and leave his desk for coffee. He was in the mood for checking up on everything in general. Doing rounds was actually a way for him to relax – unless he found something messed up. He filled the large mug, and added the right amount of sugar. By the time the coffee was gone he should be at engineering, and they always had excellent coffee for a refill. He walked out of his office with a smile on his face, looking forward to small talk with anyone he encountered. It was amazing how much practical information you could find out with small talk. It was how he kept up with the personal lives of the people he worked with. He thought about his niece, who was in college now. What was the next holiday coming up? He had to make sure to take the time off for a visit.

Chapter 14

In With the New

1

December 17, 2012

Inside Trailblazer's comm center were several people, including Grilik Munen and Base Commander Travellor. They were now watching one of the large monitors on the wall displaying the video from one of the Ganaphe' shuttles that flew ahead of Ebb and Flow as they headed for their planned demise. The shuttle flew at a greater altitude than the LRO satellite so it wouldn't be detected. The video they watched showed a wide angle and was presently centered on Ebb. It was moving so fast over the moon that the surface was just a blur. When it was in position over the calculated impact site, the shuttle stopped and zoomed in its camera so that detail could be seen. Ebb anticlimactically impacted the side of a mountain near the Moon's north pole, followed by Flow about thirty seconds later. There were no large explosions. Only minor displacement of surface material. In the comm center there was a sudden combined exhalation of relief. No one said it, but everyone knew that there was now less risk of their mission being detected. There were now two less eyes in the sky that they had to track and avoid.

"This calls for a working man's toast." said Travellor. "I'll get the coffee, you guys get the paper cups."

"I agree." said Munen. "The GRAIL satellites were an excellent concept by your people. They now have a detailed mapping of your Moon's structure. No doubt similar devices will be sent to other planets. A toast to a great achievement is fitting."

2

The telemetry stopped coming in to NASA's Deep Space Network Stations from the GRAIL satellites. They had reported all functions normal prior to performing their last maneuver that brought them into a rapidly decaying orbit and subsequent crash into the Moon's surface at over thirty-seven hundred miles per hour. "It had been a successful mission in all aspects." said Maria Zuber of MIT, the principal mission investigator.

During the time the satellites were still performing their primary mission of mapping the Moon's gravity to learn more about its internal composition, the secondary GRAIL MoonKAM mission was also underway. The strange spelling of the mission name 'KAM' stood for Knowledge Acquired by Middle school students. Led by Doctor Sally Ride, America's first woman in space, this program allowed students from around the world to select areas of the Moon to be photographed, with the detailed images being made publicly available for study on the MoonKAM website. Trailblazer Moon Base also monitored the signal stream from the satellites, and every image sent back to Earth was analyzed to make certain that the existence of the base had not been compromised. As it turned out, the base had not been detected thanks to the Ganaphe' camouflage system. Had anything revealing been photographed, there would have been only a few of seconds for the Orysta to transmit a signal to disrupt that part of the data stream. The interfering signal had to come from the Ganaphe's communication equipment since their signals traveled faster than regular radio waves, and had to catch up to the already sent signal from the satellites. This was a very difficult trick to pull off, requiring both a signal capable of traveling faster than standard electromagnetic waves and a computer that was fast enough to analyze the images and make the decision to intercept within a few milliseconds. The Orysta and its main computer was the only system with those capabilities.

3

March 5, 2013

Trailblazer Moon Base station commander Anthony Travellor leaned back in his chair and gathered his thoughts. The computer screen in front of him showed a flashing cursor and the word 'Ready'. It had taken him a while to get used to speaking his reports instead of typing them. Typing was slower, which gave you time to think and organize your thoughts as you typed. Speaking required you to have the organizing completed before you started. The Talk-into-Text program written by 361 software engineers had formatting choices built in, so he didn't have to worry about headings and accepted formats. He just selected 'Status Report' and the computer would do the rest. He hadn't trusted it at first, thinking he would have to tell the computer where to put punctuation, or start a new paragraph, but this software did a good job of handling most of that. He would only have to review and make a few minor changes afterward.

"March the fifth, twenty-thirteen." said Travellor, as he watched '05MARCH2013' displayed on the screen as the computer interpreted and formatted his words. "From Trailblazer Moon Base Station Commander to Operation 361 Space Ops Command."

The computer screen showed 'From: TMBSC To: OP361SOC'. He continued speaking.

"Mission Status Update and Review. Item number one."

Satisfied that it looked correct so far, but still not completely trusting the software, Travellor continued.

"Trailblazer Moon Base is now at a stage of development that would only have been considered to be a fantasy at one time. Originally envisioned as a habitat designed to primarily keep its inhabitants alive, and secondarily as a test base for off world operations, the base has advanced so far beyond establishing a simple outpost on the moon that even those of us who planted the flag are amazed on a daily basis. Though on a smaller scale, the base is now a habitat that operationally can challenge our most advanced military and scientific research facilities on Earth. Once 361 architects were set loose from the restrictions of our own technology, they designed (no doubt thinking it more of a mental exercise than a practical one) an operational structure that will serve for tens of years to come."

"TMB is both a Research and Development center, and on a limited scale a Fabrication and Testing center. As such we are at a point where we need to increase the number of personnel on station in order to meet our future goals. Transient staffing is no longer adequate for continued development. Presently most of the structure remains empty and unused. The base is ready for them."

Travellor took a sip of coffee, and tried to organize in his mind how he wanted to word the next part of his report. It could cause trouble in what is presently a clockwork operation.

"I realize that our agreement with the Ganaphe' restricts the number of personnel we can keep stationed on the base. That agreement was made at an earlier stage of our relationship, and was understandable as to why they demanded that restriction. We can not overlook the fact that our purpose for being here has greatly changed from the original concept. Our mission now is to continue to advance our capabilities in space operations. To do so demands we have more people on station. We must approach the Ganaphe' to change that part of our agreement, and to do so in a way that will keep both parties satisfied."

'I certainly hope someone can figure out a way,' he thought, *'because I can't.'*

"Item number two." he continued. "Since we lack the technology and engine capabilities of the Ganaphe', we are not at present capable of making repetitive controlled and undetected landings on Earth. We still do not know how their shuttle engines work except that gas reaction thrust is not used by them. Consider these factors. Landings using techniques similar to those used in our space program would expose our existence, and would be very restrictive in landing locations. This is not even considering the dangers involved in high speed penetration of the atmosphere, as we sadly know from our own STS program history. Our ships operating from TMB were assembled on location, and did not require an engine capable of overcoming the Earth's gravitational force. Our present engines are capable of propelling our ships away from the moon without excessive fuel consumption, and allow them to travel a relatively great distance in space. These engines are not capable of leaving the Earth's gravitational pull."

"With those factors in mind, I propose a two program approach on the development of our own ships. One program for developing extraterrestrial ships that are not capable of atmospheric flight. This program will have a limited, and hopefully short lifetime. Operating from TMB, this will give us the capability to expand exploration of our solar system now. Although they will not be able to enter the atmospheres of other planets, they will give us the ability of pinpoint delivery of instruments and satellites, and scientific measurements and tests that can be modified on location in real time (avoiding last minute surprises). These ships should be designed for instrumentation, payload, and speed. The second program should focus on a ship design capable of leaving and re-entering Earth's atmosphere under its own power, with controlled decent, and landing capability at any normal flight station. It should be able to reach TMB in hours. Avoidance of detection would be a definite benefit."

"This will not be an easy task, as you are no doubt thinking right now. But we have to consider that the Ganaphe' will not always be here. If not for their suffering a series of bad circumstances (Lucky for us), they would probably have already left on their journey back home. Remember that they have been away from home and family for over six years. One day they will have enough of the puzzle pieces to leave and they will not hesitate. It's only a matter of time before the Orysta is freed, and they have devised a propulsion system worth taking the risk on (Probably a Cove engine!). We must plan now for the time when the Ganaphe' are not around." Travellor grew melancholy at the thought, and added "I'll be sorry to see them leave – every one of them."

"Item number three. GRAIL is gone, but Jade Rabbit is here. LADEE will arrive soon enough and the LRO continues to fly above us. The Moon will continue to be the test bed for space exploration for any capable country on Earth for some time to come. I can almost envision a sky full of orbiting satellites, and a surface covered in crawling robots. Sometimes I think we should build a very large NO LOITERING sign and make it visible to all comers. But that is not practical. As of this time we do not have the ability to camouflage the base without the Ganaphe'. We need to develop this technology or figure out another way to accomplish this."

"Item number four. I like knowing which way is up and which is down. I could probably get used to hopping around, but walking is more practical. Again, it is Ganaphe' technology that supplies us with Earth comparable gravity. Again, let me state that they may not always be around – and their departure may be sooner than we want to believe. I would suggest we try to buy whatever creates that gravity from them, but I doubt they would want to travel between galaxies without gravity on their ship. Viable option – Find out if they can build a gravity generator for us. 361 has more resources and talent available than any other organization in existence on Earth. The question is can they build such a device for us using our technology? The next question – would they? I may be wrong but I suspect that Orysta has the necessary information to build such devices in its data banks."

"Item number five. It should be a consideration of all future plans that they be conceived and executed sans Ganaphe'. We depend on their space craft and power generation systems for too much right now – it's time to wean our selves off of that dependence. Mission Report Ends. Anthony Travellor. Trailblazer Moon Base Commander."

Travellor took a large sip of his coffee, and reviewed the formatting of the message. It looked good. He could pick a few nits here and there, but what showed on the screen got the message across. He tapped a few keys on the keyboard, and the message was encrypted and transmitted to Earth. There was probably going to be some blow-back from this. Everything was running smoothly between 361 and the Ganaphe' – so why fix it if it ain't broke. His instincts were telling him something different. The Ganaphe' had been marooned for over six years, on what should have been an eight month job. If it was him, he would have been itching to get back to 'civilization'. No doubt access to Earth had made things more bearable for the Orysta's crew, but there was family and loved ones back home who would be worried or even thinking the crew was dead. The need to get home pulled from both directions.

And where in Hell was the rescue ship that should have been looking for them? True, a galaxy was a large area to search – but six years? Certainly a people used to traveling between galaxies had developed an effective way to search one. Something must have gone wrong.

4

The doorbell sounded and Travellor, his thoughts lost in the daily report he was reading in his quarters, instinctively gestured to open the door. It took several seconds before he realized that no one had entered his quarters, and he turned to look at the entrance. Mersuul stood there staring at him, but not entering. He was confused by her facial expression, which was a mix of anger, aloofness, and doubt. He stood up from his desk and walked over to her, still trying to figure out what was going on.

"Why… aren't you coming in?" he asked.
"Because I was not sure you would want me to!" she spat.

His eyes opened wide in surprise, and his body involuntarily jerked slightly back. Now he was even more confused. Especially since he considered his quarters to be their quarters – together. Mersuul spent most nights with him here. He thought she felt the same way. Because of her duty assignments she hadn't stayed there the last two nights, but had stayed at her own quarters on the Orysta. Now that he thought about it he realized that for those last two days she had been very curt and formal when talking to him. He had been so busy himself that he had thought it was just his imagination.

"Why wouldn't I want you to?" he asked carefully.

She touched the screen of the tablet in her hand and scrolled a few times, then began reading with an angry tone in her voice.

"We have to consider that the Ganaphe' will not always be here. If not for their suffering a series of bad circumstances (LUCKY FOR US !!!!.), they would probably have already left on their journey back home… As of this time we do not have the ability to camouflage the base without the Ganaphe'. We need to develop this technology or figure out another way to accomplish this… IT SHOULD BE A CONSIDERATION OF ALL FUTURE PLANS THAT THEY BE CONCEIVED AND EXECUTED SANS GANAPHE'…"

"Whoa – whoa – whoa! That's the report I filed last week? How did you get it?"

"Commander Farber-Chatwell had enough respect for us to forward this to the Grilik. He said it brought up many issues that need to be discussed." she answered, with obvious anger in her eyes. "Respect that you did not have enough of to tell me yourself!"

Travellor unconsciously shook his head, still confused.

"I had no idea you had any interest in my mission reports, and they have nothing to do with you. What do you mean didn't tell you myself? Tell you what?"

"That you want to disconnect contact with us." she said with tears now running down her cheeks. "That you do not want us around now that your base is running well."

He was stunned into silence. It was a while before he could talk again.

"That's what you got from my report – that I don't want Ganaphe' around – that I don't want YOU around?"
"That is what you stated in your report."

The hallway outside seemed to get very busy, for a hallway that normally had little traffic. People who walked by made an effort to look straight ahead as they passed. Travellor leaned back against the door jam and smiled.

"Would you please come in, and let me explain it to you?" he asked.

She hesitated, pursed her lips, and slowly walked into the room.

"There is nothing to explain. It is all in the report." she said.
"I think I know what is going on, and if I'm right it makes me very happy."

Mersuul did not respond, but just stood there with her arms at her side, not looking at him.

"There is nothing in that report that says I don't want Ganaphe' – and especially YOU around. Only a person who is emotionally overly sensitive could take it that way."

She spun around quickly, ready to say something but stopped when Travellor put up his hands in a gesture of surrender.

"Before you say anything, let me finish first." he said. "I guess I have never said it to you – probably because I didn't think it needed to be said, but here goes. The reason you are wrong is that I am in love with you. I can't imagine you not being around – not being with me. If the Orysta was repaired tomorrow and you all could go home, I would ask – BEG – you to stay. I thought you knew that. I'm sorry that I never said it before. I guess it was because I wasn't sure as to how you felt about me."

Travellor waited for Mersuul to respond, but she just stood there looking at him. The anger had gone from her face, and now there was no expression at all. She just stood there staring at him. After some time had passed he began to worry some thing was wrong. He took the tablet from her and put it on the desk, and then took hold of both her hands.

"Mersuul… are you alright?" he asked, just as her hair flashed in a series of iridescent colors. "Wow! I've never seen that before."
"What?"
"Your hair just changed like a color light show."
"Oh," she said, "that. It is all right. Do not worry. I am fine." Her words came out without emotion or expression, like she was in shock.

She pulled her hands from his, moved around him, and walked out of the room. He was about to ask if she was sure she was alright when the door closed. '*That's not normal.*' he thought. He went to his desk and tapped on the comm.

"Medical – this is Travellor."
"Hello Commander," came the reply, "this is Doctor Blin."
"Oh good. I'm glad you're there doctor. Would you please have a look at Mersuul. I'm not sure she is well."
"Why is that Commander?"
"Something strange just happened. We were talking, and her hair rapidly changed colors, and then she just walked away like she was in shock."
"What were you talking about?"

240

"We were sort of having an argument. Well a one sided argument. And I told her about my feelings for her, and then it was like someone turned off a switch. Then her hair turned into a rainbow…"

Travellor stopped talking when he heard laughter coming over the comm.

"What's so funny doctor?"

"I am sending you some files on Ganaphe' physiology Commander. Look under the section on Emotional Responses of Reproductive Age Females. You will find the answer to your confusion there." she said, continuing to laugh. "After you have read that, if you still have more questions you should talk to Mersuul. Have a nice afternoon."

The comm went silent, and the promised files showed up on the computer screen. Travellor opened the first one and began reading.

5

June 11, 2013

Doctor Toisae-sil-Blin sat in surprise as she looked at the medical file on her screen. How long had it been now – over three decitans at least. She quickly read the reports of the monthly exams, and nodded to herself in agreement with the conclusions of the doctors and other specialists that wrote them. It wasn't surprising that it had taken this long – in fact everything she read showed an exceptional rate of progress. Considering the patient's initial condition, four to seven decitans would not have been unexpected. Toisae could remember her face clearly – what it had looked like when they operated on her that is. Two medical teams had operated in rotation on Dolores del Rio, for over eighteen heelas, repairing damaged bones, organs, and blood vessels. When del Rio was taken off of the shuttle that recovered her from space, Toisae thought her chance for survival was

241

extremely small. Everyone did. The only way to describe her condition was to say that her body had been ruptured. So many things were damaged, torn apart, leaking, swollen, bleeding,… she could go on for some time with descriptions of del Rio's injuries. Ruptured! That seemed to be the appropriate word.

During the operation she had kept wondering not if del Rio would live, but when she would die. There wasn't one area of her body that didn't have something damaged. She had been brought into the operating room just a hair's width on this side of being alive. Some organs had to be completely regenerated, as did sections of the skeleton where the bone had been fractured into pieces so small there was no way for them to re-establish a cohesive structure. Microscopic blood vessels had to be repaired or rebuilt – that was the most time consuming, even with the medical computer performing the process. It all took time to do, and time had been working against del Rio's survival. Several times, while Toisae was resting as others continued working, she had shed tears for the injured woman floating in the operating chamber, already accepting that she would die. Just thinking about it now almost brought another tear. But against all those odds, slowly as they worked they could see the black and purple extremities turn to a more promising red tone. Slowly, one by one as they repaired the organs, the body chemistry became more normal as the waste of undetected damaged cells began to be processed by those repaired organs. As body part after body part became functional del Rio began to look almost human.

The medical team had thought it certain she would lose her eyesight, but Toisae decided to try something that came to her as she worked on the motionless body. The whites of the eyes were now completely dark red from the blood vessels that had been torn apart and leaked into the eyes. She removed the intra-ocular fluid while the blood vessels were being repaired. The fluid was highly contaminated with loose blood cells, and Toisae instructed the computer to deconstruct those blood cells and then remove the constituents from the fluid. After the vessels in the eye were again carrying blood in the normal manner she replaced the fluid, and hoped for the best.

Lower arms and legs, down to the fingers and toes changed from dark purple to a bright red as blood again began to nourish her body. Bruises all over her body slowly faded. She began breathing on her own again. Her eyes danced under her eyelids as the nerves in her brain were repaired. Her joints, which were still swollen stiff, now showed all the necessary structures to work again when the swelling was gone – one of the things her body had to do on its own. There were things that had to be left to the normal healing process. The list went on and on. By the time they were finished, del Rio was surviving on her own. When they carried her to the shuttle for the flight back to Earth for long term care and rehabilitation she looked like she was eighty plebals overweight due to the overall swelling.

That was the face Toisae remembered – the round and bloated one. Now she looked at a series of photographs that showed a time lapse of the woman's face from then until now. She would not have recognized del Rio today as being the person she operated on. Going to the end of the record she looked at the general health status. Strength and stamina were better now than when she was first assigned to the base. It must have taken unbelievable determination and will power to push herself to achieve this level of fitness in such a relatively short time. Even more surprising was del Rio's request to come back to the moon and her old job. Toisae found that very impressive. She spent some time reviewing the psychological evaluations which all looked very good. At the end of del Rio's record she appended her recommendation that based on review of her physical and mental evaluations there was no contraindication to del Rio being given her old posting.

6

January – 2014

Kalinor Gorheel-sil-Planna sat in the command chair on the bridge of the battle carrier Eowaar. It had taken a long time and a lot of work to get there. He had devoted himself to the service of his planet, and had placed his life at risk many times, as the various scars on his body attested to. He loved this ship as any living creature could love an object. For a machine designed to destroy and kill the Eowaar was esthetically a work of art. She was beautiful in all her functionality! Equipped with the latest weapons and technology, the Eowaar was regarded with fear and awe throughout the known galaxies. Fear if you were an enemy, and awe if you were being protected by her. She was a technological marvel. She was designed to survive.

The Eowaar was still a relatively new vessel by military standards – just twenty decitans old – but construction of larger and more powerful vessels were already in progress. She also had scars on her body. During her short existence the Eowaar had been in forty-three skirmishes (her attackers had to be the most stupid of peoples), thirteen battles (decisively won at the cost of many 'dents and scratches'), and one inter-galactic war which had seen several pieces of her superstructure blown off and the lives of many good people lost. Even with huge pieces of her missing she was able to continue to fight and provide life support and protection for those still alive within her – and destroy the enemy. Planna was as proud of her as he was of his own record. He had even more pride in the thirty-five thousand member crew of the ship, most of which had been with her throughout her battles. At this time in the Eowaar's existence she carried a mixed crew made up of the older, tempered by experience, and the younger, highly motivated. But it was the lives of those that had been lost that conditioned his pride and boosted Planna's sense of caution. Space could be a dangerous place – and there was a lot of space in all the known galaxies. There was more of it, still unknown, in the universe.

This time they were not on a mission of conflict but on a rescue (hopefully) mission. A commercial mining ship had been missing for decitans. This was a rare occurrence these days, as ships had many ways to let people know where they were, or call for help. But the Orysta had filed a mission plan for the Vialactea galaxy, which was mostly uncharted with an indigenous species that had not yet achieved space travel. This galaxy had no communications relays or established outposts. Although it was not one of the largest galaxies in the universe, it was large enough to make finding a nardle in a ploon seem like a very easy task.

When the Orysta was first declared overdue, the mining company immediately sent out a Search and Rescue ship to find out what had happened. They knew the flight plan of the Orysta, and had no doubts about finding her. But when they drew near this galaxy and found no emergency beacons they knew something very bad had happened. They searched for the decay trail from the ships propulsion system, which should have still been detectable, but found it had stopped suddenly part way into the solar system. That, and the total lack of beacons lead them to believe the ship had met with a catastrophic failure. They were faced with two options. The first was to continue on to the planned destination, which would take a very long time at the slower than light speeds they were legally required to travel at in the system. The second option was to return home and mount a much larger search operation consisting of many more ships. They could do this and return here in less time than it would take to get to the moon of the third planet. With many smaller dedicated search vessels, which would not be speed restricted, they could search the complete solar system in a very short time. They saw the second option as the only real choice.

Four thousand IGT search vessels, which are funded and maintained by the signatories of the IGT, were missioned for the search. It didn't take long. The wreckage was found scattered throughout the rings of the sixth planet. There was nothing big enough to be identifiable as the mining ship, but the materials were unmistakable and there was enough of them. Traces of fuel and some parts of the thrust conversion chamber were found. The conclusion was that there was a destructive event so violent that the ship was shattered as it broke apart. The pieces either traveled into or were pulled into the rings. No bodies were found. No intact escape pods were found. The Orysta was the only ship with a flight plan to this solar system.

Families of the crew members were notified and mourned their loss. Life went on as it will. Decitans later the truth of the Orysta was learned, purely by accident, when a gang of pirates made the mistake of attacking a prototype of the newest (and most secret) IGT multi-role fighter interceptor.

The new ship had amazing range, armament, maneuverability, computational capabilities, and a highly classified sensor array – and none of it could be seen from the outside until the ship configured itself for battle. The prototype executed its operational test flight fully armed with all systems working, and with a highly trained and combat experienced pilot. One pirate support ship and nine attack ships saw it as easy prey – they were wrong.

By the time IGT support vessels had arrived all nine attack vessels had been destroyed and the mother ship disabled (if you can call being blown open disabled). Seventeen unconscious pirates were taken into custody. The penalty for piracy is summary execution, but several of them tried to bargain for their lives with the story of the Orysta.

These pirates were part of a larger pirate organization that had been hiding at the outside edge of the Vialactea galaxy, knowing that no one traveled there. After a successful attack on another mining ship in a nearby galaxy, they had killed the crew thinking they would plunder the cargo and be rich – but the cargo hold was empty. They stripped it of equipment and ended up with a battle damaged and barely operational cargo ship which was of little value to them. That was when they detected emergency beacons from a vessel in distress. They suspected this was another mining ship, and maybe this one had a full cargo load.

As they followed the trail of beacons they picked them up and disabled them, not wanting the signals to attract any defense forces to the area. The trail of beacons pointed to the moon circling the third planet, so that's where they went. After spending almost half a vheen searching that moon they still couldn't find the ship. They really wanted that cargo, whatever it was. That's when their leader came up with the plan to throw any rescue vessels off the trail. They would blow up the damaged cargo ship they had, sending the pieces into the rings of the sixth planet. Anyone looking for the Orysta would find the debris of the other ship and make the obvious conclusion. That would end the search. Then when they had more time, the pirates would come back and do a more thorough search of their own.

The captured pirates were still executed of course. Not to do so would be to commit suicide by IGT law. The pirates knew that. But what man with nothing to lose isn't going to try to save his life, no matter how futile the attempt. No one in the interconnected galaxies had the right or the authority to allow a pirate to live – no one!

Now that the Eowaar was in the planetary zone of a non-signatory solar system she was required to travel at slower than light speeds, this also per IGT law. There were no navigation aids or up to date charts of the area. Planna had over twenty-three hundred intercept craft on board, and all but seven were presently operational. He would have to personally talk with his maintenance chief about that. Not that having only seven ships down was bad. Most other commanders ran with a much higher percentage of inoperable interceptors. But the one-on-one would serve two purposes – letting the man know that Planna was aware of everything on his ship, and keeping a personal connection with one of his most important subordinates. The maintenance chief had to be kept on his toes, but he also had to be kept happy as well.

Those much smaller ships did not have to restrict their speed as they flew. He ordered fifteen hundred of them to begin a grid search of the system while the Eowaar traveled directly to the mission destination. That left enough interceptors on board to protect the Eowaar in case they ran into an unforeseen problem. The interceptors were small, fast, and well equipped to defend themselves and they could stay on mission for long periods. If the Orysta had been forced to change its destination, his interceptors would find her – but it would be slow. It would take a lot of time. He didn't know if the crew of the Orysta had that time – or even if they were still alive. This could become a very long mission.

Planna had made a promise to find out what had happened to the Orysta, good or bad. He meant to keep that promise. He studied the three dimensional depiction that floated in front of his eyes. Normally used to track events in a battle, the chart now showed this solar system, its planets, their moons, and any object larger than a man's head. It also showed the present position of all of his interceptors, each with an ID tag indicating the type of ship, its operational condition, system coordinates, and lastly the names of the crew members on board. There was a lot more information associated with each interceptor but those pieces of information that weren't vital at the moment were not displayed. As each crew transmitted a report the miniature depiction that represented their ship turned bright blue to catch the viewer's attention. Planna saw several turn blue, and knew the strategy team was analyzing the transmitted data before informing him of it. So far they had not notified him of anything that seemed important.

7

Second Lanor Giell-sil-Dhona was surprised by the alert on his HUD, indicating a power source on the surface of the fourth planet from this sun. The surprise turned to fear because the power level indicated was extremely weak. Then there was a second alert for another power source, also very weak. As his ship got closer to the planet he picked up more very weak power indications, and electromagnetic transmissions. His fear level elevated as he wondered if the Orysta had broken up and crashed on the planet.

His ship's defense computer automatically switched on the camouflage system, and there were more weak power indications and transmissions on his screen but this time they were orbiting the planet. As he approached close enough for visual contact he spotted one of the sources. It was a satellite. Then he spotted another satellite, and an alert showed for a third one. Then another – and another – and another. Now more surface power indications were alerting on his screen. '*Have the Vialacteans developed space travel?*' Dhona wondered. '*And why are the power levels so weak?*'

By the time he had circled the planet once he had found dozens of power indications on the planets surface. He realized what he was seeing now. This planet is the closest to the inhabited third planet. Just like in his own people's history, they were sending probes to study their neighbor and develop their space technology. As it always seemed to be, it was his luck to get what was probably the busiest planet in this solar system. All of these probes and satellites complicated his search. He had no way of knowing if the power indications were from a Vialactean probe or from a destroyed Orysta. He would have to enter the planets atmosphere and perform a low level search of the surface. Reflexively he touched the display screen on the communications panel, and a report of everything that he had discovered so far was sent to the Eowaar.

"High speed atmospheric entry configuration." he said out loud.

He looked at the surface of his ships wings and saw the protruding antennas and sensors withdraw into the structure of the ship, and cover plates slide into place to close the openings. Then the wings changed, shrinking in from the obvious extended airfoil shape to short stubs one third the size. His secondary weapons ports were now unavailable, though he wouldn't be needing them on this mission.

"Interceptor configured for high speed atmospheric entry." said his ship's computer.

"Proceed to grid pattern search. Zero point one larn above ground level. Detect, identify and document all power sources."

The interceptor took a nose down attitude while maintaining its present speed. It was only a couple of fracins until it made contact with the thinnest part of the atmosphere. When it did, the ship's engines reduced power, and it slowly took a nose up attitude. Gravity was now playing a role and pulling the ship down at an accelerating rate. Dhona looked at his wings and saw the normally dark color of the ship's skin begin to heat up and glow orange. He wasn't worried about it though. The interceptor was designed to operate in a full power straight-in dive through the atmospheres of most planets they visited. But powered dives like that came with their own risks, and you didn't take that type of risk on a search mission. Parts of the ship glowed red now from the heat caused by atmospheric friction.

It would be another fifteen to twenty merlots before he was down to the requested altitude to begin his search. He checked the ground mapping display. Most of the planet was a rugged rock and iron oxide desert marked by volcanoes and impact craters. It did have large ice masses at each of its poles, but the atmosphere was too thin and cold to support liquid water. If the Orysta had landed here they would have run out of food a long time ago, and there was nothing on this planet to sustain them.

8

It had taken over two heelas but the search of the planet was complete. Dhona was tired and hungry. He looked down at the side pocket where he kept his flight kit and the energy cakes that pilots referred to as 'flight fuel'. They would get rid of your hunger, but didn't taste very good. You would think that in this day and age someone could make a better tasting energy cake. Dhona decided he would rather wait until he was back on board the Eowaar where the food was excellent. He checked his fuel. There was enough to get back to the ship, but with very little reserve. Having to spend all this time tracking down Vialactean probes and rovers angered him, but he had had no choice but to do so.

He was about to initiate a climb when he suddenly had an idea. It would probably get him into trouble with his squadron commander, but he couldn't resist. '*Now where was that nearby damaged rover that was still transmitting a signal?*' he wondered, as he scrolled through the log that documented all the objects he had found. It only took a few fracins to find it, and placing his fingertip on the information he dragged it across the display screen to the icon for the navigation computer. Planetary coordinates immediately popped up on the screen. He touched the GO TO button and the ship smoothly banked and accelerated, heading for the location of the rover.

9

Dhona checked his ships systems as he approached the Vialactean exploratory vehicle. Camouflage was operational. Gravity Compensation was operational. Thrust vectors set to zero. He scanned the nearby area for other probes. There were none. As a precaution he activated the retention bands, which wrapped around his torso and legs and held him securely against his seat. He was now approaching at a crawl.

When he was in position he held his interceptor above and slightly behind the rover, and studied it for a while. He liked it. It was inactive at the moment, so this would be the ideal time to do something. Smiling with appreciation for the design, he understood what most of the systems on it were for. He could also appreciate what it had taken to get this machine to this planet, intact and operational. He remembered learning in school about similar systems his own people had constructed and launched into space when they began their explorations.

"Lanor Dhona, this is Eowaar control." came the voice of the flight controller over the comm.

"Control, this is Dhona. Go ahead." he replied.

"Sir, what is your status?"

"Just finishing search of the planet. Will be returning soon."

"Lanor, please transmit your latest report before returning to the ship."

"Will comply. Transmit report before returning to Eowaar."

If he had to send a final report, Dhona thought it best to do it before playing his joke on the Vialacteans. Of course his actions would still be recorded right up until engine shutdown on the ship, but this part would be the last thing on a long report. Most likely no one would even pay attention to it.

He checked the temperature outside and found it was surprisingly comfortable, then sealed his helmet. If this had been at the planets dark side the extremely cold temperatures would have adversely affected the interceptors interior. Although his suit would have kept him alive, he would have had to explain why he had opened his canopy.

"Open canopy and invert attitude along longitudinal axis." he said.

251

The canopy slid back, and there was a slight rush of air as the pressure differential between the atmosphere and the ship's interior equalized. Then the ship slowly rotated until he was looking down at the planet's surface.

"Descend to ten limms, at point one limm per fracin."

Slowly the interceptor got closer to the ground. As it did so, Dhona looked around for an appropriate object to use in his plan. He had almost reached his designated altitude when he spotted it. A jelly doughnut shaped rock about the same size as the palm of his hand, near to the rover.

"Descend to five limms at same rate."

In a short time the ship stopped and hovered in place. Dhona carefully took hold of his side arm. He didn't want to drop it. In his upside-down position, he adjusted the weapons power level to minimum and aimed at the rear edge of the rock. He fired and the blast of energy knocked the rock up into the air and forward. It flew over the rover and landed in front of it. Dhona couldn't see where it ended up.

"Ascend to ten limms at same rate."

The ship slowly rose higher and Dhona saw the rock had landed close the machine. But it was upside-down making it obvious it hadn't been there before. Frustrated by this minor glitch in his plan, he resigned himself to leave it alone. He was out of time, and by now very low on fuel. He directed the ship to upright itself, close the canopy, and slowly continue to rise upward. When he was far enough away, he initiated his flight back to the Eowaar.

Chapter 15

Moving In

1

April – 2014

Erika Aimsler drove her now four year old Mercedes convertible onto the long driveway of her uncle's home. She was a wealthy young woman who could afford to buy a new car whenever she wanted, but having the newest and shiniest didn't interest her. With the money she had inherited from her parents estate Erika could have spent the rest of her life in lazy luxury. But with all the interests she had developed from her family's influence she would be bored living like that. She understood how fortunate she was, and that even a four year old Mercedes was a financial luxury out of reach for many people. She made sure that the vehicle ran as well now as it did on the day it was purchased. That was a lesson she learned from her uncle Tony – keep your tools in good condition.

She liked being in the mountains of Montana. It always made her feel like she was on vacation, which was usually the situation when she had come here in the past. But even after the long drive, there were still tears in her eyes. It had been very difficult saying goodbye to her aunt and uncle. They had effectively been her parents for the last eight years. They took her into their home, and treated her like a daughter, with as much love as they gave their two sons. They had seen her through the slow healing of her heart after the loss of her father and mother. Guided her through her final teen years, and her first date, first boyfriend, high school graduation, and college. When she pulled out of their driveway to come here, she had cried so much she didn't think there was any moisture left in her body. In her mind, she could still clearly see them and her cousins waving goodbye, all with tears in their eyes. She was already looking forward to visiting them on holidays.

As her car came within fifteen feet of the garage doors they automatically opened and she drove in and parked next to the blue pickup. She liked the automation her uncle had built into the property. There were sensors everywhere, both in and outside of the house. Grabbing her purse, she went to the house entrance and heard the lock unlatch as she got close. This automatic response of the security system was triggered by the beautiful birthstone ring her uncle had given her when she had graduated High school. The ring was very light in weight, and made of a space age ceramic material. It acted as an 'identification badge' of sorts, communicating her presence to the house's automation computer. If anyone was home, her arrival would be announced to them over the distributed speaker system.

A smile grew on her face, because now she would be scrutinized by what she considered to be the real security system of the house. This was the real test that you belonged here, and weren't an intruder. Her smile grew bigger as she walked through the door, knowing what was waiting for her. She looked down, and in front of her was a baby triceratops dinosaur, about as big as a medium sized dog. This small robot had started out as a simple robotic toy, but over the years had been extensively modified by her uncle. The camera eyes of the little robot pointed at her face for a second, then it started wagging its tail and making a yipping noise like a happy little puppy – its facial recognition software had matched her face. It then sat down in front of her, and raised its front paws.

"Erika is home." it said, several times, in an excited child like robotic voice.

The little robot then sidled up to Erika and rubbed against her leg. She leaned over while laughing at its antics, and scratched the top of its head with her fingertips. It purred like a contented kitten. Erika laughed a little harder at that. Every time she came here, she found the little dinosaur's personality had been expanded in one way or another. It kept getting more lifelike.

"Hello Vicious." she said to the dinosaur, "I'm happy to see you too."

She knew that her uncle had programmed Vicious to only show these responses when it recognized her. With other people, Vicious acted more simple and robotic. She loved that her uncle had put in all that time and effort to make her happy when she visited. But then, as far as she was concerned, he was the greatest uncle in the world!

Vicious was correct about her being home. Her uncle had recommended her for a job with the same company he worked for, and they had hired her. Her Engineering degree, and personal skills were just what they were looking for in an entry level position. She had to go through a comprehensive background and security check before she was offered an employment contract. Since the job required a lot of travel and long periods of being away it made sense for her to move in with her uncle instead of getting her own place where she probably wouldn't have time to get comfortable in.

Vicious wasn't just an entertaining toy. He was the mobile extension of the house's security system, and also had his own internal and independent computer system. At night, the little robot would prowl around the house and outside property searching for anything that didn't belong there. It had IR and temperature sensors for heat detection (calibrated so that it could report actual temperature), distance calibrated variable focus lenses for eyes, hundreds of stored images in its non-volatile memory which it used for visual recognition, ultrasonic transducers for distance/proximity measurement, several microphones around its body for sound detection and direction determination, and its cute little horns could deliver a fifty thousand volt electric jolt.

Vicious also had scanning lasers projected from each eye, each modulated at a slightly different frequency. This allowed three dimensional mapping of a relatively close object by measuring distance to object's features with the lasers and combining the two maps together. Sensors on the bottom of its feet could detect moisture content (which had come in handy when the water heater sprung a leak last year) and surface texture and temperature. It also had a vocabulary of over one hundred words and phrases which it could translate into ten different languages, had voice recognition capabilities, and was in continuous contact with the house computer via UHF and WiFi radio links.

The electronics package in Vicious was enclosed in a hermetically sealed box, which also contained the rechargeable battery. The battery was capable of powering the robot for up to thirty-six hours, but Vicious was programmed to self dock in his charging station and recharge when power levels dropped to twenty percent and the house inhabitants were active, or the property was determined to be secure.

Its programming also included 'Abnormal Attitude' algorithms which allowed Vicious to compensate for faulty sensors by making related measurements with its other sensors. If its ultrasonic module failed, it could measure distances by using the calibrated focus function of its eyes (lenses). Faulty temperature sensors could be compensated for with its IR sensors which could create a temperature map of the environment. If either of the radio links went down, it could continue communications using the other one. And since Vicious was the mobile sensor of the security system, it had a fail-safe package built in – an embedded stand-alone transmitter that sent an emergency 'Under Attack' signal. If three or more sensors malfunctioned, it was assumed that Vicious had been intentionally damaged, and the signal triggered every alarm and defense mechanism of the house – sirens went off, lights went on, selected doors and windows locked, and programmed communications went out over phone and satellite systems to the security company and Erika's uncle. There were even some more 'active' defense mechanisms that her uncle wouldn't tell even her about – something about keeping her legally immune from liability. The house was highly automated, and her uncle could monitor and control all of its systems from wherever he was at the time – assuming that location had communications to the rest of the world.

This all made sense, and seemed very reasonable to Erika. To this day, her uncle's job was still a mystery to everyone who knew him. The long periods of being incommunicado made her suspect he was working deep underground or surrounded by very rugged terrain, where communications and travel would be difficult. It had gotten better over the years – From being out of touch for weeks at a time, it was now down to almost daily video chats. Being away for so long and often meant a high-tech house was only practical. He was a technical specialist, knowledgeable in many fields, and often worked with experimental technology that was unknown to most of the world. He loved his job, and the thought that she was soon to be working with him, and exposed to his secrets, excited her.

She had gotten the job because she met all the qualifications – a recommendation from an associate in good standing (her uncle), an educational background related to the work (degrees in both Mechanical and Electrical Engineering), and successful completion of job interview and background check (which no doubt was fairly boring since most of her life had been spent in school). What Erika found curious was that her new employer seemed highly interested with her familiarity with weapons – no, that wasn't it exactly – it was the fact that she was both comfortable and capable with weapons. They also seemed very impressed with her love of camping in the wilderness – which Erika took as an indication that she would be working someplace that wasn't close to civilization. Even to this day, the work location was still a mystery since her uncle had made it clear he would tell her about it when she moved in – he loved to keep her in suspense. But it really didn't matter much to Erika. She would be working with her uncle which was all she needed to know. She would also be the newbie, so she expected to be given all the grunt jobs. Still not a problem – she was willing to earn her place.

Her uncle had taught her about firearms, and she was one of the few people her age (maybe the only one her age) that had actually operated and fired the quad fifty caliber machine gun fire control system that had been standard equipment on the tail of D model B-52 bombers. The experience had been a birthday present from her uncle. Those aircraft had been decommissioned long ago, but some of the weapon systems had been scavenged piece by piece and re-assembled by firearms collectors.

257

Although it lacked the automatic radar tracking and targeting computer, the one she was able to fire had fully functional guns and hydraulics – and it was a kick in the pants, literally – because when those guns went off the whole gun mount shook violently, and she felt it through her whole body. When she got home that night, she couldn't stop talking about it to her cousins. Nothing says Happy Birthday like firing off several hundred rounds through a quad fifty cal! Over the years her uncle had also taught her to use handguns and rifles of various types, and she was a proficient marksman.

2

"Where's Uncle Tony?" asked Erika.
"*Uncle Tony not home.*" said Vicious, "*Mersuul is home.*"

Erika tried to remember who that was, but wasn't familiar with the name.

"Who is Mersuul?" asked Erika, just as she walked into the living room and noticed the sleeping woman stretched out on the couch.

The woman was beautiful, but there was something strange about her that Erika couldn't identify. Something strange other than her hair. '*Oh my gosh,*' thought Erika, '*her hair is iridescent. I'll have to ask her how she did that when she wakes up.*'

"*Mersuul is friend.*" replied Vicious.
"So… Uncle Tony has a girlfriend, huh?"
"*Mersuul is Vicious girlfriend.*"

Erika chuckled, knowing that her uncle had anticipated her question, and intentionally programmed that reply. He was very good at that, anticipating things and preparing for them beforehand.

"So she's your girlfriend, huh?" Erika asked, tickling Vicious under the chin. The robot's right rear leg moved rapidly up and down, like a dog getting its belly scratched. She chuckled again. That was a new response for Vicious.

Erika quietly left the living room, trying not to disturb the sleeping stranger, and went to the kitchen to make a pot of coffee. She had little doubt that if Mersuul was uncle Tony's girlfriend, she was a coffee drinker. It had finished brewing by the time she had gone back to the car for her luggage, and placed the bags in her room.

A sleepy Mersuul walked slowly into the kitchen as Erika was spooning sugar into her cup, inhaled the aroma and smiled. She opened her mouth and spoke, but it sounded like a foreign language to Erika. A second after Mersuul stopped speaking, the voice of the house computer came over the speakers.

"*I love the smell of coffee just brewing.*" it said.

It took a few moments for Erika to realize the house computer was translating for Mersuul.

"Oh. OH! Yes, me too. You mean 'fresh brewed' coffee." Erika said, still surprised. She didn't know the house computer was programmed to translate languages. Her uncle had been very busy since she last visited.

Mersuul looked closely at Erika's mouth, studying it.

"Fresh brewed." she mimicked in a clumsy but accurate copy of Erika's words. "Fresh brewed."

"Yes," said Erika, "fresh brewed. I just made it. Would you like some?"

The house computer once again spoke, but this time in the

unfamiliar language – It was translating Erika's words for Mersuul. It wasn't like any language Erika had ever heard before. Mersuul's eyes went to the ceiling, where the speakers were mounted, as she listened to the translation. Then she smiled, and nodded yes. Erika took another cup from the cupboard, and poured coffee into it. Mersuul added sugar and just a touch of creamer. Erika pointed to the kitchen table and they each took a seat.

"Do you speak English?"

"Some. A little." she said. Then she reverted back to her own tongue and the house computer translated. *"Your uncle is much better with language than I am. Tony show me coffee. Very good. Warm. Warm me up."* came the computer's voice. *"I show Tony bliml. Bliml better than sugar and cream. There is no bliml here."*

"Blimal? What is blimal?" asked Erika.

Mersuul listened to Erika's question being translated, and replied.

"Bliml like sugar and cream, but one and better." translated the computer.

Their conversation continued, as they drank more coffee and enjoyed some pound cake that was in the refrigerator. As Mersuul became more comfortable with Erika she began to use more English words to express herself. Erika had to mentally compensate for Mersuul's grammatical idiosyncrasies as they spoke, and realized the other woman was probably doing the same thing. As their conversation continued, Erika finally realized what it was that looked strange about the other woman. There was a very slight and almost imperceptible blue tinge to her skin. She would have to ask Mersuul about this later. For right now it was enough to enjoy the company, coffee, and pound cake.

3

They had moved to the living room couch, and over an hour had passed as the two got to know each other. As they continued, Erika realized there were some strange statements Mersuul had made, that couldn't be attributed to being lost in the translation.

"I have to ask," Erika said, "I notice that your skin has a very light blue coloring. Are you alright?"

Mersuul smiled.

"*Most people do not notice that.*" she answered. "*It is because of your low oxygen level. Four percent more oxygen is normal for me. Your air make me sleep some times and I do not feel enough energy.*"

'*Another strange comment.*' thought Erika. She wondered what Mersuul meant by "your low oxygen level".

"You live some place where the oxygen in the air is four percent higher than normal? Where do you come from?"

"*I cannot say. Your uncle will tell you.*"

Erika's eyes widened in surprise. '*OK,*' she thought, '*this is even stranger.*'

"You can't tell me, but my uncle can? Do you know how strange that sounds?"
"*I do not have permission... authority... to tell. Tony will tell.*"

Erika's curiosity rose. She was with a strange (in more ways than one) person, who spoke a strange language, and couldn't give information

261

about herself but her uncle could. This was a new situation for her. Then she looked at Vicious, as the little robot was walking by on its security rounds, and had an idea.

"Vicious," she said to the robot, "where does Mersuul come from?"

Now it was Mersuul's eyes that widened in surprise.

"Tony say you are very smart. I did not expect that." she said in English, smiling.

Vicious' head turned toward Erika, and when it recognized her, the little robot walked towards the couch. They both waited for Vicious to answer the question. It took a few seconds before the robot responded.

"*Unknown.*" said the little dinosaur's computerized voice.
"Vicious, tell me everything you know about Mersuul." Erika prompted.
"*Mersuul is Vicious girlfriend.*" the little dinosaur said.

It took a couple of seconds for the house computer to translate Vicious' words. Mersuul laughed and Erika shrugged.

"It was worth a shot." she said to Mersuul. "So when is uncle Tony supposed to be back?"

Mersuul looked at the clock on the fireplace mantel, like a child who was just learning to tell time. She still had difficulty translating the two systems of time she had to deal with. Then her expression relaxed as she thought of another way to answer the question. The computer again translated for her.

"*He will be back before dinner.*" she said with a self satisfied expression. "*I do not use your time very much so I forget to tell your time*

262

easy. He went to get bar bee Q steaks."

Erika wondered what time system Mersuul was used to. She thought everyone used a twenty-four hour system, whatever country they came from.

      The next couple of hours went more like two new friends getting acquainted. Mersuul helped Erika unpack her bags, and Erika helped Mersuul refresh her memory on reading a clock. They even had time for a quick driving lesson for Mersuul, who claimed she didn't get much opportunity to drive a car – and yes, she did like convertibles. In the back seat sat Vicious, who acted as a remote translator node via his radio link with the house computer.

      It was during this driving lesson that the two seat home-built aircraft, with Anthony Travellor at the controls, dropped down and kept pace off the right side of the car. It flew twenty feet above the ground, and close enough for Erika to see her uncle smiling and waving. After a couple of minutes the plane accelerated and climbed, heading towards the house. One of the reasons her uncle had built his house here was that property was affordable. He had cleared a two thousand foot private landing strip in the back. "Property and privacy" he always told her. Those were the primary reasons he chose this area.

      By the time they had garaged the car, and came out the back door, Travellor was already tying down the plane. Erika ran to her uncle and wrapped her arms around him so tightly that her hug forced the air out of his lungs. He returned the hug and kissed her cheek, as he lifted her off the ground.

      "Ohhh… It is so good to see you." he said.
      "I missed you so much." she replied.

Erika closed her eyes and enjoyed the warmth and security she always felt when she was with her uncle. The hug went on for several seconds more before they released their hold on each other.

"How are you, beautiful?"

"I'm fine, uncle Tony. How are you?"

"Much better now that you're here. I see you've met Mersuul." he said, as he watched the other woman approach.

"Yes. We've been having a good time, and I have a lot of questions about her. She says she can't tell me anything about herself but you can. What's that all about?"

Travellor reached a hand out to the approaching Mersuul, and she briefly spoke to him as she took it. This time they weren't near the house computer or Vicious, so there was no translation for Erika. Travellor replied in that same strange language.

"No fair." said Erika. "I don't understand what you're saying."

"I'll fix that." said Travellor. "I have a portable translator in the house. That will work until we get you a more permanent unit."

4

Barbecued steak and sweet potatoes cooked on the grill, with a glass of wine and a setting Montana sun made a great end to an enjoyable day. The wrist translator Travellor had given to Erika was faster than the house computer, which made conversation easier. As they lounged lazily in the cooling evening air, they took turns taking pictures of each other and laughing about the language problem until the sun was completely down.

Cleanup didn't take long, and they were soon in the living room and continuing their conversation. Erika was in the mood for some answers, and she thought this would be the right time.

"OK, let's clear up this mystery uncle Tony. Where does Mersuul come from, and why couldn't she tell me?"

Her uncle smiled at her curiosity, and hesitated before answering.

"I would like to tell you, and relieve your curiosity, but that would ruin the surprise. Tell you what, give me until you start your new job, and everything will be made clear."

Erika knew that look on his face. It was the one he had when he was planning a surprise for her.

"Seriously?" she said. "You can't just give me the name of the country she comes from?"

"If I did," he replied, "I'd miss out on all the fun of seeing your reaction when you found out."

"So this has something to do with my new job then?"

"Yes."

Erika was getting suspicious, and her mind shifted into high gear. This was a game they had played many times before, with her uncle challenging her to accomplish or figure out something. He challenged her often, but he always made it interesting. Most of the time the conclusion was something that completely surprised her. She was determined now – she would win this game!

"What do I get if I figure it out for myself?" she asked.

Travellor's eyes became as big as his grin. His niece was never one to back away from a contest of wills. He enjoyed their little games, as he knew she did.

"If you figure it out, you will get to see me in the GREATEST state of shock that I have ever been in my life… AND I'll take you out for ice-cream."

"ICE-CREAM! Yes, you promised me ice-cream." said Mersuul.

"I did, didn't I? OK, tomorrow I'll take all of us for ice-cream." Travellor replied.

5

Travellor, Erika, and Mersuul lay on their backs, on the dusty ground. They wore protective glasses, and ear plugs. They had reversed their baseball caps so that the bill didn't block their view, but that didn't keep the dirt from working into their hair as they positioned their heads to line up the shot. The morning sun was still low enough to bother their eyes, which made things more difficult. It was the final round before getting cleaned up and going into town for lunch. Erika had enough practice to re-familiarize herself with the weapon she had selected – a Browning Hi Power. She liked the all metal design. It was heavier than the Glock Mersuul had selected (and was very good with). The gun's extra mass that normally helped to absorbed recoil, allowing her to get the sights back down and on target faster, now worked with gravity and against her. Her uncle had selected the Beretta, also an all metal gun. With the sights lined up on target, upside-down, they listened for the timer to beep – then fired. Six shots each. Ten seconds later the timer beeped again, signaling the end of the round. They each checked their targets, and then looked over at the others.

"YES! Yes, yes, yes!" screamed Erika, happily. "I win!"

Still on her back, she released the magazine and placed it on the ground. Then she locked back the slide, verified the chamber was empty, and placed the gun on the ground, barrel pointed down range. She jumped up, and started dancing around. Mersuul and Travellor stood up more slowly, and brushed the dirt off their clothes.

"HE'S MINE. HE'S MINE. HE'S MINE. HE'S MINE." Erika continued, with a very big smile on her face.
"Yes he is." said Travellor, chuckling at his niece's exuberance.

266

He felt a touch of nostalgia, as he watched his twenty-two year old niece acting like a little girl on Christmas morning, the way she had before her parents had been killed. He remembered that last Christmas when they were all together – when his sister was still alive. He thought about how Erika looked so much like her mother. Then he shook off the sadness and brought his attention back to the present.

"Mags out, chambers clear." he said, as he and Mersuul completed the safety procedure.

They picked up their equipment and walked over to the weather worn wood table, and placed the weapons there. Travellor placed the guns in his range bag, with the extra magazines and ammunition. Erika continued jumping around exuberantly, while she helped Mersuul pick up the brass from the ground. Travellor couldn't stop smiling as he watched her. Not many things made him as happy as seeing his niece happy.

Mersuul studied him as he watched Erika. His love of his niece was one of the things that attracted her to him. She was also very close to her family. As she thought about them, she became a little sad, and wondered when she would see them again. It had been a long time since she had seen home. There was even the possibility that she may not get back for a very long time more – if ever.

They headed for the house, and Erika reached it minutes before the others. Mersuul took Travellor's hand as they walked.

"Did you allow her to win?" she asked.

"Oh no. I stopped doing that when she was eight. Erika is very good at anything she puts her mind to. She had a good day at the range, and I was a little off." he answered, smiling at her. "I was going to give him to her anyway – but don't tell her that."

He held her hand a little tighter, and realized how much he enjoyed having Mersuul with him.

By the time they reached the back door, Erika was coming back out with Vicious walking next to her.

"Tell him! Tell him! Tell him!" she said excitedly.
"OK – OK." said Travellor, laughing at his niece's excitement.

He put down the range bag, and squatted in front of Vicious.

"Administration mode." he said to the little dinosaur.

Laser grids projected from the robot's eyes, onto Travellor's face, as Vicious ran identification protocols.

"*Vocal and facial recognition complete. Administration mode active.*" said Vicious, in an all business tone of voice.
"All command and control authority is immediately transferred to Erika Aimsler." instructed Travellor. "Confirm Compliance."
"*All command and control authority has been transferred to Erika Aimsler. Presentation of administrator required for completion.*" said Vicious.

Erika reached down to pick up Vicious.

"NO!" yelled Travellor, causing his niece to jump back. "Not yet, sweetie," he said chuckling, "unless you want to get a sudden shock. He is in maximum security mode right now. Until he accepts or rejects the transfer of control, he is operating as an independent agent. Squat down in front of him so he can verify your identity."

Travellor moved aside and Erika kneeled in front of Vicious.

"Hi Vicious." she said in a happy tone. "You're mine now."

With initial facial recognition confirmed via the cameras in the robot's eyes,

Erika's face was scanned by the projected laser grid. Her image was mapped, and the robot's internal memory record was updated.

"Vocal and facial recognition complete. Erika Aimsler confirmed. Records updated. Command and control authority transfer complete." said Vicious.

"NOW – he's yours!" said Travellor, as he stood up.

"YAY!" said Erika, and she leaned over the robot, and placed a kiss on its head. She then scratched under the its chin, and it purred.

Mersuul looked puzzled at the sound coming from Vicious.

"I have never heard it make that sound before. I have petted it on its head." she said to Travellor.

"It's programmed to only make those type of sounds for Erika. It doesn't even do it for me."

"Will you build another to guard the house?"

"No need to. Vicious was a great addition to the security system, but over the past few years I've installed sensors all around the property, and automated the house to a level that almost makes him redundant."

She looked at Erika and Vicious, and smiled at how cute they looked together.

"Vicious is like a pet. A very useful pet." she said. "And you can take him with you to travel. Sometimes I forget it is a machine."

Travellor looked into the eyes of his beautiful companion. *'Note to self – '* he thought, *'build a robot for Mersuul.'* He moved closer and kissed her lightly on the lips.

"Alright," he said, "Let's get some lunch. We'll take the Cherokee. Mersuul needs to build up her time, for her private pilot test."

6

Mersuul slid her hand caressingly over the metal skin of the Cherokee as she performed the preflight check of the aircraft. Erika watched her as she did this, and realized there was a sense of reverence in Mersuul's actions.

"You really like this plane, don't you?" she asked Mersuul.

"Very much. This is flying as it used to be. Only collectors and museums have aircraft like this back home."

"You don't have anything like this?" Erika asked, very confused. "You mean, you don't have any private aircraft?"

Mersuul smiled broadly at her.

"We do not have anything… what is your word for it… anything as CLASSIC as this."

Erika stuttered slightly with confusion.

"This plane is just a few years old. It's got the latest glass cockpit. I mean… I guess you could call the design a classic. The basic airframe was designed a long time ago."

"Yes." Mersuul agreed. "It is not the plane. It is the technology. Our air vehicles do not use atmospheric lift. They have not for generations."

Erika was very confused, and wasn't sure if Mersuul was having fun with her.

"Your air vehicles don't use atmospheric… What?… What does that mean? What kind of aircraft do you have?"

Mersuul stopped, and looked hesitantly at Erika.

"You will have to ask Tony. I cannot tell you."

"WHAT???..." stuttered Erika, not sure if she was misunderstanding what Mersuul was trying to tell her.

She wondered if something was getting lost in the translation. She turned to her uncle.

"Uncle Tony, I want an answer. What does she mean they don't use atmospheric lift?"

As she looked at him, Erika realized he had been laughing at their conversation for some time.

"All in good time." he said. "All in good time. Besides, my time isn't up yet, and the answers are related. He turned to Mersuul and asked "Preflight all done?"

"Yes."

"Let's go." he said. "I'm hungry."

They climbed into the plane, and fastened their safety harnesses. Mersuul performed a soft field takeoff with a simulated obstruction at the end of the runway. It was only a short thirty minute flight, and it was VFR all the way. She had spent enough time in the local airspace to be familiar with the landmarks, and had no problem navigating to the airport.

"Uncle Tony, how did you meet Mersuul?" asked Erica, out of mild curiosity.

"Oh..., met her at work. She was part of the group that saved the life of one of my men."

Erika's eyes widened in surprise.

"How did she save one of your men?"

"Can't tell you." he said chuckling.

Mersuul looked at Travellor and shook her head. She knew he was having fun keeping his niece in suspense. It was only several hours more before she found out what the secret was. It would take her days after that to adjust to it. She returned her attention back to flying the plane.

7

First Day At A New Job

It was four in the morning when the alarm went off. Erika had a hard time getting out of the bed. It was so warm and comfortable, and just right for sleeping. She slowly pushed herself to get up, and start getting ready. Six hours of sleep just wasn't enough. '*Good thing I packed last night.*' she thought, as she walked into the bathroom. She looked into the mirror and thought she looked terrible. A yawn took control of her mouth, and it opened so big it looked to her like she could have swallowed her own head – well, almost.

In a few minutes she had brushed her teeth, and was standing under the shower, and she was beginning to feel awake. Why did they have to leave so early in the morning? Even in college she always had a hard time with the early hour classes. By dint of repetition, she applied some makeup and was dressed in her new flight suit. It didn't fit very well. It was like a tent someone had sewn into something resembling clothing. '*COFFEE!*' she thought. '*Want coffee!*'

Mersuul was already there, looking at a laptop screen and sipping on a steamy cup. She was in her flight suit, and the silvery material looked tailor made on her. Without looking she pointed to the pot and Erika needed no other instruction. There was an empty mug already waiting for her. '*Excellent.*' thought Erika, '*No thinking required.*' The first sip was like liquid wakeup. Her mouth was very happy with the sweet warmth.

Just as Erika was getting comfortable in a chair, her uncle came through the back door at what seemed like rocket speed to her – but almost anything seemed like rocket speed at the moment. Her brain just didn't want to wake up. She worried that she was going to make a bad impression on the first day of her new job.

"Bags are outside and ready to go." said Travellor. "We have ten minutes before we leave."

"It will only take me a few minutes to put my boots on and get my overhead bag ready." Erika said, suddenly noticing that Mersuul was looking at her and smiling. "What?" she asked, looking back at her and returning the smile involuntarily.

"TEN MINUTES!" said her uncle, a little louder than before.

He was smiling at her also. There was obviously a conspiracy going on.

"Why are you two…"

"TEN MINUTES!" said her uncle again, cutting her off. His smile got bigger.

"ALRIGHT." she said. "Ten minutes! I got it. Jeez."

"COFFEE." said her uncle, as he robotically turned to the counter.

"This flight suit doesn't fit very well, Uncle Tony. Couldn't you find something closer to my size."

"I can fix that." said Mersuul. "Stand up."

Erika stood up, but doubted Mersuul could do much with all the excess material she was wearing. Erika took a big gulp of coffee, and slowly swallowed it as she waited for the fitting she didn't think would help much.

"Press the top spot." said Mersuul, pointing to the three purple dots at the upper left chest area.

"Press this?" Erika asked, with a doubtful expression on her face.

She pushed on the small spot, and immediately she felt the material of her suit get warm. Her eyes opened in surprise and the suit began to shrink. In less than a minute, all of the excess material seemed to have disappeared, and the suit formed a close fitting outfit on her body. *'Maybe a little too form fitting.'* thought Erika, as she noticed how much of a second skin it seemed to be.

"Now tap the lower left spot."

Erika did this, and with each tap the suit loosened slightly overall.

"Tailor made!" said Travellor. "Where's the jacket?"
"In my room, with the boots."
"They also have the same fitting mechanism." said Mersuul. "After you put them on, press the top spot. The clothes will remember your settings. When we have more time, I'll show you how to customize the fit. Men like to loosen it up between the legs. Women like to loosen it up around the chest."

As Erika compared her outfit to Mersuul's, she noticed for the first time that they had names imprinted across the upper left chest area. Mersuul's was different than hers or her uncle's. She had E. AIMSLER written in caps, and below that were symbols she didn't recognize. Her uncle had A. TRAVELLOR with some different symbols underneath. Mersuul had the strange symbols on top with M. VAANA underneath.

"FIVE MINUTES!" yelled Travellor, making both women jump.
"ALL RIGHT!" said Erika, moving to her room. "I only have to close my bag and I'm ready! VICIOUS?" she called loudly. "WHERE ARE YOU?"
"He's with the bags." said Travellor. "I've packed his charging station, and some spare parts also."
"Thanks Uncle Tony." she called back to the kitchen.

Mersuul followed behind her, to see if she could help.

8

"Aren't we taking the Cherokee?" asked Erica, as they walked passed the hangar and into the copse of trees.

"Cherokee won't get us where we are going – although Mersuul would be happy if it could." said Travellor, maintaining the smile on his face. Mersuul was also smiling as she nodded in agreement.

They were following a worn path that Erika knew hadn't been there the last time she visited. They had gone about thirty feet into the copse when suddenly they were standing on a concrete floor that just appeared from nowhere. They stood in a small room made of transparent walls, which was attached to a larger structure. The building was furnished with a small couch, some chairs, and there was a small table with a coffee maker next to a bottled water dispenser. It reminded Erika of the FBO at the local airport.

At one end of the room she saw the rest of their bags, and a number of plastic barrels and wooden crates. Vicious was moving from there towards them. Looking through the transparent windows of the room, Erika could see that there were two equally spaced circles painted on the floor of the structure. Each circle had a large letter H painted in its center. Eight red lights which were almost flush to the ground, were located around the edge of each circle. She tapped on the window – it was a thick polycarbonate material.

The structure was enclosed on all sides, and the doorway behind them seemed to be the only entrance. The building hadn't been there before – shouldn't have been there now. She could clearly see all the stars of the early morning sky when she looked up. Erika spun around, looking at her surroundings again.

"This can't be here!" she said. "We flew over here yesterday, and this wasn't here!"

She stopped turning around when she saw her uncle's face. His smile was much bigger now. Mersuul was looking at him and shaking her head like you would at a child who was playing a practical joke. She nudged him with her elbow.

"Tell her, now. You have had your fun."

"Oh, but this is once in a lifetime. Look at that expression on her face!" he said, as he was enjoying her confusion. "And she hasn't even seen the good stuff yet."

"It is camouflaged from view overhead. Anyone flying over would only see trees." said Mersuul, again shaking her head at Travellor.

"That's very effective camouflage! So we're going by helicopter?" asked Erika.

"Nope." replied her uncle. "You are going to love this! What time is it?"

Travellor had just finished speaking when the red lights around the landing circles began flashing.

Mersuul sighed. "Just as I had become comfortable here, it is time to go back to work."

Travellor and Mersuul were looking up to the sky, and Erika did the same. She still couldn't see anything but the stars – except… Strange, there appeared to be a black hole in the sky – and the hole kept growing.

Then a low frequency sound could be heard. As the hole kept getting bigger, the sound grew a little louder. It sounded like a dry, low level roaring, and Erika noticed neither her uncle or Mersuul seemed bothered by it. As she stared up at the hole it began to grow lighter until it changed into a glowing hole in the sky. It wasn't bright enough to hurt your eyes, but against the dark sky background it was very obvious. Then the glow that had been above them lowered into the structure.

Erika felt a thump from the ground as if something had contacted the floor, and the glowing shape that hovered several feet above the ground began to dim. Soon it was gone. She moved closer to her uncle and took his arm. It wasn't fear she was feeling exactly – more like the anticipation of the unknown. He turned and smiled at her.

"Keep watching." he said, and turned his head back to view the seemingly empty room.

But there was nothing to see. She look out and saw just the walls of the structure and the open sky above. She was feeling confused when suddenly she involuntarily jumped back as a large elongated oval shaped object appeared from nowhere. The object had windows, and through them she could see people inside, all wearing flight suits similar to theirs. It was held up by six legs with bristle brushes on the ends – the bristles were very thick, each being as big around as her wrist. She didn't realize that her eyes were wide, and her mouth open, as she moved closed to get a better look.

"It's an aircraft!" she said in surprise.
"Is that great camouflage or what?" said Travellor.
"It doesn't have any wings!"

Erika heard a clunk and thud, and a door opened on the side of the craft. Stairs extended to the floor, and the four men inside started down. They waved to her uncle and Mersuul as they spotted them. Just like any traveler getting off of an airplane, they carried luggage with them as they came out. As they gathered outside the ship, Mersuul took Erika's hand and led her into the hangar.

"Come. They all want to meet you. Tony talks about you so much, everyone thinks of you as family."

Chapter 16

Starting The New Job

1

"Scan flight path for traffic." said Travellor.

"*Flight path clear within twenty-five mile radius up to thirty-five thousand feet.*" said the computer.

"Looks like we're good to go. Everyone seated and secure?" he asked, even though he could see that Erika and Mersuul were.

"There are no seat belts." replied Erika.

"None needed. I'll make sure you have a copy of the shuttle's flight manual available to study in your free time."

It was checklist procedure – everyone seated and secure – asked by the pilot and confirmed by passengers before takeoff. Unlike an airplane, there were no seat belts in the shuttle. The seats themselves had the capability to surround and restrain your whole body during an impact resulting in up to an instantaneous ninety G deceleration. The skeletal structure is held in position so that no damage to the spinal column occurs. It was a safety system Travellor had wanted to get integrated into aircraft on Earth, but it required computer processing speeds and electro-mechanical devices with response speeds far beyond that capable by Human technology. Even the supercomputers couldn't reach that speed, and the ship's processor was smaller than an olive. In fact, it looked like an olive. Ganaphe' electro-mechanical technology was structured in three dimensions, and their components took on odd shapes defined by their function.

"Doors and access points secured?" asked Travellor.

"Doors and access points secured." replied Mersuul in confirmation.

"Checklist complete. Here we go. Manual control to pilot."

"*Pilot has manual control – confirmed.*" said the computer.

Several of the display panels in front of Travellor changed from displaying monitored parameters to control indicators.

"What's in the metal barrels?"

"Water." said Travellor.

"There's no water on location? Couldn't we use filtration systems? Transporting this much water must be expensive."

"There are some magmatic water sources that we could use in an emergency," said Mersuul, "but getting to them is very difficult. It is much easier to bring water from here. We do recycle most of it, but there is always some loss that we cannot control."

"So we're land locked?"

"Ohhhhh yessss." said Travellor. "You could say we are definitely land locked."

Erika had been on an almost non-stop questioning binge since they had started loading the supplies on the ship. Only this time she was actually getting answers. They had loaded on a lot of cargo before taking off, but the ship rose into the still dark sky without any noticeable strain. Travellor was piloting the ship, and Mersuul was sitting back and watching him.

"So how come you're not letting Mersuul fly, Uncle Tony? Are you already qualified in this ship, Mersuul?"

Travellor broke out in a wide smile, and looked back at his niece.

"I'm flying because I'm the student in this ship. Mersuul is my flight instructor. She may look like she's just relaxing, but don't let her fool you. She is very critical and strict with her students."

279

"Do not say it like that. You make me sound terrible." said Mersuul. She looked at Erika. "I am demanding of my students, yes, because I want them to know everything that may save their lives, or what can kill them."

"Oh!" exclaimed Erika, with wide eyes. "Wow. Will you teach me also?"

"It is required that all personnel know how to fly the emergency vehicles on the ship, in order to increase the survival chances of all the crew. After you are settled, flight training will be part of your required education."

What Mersuul said about required education didn't surprise Erika. There was always something to learn on any new job. Since her early college years she had realized that anyone in a technical field will continually have to keep up with changing technology – in effect, never getting out of school.

They had broken through the cloud layer they were in, and the sky was suddenly a light blue. There was one very large and bright star high and on their left. It was an amazing view. They kept climbing and it seemed to Erika that their speed was increasing, slowly and steadily. Soon the clouds below them looked like a carpet of fluffy cotton. The sky kept getting brighter.

"What's our altitude?" asked Erika.

"Going through forty-five thousand." said Travellor.

"Did we file a flight plan?" she asked, knowing that all aircraft at this altitude had to be on an IFR flight plan and in contact with flight controllers.

"No flight plan, sweetie." said Travellor as he turned to look at her. "No one can see or detect us, and it's very important to keep it that way. It will all make sense when we get there. But don't worry, we can keep track of all other aircraft around us."

He pointed to a panel displaying little three dimensional aircraft that moved around as if they were in a choreographed ballet. A line ran through them longitudinally, which seemed to indicate a projected flight path. Erika felt a slight unease about that. Why shouldn't she? She was in a strange aircraft with strange instrumentation, violating the flight rules she knew were necessary for safety, and going to an unknown destination. If her uncle hadn't been the one taking her there she would have looked for a parachute or some other way to get out. That thought in itself was crazy, so she knew she was nervous. There had been something else that Mersuul had said, that also added to her confusion. What was it? *'Oh yes,'* she remembered, she had said *'emergency vehicles on the ship'* – plural. More than one of these craft on a land locked ship. What kind of ship travels on land and is big enough to require more than one of these transports, she wondered. Maybe she just heard it wrong.

She was about to ask a question about the instruments when she realized the bright sky was dimming. She could still see the sun, but outside was definitely getting darker.

"Beginning transition to interstellar flight." said the computer.

Erika looked around for a speaker but didn't see one.

"Engage auto flight systems. Destination moon base." said Travellor.
"Automatic navigation systems operational. Destination is Trailblazer Moon Base." said the invisible woman.

'There has to be speakers around here somewhere.' thought Erika, but her visual search came to an abrupt stop when she looked outside again. It was completely dark. The stars seemed to be unusually clear.

"Uncle Tony, did it say 'interstellar' flight?"
"Hmmmm… Yes, it did." he replied with another smile on his face.
"Very nice." said Mersuul, to Travellor. "When we arrive I'm going to sign you off on the transports. You really haven't needed an instructor for some time now. Your balancing of the cargo was excellent."
"I know," said Travellor. "but it's been a good excuse to have you

come with me."

Mersuul smiled, reached over and grabbed his hand.

"I know." she said.

Erika's eyes had been continually getting larger as she realized that they had left Earth's atmosphere and were now in space. Her mind was trying to handle the information overload, and all the surprises coming at her.

"Isn't it time to start heading back down now?" she asked, "... Wait ... WHAT? ... Moon base? Did you say moon base?"

"Did I forget to mention that you'd be working on the moon?" said Travellor, with a quirky smile on his face.

"WE HAVE A BASE ON THE MOON?" blurted out Erika. "AND NO ONE KNOWS ABOUT IT?"

"Ah… well… If by 'We' you mean the USA, then not exactly. But our employer does." said Travellor.

"I … I thought I was hired by a U.S. government agency. I mean, with all the secrecy, and the background checks and all."

"You were. Only the government doesn't know the agency exists. Well that's not exactly true – they do know – sorta. It's complicated. But all will be made clear as you go through indoctrination on the base."

"*Adjusting course for avoidance of WISE satellite.*" said the disembodied voice.

"WISE satellite? The WISE satellite? Where? Where is it?" Erika asked excitedly. "I've only seen pictures of it."

The ship moved in an 'upward' direction, in relation to the floor. Erika could feel the slight increase in pressure against the bottom of her thighs.

"There!" said Mersuul, quickly pointing out the left window.

Erika saw a cylindrical shaped object with a flat panel on its back, as it seemed to drop below their flight path. It was pointing away from them, out into space.

"Its sensors could detect the heat of our ship." said Mersuul. "It is one of several satellites we have to avoid, so we are not detected. There is something else you may want to see." she said pointing out the other side of the ship.

Erika turned her head, and her mouth opened. The International Space Station looked like it was close enough to grab. She thought it was amazing and beautiful as it glowed in reflected sunlight. It was like a huge metal art sculpture hung in space.

"We fly by the station whenever we can, so that we can check it for potential problems the astronauts might not be aware of. Unfortunately we are limited to visual inspections only." said Travellor.

"They are very brave people, to risk their lives in such a primitive ship." said Mersuul. "Space travel is very dangerous even in a ship like the Orysta, which is one of the best of its class. But this…" she said, nodding her head towards the ISS, "… this is like living in a paper house during a hurricane. I do not know if I could be that brave."

It was with those words that Erika Aimsler began to feel the impact of what she was seeing and hearing. She felt light headed as the shock of realization set in.

"How… How are we doing this?" she asked. "How can we do this – what we've done? We've gotten here in just minutes."

She looked down at the floor as she tried to piece together the puzzle. Travellor looked back at his niece, and didn't like the way she looked. Now he was worried.

"Erika, are you alright hon?"

"This ship has no rockets, but we've traveled faster than any rocket built on Earth. There is almost no noise – no vibration. What makes this thing go? How can this ship have this much power? The Orysta? This isn't the Orysta, is it? The Orysta is much larger isn't it?"

Travellor got out of his seat, and knelt beside his niece. He took her hands in his, and the smile was gone from his face.

"Maybe I shouldn't have brought you here without preparing you better for this." he said as he looked into Erika's eyes. "You are perfectly safe here – as safe as anyone can be in life. You are about to see some amazing things, that very few people from our planet have seen. If you want to, you will be able to learn things that are beyond our world's knowledge and capabilities."

Erika didn't respond, but just kept looking at her uncle.

"Medical analysis of Erika Aimsler." said Travellor
"*Erika Aimsler shows signs of slightly low blood pressure and rapid pulse indicating minor condition of shock.*" said the voice.

Travellor held her face in his hands, and then kissed Erika on the forehead.

"Remember when you were six, – I think that was when you first said it – and we would look through the telescope at the night sky? I would ask you what was your favorite thing in the sky and you would point to the moon and say that it was what you wanted for your birthday present, and I told you I would try to get it for you? Every year after that you said the same thing, and I told you I would try. We'd laugh about it, knowing I would never really be able to give it to you. Remember that?"

She nodded her head. Travellor smiled gently at her stunned silence.

"I'm about to make good on that promise. I'm about to give you the moon."

Erika had already realized that the moon she saw through the front windshield was getting bigger and they were moving closer to it. Her eyes opened wide.

"OH MY GOD!" she said in a stunned tone. "OHMYGODOHMYGODOHMYGOD!"

She began to breathe more quickly.

"You…" she said looking at Mersuul. "THIS!…" she said looking around the ship. "We didn't build this did we?… I mean this ship was not built on Earth, was It? And you're not from here are you? You're an alien aren't you?"

"Yes." said Mersuul, reaching out her hand.

Erika took her offered hand, and held it firmly, paying attention to the feel of it in hers. It felt like any person's hand. On one of the display screens of the instrument panel an outline of a person appeared and numbers with words she couldn't read were displayed next to it. They all noticed when the display came one. Mersuul glanced at it for a few seconds, then turned back to Erika.

"Is that supposed to be me?" asked Erika.

"Yes." said Mersuul. "The ship's computer monitors all crew members throughout the flight. If anything changes from normal it displays the persons physiological data, so that the rest of the crew can be warned that something needs to be given attention."

"Your heart and breathing rates increased when you got excited, triggering the display." said Travellor.

Erika realized that her breathing had become heavy, and her heart rate was fast.

"WELL OF COURSE MY EVERYTHING IS FASTER!" she said loudly. "You just told me that I'm in an alien ship – WITH A REAL ALIEN! – and we're really going to the moon! Ohmygod. Ohmygod, Oh..my..god… THIS IS FANTASTIC! We're going to the moon! YES."

She leaned forward and wrapped her arms around her uncle's neck, and gave him several kisses on the cheek. She tightened her hug until he pointed to his neck, indicating he couldn't breathe.

"Your uncle does know you very well." said Mersuul. "I was worried for a while when you first realized what was happening, and your metabolism changed. I thought Tony had made a mistake not to prepare you for this."

"How long have we known each other for?" asked Travellor with a smug look on his face. "When will you ladies ever learn?" he asked jokingly.

"You are wonderful." said Erika, tightening her hug briefly. "A little arrogant, but wonderful."

Mersuul looked at the two of them and couldn't help smiling.

"I think I will have that added to his official medical record – 'Wonderful but arrogant.'" she said, looking at Travellor with affection in her eyes.

Mersuul pushed one of the buttons on the arm of her seat, and a touchboard came up from the side and positioned in front of her. She started entering data. A few minutes later the touchboard retracted away.

"There!" she said. "The first official report on your moon base record. I was ordered to evaluate your reaction to everything you were told about the operation. Your new employer will be very happy, as will Grilik

286

Munen."

"MY new employer? Don't you work for them also?" asked Erika.

"It is a joint venture between my company and yours. That will be explained in your indoctrination training, which is very thorough."

"I can't wait." said Erika. "What's a Gril…"

"Grilik. It is the same as Ship's Captain in your language."

Erika looked out of the ship at the moon. In just the few minutes that had passed since she last looked, it had become much bigger than before.

2

"Trailblazer Moon Base, this is Travellor in shuttle two. We are ten minutes out. Request active approach. Over."

"Shuttle two, this is Trailblazer. Welcome back Commander. Active approach is D for Delta. Satellite avoidance in effect. Over."

"Approach Delta with satellite avoidance." confirmed Travellor, as he tapped on the display screen in front of him to select the approach pattern.

As the shuttle approached the moon it filled the forward windows, and soon Erika could make out smaller details of the landscape. The the shuttle flared and began traveling horizontal to the surface, getting closer with every second. Their speed slowed and she could clearly see the surrounding terrain. Erika looked farther out in front of the ship and could see the rise of a crater's outer edge. They were flying slightly higher than that, and overflew the crest. She was not expecting what she saw next. The huge circular structure that stuck up from the ground. It was covered with windows that bled light into the surrounding darkness. As she stared, Erika realized her mouth was open – again – something she had been doing a lot since they left Earth.

"What – is – that?" she asked.

"That is Trailblazer Moon Base. Your home while you are at work." Travellor said. "Wait until you see inside."

"Orysta, this is shuttle two on approach for landing." said Mersuul.

"There are people outside!" Erika said, pointing at a group moving on the moon's surface.

A voice came over the comm, speaking in Mersuul's language. It took a few seconds before Erika's wrist device translated the acknowledgment in English. She scanned in front of the shuttle, and saw light coming out of a rectangular opening in the ground.

"Is the Orysta underground?"

"Yes." replied Mersuul. "You are going to learn a lot about her in your training."

"That's one way to stay hidden."

"Unfortunately, that was not intended." Mersuul said with a tone of unease in her voice.

"Shuttle two, Trailblazer Approach. Commander, Grilik Munen requests that you dock in the Orysta."

"Dock in the Orysta. Roger that. What satellite are we exposed to?"

"Sir, LADEE is below three hundred feet above ground level at thirty-six hundred MPH. This looks like its farewell orbit."

Travellor became quiet for several seconds. Mersuul looked at him in anticipation of his thoughts.

"What are you thinking about?" she asked.

"I've never seen a dying satellite up close before." he said with a smile. "I'd like to. I'm sure Erika would also." He looked back at his niece, who was nodding in the affirmative. "Approach, shuttle two will be deviating from course and delaying our arrival. We're going to do a little sight seeing."

"Shuttle two, roger. Contact approach when ready to land."

"Will do. Over." He tapped the display screen and said "Plot course to overtake and parallel LADEE satellite. Maintain three hundred feet AGL."

"Course plotted and intercept initiated." said the computer.

The sudden acceleration from their relatively slow speed was felt by all three, even with the ships inertia compensation in operation. The view of the Moon's surface blurred again as they quickly went around to the far side of it. They couldn't see any details of the ground but suddenly ahead and on their right side came a reflected glint from their forward lights.

"Illuminate all quadrants, full power." said Travellor.

The powerful external lights of the ship flared on. They still couldn't see details, but a ghostly gray reflection from the surface followed directly below them. On their right, and clearly illuminated was the LADEE. Covered with solar panels and gold protrusions, the satellite reflected blue and purple as it rotated. They caught up to and paced the satellite. Slowly it began to fall below the shuttles flight path.

"Bank twenty degrees right. Call out speed in MPH." said Travellor.
"Ground speed is three thousand six hundred twenty-seven miles per hour." said the computer, as the shuttle rotated on its longitudinal axis.

With the ship banked, they were able to continue viewing the satellite as it dropped closer to the surface.

"Reduce speed to maintain two mile separation. Pitch thirty degrees down. Cancel bank angle."

Now the shuttle pointed downward and fell behind the LADEE. They could see it clearly through the front windows.

"Satellite will impact surface in ten seconds."

"On impact drop speed and hover over impact zone." commanded
Travellor.

The satellite kept getting smaller as it descended to the surface.
Mersuul wiped a finger on one of her display screens and the image in front
of them was magnified until they could see the satellite's details again. It
seemed to be losing altitude faster now – and suddenly it was gone. It just
seemed to disappear. The shuttle decelerated so quickly that this also was
felt by the three of them. It hovered over the impact zone. Travellor
regained manual control of the ship and lowered their altitude. In front of
them was a relatively small crater with a cloud of dust hanging above it.

"Wow!" said Erika. "There's nothing left."
"Interesting." said Travellor. "Did we record it?" he asked, looking
at Mersuul.
"Yes. Ship's data and video."
"Excellent. Now that's something not many people have ever seen."

3

The shuttle flew over the opening in the ground and hovered. Then
it slowly descended. At first Erika could only see bright light below and a
vertical shaft they were descending into. As the shuttle got lower the details
of the shuttle bay became clear, as did people working there. The landing
was handled by the shuttle's computer, but the shutdown procedure was
performed manually by her uncle and Mersuul.

"Orysta, this is Navigator Mersuul-sil-Vaana. Record in the ship's
logs that Commander Anthony Travellor is now authorized to fly as Pilot In
Command of the Orysta's support vessels. Authorize with my name, on this
date."
"*Navigator Mersuul-sil-Vaana recognized. Ship's log updated to*

reflect status change on record of Anthony Travellor, Commander, Trailblazer Moon Base."

"Who was that?" asked Erika as she stood up from her seat. "Why do they keep calling you 'Commander' uncle Tony? You left the military years ago."

"There is so much to tell you." Travellor replied. "For the next few weeks you will probably go to bed mentally exhausted from everything you are going to be exposed to. But on the plus side, you will probably sleep like the proverbial log."

"You did not tell her what your job is?" asked Mersuul, in a shocked tone of voice.

"It would have been a little hard to tell her that without telling everything else that goes with it. Come on, let's get out of here. They're waiting to unload the cargo."

As they stepped out of the shuttle, there were three men waiting for them. The one standing farthest away snapped to attention and saluted. Travellor returned the salute. Erika stayed close to her uncle.

"Welcome back." said the smiling man at the front of the group. "Is this your niece, Commander?"

"It is." replied Travellor. "Erika, this is Grilik Munen. He is the captain of the Orysta."

Munen nodded his head and extended his hand to Erika.

"It is nice to finally meet you Miss Aimsler. Your uncle has told us a lot about you. This is Benua-sil-Plessa, Chief Engineer of the Orysta." he said indicating the bearded man next to him.

"It is nice to meet you Miss Aimsler. I have been looking forward to your arrival." he said in excellent formal English. "We will be working together on your first project here, after you have finished orientation."

"It's nice to meet you also." said Erika, shaking both men's hands. "I can't wait to get started." she said with a big smile. Realizing that she would be working on an alien space ship with an engineer from another universe, she forced herself to hold back her excitement.

Travellor was surprised by the statement that Erika would be working with Plessa. That was not her original assignment. He decided not to say anything until he found out more about it.

"And this is Joshua Kibbee, head of security on the moon base, and the same in an advisory capacity to the Orysta" said Travellor.

"Commander. Miss Vaana." he said, nodding to Travellor and Mersuul. Then he took a step closer to Erika. "It's a pleasure to meet you Miss Aimsler." he said, offering his hand. Erika shook it with a smile.

"It's my pleasure to meet all of you." she said. "I can't tell you just how thrilled I am to be here."

"I hope you do not mind my diverting the shuttle to land here." said Munen. "Our water system had a problem, and we lost a considerable amount. I knew you were bringing more on this trip. It made sense to have you land here."

"I agree." said Travellor.

"I will be happy to show you around the Orysta tomorrow, miss Aimsler." said Plessa. "While I show you around we can talk about the project I would like you to work on."

Now it was Mersuul's turn to be surprised. She had worked with Plessa for a long time, and tour guide was never a title she would associate with him. Plessa was a social enough person but not the type to offer to host visitors.

As everyone conversed, they left the landing bay and headed through the connecting passage to the base. Erika couldn't stop moving her head as she took in all the new sights. One sight quickly grabbed her attention as they stepped from the passage and into the reception area of the moon base. There was a sign that said 'Welcome to Trailblazer Moon Base', and below a large picture of a smiling man in a space suit. The caption underneath read 'Anthony Travellor' and 'Base Commander'. It finally hit her. She had dismissed all the people calling him Commander as being a courtesy title, like many retired military personnel who continue to be referred to by their rank. She realized that wasn't the case here. Her uncle was in command of the moon base – the first operational base established on the moon! With her eyes locked on to the picture and not watching where she was going, she tripped a little but quickly regained her balance. Everyone stopped to make sure she was alright. She looked at her uncle, who looked back at her.

"Oh yeah," said Travellor, "I keep forgetting that picture is there."

"You... you're in command of this operation? You run this place?"

"Well, everything outside of the Orysta. I guess I sorta run this place."

"You did not know that your uncle commands this base?" asked Plessa, with as much surprise on his face as Erika had on hers.

"She did not know the base existed until a few minutes ago." said Mersuul. "Erika has had many surprises today."

"C'mon. There's more to see." said Travellor taking Erika's hand. "I'll just give you the quick tour now. You'll get the complete tour in orientation."

"No uncle Tony." she said, letting go of his hand. "I don't want people thinking they should give me special treatment because we're related. From now on, please don't tell anyone that I'm your niece."

"OK." he said, looking a little proud. It was what he expected from her.

"I would appreciate it," she said looking around at her companions, "if all of you also would keep that to yourselves."

As they walked deeper into the building Erika tried to take everything in. Some areas looked like they came out of a SciFi movie, while others had been deliberately designed to have a down home feel to them. She could tell the base was huge, and that what she had seen so far was just a small portion of it. It amazed her that an operational base this big could even have been built here. But of course, it really couldn't – not with present space travel capability. That is, not with Earth's present space travel capability. The aliens had to have had a big hand in getting materials up

293

here. And then there were those little objects that moved back and forth over the ceilings and walls that she found so captivating.

"What are those things?" she asked. "Those small moving things on the ceiling?"

"Those are some of our maid bots." said Travellor. "They travel over the walls and ceilings cleaning off dust and contaminants. They also emit UV light to kill any viruses. Saves having to have someone do the job manually. We also have other robots of different shapes and sizes that do various housekeeping chores. You'll see them moving around the station."

"How do they stay up?"

"I applied a little Ganaphe' technology to them. Their treads are made from a material that can cling to almost any surface, and still easily release its grip. I gave them mini tank tracks made of that material. Their only purpose is to clean off the walls and ceilings. You'd be surprised how much of a difference that makes in keeping this place clean. We have about a hundred and twenty of them."

"Ganaphe'?"

"Oh – sorry. I never explained that." said Travellor. "Mersuul, Grilik Munen, Chief Engineer Plessa, and the crew of the Orysta are Ganaphe', from the planet Taloraicia. It will all be covered in orientation. Usually orientation is handled before you come to the base, but with the tight time frame from your graduation to your being available for work it made more sense to do it on site. Your first week here is nothing but orientation, so you don't have to worry about anything else. And yes, that is special treatment for you,… and a couple of other new people – Sorry. I promise I won't do it again."

Erika looked at him with a mixed expression of appreciation and suspicion. She was determined to make sure he didn't do it again whether he wanted to or not. Mersuul looked at him with an expression of doubt. Travellor couldn't believe what he saw on their faces. He didn't understand how they could doubt him, but decided it was best to just continue walking and remain silent.

"You know, some of these robots would be great down at the house."

"Can't do that. Our agreement with the Ganaphe' allows us to use their technology here, but we're not allowed to take any of it to Earth. It will all be explained in orientation."

"I know I'm asking a lot of questions, and I'm sure all will be explained in orientation, but there is one thing I find very odd. I was sure that walking would feel different on the Moon, with the lesser gravity, but it feels just like walking on Earth as far as I can tell."

"The Orysta generates a gravity field." said Munen. "It can be shaped and extended from the ship. It can be very useful in our mining operations. We now have it configured to provide normal Earth gravity on the ship and the base, but when you go away from the crater you will experience normal Moon gravity."

"You can create gravity?" Erika asked in an excitedly louder voice, looking back and forth at Munen and Plessa.

"The Ganaphe' have technology that is far ahead of ours." said Travellor. "We're fortunate to be able to use it."

4

"Sorry unc..uh, Commander, but I'm just too tired tonight." said Erika.

"OK sweet... ah, miss Aimsler. Get some sleep. I can't wait for this week to be over."

"Commander, is anyone else there with you?"

"Just Mersuul."

"Good. I love you uncle Tony. Goodnight."

"Goodnight sweetie. Sleep well."

The comm went silent, and Travellor looked at Mersuul.

295

"How can she be so tired from Orientation? What are they doing to her in there, sending her outside every day?"

"It is not only the Orientation. After instruction she has been going to the Orysta and spending time with Plessa. She wants to get started on her duties as soon as she is cleared. She has been learning everything that is allowed about the ship."

"AND THAT'S ANOTHER THING." he said loudly. "How did Plessa get the idea she was going to work with him. I have her assigned here on the base."

"It was your idea." answered Mersuul as she took his arm and led him to the table. "Dinner is ready."

"My idea? Not my idea!" he said, gathering the individual plates and putting them aside. "We don't need these." He moved the sweet and sour pork and rice to the middle of the table, and stabbed a piece with his fork.

"Yes, your idea." said Mersuul, picking up her chopsticks. She was determined to master their use. "It was your idea to offer Grilik Munen twelve employees of his own if he would allow twelve more people on the base. That was your solution to the limit of the original agreement. There was a meeting on Orysta and Grilik Munen agreed that we could use more help, so he accepted the change to the agreement."

"What? When did this happen? Why wasn't I informed? I AM supposed to be the base Commander here."

Mersuul smiled at her success at getting a piece of meat to her mouth. She savored the flavor, then her expression changed to determination as she tried to do the same with the rice.

"It happened the day before we arrived. Grilik Munen spoke with Commander Farber-Chatwell to finalize the agreement. Plessa was also there. I believe you will be getting the official notice in the morning – there were still problems with the contract language that had to be worked out."

"Huh! So Munen liked my idea. It took him long enough. I told him about it more than a week ago. We're getting twelve more people –

EXCELLENT!"

"Yes, it was a very good solution to the problem. Everyone is happy."

"Great. Now tell me why Erika will be working with Plessa."

Mersuul gave up on the chopsticks and picked up a fork. She scooped up some rice and a piece of pork.

"Farber-Chatwell had informed Grilik Munen that Erika would be considered one of the twelve people who would be assigned to you, and that she would be arriving early with us. Plessa wanted fresh eyes on the problem of freeing Orysta. Grilik Munen and Plessa requested Erika's educational background and employment evaluation. Plessa liked what he read and wanted her, so Grilik Munen made it a final condition of the agreement that she be one of his twelve new employees."

Travellor stopped chewing and stared at her.

"They stole her from me! They stole my niece from me! They obviously planned it for days."

"They... negotiated her from you." said Mersuul, chuckling with a full mouth.

5

Doctor Sylvia Krather entered her office and was very pleasantly surprised to see a large bouquet of beautiful flowers in a crystal vase on her desk. She sat down and found a box of chocolate truffles in front of the vase. She picked up the note attached to the chocolates and read 'Thank you Doctor Krather. I owe you for my life. Please allow me to buy you dinner this evening and say thanks properly. I've invited the other medical personnel that I also owe thanks to. Commander Travellor and Grilik Munen have arranged for everyone to have the time off. Nineteen hundred *hours Earth time in the banquet hall. Dress is casual.'* It was signed by Delores del Rio. A smile widened on Krather's face.

She had reviewed del Rio's medical file, and those of twenty-two others of the new personnel to be stationed on the base. It made her glad that del Rio's request to be re-stationed here had been granted. It didn't surprise her though. Farber-Chatwell always looked out for his people and he would have considered del Rio's assignment here as part of her recuperation process. She felt a sense of admiration for del Rio, who could have remained on Earth and taken another assignment there. Instead she chose to come back to the edge of space exploration, even with all its dangers. Only the brave made choices like that. She also felt appreciation for Farber-Chatwell. He took care of the people who worked for him. He was a good man in many ways, and she enjoyed the personal time she spent with him.

She opened the box and looked at the variety of sweets that all looked delicious. She picked one from the middle and took a bite. Her eyes closed in pleasure as the taste and unbelievably smooth texture wrapped around her tongue in one small but wonderful moment of gourmet bliss.

6

It was over! One week of orientation – eight days actually, since someone decided she should be checked out on the basics of the Ganaphe's weapons systems. More than likely that was her uncle's idea. But now it was over. She had had to learn to use the technologies of Trailblazer Moon Base and the Orysta – and what amazing technology it was! How could her uncle have kept this all from her – have not even hinted about it!

In the past week she had done things that very few people in the world had done. She had walked on the surface of the moon, traveled at near-light speeds to close-by asteroids, had gotten a few minutes of time at the controls of both Ganaphe' and human designed space ships, had performed extra-vehicular activities from a Ganaphe' shuttle, had studied the structural design of the moon base and the Orysta, had learned a smattering of Galya (the language of the Ganaphe'), and had learned unending amounts of safety procedures (Living on the moon was very dangerous). She had learned the danger aspects of all of the above and also learned what bliml was, and that they had run out if it some time ago.

Last but not least, she had one of the few remaining spare universal language translators implanted just behind her ear. It not only translates languages from planets she has never heard of, but has also been programmed with all of Earth's major languages. Apparently, because there were only a few left after these were implanted in the original Trailblazer team, they were no longer distributed to personnel. New personnel on station are now issued comm badges with a built-in translator of Human-Ganaphe' design. These are not as powerful as the Ganaphe' translators and only handle a half dozen languages, but do work very well.

That was all over now. Now Erika could concentrate on the problem she had been made aware of when she first arrived here – freeing the Orysta. She had been learning a lot from Plessa, and the ship's Chief Engineer may have "let slip" some technical specs on the ship that should have been restricted by the IGT. *'Oh, yes!'* she thought, *'Let's not forget the IGT. How was anyone supposed the learn anything in a first contact situation without violating that piece of work!'* The thought brought a slightly angry expression across her face.

She had studied the recordings of the first attempt. It was a good try, but it was strictly a brute force effort. There was no finesse in it. Freeing a stuck ship with no flight capability is a lot more complicated when you have all that surrounding material trying to hold it back. Even a ship as strong as the Orysta had been damaged in the attempt, and it is a very well built ship. She had already considered several methods, and none seemed suitable by themselves. This was going to require implementing multiple methods together, and she had an idea of how it should be done. She still had more research to do, but not tonight. Tonight was a special dinner, and she was going as Plessa's guest. This was her first social event on the base, and it was perfect timing.

7

It had been at least ten minutes since she had entered the hall, and Erika was still in a state of mild awe of the room. Most parts of the base she had already been in looked like what someone might expect a moon base to look like. The Orysta looked like what someone might expect an intergalactic space ship to look like. But this banquet hall was completely out of place on the Moon. She had been in many elegant and extravagant estates around the world, owned by some very rich people, but the style and elegance of this room was unbelievable. She had a good idea what the hand carved exotic woods that furnished this room must have cost. This type of workmanship just wasn't done anymore. The time and skill it had taken to create the furniture, walls, and ceiling was from long gone eras of kings with untold wealth. Even the rich countries of today did not have the imagination required to produce this level of elegance, not to mention finding the artisans to do it. She looked very carefully at the crystal goblet in her hand and compared it to another one on the table. No two were exactly alike. Each one had been hand made. And this was a casual gathering. She wondered what the formal ones were like.

Erika sat at a table with Plessa, Grilik Munen, Tahn-grilik Califas and all the other crew members of the Orysta on her right. They had asked her to sit with them since they considered her part of their team. On her left was her uncle and Mersuul, the original Trailblazer mission crew, and all the other moon base personnel except for the recent arrivals (who were covering duty stations as part of their training). As she continued around the table she recognized Doctor Blin and her staff of transient medical personnel who rotated between Earth and the Moon. At the head of the table was tonight's hostess, Specialist Delores del Rio, and sitting next to her was Doctor Sylvia Krather.

It had surprised Erika to find out that del Rio was paying for all the expenses of tonight's dinner. After her life saving surgery she had spent many weeks in a medically induced coma. After being brought out of that there were years of rehabilitation to strengthen her body and mind. When she was deemed fit to return to duty, she spent more years physically pushing herself until her levels of strength and stamina were better than before her accident, all the while working a regular job back home. She had been receiving her full salary throughout it all (which Erika thought was abnormally generous of her employer), and since her belongings had been placed in storage she had no expenses until being released from the hospital. The money kept accumulating in her account until that time. Most people would just have kept it, but del Rio was so grateful for everyone who had saved her life, that she wanted to show her appreciation. She didn't know the exact figures, but Erika guessed that the cost of this evening's gathering was at least two years worth of paychecks. It's not cheap getting food and drink shipped to the Moon!

Erika leaned over towards her uncle, and spoke in a low voice.

"Commander, may I speak with you?"

"Miss Aimsler." he said, also in a low voice and with a large smile on his face. "What can I do for you?"

She looked around quickly, and saw that only Mersuul was paying any attention to them.

"Do you remember the conversation we had about special treatment for your niece?" she asked, now in whisper.

"I remember very clearly." he answered, wondering what she getting at.

"Well, I had one of the few remaining implantable translators put in. Don't you consider that special treatment?"

"I certainly do consider that special treatment!" he said, wide eyed with surprise. "But I didn't have anything to do with that."

Erika was surprised by his answer. She had been sure it had been favoritism shown to her because of her uncle.

"Wait a minute." said Travellor with a suspicious look as he slowly turned to Mersuul. "What do you know about this Mata?"

"Who's Mata?" asked Erika.

Mersuul gave a knowing smile to both of them.

"It was Chief Engineer Plessa who requested that she be given one. He thought that her work with him was too important for her not to have the most efficient device. He didn't want any misunderstandings in their work together." she said.

"This is Mata." said Travellor. "My own personal Mata Hari. She knows everything and never tells me any of it."

"Oh! So it was Plessa's idea. Great. That's OK then."

"I did not inform you of this because it seemed reasonable and unimportant."

"Uh huh. I'm keeping my eye on you." he jokingly said to Mersuul. "See," he said turning to Erika, "no special treatment from me. So how is the job going?"

Before Erika could answer, the dinging on a crystal goblet caught their attention.

"I'll tell you later." Erika said.

It was time for the hostess to perform her duties, and Delores del Rio stood up while tapping a fork against her glass to get everyone's attention.

"Good evening everyone." said del Rio, "Thank you so much for coming tonight, and allowing me to say Thank You to the people who saved my life. All of you had something to do with my being here tonight. I couldn't say Thank You enough times to properly express my gratitude. Some of you flew into space to find me. Some kept the communications links going to the right people. Some watched and prayed for me. I was lost in space, and getting further lost by the second. It was the worse case of finding a needle in a hay stack, and you kept at it until you found me.

302

Thank You." she said, finally stopping for a breath. Her eyes started to wet.

"When I was brought back and taken to medical, I was a mess. A terrible mess. I know because I was allowed to review my complete medical record of that time. Under the guidance of Doctor Krather, the medical team worked around the clock, repairing piece by piece – literally – all the damage that had been suffered by my body." Del Rio sniffed and a visible tear flowed down her face. She continued, "If it wasn't for the medical technology on the Orysta I would be dead. Even with every amazing thing their medical equipment was capable of, I was still a mess after they had finished. After I had read my medical file I couldn't believe that I had survived." Her lips pursed, and she choked up a little.

"You should have seen the pictures of me – I did. I was barely recognizable…, I…, Excuse me for a second." she said, trying to regain her composure and clear her now closing throat. She took a tissue from her pocket, and wiped her eyes and nose, and then continued. "During the years of rehab I learned more about what everyone did during my rescue. Thank You – again. I can't say it enough. Those of you who knew me more personally will notice small changes in how a look. My face is a little rounder. Some of my movements have a glitch in them. My eyes are not the same color anymore. There are some other minor differences, but none of it affects my functioning. Today I am actually stronger than when I first came here. I could go on, but you get the idea." She took a sip of water and cleared her throat. "Sorry… something in my throat."

"So tonight is my way of saying Thank You, in a small way…" She choked up, then took a minute to gather herself. "Enjoy this dinner with all my gratitude. Thank You again. Let's eat!" she finished with a smile, as the tears flowed freely now.

Erika looked to her uncle and Mersuul with a questioning expression.

"What happened to her?" she asked.

"That is a hellova story. We'll tell you the whole thing later. There are lessons to be learned by that incident."

"Yes." said Mersuul. "I helped transport her to Earth after the

303

operation. She is correct. She did not look like a person, and she was barely alive. I do not think anyone expected her to survive. Doctor Blin told me that they had to perform procedures no one had tried before. That is how badly she was injured. I understand that she had to learn to control her body again, like a newborn. She appears to have overcome all the problems. It is amazing."

Krather gave del Rio a hug, and said something no one else could hear. The tears stopped coming out after a while, and a smile took over del Rio's face. Then the serving staff zoomed into action, and several large covered silver trays were rolled out on serving tables and stationed against the wall. The covers were lifted to reveal a small roasted pig on one, surrounded by baked fruits and vegetables. Another had squares of deep dish pizza with various toppings. A third had hot dogs being cooked on rotating steel rods and surrounded by buns and condiments. A fourth had a large roast beef with bowls of sauce, and steamed vegetables around it. A fifth had a stack of steaks surrounded by French fries and hot biscuits with lots of butter. A sixth had various fresh vegetables surrounding a large bowl of salad, and several kinds of dressing.

At the end of the line of the food tables was the bar, with any type of beverage you could want, and prominently displaying large champagne bottles ready for their corks to be popped. It was more food than they all could eat, but nothing remaining would go to waste. Before it was gone everyone on station would have a chance to try some of each item. Food was never wasted out here.

Everyone got up to go choose the culinary delight that would satisfy their taste buds. The conversation level rose and everyone began to relax and enjoy themselves. One by one people were going over to del Rio and personally welcoming her back. When either a shuttle crew member from one of the ships that searched for her or a member of the medical team that had worked on her came up, del Rio gave them a long hug and thanked them again. With each hug came more tears as emotions of happiness and gratitude swelled within her.

Chapter 17

A Busy Month

1

August – 2014

*"If you want to find the secrets of the universe,
think in terms of energy, frequency and vibration."*
Nikola Tesla

The meeting took place in the Orysta's planning room because the ship was the focus of the problem, and because the three dimensional image capabilities of the projections would make the concept clear to everyone. The idea was conceived by Erika Aimsler, and developed with the help of Chief Engineer Benua-sil-Plessa. They had spent weeks refining the concept and working out the details of its execution. They had used the ship's main computer on an almost twenty-four by seven basis calculating and confirming the concept. Now they had to get the plan authorized by both the ship's Grilik and the Commander of the moon base. They had kept the overall idea a secret until they were sure of success – or at least a ninety percent chance of it. This wasn't easy to do since Grilik Munen would often ask his chief engineer about the project.

In the room were Grilik Munen, Tahn-grilik Califas, Commander Robert Farber-Chatwell, Moon Base Commander Anthony Travellor, and a special guest visiting the moon base for the first time – Ransen Ramsdel. No one else on station knew much about Ramsdel but both Farber-Chatwell and Travellor listened closely when he spoke. Rumor had it that Ramsdel was the man responsible for making the operation here financially possible. Judging by the pay scale and benefits packages for 361's employees he was doing one hell of a job. This was a small gathering, to judge the response of those in authority. If they accepted the plan almost everyone on station would be involved in some way. When Erika was ready for her presentation, Plessa got the attention of the others.

"Everyone, let us begin." he said in a voice loud enough to override the ongoing conversations. "Miss Erika Aimsler of, I am pleased to say, the Orysta team," he paused to smile at her, "and I, have developed an idea to lift the Orysta from the crevice she is in. Since Miss Aimsler came up with the concept she will be giving the rest of the presentation."

Plessa moved away, with a wide smile on his face, looking like a proud daddy showing off his child. Erika stood up and moved to the front of the room. She had a small smile on her face, but hers was a sign of nervousness. It wasn't presenting the plan to this group that made her nervous, it was the possibility of having it rejected.

"I've read the report on the first attempt at getting the Orysta out of the position it is in. At the time there were two shuttles from the ship and four from the base. The combined lift generated by all of them should have been enough to lift the Orysta if it wasn't being held by tons of rock and soil. To compensate for that explosives were used to loosen the soil's hold on the ship. Unfortunately it didn't work. I believe the concept was basically sound. The problem with the attempt was that all the earth…, or in this case, all the moon that the explosion loosened up didn't stay loose long enough for the Orysta to be pulled free."

"The idea that I suggested to Chief Engineer Plessa is demonstrated by these Youtube videos. Of course, this is the general concept in its simplest form. They show what we intend to achieve, but with a different principle than what is used in the videos. I will explain as you watch it." she said as she gestured over the table with her hand.

A video began to play. Since it was a two dimensional image, the Orysta's main computer displayed it in a unique manner. The video was displayed in a single plane of polarized light. That plane was replicated and rotated one half of a degree until a cylinder of projections was created. The resulting effect was that anyone looking at the projection would clearly see only the plane that was perpendicular to their eyes, so that everyone saw the same thing and from the same perspective.

The video showed a metal plate supported on an audio transducer. Grains of sand were then sprinkled on the plate. The demonstrator then fed the transducer with different sound frequencies causing the plate to vibrate at that frequency, and the sand grains to move to form different geometric patterns on the plate. As the frequency was changed, the sand danced over the plate to coalesce into different patterns.

"On this first video you see a sound frequency signal causing a metal plate to vibrate. The sand particles come together to show you a visual presentation of what different sections of the metal plate are actually doing. Notice that it does not vibrate as a single unit as you might imagine, but has different areas of the plate acting as separately vibrating sections. Notice also that as the frequency is changed the shape and size of these vibrating sections also changes as they interact with each other. Now let's watch one more video."

She gestured with her hand again, and a different video began to play. In this video small, light foam particles were held suspended in the air by sound wave energy emitted by strategically placed speakers, where they formed and maintained a geometric pattern while being levitated. The intact pattern was then moved around to different positions in the air when the energy level was varied in each speaker. The video became more interesting to those watching when different heavier items such as electronic components, hardware, and various plastic parts were levitated and manipulated in the air. The group quickly began to realize the practical applications of what they were watching.

"This second video," she continued, "shows materials of different size and density being levitated and moved around by sound waves generated by the surrounding speakers. What material, and how much of it that can be manipulated depends on the frequencies of the sound and how powerful the sound waves are. Of course, in both of these videos even the heaviest object being moved and levitated are still relatively light."

"So much for the introduction." she continued. "Now to the point. By applying a similar technique to what you just viewed, we believe we can shift the moon material pressing against the Orysta. We believe, and our experiments have shown, that moving this material just a fraction of an inch and keeping it in motion will remove the pressure on the ship's hull, and we should be able to lift the Orysta out of its prison."

"Of course the problem we have here on the Moon is the lack of an atmosphere for the sound waves to propagate through. Any gas molecules held by the moons reduced gravity are so few and far apart that sound waves can't travel through them. But the Orysta has a very special capability that will allow us to achieve the same results. The Orysta can create and control gravity waves! It is with gravity waves, or to be more precise a gravity field, that we will place the ground material in motion, and keep it in motion while the ship is lifted from the ground."

Everyone's eyes were wide with surprise and excitement – especially Grilik Munen and Tahn-grilik Califas. The thought of having their ship free again had their hearts beating quickly. The room was silent, but for just a little while.

"You've already tested this?" asked Travellor.

Erika's smile widened. She knew her uncle would be the first to ask the question. She had even bet Plessa that he would.

"Yes, on a small scale." said Plessa. "We will have to reconfigure the ships field projectors, but that will not be difficult to accomplish."

"It will take a tremendous amount of power, but we can do it." added Erika. "The Orysta is capable of generating an unbelievable level of energy by Earth standards. This ship, in its present damaged condition, is amazingly capable of supplying the peak power requirements of the entire North American continent on a continuous basis, for a period of twenty months or more. It's mind blowing! During the attempt we will have to eliminate the field extending to the base for the short period of time it takes. All personnel will have to be aware that they will be under the influence of the reduced gravity for that period. Even within the Orysta normal gravity will be suspended."

Her statements hit Travellor, Farber-Chatwell, and Ramsdel like a shock wave. It just couldn't be possible for a single machine the size of the Orysta to generate that much energy. Their first thought was that Erika was either exaggerating or mistaken. Travellor stared at his niece, and soon realized she was stating the facts as she knew them. She had been working closely with Plessa, and no other human had before been given the information on Ganaphe' technology that had been made available to her. His mouth hung open at the realization that what he had believed the Ganaphe' capabilities were hadn't come close to the reality. Why hadn't he realized this before. He – no, not only he – everyone had become so comfortable with what the Ganaphe' had shared with them that they failed to consider how much more they were capable of.

It made sense now that he thought about it. How else could you move a ship this size through galaxies, and in practical time periods, without tremendous amounts of energy. And from what the Ganaphe' had told him about their war ships the Orysta was a comparatively small vessel! He sat silently in thought as the others conversed with each other.

"That's the simple explanation of course. There is a lot more to it, but that's the basic idea." finished Erika.

"How will you lift the ship?" asked Califas, excitedly. "The Moon Base ships no longer have the same engines that were used for the first attempt. I believe the new engines are not suitable for this application."

"That is correct." said Plessa, as he gestured over the table. "We are all familiar with the Orysta's present situation." Several small images appeared high over the table. He touched one and dragged it downward. It blossomed into a larger image of the Orysta, complete with all the rocks, gravel and sand pressing against its hull. "Indicate attachment points and show shuttle craft positions during first recovery attempt." he instructed the computer.

Now six bright red spots showed on the upper part of the hull. Dark blue lines went from them to the smaller images of the shuttles. Plessa continued.

"For our first attempt we ran cables from the attachment points to the six ships above the surface. They provided the lift necessary for the attempt. Most of you are familiar with this." Plessa gave everyone time to look at the image.

"So that's what you did." said Ramsdel, looking closely at the image. "I'm sorry I missed that."

"Then you will be here for the next attempt." said Farber-Chatwell. "You need to spend more time here to get first hand knowledge of the operation."

Ramsdel shook his head in agreement, while still studying the image.

"Show Aimsler frame" said Plessa.

The six shuttles disappeared from the image, replaced by a dark rectangular frame structure, internally divided with cross members into a three by five array. Projecting downwards at each cross member intersection were short stubs that ended in rocket nozzles. Twenty-four of them.

"Please continue Erika." said Plessa.

"There are twenty-four solid-liquid hybrid fuel rocket engines that will supply the lifting force to pull the Orysta free of the ground. The solid

310

fuel is contained in the chambers above the nozzles. The fluid oxidizer is contained in the hollow frame. By using the frame to hold part of the fuel supply we can carry more total fuel and extend the maximum burn time. Commander Farber-Chatwell has supplied us with the performance specs of the rockets, and has confirmed that the thrust control modifications we need will not be a problem to add. As in the first attempt, power output of all rockets will be monitored and controlled by the Orysta's main computer, since it has the processing power to monitor and control them in real time."

"Also, as in the first attempt," she continued, "explosive charges will be placed. However, since gravity waves will be the force that keeps the smaller materials fluid, these charges will instead be used to fracture the large rocks and boulders that are in direct contact with the hull. They will be more powerful than before, but there will be fewer of them. This increases the possibility of outer skin penetration but Chief Engineer Plessa believes it will not cause any damage that can't be repaired."

She took a sip of water to soothe her dry throat, and gave everyone a few seconds to think about what she had told them.

"There is one more major item to consider. There is a break-free point where the grip of the surrounding soil will suddenly give way, causing the ship to quickly shoot up and out of the ground. The ship would slingshot up before the thrust of the rocket engines can be cut off. This is a limitation of the engines and not of the computer controlling them. If we cut the engines when this happens the ship will impact the frame. The damage could be serious. If we leave the engines throttled up the frame will pull the ship away from the moon. Since the Orysta is not capable of normal flight and landing, it could be very tricky trying to bring her back to the surface without damage. So we propose an alternate option, which you will have to decide on. We believe the best choice to get the Orysta safely on the surface is to quickly shut down the engines at the first indication of the break-free point. The computer can easily detect this by monitoring the vertical rate of motion. Also notice in this simulation that as the ship is being lifted, the still fluid ground materials will flow under the ship, filling in the cavity that forms below and automatically building support underneath the ship."

Erika touched the projected image and it played like a movie, showing the ship being pulled up by the frame with its engines glowing white, and the soil and rocks flowing in underneath it. Then the engines went dim and the ship stopped rising.

"Because of this back fill the ship cannot fall back down. We estimate that the break-free point will be six to ten feet below the surface, so this is where the ship will rest at engine shutdown. We can't estimate any closer than that because of the variation in material surrounding the ship. But with the ship at that level, it should by easy to remove the remaining ground material, and build a lifting frame to mechanically raise the ship the rest of the way. Thirty-six hours after the start of the attempt the Orysta should be free and on the surface, standing on its landing gear. Chief Engineer Plessa has all the calculations and test results. The decision is yours to make." she concluded, as she looked around at the faces looking back at her. She suddenly realized she was tired.

Munen and Califas called Plessa to them and began discussing more of the details. There was a lot of preparation to be done if the plan went ahead.
Travellor looked at his niece, who had sat down in a chair at the front of the room. Vicious had moved next to her, and she stroked the robot's head like someone might do to a pet. He could tell she was physically and mentally drained. She must have pushed herself to make this presentation, and now that it was over the exhaustion was taking over. He wanted to go over and put an arm around her, but she wouldn't like that with everyone around. He had promised to treat her like any one else. It was a very difficult promise to keep.

2

Erika couldn't remember the last time she felt this tired, if ever. It wasn't just physical. After the presentation of the plan to lift the Orysta from the ground, she had decided to take up the open invitation from Mersuul to use her quarters on the ship. Her mind was fatigued and she was aware that her thinking was slow. She was especially aware of that after making the mistake of standing in the shower and telling the computer to '*Give me everything you've got.*' The resulting impact of water was not what she was expecting. She was sure she swallowed most of the Orysta's water supply before being able to order the computer to turn the shower off. There was a lot about living on the ship that no one had told her – like drowning in the shower! Or maybe they had mentioned it, but with her thinking so impaired it was hard to remember. '*The Orysta gets kudos for its hair dryer.*' she thought. '*It took only a couple of minutes.*' She knew she was hungry, but was too tired to be bothered with eating.

"Goodnight Vicious." she said as she slid onto the bed.
"*Goodnight Erica.*" replied the little robot. "*Sleep well.*"

She lay down and closed her eyes, thinking that the bed was surprisingly comfortable. As she began to fall asleep she realized how perfect the room temperature was, and that she didn't need any covers. Then for some reason she opened her eyes and looked down at the bed. It was ten inches below her. Her body was floating in the air, perfectly supported at all points. It was unbelievably comfortable.

"I have to get one of these." she mumbled, while closing her eyes again. "Vicious, remind… me to get …"

She never finished the sentence. Sleep had finally caught her. It was eleven hours later when she woke up.

3

"Hi aunt Jen. Hi uncle Phil. Hi guys."

"Hi Erika. How are you?" came the delayed combined reply over the computer screen. They were all trying to adjust to the lag between remarks.

"I'm doing alright. How are you?"

"Erika, sweetheart, you look tired. What are they doing to you there?" asked her aunt. "Don't they give you any time to rest?"

"Oh, that's my fault." she replied, letting out a deep breath. "I've been so involved with my work that I've been pushing myself. Putting in a lot of hours. I'm working with a really great mechanical engineer. I've learned a lot of new things. Do I look that bad?"

"Well your eyes are dark, and you look like you could use a good nights sleep." said her uncle Phil. "And maybe some time on a beach. I thought Tony would take better care of you."

"Can't blame Uncle Tony." she said. "I told him when we arrived that I didn't want anyone to know I was his niece, and I didn't want special treatment. But it's OK. I've got some down time for the next couple of days, and I plan to catch up on my sleep."

"How is Tony?"

"He's fine. I'm having dinner with him tonight. He's been very busy also. There is no lack of work around here. This place is like a bee hive."

"When are you coming for a visit E? I miss you." said Ernst.

"I miss you too. All of you. I want to give each of you a big hug. Probably won't be able to get some time off for a month or two. I'll talk to uncle Tony about it, and let you know. So what have you all been up to?…"

4

Travellor heard the page tone from the comm box and pushed the answer button.

"Commander, this is Browning in Comm. Orysta's number two shuttle is approaching the base."

"Number two? They've been gone for days. Wonder where they've been."

"Sir, the General is aboard. He requests that you meet the shuttle outside when they arrive."

"Outside?"

"Yes sir. They won't be landing in the Orysta."

"E-T-A?"

"Forty minutes."

"Tell him I'll be there."

"Will do."

Travellor took a last sip of his coffee, and left his office. It would take him about thirty minutes to suit up and get outside. That would leave him ten minutes for a quick visual inspection of the base while he was out.

5

Travellor had just finished his walk around the structure when the landing pad lights turned on. When he looked up he couldn't see the shuttle clearly. It was obstructed by a large dark object underneath it. When it was closer to the ground he could see the shuttle piggy-backed on top of it. Landing gear then dropped from underneath the dark object, and it made contact with the ground.

"Travellor? Is that you?" came a voice in his helmet.

"Yes General. What have you brought me?"

"Stand by. We have to uncouple from the other ship."

That caught Travellor by surprise. He wasn't notified about a new ship, or that it was being delivered to the base. Not to mention the fact that it was already completely assembled, something that was normally done in the base hangar. What surprised him just as much was its size. Taking into account its manta ray shape, he guessed that internally it was as large as one of the Orysta's shuttles. It took a few minutes, but slowly the shuttle lifted off from the top of the new ship and landed next to it.

The shuttle's door opened and one person got out of it. When he was clear, he waved back at the shuttle, which lifted off and flew to the Orysta's open access doors.

"Hello Commander." said Farber-Chatwell through the comm link."I've brought you a new toy. Let's get a crew out here and tow it inside. I hope keeping one of the Ganaphe' shuttles for so long didn't inconvenience. We had to travel a lot slower than normal with it attached." He turned and looked back at the ship. "I think we got it here without scratching the paint."

6

The hangar bay was noisy from the conversations of people who had time from their duties, both human and ganaphe'. It had been a constant rotation of faces once the word got out about the new ship. Some had been here more than once. Everyone was curious about it, and apparently not even Grilik Munen had been made aware of its existence. For the first time in the moon base's short existence a completely assembled and operational ship had been delivered there. People were curious about that also. Was this to be the new modus operandi for the base? No details had yet been released about it.

"It's beautiful!" said John Smith. "I can't wait to get my hands on the controls."

"I wonder what nav and instrumentation is like." said George Washington. "You can bet this is not like our present ships. One of the techs said it had an experimental quantum computer that is interfaced with all the systems."

"You're right, and we're the ones who get to fly it first."

"You think so?"

"Hell yes! We have seniority on this base. We BETTER be the ones, or I'm gonna have a word with the brass. Huh! Look at this. It looks like most of the skin has been dimpled – like the outside of a golf ball."

"You are absolutely right. We should have first shot at it. I wonder if they've programmed the flight simulator yet?"

"Don't think so. The flight lab guys are over there. That dumbfounded look on their faces tells me they're as surprised by this as everyone else."

"And speaking of the brass, I don't see any of them here."

"Kibbee said there was a big meeting going on. They're all probably there."

"What the hell!" said Smith as he looked at the ship's trailing edge. "What are these holes for?"

7

"OK. I think everyone's here now." said Farber-Chatwell as he looked at the assembled group.

Around the conference table were all the command level personnel, several engineering staff, Mersuul-sil-Vaana, Brighde Balfour, and Erika

Aimsler who was there at the request of Chief Engineer Plessa. Travellor smiled at his niece across the table, but said nothing to her. She returned the smile. The projector was turned on displaying an image of the new ship. It wasn't as impressive as the three dimensional depictions on the Orysta but it would get the job done.

"This is our latest ship design. I call it Travellor's Folly…"

"WHAT! Whoa. Wait a minute." said Travellor. "Why is it my folly? I didn't have anything to do with that."

"… As I was about to explain," continued Farber-Chatwell, "over sixteen months ago Commander Travellor submitted a report which outlined several programs that he felt 361 should undertake immediately. The basis for this report was his belief that Orysta personnel and ship would not be around for much longer. He speculated that within a relatively short time the Orysta would be freed of its prison and that an alternate means of propulsion would give you the option of attempting the journey home."

"Although the report was not discussed much with the Commander after he submitted it, it was disseminated to a wide group at 361. No one could argue with its premises. It stated what many had known but didn't want to think about. Doctor Eckelberry Cove was one of the people that had read the report, and he told me it motivated him to many restless nights. He is a brilliant man as we all know, and this ship is the result of those lost hours of sleep."

"The Commander suggested we develop two separate flight platforms. One for atmospheric use and one for space. Cove is a man who values efficiency, and developing two different space craft, as the Commander suggested, made no sense to him. He felt that developing one ship that could operate both in and outside a planetary atmosphere made more sense than having two separate designs. Who was I to argue with Eckelberry Cove? I had him submit a proposal to accomplish this, and gave him the resources he asked for. This ship is the result. I'll cover the major features today, but more detailed documentation is available to all here. There are some classified systems, but they shouldn't keep anyone from

318

understanding the design."

Farber-Chatwell pressed the button on the remote control, and the image on the screen changed to a rear view with labels indicating various features on the ship.

"Lets start with the propulsion systems. This ship has two. The eight holes spaced along the trailing edge are the Ion Drive system. We studied what NASA has developed in their Evolutionary Xenon Thruster program, and Cove made some modifications to their system. The result is the Forced Ion Pulse engine. This is a high capacity, sustained output, compressed Ion Drive, capable of accelerating the ship to speeds beyond the two hundred thousand miles per hour achieved by the primary engine, for very long periods of time. This is a secondary system. Once the ship is accelerated to speed by its primary propulsion system the ship switches to Ion thrust for efficiency. Its main function is to compensate for gravitational influences when the ship is close to a planetary or other large body."

"The primary propulsion system is this engine." he said, using his laser pointer to indicate the much larger variable duct exhaust nozzle. "This is the business end of the latest Cove engine. We've had it under development for the last six months, and Cove has been thinking about it for a lot longer than that. It's a good thing that 361 owns a lot of the companies that forge and fabricate the necessary components or we would never have completed it this quickly. When he was ready to build it, we prioritized the program. It's been extensively tested to failure. The engine is capable of safely developing two point five million pounds of maximum operational thrust..."

The voices immediately rose around the table.

"Excuse me General." said Plessa, with a touch of disbelief in his voice. "Are you certain you mean 'million' pounds of thrust? In an engine that size? Is it a one use only engine?"

Murmurs of agreement came from most in the room. Farber-Chatwell broke into a big smile. He half expected the reaction.

"Million pounds of thrust is correct, and no it is not a one time use engine. Of course, it takes several minutes to reach that level of output. To instantaneously put out that much thrust would destroy the ship – and the engine. There are safety backups built into the engine that will stop the pilot from accidentally or intentionally doing that, controlled by an experimental quantum computer that interfaces with all of the ship's systems. If continuous acceleration is commanded the engine will put out maximum thrust as quickly as it can safely do so. 'Safely' being defined as without destroying the ship."

"What's the TBO on the main engine?" asked Travellor.

"When operated in space at seventy-five percent max thrust, the TBO is estimated to be over six months. That's six months continuous use! In atmosphere it drops to about one-sixth of that. We expect a much longer operational life when used under normal conditions. The ship when fully equipped and crewed can carry enough fuel for forty-four hours of continuous max output engine operation. It's not designed to travel outside our solar system. It's a damn good first step in our inter-planetary spacecraft evolution, in my opinion."

Erika Aimsler had sat for the last few minutes with her mouth open, as had most of the others in the room. She had familiarized herself with the Cove engines presently being used on the base, and this was light years beyond those. She performed some mental calculations. At perigee, when the moon is closest to the Earth, this ship could travel that distance in less than three hours if it performed as claimed. That would make it almost as useful as a Ganaphe' shuttle. She looked at the others in the room who were conversing with each other about what they had just heard. Then she looked at her uncle who was sitting quietly in thought with a hand on his chin. His lips were pursed as he stared down at the floor. He wasn't very happy about this development. It was then it struck her that his prediction about the

Ganaphe' was closer to coming true. She was going to help them free their ship, and this new Cove engine, maybe modified or made larger, might be the engine they decide to use to help them begin their journey home. Then she looked at Mersuul, who also was staring at her uncle. She had a conflicted expression on her face. She too had realized the same thing.

"Let's continue." said Farber-Chatwell. "Since we do not yet have the ability to camouflage our ships, the Folly is designed with the latest stealth technology. In keeping with that the weapons systems are carried internally as per the F-22 fighter. It also has external hard points for attaching additional systems and loads. For added strength, parts of the structure of the ship are made using a manufacturing technique that emulates bamboo. For those not familiar with that, the alloy grain size gradually increases from the outside to the center, giving added resilience. We have researchers at North Carolina State University to thank for that idea. I'll be visiting that campus in the near future, to see if there are any good candidates for 361 to hire."

"Flight training will begin next week. Simulator software should be completed by then. I am expecting the first test flight from here to take place as soon as pilots are qualified. In the mean time flight crews will begin learning the instrumentation. The Folly is a prototype ship, with prototype engines, and several prototype systems. Although everything has been well tested separately, it has not been field tested as a system. I believe it's obvious to everyone that this testing will be dangerous – but then it usually is."

8

"Terrain mapping complete."

"Message received base four. Return to landing bay." replied Brighde Balfour from the flight control center. The updated three dimensional terrain mapping data would be used by the Orysta's computer

321

to camouflage the ship when it was back on the surface. "Orysta one and two. Position Aimsler frame when area cleared."

"Orysta one confirms."

"Orysta two is confirming"

Balfour moved around the control center almost as if nothing had changed, primarily because of the weights she had borrowed from the gym and belted onto her waist. Trailblazer Moon Base was now operating at moon level gravity. Some people found hopping and skipping around entertaining, while others found it annoying. They had long ago taken for granted the Earth level gravity that was maintained by the Orysta, forgetting that it was not natural here on the Moon. Now the gravity field from the ship was no longer extended to the base. They were also disconnected from the ship's power feed, operating on base power systems which would serve as a good test of the base power generation capabilities.

Balfour looked at the two Ganaphe' shuttle craft hovering above the crater's edge, with the rocket frame hanging below them. The base was on the far side of the Moon now, but the very bright outside area lights illuminated the scene. She watched the area closer to the base and saw base shuttle four clear the airspace and smoothly slip through the landing bay entrance. She loved working with crews of this high caliber. It kept communications to a minimum. Everyone knew their jobs and how to do it.

The Ganaphe' shuttles slowly moved into position. Balfour's attention moved to the younger woman who was looking out the transparent dome at the activities outside. She could see the tension and nervousness in her posture, which wasn't surprising. The plan belonged to Erika Aimsler, and if it failed it would be her failure as much or more than anyone else's. That would be the way it would be seen anyway. If Balfour was in her position she would be just as tense.

The steel reinforced carbon fiber frame with its twenty-four attached rockets was gently lowered to the ground, where members of the Orysta crew were waiting to attach the cables. Balfour waited for them to notify her when they were ready.

"You're not going to be on the Orysta with Engineer Plessa?"

"Grilik Munen said it would be too dangerous. He didn't want me inside the risk zone. But I can monitor everything on your displays here."

"That's understandable. All of the Orysta crew except for Munen, Califas, and Plessa have left the ship."

"Yes,… but I still feel like I should be there."

"You know, I've spent a lot of time with the Orysta crew getting ready for this event. They all think very highly of you – especially Plessa. None of them would want you in any danger. Let me rephrase that – in any more danger than what comes with living on the Moon."

They watched together as the frame touched down, and the cables were attached. They listened to the two crews coordinating their actions. Then the shuttles lifted the frame until the cable were taut, and then moved sideways out of the trajectory path of the frame.

"Grilik Munen, this is shuttle one. Both shuttles are at cable tension and holding." said the voice on the radio.

"Commander Balfour this is Grilik Munen. We have completed the checklist and I am turning control over to you."

"Message received Grilik Munen. All personnel, this is Flight Commander Balfour. Operation Second Chance is in effect. All personnel to assigned stations. All safety protocols are in effect. Stand by for further instructions."

Balfour had just finished speaking as the outside crew entered the access door to Trailblazer base and secured it. The area of operation was now clear of all equipment and personnel.

"Orysta, please confirm your computer has control of the frame engines." said Balfour.

"This is Califas confirming Orysta has computer link and control of frame."

"Thank you Tahn-grilik. Maintenance team, report status."

"This is Valian. Maintenance team confirms all systems disconnected from Orysta. Access door secured."

"You ready for this?" asked Balfour, looking at Erika.

"I've got all my fingers and toes crossed." she answered.

"OK. Here goes." Balfour tapped the comm button. "Orysta, give me minimal output from the four corners please."

A couple of seconds later the four corner rocket engines ignited and glowed dimly. The tension on the cables increased. Erika thought she could hear the cables straining but knew it was only her imagination.

"Shuttles one and two, report."

"This is shuttle one. Frame is holding tension on its own power."

"This is shuttle two confirming."

"Good. Excellent! Shuttles one and two, disconnect from frame. Maintain hovering position outside of the operation zone."

The two ships disconnected their cables from the frame, and moved back to their original position over the crater's edge. The frame held stable in the position they had left it.

"All personnel, this is Flight Commander Balfour. Please put on your safety glasses or view only from a prescribed location. Do not look directly at the rocket engines with bare eyes. Orysta, the operation area is clear. The frame is holding stable. I am returning control over to you. Keep communication channel open throughout the operation. Please confirm."

"Flight control, this is Munen confirming. We have control of the operation. We will maintain communication channel open."

Balfour sat on her chair and rolled it over to Erika.

"Nothing to do now but watch. Did you bring the popcorn?" she joked, drawing a small smile from Erika. "Glasses on everyone." she said to the others.

9

Several minutes passed in silence. Outside, the area lights illuminated the inside of the crater like it was daylight. Erika looked over to her uncle and Mersuul, who were standing side by side as they looked out at the floating rocket frame. She noticed he was holding her hand, which was something he never did while on duty. That was when she knew that he both feared and hoped for the success of the attempt. With the Orysta free of its prison, his prediction of the Ganaphe' going back home might happen sooner than he wanted. It wouldn't be that difficult for them if Cove's new engine performed as it was expected to. They could mount three or four of the engines to the Orysta to achieve enough performance to get to inter-galactic trade lanes in just months. All they would need to do then would be to make radio contact to request a rescue – a rescue that would arrive at inter-galactic speed. They could be back home with their families in less than a year. The thought made her a little sad. She was just getting to know these people, and she had become very fond of Mersuul.

Mersuul and her uncle were both in space suits with their helmets on a nearby desk, just in case. Lifting the Orysta was a dangerous endeavor, and if anything went wrong all hands had to be able to give assistance as quickly as possible. Erika noticed Mersuul's iridescent hair, which always seemed brighter when the woman was near her uncle. Ganaphe' women of reproductive age had that coloring in their hair. An evolutionary holdover from when their home world was mostly dark, before it was pulled into stable orbit with their two suns. What a geologically violent era that must have been. There was no doubt about what was on Mersuul's mind, and Erika wondered if her uncle felt the same way.

"Bringing all engines into operation." came Plessa's voice over the speakers.

The nozzles of all the other engines illuminated and glowed like the four that were already active. Even in the bright area lighting the engines could not be looked at without the protective glasses.

"Instruments indicate all engines functional. Performing low level short term throttle control test."

Half of the engines' output flames grew longer and brighter, like blow torches that had their valves opened up, and then diminished again. Then the other half was tested.

"Computer indicates that three engines are not generating design thrust. Performing full output test to calibrate engines." said Plessa.

The flames of three of the engines grew longer and very bright, and the frame seemed to strain slightly against the cables. Then the flames diminished again.

"Engine calibration procedure was successful, and compensation factors calculated. Main computer indicates the Aimsler frame is operational and ready. Extending gravitational field around the Orysta... Gravitational field at full strength and holding." stated Plessa.

"Commander Balfour, this is Munen. The Orysta is ready to initiate extraction if you are ready on the surface. Please indicate your status."

"All surface assets are in place and ready Grilik Munen. We'll take our cues from your lead." replied Balfour without hesitation. She had already confirmed everyone was on station and ready.

10

Orysta's Chief Engineer performed a visual check on his instruments. At his station he could monitor the output thrust of the frame's rocket engines, the frame's elevation above the ground, a digital readout of the stress on the lift cables, the amount of pressure imposed on the hull by the surrounding rocks and soil, and the distortion forces on the ship's superstructure. Behind his station, located where all three crew members could see it, was a three dimensional depiction of the Orysta in its predicament. Surrounding the ship was a transparent pink, elliptical, hollow cylinder with thirty foot thick walls, that depicted the gravity field. The pink extended below the Orysta and went upward to several inches above the ground, but did not touch the ship. The gravity field was completely external. If it had been extended internally the forces they were about to generate would have caused tremendous damage to the Orysta.

"We are ready Grilik." he said.

"The ship is under your control." said Munen. "Intul and I will help you monitor the instruments and yell if we see anything abnormal."

Plessa nodded his confirmation.

"Commander Balfour, this is Plessa. We are ready to initiate the operation."

"Understood Engineer Plessa. Communications will be broadcast base wide. Proceed at your discretion."

Plessa looked one more time at his crew-mates, getting a nod from each of them. Then he adjusted the controls on his display.

"Initiating optimum resonant oscillation of the gravity field." he informed them.

The pink cylinder on the three dimensional depiction started moving out and in at an increasingly faster rate, becoming less distinct and slightly more transparent. It took only a brief period to achieve the optimum oscillating frequency that Plessa and Erika had determined through experimentation. Inside the ship they could hear a scratching noise coming from the outside, which then turned into a constant high pitched hum. They felt the ship shift and drop a little.

"Initiating programmed computer control." he said, tapping his control screen.

The Orysta's main computer adjusted the combined thrust on the Aimsler frame until the ship was stable in its position.

"Gravity field optimum resonance achieved." said the computer.

The soil in the gravity field was shifted in and out under the influence of the alternating positive and negative gravity field. At the optimum resonant frequency the granules moved at different rates due to their differing sizes, and bounced of each other. Unable to make continuous contact with the adjacent piece of soil, the ground became fluid. It moved in waves and ripples. On the Moon's surface, above the Orysta, the ground resembled an undulating swamp.

"Ready to trigger explosive charges." said Plessa to his companions. Then directing his words to the moon base he said "Miss Aimsler, please trigger the explosives now."

In the flight control center, Erika heard his words come over the comm system. In front of her was a display screen displaying only a yellow rectangle with the words 'Explosive Charges' written in the middle. Since Erika would not be allowed on the ship during the operation, Plessa came up with this solution to make her part of it. She touched the rectangle with her finger. It turned red.

Her action was immediately felt on the Orysta as the large rocks pressing against the ships hull were blown apart causing them to strike the ship with powerful hammer blows. The ship rocked and vibrated for a few seconds. Califas, who had been standing at the time, was knocked off of his feet. He pulled himself back into his seat.

"Explosives sequence concluded. Beginning lift sequence." said the
computer.

On each of their screens replicating the Engineer's control panel the rocket
engine throttle controls moved to maximum.

The glow of the rocket engines suddenly changed from their
relatively dim red-orange glow to a blindingly white explosion of light.
Everyone in the flight control room had to cover their eyes or look away.
The illumination by the rocket engines turned the area into a surreal
monochromatic landscape – everything was white, with little detail. If this
part of the Moon had been facing the Earth, anyone looking with only their
bare eyes would have noticed the flare.

It was slow at first, but the Orysta definitely began to move upward.
Even Plessa, who had been one of the two people to put this event into
action, was wide-eyed in pleasant surprise as the ship began to move. His
instruments verified each incremental change in their position. The
movement was not constant as the ship moved through differing materials,
sometimes accelerating and sometimes temporarily thumping to a stop –
but it kept moving upward. Munen and Califas began to scream in
excitement.

11

"It is working! Orysta is being lifted!" said Mersuul.

Erika strained to see what was happening. Her eyes had adjusted to
looking at the brightly illuminated scene through the glasses, and she
watched her plans work as she had designed. She also was feeling the
excitement. The cables attaching the ship to the rocket frame were color
marked every three feet, to give a visual reference, and she could already
see the first mark – and it was continuing to rise. The surface of the ground
had begun to bulge upward.

"Orysta, this is Balfour. We are seeing positive motion up here!"

"YES!" came the reply from Plessa, with encouraging screams in the background. "We are moving! We are coming up!"

The excitement had spread throughout the base. The communication between the ship and flight control center was being piped through every speaker. Those who could, stopped what they were doing to listen. Those near a window tried to see through the bright light of the rockets. The ship was rising at a rate of one foot per minute and accelerating. It wasn't long before the second mark was seen on the cables. Happy, excited yelling was all that was coming over the comm from the Orysta, encouraging the ship to keep on going. The rest of her crew now looking through the windows in the Engineering lab were also yelling in excitement.

Travellor winced as his fingers were being squeezed by both of Mersuul's hands. He looked at her, but she didn't notice. Her attention was completely focused on the outside, and she had no idea she was squeezing his hand that hard. He didn't say anything, not wanting to interrupt the triumphant moment. He could take a little pain – for her.

As the ship continued its upward journey both Erika and Balfour had slowly begun to rise from their chairs. Soon they were both standing, their hands pressed against the console as they unconsciously leaned forward. Erika was taking short breaths in her excitement, which grew with each new inch of cable that became visible. It was working. Her plan – her design – her idea and solution was working!

"Outer hull penetration." came the computer's voice over the comm. *"Damage terminated."*

The words were like cold water over Erika's head. She tapped the comm button.

"Orysta, report status." she blurted.

330

"Outer hull was penetrated." came back Plessa's voice. "Minor damage within safety limits. It does not affect extraction. Operation is continuing."

The entire base seemed to release a communal sigh of relief. Everyone had been briefed that the ship might be damaged in the attempt to raise it. For a moment they worried the operation would be stopped. Plessa's reply gave reassurance it was still possible to get the Orysta on the surface. Everyone's attention was soon back on the outside of the base.

"Elevation plus one point five limm. Rate of climb two limms per mirlot." said the computer.

12

The average rate of movement had stabilized at two limms per mirlot, or approximately two yards every two point eight minutes. This progress varied now and then as the ship pushed through materials of different density. It had taken twenty-four minutes to raise the Orysta fifty-four feet, and it continued to rise. That wouldn't last much longer. That thought had just passed through Erika's mind when the rocket engines reduced their thrust level. Orysta's computer had determined the ship had reached break-free and throttled them back. The thrust level now would hold the ship in position while the ground stabilized.

Erika watched as the four foot high mound of soil that depicted the Orysta's outline vibrated and slowly ebbed away as the still fluid soil moved down to fill the empty space below the ship. Some minutes passed, and where the mound had been was now a slight depression in the shape of the Orysta. Soil particles bounced around on the top of that depression, indicating the gravity field was still operating.

"Flight control, this is Munen. We have reached the break-free level. WE'VE DONE IT! WE'VE DONE IT!" came the excited call.

Erika could imagine the Orysta's crew jumping up and down in happy celebration. That was when all the tension and fear of failure hit her. While everyone in the flight control room was happy and screaming and clapping, and she herself was smiling broadly, the tears flowed uncontrollably from her eyes. Her body began to shake. It wasn't anything she could control. Her adrenalin levels were high from all the emotions she had been feeling, and now her body was burning up that adrenalin by vibrating her muscles.

She felt arms around her shoulders, and saw that it was Mersuul who was holding her. There was a big smile on her face, and Erika couldn't help but smile back.

"Do not worry. The shaking will pass. Your body is reacting to everything that has happened."

"I know." said Erika, nodding her head. "I just don't know why I'm crying."

"Tears of joy."

She looked at Mersuul and saw tears in her eyes also. Then she looked at her uncle who had a huge smile on his face. Then he gave her two thumbs up.

"Reducing gravity field." said Plessa, over the comm. A few seconds later he said "Gravity field terminated.", followed by "Orysta is stable. There is no motion."

Another cheer went through the room.

"Initiating landing of Aimsler frame by computer control." said Plessa.

The thrust of the rocket engines diminished until the frame began to slowly come down to the ground. The computer control was so good the frame landed softly. Then the engines shut down completely.

"Commander Balfour, this is Munen. You have control of the final phase of the operation."

"Roger, Grilik Munen. I have control. Shuttles one and two, take your positions over the frame. Ground crew – attach the frame to the shuttle cables when they are in position."

"Grilik Munen, this is Travellor. How far below the surface is the Orysta?"

"Commander, the Orysta is one point three limm below the surface. I could clean away that amount of soil with a dust pan. Over."

"Wow!" remarked Travellor to Balfour. "He's in a good mood."

Everyone was in a good mood. There's nothing like a successful operation to make people feel good.

The cleanup of the operation took less than three hours. The mining crew quickly established a path down to the ship. Power conduits from the Orysta were run up to the surface and over ground to the moon base. The radar terrain mapping data had been translated by the Orysta's computer and the camouflage was again operational. Anyone looking down onto this area would see the same surface features that were there before the operation. A surface passageway would have to be built to the ship once it was completely out of the ground, which would be accomplished within forty-eight hours, since the hydraulic jacks needed for the job only had to be positioned around the ship and attached to the hull. But that was for tomorrow. Tonight was for celebrating.

13

"That was a nice gesture by Munen, to make Erika an honorary crew member of the Orysta." remarked Travellor. "I'll have to thank him."

"He did not make her an honorary crew member. He made her an actual part of the crew. It is within his authority as Grilik of the Orysta to do so. Her name is now logged in the ship's record as a crew member." said Mersuul, as she wrapped her arms around his neck and kissed him lightly on the lips. "It was suggested by Chief Engineer Plessa, and everyone agreed it was an appropriate way to show their gratitude for what she has done."

"Hmmm… And what exactly does it mean for her to be a crew member of the Orysta?"

"It means that she will receive an appropriate share of the profits generated by the mining operation from this time forward. If we continue to mine crystal-flow in the quantities that we have been, her share would be a significant amount of currency. When we return home an account will be created for her."

"Yes… when you return home." he said, the smile disappearing from his face.

Mersuul looked into his eyes, her expression now serious.

"You are both my greatest pleasure in life, and my greatest problem." she said, knowing an explanation wasn't necessary.

"As you are to me." he responded, pulling her tightly to him and placing his face against hers. "You know that Erika is already a fairly wealthy young woman. She doesn't really need the money."

"I know that she is, but the money she makes as a member of the Orysta crew will be accessible to her on any IGT signatory planet. Her biometric information is in Orysta's database, and that is what we use for identification."

"Huh." he grunted. "So now Plessa and Munen want her to go planet hopping with them. Why is it that Plessa always seems to be trying to steal my niece from me?"

"She reminds him of his daughter." she said with a touch of sadness in her voice. "He has never been away from her for such a long period of time before. He is homesick. We all are."

"Yes…, I know your are…" he said, with an empathetic look on his face.

Mersuul noticed his expression and held Travellor in a hug, with her face against his chest. He wrapped his arms around her and pulled her tighter to him.

"You keep me sane." she said. "You are the happiness that counteracts my sadness. Whenever I imagine going back home, you are always with me."

14

Erika had completed feeding the terrain mapping data to the four ground moving robots. They would now recreate the landscape features that had existed before the Orysta was lifted. It was the last item on her to-do list for the day. She left her duties and her computer in Mersuul's cabin, quickly changed into her sweats, and told Vicious to follow her. Minutes later she and Vicious entered the moon base's solarium.

Inside, they were all naked – all seven of them, laying on their towels on the sand. They preferred it that way, to get an over-all tan. They could have worn bathing suits if they wanted. It was their choice. But why do things half way? Surrounding them was a blue sky, and at their feet were waves splashing on the shore but never getting anything wet. The palm trees swayed in a gentle breeze which flowed over their skin. Erika stripped down and hung up her clothes, then found a spot next to Mersuul to spread her towel. Vicious sat down next to her.

It was Friday evening back on Earth. Once a week, on calendar Fridays, from four to eight in the evening, it was Ladies Night in the solarium, where the tropical beach of the week was recreated with all its sounds and smells. The projection was so real, people often forgot they were on the moon. When you are outnumbered by ten to one, small concessions like this were a welcome sign of appreciation. Even work schedules were manipulated if possible, so that all the women could spend the time together. It built morale and engendered appreciation of all of the different skills needed to keep the base operational – and it was fun.

All personnel on the moon base were required to spend thirty minutes, every other day, in the solarium for health purposes. Vitamin D, supplied by a pill, just wasn't the same as that created by the body itself, when exposed to sunlight – or even artificial sunlight. Ladies Night had become an established social event. Gossip and suntan lotion were the main items shared, but very often it was an experience at work. Every work day experience on a moon base was valuable knowledge. It could save your life. But tonight was more of a 'Put work out of your mind' type of night, filled with laughing and joking.

"I was in the Commanders Office this morning when Security Supervisor Kibbee came in to give his morning briefing. He was in a very good mood for some reason. The first thing he said to the Commander was that he thought a security team should be posted in here during Ladies Night and that he was volunteering to be one of the team." said Mersuul with a laugh. "The request was denied." she said, now laughing harder.

They all began laughing at the story. The men were always trying to get into the solarium during Ladies Night.

"He knew it would be denied, but he was in a very good mood. I wonder why that was?" asked Mersuul as she looked over at del Rio, who kept quiet with a big smile on her face. "You wouldn't know why he was so happy, would you Delores?"

They all laughed at del Rio's not so secret romance with Kibbee.

"It is good to know that men are men wherever you find them." said Toisae, and they all laughed again.

The rest of the evening continued in that tone. Someone had brought wine and some bread and cheese. That added to the lubrication of the gossip, as new and old stories were told. As the time passed they were all relaxed, happy, and ready for whatever else the evening would bring.

15

Munen sipped from the hot mug, and looked out the window of the moon base control tower at what he thought was the most beautiful sight he had seen in decitans. It had been that long since he had seen it. The Orysta was on the surface, supported by its own landing gear. It was scratched and dented, and bore a scar of repair where the outer hull had been breached, but all of that only gave the ship more character. He thought she was as beautiful as when he first saw her. It was in fact his home, and had been for over five decitans. Even though unoccupied rooms in the moon base had been made available to him and his crew, it was still his own cabin on the ship that he went to at night.

Of course, a cup of garva with a touch of bliml had been replaced by coffee with sugar and cream, and a few other items they had run out of were now being substituted by items from Earth. Still, the Orysta was his home. The cosmetic deformations would all be taken care of when they returned home – and he WAS going home! He knew that now more than ever, by the fact that she was free of her prison and that Eckelberry Cove was designing engines with enough power to make it practical to attempt the journey out of this solar system, and into the inter-galactic commercial trade lanes. It would take longer than normal to get there, but once they could establish communications with an IGT ship their journey would be almost over. And they would be returning with a very profitable load of crystal-flow in the cargo hold. He took another sip of coffee, and thought '*I should bring back some of this for the family to try.*'

Chapter 18

The End of August

1

X-ECN-1

Travellor felt the vibrations coming up from the floor and through his desk. He was close enough to the hangar bay to feel them as the engine on the new ship was being tested. Even though the vibrations would not reach all of the areas of the base, being damped out by the buildings structure, he wondered how the people in the Analysis department were handling it. They were directly above the hangar. Each test only lasted a few seconds, but it had been going on for hours now.

The X-ECN-1 (eXperimental – Eckelberry Cove New engine – 1), also dubbed the Travellor's Folly, was being fitted with equipment and tested to the strict standards of the moon base flight technicians. Their personal standards were so strict that even acceptable tolerances were not good enough for them. That was one of the reasons these people were stationed here. They demanded more of themselves and the others they worked with. This sometimes caused friction between them and the flight crews who were eager to get on with the mission. The technicians always won though. They had the only argument that flight crews couldn't argue with – they did it to make sure the flight crews came back alive. Who could argue with that? That didn't stop the crews from starting arguments they already knew they would loose. After all, a good argument helped release tension – sometimes. For those crews that refused to accept the inevitable there was the argument of last resort – the technicians simply pointed to the large piece of twisted metal that hung above the hangar doors. Next to it was a picture that showed that same doorway when it had been blown out,

338

the metal structure bent and torn, and the door completely missing. Everyone knew the story behind the picture, and the woman who was lucky to have lived through it. It was one of the first bits of base history they learned when coming on station.

There was no friction between the crew and technicians, with anything concerning this ship. There were just too many new systems on it, and all were to be tested in actual conditions. They had already been tested as sub-assemblies. Now they had to be tested as a whole, in the actual operating environment of space. If the engines performed as advertised – and no one doubted that they would – the ship would be far enough away from the base that rescue could take longer than the time the crew would have to survive. A catastrophic failure could occur in minutes – or seconds. In such a situation they crew did have the option of bailing out. Their suits could keep them alive long enough for help to arrive – possibly. If the situation caused damage to the ship and their suits, there would be no time for a rescue.

A Ganaphe' shuttle would be accompanying the X-ECN-1 on its maiden flight. Navigation and communication equipment from the Orysta was being installed in it now, and Tahn-grilik Califas would be part of the crew. This had become standard practice now, and everyone appreciated the support from the Ganaphe'. The X-ECN-1 had been designed with a separate electrical sub-panel designed to accept the Ganaphe' equipment, and make the job of interfacing it to the ship much easier. The shuttle and the X-ECN-1 would have their flight computers linked so that the shuttle could track and trace the ship wherever it went. That was the best case scenario anyway. If the two ships lost each other the shuttle would at least have an idea of where the other ship was headed.

The time was getting closer – maybe just days now. The imaginations of everyone on the base were working overtime. Travel at the speeds predicted for the new engine would bring interplanetary travel into the realm of practicality. No longer would people need to rely on long range space telescopes, satellites that take years to arrive, or artists renditions to see what the planets looked like. They would be able to see them with their own eyes. Yes, that would also bring with it danger, but danger never stopped the human race from attempting the presently impossible. There was always someone who believed the goal was worth the risk.

Travellor was tempted to go down to the test area and watch for a while, but he didn't want to inadvertently get in anyone's way. The operation down there was moving fast. No one would say anything to the base Commander, but he might interrupt the smooth flow of the operation. It was just his curiosity that kept bringing his mind back to the new ship. He wouldn't mind flying it himself, sometime. It looked sleek and fast. Instead he kept forcing his mind back to the paperwork in front of him. '*The hell with it.*' he thought. '*I AM the base Commander. I AM allowed anywhere on the base that I want to go. This job comes with a few perks.*' He got up from his desk, checked himself in the mirror, then left his office for the hangar. He felt the vibrations through the floor again and sped up his pace. He wanted to see what that engine looked like at full burn.

2

"Six of your people. I need them immediately, if possible." said Munen, smiling broadly with almost uncontainable glee.

"What do you need them to do?" asked Farber-Chatwell over the video link, his face displayed on the large wall mounted screen.

Califas, Plessa, Erika, Mersuul, and Mengu-sil-Valian were also seated in the office. They all knew what the excitement was about, and it showed on their faces.

"I want to put more of my people on the mining team to increase the production rate. I need six temporary personnel to take their places at those stations on the ship. They will be monitoring and adjusting the equipment, and we can train them quickly in what needs to be done. Technicians would be best suited for the duties."

"That's a large part of our staffing." said Travellor. "Technicians will not be easy to replace quickly. It must be important."

"It is! We have found... you have a name for it... the mother lode of crystal-flow. You will not believe where it is."

Travellor and Farber-Chatwell looked at the others as they nodded their heads in agreement.

"Mother lode of crystal-flow? How much are we talking about?" asked Travellor.

"As much as or more than the amount we presently have in the cargo hold. It's all in one location, and we are sitting on it – literally."

"WHAT?..."

"How much?..."

"Yes! At least equivalent to the amount that has taken us years to find. That is why crystal-flow is so expensive. No one has ever found it in such a concentration before."

"It is all because of the Aimsler Method!" interjected Plessa.

"The Aimsler Method. What is the Aimsler method?" asked Farber-Chatwell.

Travellor looked at his niece, who sat quietly with a very pleased look on her face. The Ganaphe' looked at her with an expression of pride.

"Miss Aimsler's procedure to free the Orysta has also become a new method of mining. From what we have determined by our measurements, her idea to turn the ground into a continuously agitated fluid caused the various materials to separate into layers according to their density. This makes it very much easier to find and obtain the crystal-flow. This method is also suitable for mining much more than crystal-flow. It will change the mining industry."

"Clarify something for me," said Travellor. "Where did all of this crystal-flow come from?"

"It was always there," said Plessa. "In the crevice where the ship was trapped. We never thought to look for it in the area we were trying to escape from. Our only thoughts were to free the ship. Mining around it did not enter our minds because it might have endangered the ship."

"Any questions General?" asked Travellor, looking at the video screen.

"Grilik Munen and I can work out the financial agreement between us later. The personnel issue is your decision, Commander. Can you spare six technicians to work with them at this time?"

Travellor turned his computer monitor to face him, and pulled up the base work schedule. It took him a couple of minutes to organize his thoughts.

"How long will you need these people for?"

"I can not say exactly." answered Munen. "At least one month and no longer than four months."

"That's a long time to be short on technicians. Especially with the ongoing programs." said Farber-Chatwell.

"Yes…, very true." said Travellor. He locked eyes with Munen. "I will assign six technicians to work with you starting tomorrow," he said, "BUT… in exchange for this loan of personnel I want the staffing limits for the base increased by six new permanent positions. While my technicians are on loan to you, their compensation and benefits will be paid by your company. Their work periods will meet all of 361's requirements for down time, workplace safety, and proper work environment. You will give me weekly status reports on their wellbeing and performance. Any of your personnel already scheduled to assist us in projects that are already on the calendar will do so as promised. Also, the technicians on loan will be rotated every two months so that more of my people can become familiar with your equipment. Is that agreeable to you?"

"Yes, it is agreeable." said Munen immediately.

"Whoa – hold on. You didn't even think about it. That must be some mother lode you've found." said Travellor, as he glanced at Erika and Mersuul.

Both women had expressions of pride on their faces. At first

342

Travellor didn't realize that he was the object of that pride, and then he felt a little flattered even though he didn't know why. He brought his thoughts back to business and turned to Munen.

"I have already thought about it before coming with my request." said Munen. "My crew had advised me on what to expect from you."

Travellor looked back at the two women.

"They did, did they?"

"Alright then." interjected Farber-Chatwell. "Grilik Munen and I will work out the left over details. I'll start processing six new people for you Commander. If anything else comes up we'll figure it out as we go along."

3

"I told them what you said Commander, but they insisted on talking to you directly." said Balfour.

Travellor looked at the two pilots, who had an 'I can convince you to change your mind.' look on their faces. John Smith and George Washington could barely contain their agitation at the hold order for the first test flight of the X-ECN-1. They tried to maintain a professional decorum but Travellor could see they were ready to burst.

"I don't mind you coming here to vent your frustration. I can even understand it. But I have no control over this, gentlemen. I have a boss and you have a boss, and my boss has instructed me to tell you that the test flight is on hold for now – which I have. Cove has designed some new instrumentation for the ship, and some mods for the engine. He wants them installed for the first flight. I know you want to get your hands on that ship. Hell, I want to get MY hands on that ship."

"Sir, I think…"

"They're making updates to the simulator software as well." said Travellor, holding up his hand to stop any comments.

"Sir, we are ready to go. We are trained. WE – KNOW – THAT – SHIP!" said Smith, emphatically. "There is no reason why we shouldn't be running that test flight right now."

"He's right, sir." said Washington. "We could be testing the airframe and mechanicals. No new instrumentation is going to make a difference with that."

Travellor leaned back in his chair. He had to tell these men they weren't going to get what they wanted. The problem was that he wanted the same thing. Ever since that ship was ferried to the base he'd wanted to take it for a little Sunday afternoon joy ride – not to anywhere far – just to Mars for brunch with Mersuul and Erica. But that was just a daydream.

"Cove is coming here himself to supervise the installation of the new instrumentation. Until that's done, the simulator is as close as you're going to get, and I want you on that simulator. I want you to know that ship better than any other craft you've known before. There's great potential in that new engine – and proportionately great risk. I know it's frustrating, but until Cove says it's a go, that ship stays grounded."

The two men groaned at the inevitability of Travellor's response. They knew it would end this way, but they felt they had to try. They got up to leave, slowly followed by Balfour.

"I will try to get you a definite schedule gentlemen." he said as they moved to the door. "Please stick around Flight Commander. I need to talk to you."

"Yes sir."

As the door closed behind the pilots, Travellor turned his attention to Balfour. She declined his offer of coffee and sat back in her chair.

"You haven't been read in on this delay, have you Flight Commander?"

"No sir. No explanation was given to me."

"Then I'll make the decision to tell you. Here's the deal." he said as his head went back and he looked at the ceiling. "Genius apparently can sometimes get ahead of itself. Luckily for us Cove was smart enough to know when he screwed up. Also luckily for us he knew how to fix his mistake." His gaze came forward and he focused on Balfour. "That ship is potentially more dangerous than even what we already thought it was. So it's important for you to hear me clearly. No one, absolutely NO ONE is to leave the ground in the Folly. That responsibility is yours. I don't care if you put padlocks on the landing gear or bolt it the ground. Until Cove has cleared that ship for flight it is nothing more than a fancy arcade game."

"I understand sir. I will make sure of it when I leave your office."

She got up to leave.

"And Commander, don't be hesitant to come down hard on anyone you think might want to take that ship for a spin. Ground them if necessary. I'll back you."

Chapter 19

Preflight

1

September – 2014

Marisa "Radio" Herrera Delgadillo sat quietly in the shuttle and watched out of the view port as they got closer to the X-37B. The U.S. Air Force's flying test platform had been orbiting the Earth for twenty-one months, being tracked by the military control team as well as many civilian techies wanting to show their peers how good they were at finding the highly secret ship. There were also some countries that were not friendly to the U.S. that also tried to find and track it. The X-37B changed altitudes and orbits under the control of its operators on the ground, making it hard to find but not impossible.

Radio had volunteered for this mission because she wanted to see the Earth from this closer distance – closer being defined as not as far as the Moon. She checked her camera in its protective crystal-flow case made especially for her by her Ganaphe' friends – with the understanding that it was just on loan. Even a small case this size was worth a lot of money when it was made of crystal-flow. It would eventually be re-melted and used for other purposes, but for now it protected her camera from space radiation. She made sure it was turned on and in video mode, then attached it to the side of her helmet. This video would be used in future training of moon base personnel, and she was more than happy to be the one to mix a little business with pleasure.

Being an amateur photographer, she had chastised herself for passing up past opportunities to get pictures like this and she wasn't going to miss this chance for pictures of her home planet. She was using the term 'home planet' more often lately. Her knowledge of the universe and the many different species that existed in it had been expanded by the education from the Ganaphe' friends who were now part of her every day life. There were a lot of 'home planets' out there. Earth was hers – and from this altitude it looked beautiful.

The Ganaphe' camouflage system kept the shuttle from being detected by eyes and instruments, even as close as they were. Slowly the shuttle pilot maneuvered closer to the X-37B, until they were in jumping distance of the ship. This would not take long if everything went well. The shuttle flew aside and pacing the other ship.

"Prepare for extra-vehicular activity. Everyone place their helmets on. Confirm when you are ready." said Tahn-grilik Califas who was piloting, as he set the shuttle to computer control.

Tonio Vargas attached his helmet, then checked Radio to make sure hers was secure. They had been part of the same team since the beginning, and he wasn't going to lose his friend now. He had more than an education on the universe to thank the Ganaphe' for. They had saved his life. He had come very close to having the distinction of being the first man to die on the Moon. After both were ready they gave a thumbs up to Califas.

"Equalizing the craft." said Califas.

The sound of air being sucked and compressed for storage in tanks reminded everyone that they should check their individual air supply. This method of storing the shuttles internal atmosphere reduced the loss of air when the ship had to be opened to space. Air, like water, was always in limited supply when traveling through space. You couldn't save it all, but could reduce the amount lost. They waited as the ship's internal pressure became a vacuum.

Vargas removed the small, almost flat rectangular shaped device from the shelf, and checked the display screen on it to verify the instrument package was working correctly. It was designed to take various measurements needed by Eckelberry Cove so that he could complete the design of updated instrumentation for the X-ECN-1. It was painted a mottled gray color, and he wondered why that was. He handed it to Radio, who attached it to her arm. Several seconds later the air compressors completed their job.

"I am ready to go, Tahn-grilik." said Radio.

"Good. Remember, it will only require a gently push to get you across to the other ship." reminded Califas.

"Yes sir. You've trained me well. I won't fail."

"I know you will not." he replied.

Her words brought a smile to Califas' face. He had no doubts about her skills. They had practiced the procedure many times using one of the base's shuttles as a stand-in for the X-37B.

The door opened and Radio moved to the edge of the opening. She tried to remember the feel of her successful attempts during practice. Placing her hands on the sides of the doorway, she pulled herself forward with just a slight amount of force. Slowly she traveled across open space, and seconds later she contacted the X-37B. She stuck to the vehicles skin using the same Ganaphe' adhesion material that gave the cleaning robots on the base the ability to stick to the walls and ceilings. The front of her suit and the inside of her gloves had been lined with the stuff. It held her to the ship like a gecko walking up a wall. She detached her upper body from the ship and pulled the instrument package from her arm. The bottom of the package had the same material coating it, and when she pressed it to the X-37B it stuck like it was glued there. A small electric current run through the material would cause it to contract and release its grip, which it would do at the right time.

Radio tugged on the package to confirm it was securely attached. She checked the display to verify it was working, then lifted her knees from the ship and pushed off in the direction of the shuttle. She was greeted by Vargas' hands that guided her through the door. Califas slowly moved the shuttle away from the X-37B, and moved behind and clear of the other ship.

"Just like we practiced." said Radio, gleefully.

"Excellent work." replied Califas. "I'll hold this position while you acquire your photographs."

"If you don't mind, Tahn-grilik, I think I'll take them from outside the shuttle."

Califas nodded his approval, and Radio made her way to the top of the shuttle, and stood up. It was a strange sensation. She thought she should be falling from the ship, but which way was up and which was down? Surrounded by empty space and looking up (down?) at the Earth, she grabbed her camera from her helmet, adjusted its settings, and snapped her pictures. Then she turned around and just randomly took pictures of various sections of space. There was no atmosphere and no weather to obscure her view, and the stars were bright enough to pluck from space.

2

The Study Group

They were a varied group of people, each with an individual style. Consisting of men and women from academia and industry, and they were hand selected by General Farber-Chatwell. Some wore suits and ties, and some were more casual. Some dressed in shorts and sandals like they were attending a seminar in the Bahamas. They all had one trait in common – their wide eyes. Wide-eyed in disbelief. Wide-eyed in facing the unexpected. Wide-eyed trying to absorb and accept the new knowledge they were being exposed to. Their personal worlds, which so many of them had carefully crafted for a sense of security and comfort in their lives, was no longer a world – it was now a universe. And it was a universe inhabited by many other intelligent beings. A lot of the tenets they believed as truth throughout their lifetimes were being smashed – or was that expanded? They represented all the fields of modern day science from Physics to

Physiology. From Botany to Cosmology.

Erika sat in the back of the room, watching their reactions. Listening to their questions. She was certain she had accepted the truth of it all more readily than these people. She tried to take in these classes whenever she could attend. There was so much to learn. Each class seemed to be for a different group of people being cycled through the base. Some of them were friendly, but most seemed insecure or lost in all of the knew information. She had stopped trying to be friendly to them several classes ago. These people were here for one week at most, unless they were stationed on the base in the future. All of them were selected as potential moon base personnel. Those that wanted to be stationed here had to request it. It was too dangerous a posting for people who didn't want to be here. Now that she thought about it, she was never really given the choice – but then she could not imagine turning it down, especially with her uncle here.

This evening's class was on the Ganaphe' home world Taloraicia. It is a planet lush with plant life due to the fact that Taloraicia orbits two suns in an elliptical orbit. When the planet is traveling between the suns two thirds of it is in sunlight, making for short night times and long day times. This also means that plant life there is exposed to long hours of daylight boosting the growth cycle. As it circles around one or the other sun only half of the planet is in daylight, like the Earth. The orbit makes for a changing sleep cycle for the inhabitants – an alternating circadian rhythm – which is why the Ganaphe' can often go without sleep for long periods. Most of the planet's land mass is around its equator, and is mostly in a tropical climate. Vegetable and fruit growth is abundant throughout the planet's orbital cycle. Where there is a bounty of vegetation, animal life is also abundant. So it was with Taloraicia.

Theories were being broken here. *'No, that's not correct.'* thought Erika. *'Not broken. Expanded on. Re-evaluated. Looked at under the light of new information. That is a more accurate way to describe it.'* It wasn't so much that their understanding of the laws of physics was wrong as it was too limited. Not all the factors and their interactions with each other were understood. The Ganaphe' were much more knowledgeable, more advanced in their understanding, but even they had admitted there was so much more to learn and understand. *'We are going to have to write a whole new set of text books when this gets out to the world – whenever that will be.'* she thought.

Of all the new insights, new possibilities, and new truths that were taught, one stood out among the rest. Scientific examination showed that in all the known galaxies, and all the known solar systems with all the known habitable planets, life had appeared on them at approximately the same time – give or take five thousand Earth years, which in geologic time is insignificant. In effect, all known life began at about the same time. It was a stunning and mind opening revelation.

3

October 17, 2014

General Farber-Chatwell stood in back of the gathered military project heads and the technical team of the X-37B mission. He was a guest at this event – a self invited guest. When a man with Farber-Chatwell's credentials – and seemingly endless connections – wanted to be invited to a top secret military operation of this type, he was. No high ranking officer questioned it anymore. He had helped too many of them successfully overcome problems in career making situations, and they wanted to make sure he would help them in the future, if the need arose. Besides, there wasn't any technical aspect of the mission that he wasn't already aware of. They suspected he was here for a specific reason, but no one would ask directly. It didn't matter though. He had clearance to be here, and was already one of the most knowledgeable people of the X-37B project and its capabilities. He had been involved in designing some of the craft's instrumentation, and was contributory in fixing problems with the software that controlled it. How he was able to get these things done was itself classified. He was a resource for the country to use when needed, and satisfying his curiosity was a very small price to pay for that.

The long focal length DOAMS (Distant Object Attitude

Measurement System) tracking cameras displayed their views on various screens in the control room. The only thing visible at the moment was a bright white spot. The ship was still too far away to make out any details. Readouts on the screens showed airspeed, ground speed, altitude and direction of travel among many other readings. It took another minute before the small but definite outline of the X-37B could be seen as it maneuvered through the sky at several times the speed of sound. With every passing second more detail could be seen. It looked like a mini STS as it flew closer to Vandenberg Air Force Base. On board cameras showed the view in front of the robot aircraft as its automated flight system guided it toward the runway.

A few minutes later the ship followed the guidance signal of the Microwave Scan Beam Landing System to align itself with the runway. The landing gear came down and locked into place. All of it was done by the on-board computer. It all looked very smooth on the monitors. At 0924 hours PST the almost two year secret mission of the X-37B came to an end as it touched down and rolled to a stop. Technicians in trucks rolled onto the runway to check out and secure the craft. That was when Farber-Chatwell reached into his pocket and pushed the button on what looked like the remote control to his car. Before the technicians were close enough to see clearly, the small rectangular device hanging onto the skin of the X-37B released its grip and slid down the side of the ship. It landed on the sun beaten gray runway that it was painted to look like. Then the computer inside the device repeatedly expanded and contracted the gecko cloth that had held it to the ship, causing the device to crawl away from the ship and into the grass on the side of the runway – unnoticed by anyone. Recorded inside the device was the data needed by Eckelberry Cove to get his new ship into operation.

Farber-Chatwell watched as the X-37B was checked out, and then hooked up to a tow vehicle and taken into a hangar – the machine as well as the mission was classified. That was when he was sure no one had seen anything out of the ordinary. He thanked his hosts for allowing him to watch the landing, and after a few words of praise on their accomplishment he left the building, got into his car, and drove off the base. The device would be recovered tonight by a camouflaged Ganaphe' shuttle.

4

November – 2014

You couldn't tell by the pair of beat up and scuffed sneakers sticking up in the air that they belonged to a person considered to be one of Earth's most brilliant scientists. He had degrees in several fields, and has re-written some of the text books. Only a few had access to his work – at least at this time.

His father is a semi-retired and very experienced heavy machinery mechanic, who occasionally takes contract jobs across the country. His mother owns a small and profitable bakery whose customers regularly enjoy the constantly innovative culinary treats she comes up with. They are a successful middle class couple, and there is nothing to indicate that their only male child is a genius. They never talk about him as one either, and never indicate to friends and family that there was anything very special about Eckelberry Cove. Their two daughters however are often gushed about, by both their parents and their older brother.

Having helped his father with heavy equipment repairs since he was seven gave Eckelberry an unconscious understanding that being physically strong was a useful characteristic in life. He didn't mind crawling around the dirty machinery, and from observation and a lot of questions he learned many principles of mechanics and hydraulics. He liked several outdoor activities, and worked out regularly. This was a good balance to the many sedate hours he spent delving into books of various scientific disciplines. They all intrigued him, and he could see the interconnectivity of the natural sciences. In his teens he soaked up all the knowledge available to him. When he was sixteen he was the beneficiary of a college scholarship that he had not applied for. It was funded by a small technology company he had not heard of, and it paid for all expenses including a small apartment, a car, and clothing and food allowances. This was how he met Ransen Ramsdel, who was the administrator of the scholarship. His parents were thrilled by their son's good fortune, and found themselves in a position to afford better schools for their daughters than they might have been able to afford if paying for three college educations.

Eckelberry Cove just didn't look like the genius type. With his upper torso stuck up behind the control panel of the X-ECN-1, and with only his lower body visible and his feet in the air he looked less so. Maybe that was why John Smith and George Washington, whose upper bodies were also unseen and their feet also in the air, got along so well with him. The pilots were on either side of Cove, helping him hook up the wiring harnesses of the new instrumentation. Every now and then an 'ouch' or a 'damn it' could be heard, and one or the other would show himself as he grabbed another tool or fastener.

The airframe mechanics whose job it actually was to install the equipment had quickly realized they were relegated to being the backup team, so they stood outside the spacecraft waiting for any requests from the three. They would eventually have to put their heads under the panel to verify the work was done to specs – after all, it was they who would have to sign off on the installation. Not even the inventor/designer/builder of the equipment had the authority to do that, and on this moon base, run by Commander Travellor, everything was done by the rules and regulations.

Hanging above the main hangar door, for everyone to see, was mounted a large piece of twisted steel from what was the original hangar door. It was a reminder to everyone of the only major accident to occur on the base, which almost took the life of one of its inhabitants. No one wanted to be responsible for the next accident.

"Go ahead, admit it." said Cove. "First chance you had you were going to push the engine to its limits, weren't you?"

"Well… maybe." said Smith, and he involuntarily shrugged and hit a metal support with his shoulder. "OW – damn it!"

"I'll take that as a definite 'Yes'. But that's OK. That's what I expected you to do – whatever your instructions were."

"But only after a complete checkout of all the systems!" interjected

354

Washington defensively. "Everyone knows you over-design your stuff –
WAY over-design. You put a large safety margin into everything."

"You're right. I do. The problem is that you will be traveling at
speeds we've never reached before… well… if it works correctly…, and
accelerating at a rate we've never done before – at least not for any manned
vehicle I'm aware of. Today's state of the art sensors are not capable of
accurately measuring in that realm. When I realized that – when I realized
how far off the measurements would be, and that you could and probably
would exceed the design safety limits – even the over limits I designed into
the ship…" He hesitated, lost in thought for a while. "The ship would have
been destroyed, and you would have been killed – and it would have been
my fault!"

"How did you figure that out?"

"It's my brain." said Cove. "Sometimes I have no control over it.
When I'm working on a project, it never shuts down. Even when I'm
sleeping, or more accurately trying to sleep, my mind is still active – still
analyzing – still calculating. Until the conclusion of the project, I never get
a peaceful night's rest."

"I've had nights like that," said Smith, "but with me it usually
happens after I screw up."

"That is why the first thing I did when I realized my error was to
contact the General and tell him to shut down the program immediately. I
told him no one was to fly this ship until I re-instrumented it. I even
suggested that he have the engine removed from the airframe as a
precaution, but he said that everyone up here were professionals and that no
one would violate the no fly directive."

Smith and Washington both turned their faces away. They didn't want Cove
to see the guilt on them. It had only been talk after all, that they would take
the ship for a short hop. They weren't really going to do it. At least that's
what they told each other.

"I didn't want anyone's blood on my hands." said Cove in a quiet
voice. "If you had throttled this ship to its limits it would have broken up –

catastrophically." He was quiet for a while, and then his voice went louder. "Once I get these new instruments in – once we can compensate for the deficiencies in our sensors, and give you accurate readings on all flight parameters – speed – acceleration – airframe stress, and the computer can account for all of these factors, then – THEN – if you decide you want to kill yourselves – then I'll be able to sleep OK."

Cove continued working on the cable harness. He wanted his words to sink into the thoughts of the two men who would be testing his new creation. He wanted them to understand that there was danger from known and yet to be learned factors of what they were about to do. He wanted them to be cautious – and to come back alive.

5

The Briefing

December – 2014

"The ship now has the new protective Interleaved Magnetic Field generator. It generates multiple rotating magnetic fields that alternately move from an inside to outside position in reference to the ship's skin. This will provide better protection from space radiation, and because of the way the fields interact with each other they can also act as a sensor array that can be used to detect and analyze radiation." said Cove, speaking to his small audience.

In the room were Base Commander Travellor, General Farber-Chatwell, Ransen Ramsdel, the A&P maintenance team, and all flight crew personnel. As a courtesy, the Orysta's Grilik, Tahn-grilik, and Chief Engineer were invited to sit in. Everyone listened intently, trying to understand as much as they could. Of course, the pilots were more interested in anything related to flying the ship, the maintenance team was mostly interested in how it was assembled and tested, the Ganaphe' were mostly interested in the potential of the engine design as a substitute for their own damaged engine, and Travellor, Farber-Chatwell, and Ramsdel were mostly interested in the potential risk to the test pilots. Cove had to try to explain everything in a way his audience would understand.

"I have also installed an experimental Light Field Camera system that feeds into a dedicated computer. The computer is constructed of multiple mother boards, each containing sixteen multi-core processors running in parallel. This much computer power may sound like a lot, but it is the minimum required to analyze input from the LFC and display it in real time – well, relatively real time anyway – for the pilots to use. The computer is programmed to analyze the space in front of the ship and alert to any potential threats. It has its limits though. It's just one piece in the overall system of protection."

"What kind of potential threats?" interrupted Travellor.

"Asteroids, meteoroids, or any type of space debris that may be heading for impact with the ship. A collision avoidance detection system on loan from the Orysta has also been installed. We are still working on our own version of that device, but it will take a lot more time to get a functional and reliable unit."

The conversation brought back and old unpleasant memory to Travellor. One where he almost lost a friend. He shivered in his chair as the incident replayed in his head.

"In open space," said Grilik Munen, "there is not much risk of such impacts occurring. Flight near planets, asteroids, comets or other celestial bodies are where most of the danger exists. Unfortunately you can never be certain that open space is free of such dangers. Your test flight will not take you within the influence of any celestial bodies, and Califas will be on the flight with you, to monitor for any dangers."

"Excuse me gentlemen." said John Smith impatiently. "Does this mean we are ready to go or not? We've been retrofitting the ship for weeks now. Is it ready to fly?"

"Almost." replied Cove. "That is, we will be ready as soon as the paint is dried and connected."

The remark brought questioning looks from everyone.

"Connected?" asked Farber-Chatwell, as confused as the others.

"Yes Sir, connected. The Sensor Skin Paint project was successfully concluded just prior to my coming here. I thought that this would be the best real world test of it. It's being sprayed on the X-ECN-1 at this moment. Should be ready to go in two or three days."

Smith sighed and slid down in his chair, letting his posture express his feeling about this new delay.

"What does the Sensor Skin paint do?" asked Travellor.

"The Sensor Skin paint is a coating of micro-electro-mechanical-machines, fabricated using our own proprietary MEMS manufacturing process – but that's not important right now. Basically the paint is loaded with microscopic machines that perform three functions. First, they are self generating power sources, meaning no external power source is required for them to work. Second, they are condition sensors. In this function they monitor the overall condition of the coating and communicate any abnormal condition, such as physical damage, to surrounding machines. Third, if there is damage to the coating these machines can repair the damage – if it is not too severe. They are immune to radiation – up to a point. Their main purpose is to indicate contact with foreign objects that have not yet damaged the ship's skin. An early warning device is one way to think about it. A clear air turbulence detector – or in our application, a clear space turbulence detector."

"But this is not necessary for the test flight?"

"No sir, it's not. But there is no better opportunity to test it than this flight."

Travellor thought about this for a moment then looked at Farber-Chatwell, who just shrugged. He looked around at the expressions and postures of everyone in the room. They were ready for this flight, and a lot of them (mainly the flight crews) were tired of waiting.

"Two days!" said Travellor. "This ship takes off in two days – no longer! There will be no further changes to the configuration of the ship without my approval. Anything not working that isn't flight critical will be tagged and ignored. Understood?"

Cove hesitated a bit, then nodded his agreement. He wasn't used to not getting his way in these matters, but he quickly realized that Commander Travellor was not like General Farber-Chatwell. This base was not a design center. It was an operational testing center. That was what they did here. If something wasn't ready for testing, it shouldn't be here.

6

Clothes Encounters

"I assure you Commander that I didn't know the solarium was closed to men this evening." said Cove, pleading his innocence. "I would swear there was no sign on the door."

Joshua Kibbee leaned back against the wall, chuckling and barely suppressing outright laughter, as he watched Cove try to explain his actions. He thought the situation was very funny. Cove, who sat in his gym shorts and a T-shirt, looked very much like a kid who had been called into the principals' office.

"We don't have a sign on the door?" asked Travellor, looking at Kibbee.
"Uh, that's true sir. There is no sign. We never really formalized

359

Ladies Night. Never had to. Everyone on the base knows about it."

Travellor leaned back in his chair, looking at Cove. He believed what the man was saying. He believed he had walked in on Ladies Night in total innocence.

"So you went into the solarium in your gym shorts, and walked in on – how many naked women were there?"

"I…, I don't know, Commander. I wasn't thinking about counting them." he said, defensively. "I was caught by surprise, and I could only think about leaving there quickly. I remember apologizing to them, although I wasn't sure what I was apologizing for, at the time. I knew by their yelling at me that I shouldn't have been there, so I left as quickly as I could."

"Maybe not that quickly." said Kibbee, still suppressing his laughter.

"What does that mean?" asked Travellor.

"Uh, nothing sir. Forget I said that."

Travellor grabbed the computer mouse and clicked a few times while focusing on the monitor. It took a minute to confirm what he was looking for.

"You're right. There's nothing in the Rules and Regs about Ladies Night. It's never been made official." he said, as he typed an email to his assistant. "There. That will be corrected in the morning." He looked back at Kibbee. "Do me a favor and make up a sign for the solarium door. Put it on with tape if you have to, until we get one made up and mounted."

"I'll take care of that right after." said Kibbee.

"Well Doctor," he said, now looking at Cove, "you have now been officially notified of Ladies Night on the base."

Cove nodded his head rapidly up and down.

"I suggest you wait until tomorrow before you use the Solarium. Give things a while to calm down."

"Yes sir. Of course I will. Maybe I'll just pass on it this trip."

"Doctor, your going to be with us for a while. You can pass on it for as long as you meet the medical requirements in the regulations. Otherwise, you will use it."

"OK Commander. Of course." said Cove as he stood up to leave.

"Have a good evening Doctor. And remember, if you run into any of those women and they seem a little angry with you – well, the base is fairly large. I understand you're a runner so you should be able to get away." said Travellor, also now chuckling.

Cove didn't see the humor in his embarrassing situation. He walked out of Travellor's office, closing the door behind him.

"What did you mean by that remark, that Cove didn't leave that quickly?"

Kibbee broke out in a large smile, and moved closer to the desk.

"I spoke to Specialist del Rio before I brought Cove here. She couldn't stop laughing about it. Apparently none of the women could."

"So I won't be hearing any grievances about this?"

"Not likely Sir. So anyway, what she said happened was that Cove walked into the solarium, looked around and slowly realized something wasn't right. He was as surprised as the women were. They start yelling at him to get out and come back tomorrow. He's so caught off guard he's not sure what to do. Eventually his brain gets into gear and he starts to leave. Now this is the interesting part. As he's turning to go his gaze falls on one of the women, and he can't turn away from looking at her. Delores says she thinks his brain locked up." Kibbee took a deep breath and started laughing.

"Can you picture it. This young genius loses his self control at the sight of a naked woman – well…, one particular naked woman. He's so lost in what he is seeing that he can't move. After a couple of minutes, Doctor

Blin and Delores have to take him by the arms and walk him out of the room – all the while his head is twisted around as he continues to stare at this girl." Kibbee laughed harder, and couldn't continue talking.

"Oh great." said Travellor. "You said I wouldn't be hearing about this any more. Sounds like I'm going to be getting a harassment notice filed. So who was the woman Cove couldn't take his eyes off of?"

Now Kibbee started laughing harder. He tried to talk, but each time he would start laughing again. After several minutes he was able to regain control of himself.

"Well?" said Travellor. "Who is she?"

Kibbee held a large grin, but he didn't say anything. Travellor waited for the name, but after a few seconds he realized why Kibbee didn't say.

"Erika." Travellor said. "That's who it was, wasn't it?"

Kibbee just nodded in affirmation, and almost started to laugh again. He took some deep breathes and regained his composure.

"Apparently," said Kibbee, "he found your uh… naked niece to be so captivatingly beautiful that he couldn't look away. Not even as he was being pushed out of the room. But on the positive side, if she does want to complain, she'll probably just tell you about it and not file anything on paper." He was still grinning.

7

Promises

Travellor stood back, sipping his coffee, as he watched the four way conversation between Cove, the Air Maintenance Chief, and two of his younger subordinates. He didn't know the names of the younger men, and that bothered him. They hadn't been stationed here for long, but he felt it was part of his job to know his people. The combined staff on the moon base just wasn't that big that he shouldn't. Had he been so busy lately that he couldn't do this before? He would correct that error by having lunch with the men and welcoming them to the base. It was obvious that something was going on. Cove kept reviewing the papers in his hand, and the airframe technicians were answering his questions. Travellor could always recognize a problem when he saw one. Solving it was a different matter.

He walked over to the group. The Maintenance Chief saluted him, and Travellor returned the salute. His two technicians did not salute, and weren't sure what to do. They had never been in the military, and this was not a military base. Saluting here was more of a courtesy than anything else.

"Good morning gentlemen. Sounds like you have a problem. What's going on?"

"It's the Sensor Skin paint." said Cove. "It appears to have been mixed incorrectly before being shipped here. Totally my fault. I should have checked it before coming to the base."

"Can you correct the problem? Remix it?"

"Not with what we have on hand. It requires special processing equipment that doesn't damage the MEMS. The only thing we can do is have more made on Earth and sent up to us."

"This ship is scheduled to fly tomorrow, Doctor."

"It will have to be delayed Commander. It will take several days to have a new batch made up, tested, and shipped here. We also have to strip off what's on the ship now and prep it for the new paint."

"You made a promise to the flight crew Doctor. You told them they would fly tomorrow."

"I know that Commander, and I'm sorry that they'll be disappointed, but I don't see any other way."

The group went silent for a while. Travellor sipped his coffee, and thought to himself for a minute.

"And this is the only thing holding us up? All other systems are functional and ready to go?" asked Travellor.

"That's correct." replied Cove. "Once we have this fixed she'll be ready to fly."

"Where is the ship's maintenance log book?" asked Travellor, directing his question to the Crew Chief.

"I've got it here, Sir." the Chief said, handing the log to Travellor.

Travellor opened the book, and found the equipment list. He wrote at the bottom of the page, and then signed and dated it.

"Problem solved." he said, closing the book and handing it back to the Chief. "I've designated the Sensor Skin paint as non-essential equipment." He turned to the two technicians. "Gentlemen, excuse me for not welcoming you to the base formally. I'd like to make up for it by buying you lunch, and getting to know you if that's alright."

The two younger men were surprised by the invitation, but agreed to it enthusiastically. Travellor turned his attention to Cove and the Chief.

"This ship flies tomorrow as scheduled. Any problems that will interfere with that will be brought to my attention immediately. I want the flight crew notified of that. So – that settles that little issue. Anything else I can take care of while I'm here?"

No one brought up any other issues.

8

Erika was deep in concentration, and she rechecked her calculations on the tablet screen. The tablet was acting as a remote terminal, with the actual data processing being performed by the Orysta's computer.

Her uncle had been right about the Ganaphe' wanting to leave for home the first chance they got. Now, as an official member of the Orysta's crew (which still seemed strange to her) and a temporary employee of Grilik Munen and the mining company he worked for, she had been tasked with the analysis of doing exactly that. Using the projected performance specs of the new Cove engine, she was to figure out if mounting multiple engines on the Orysta could get them to the inter-galactic trade lanes, how long it would take, how much fuel would be required, and most importantly could the engines be adapted to being powered by the ship's power exchange unit or vice versa. Her mind was completely focused on the task.

Being so intently involved with a problem is not good when you are walking and not paying attention to what's in front of you. One second she was looking at the screen, and the next she was on her butt trying to figure out what had happened. She was in the passageway that connected the base to the Orysta. In front of her, also on the floor was Eckelberry Cove. He was surrounded by printouts, and an open laptop with a now cracked screen lay next to him.

"I'm sorry. I wasn't watching where I was going." they both said in unison.

"It was my fault." said Erika. "I don't usually walk without looking where I'm going."

"Actually it was my fault. I always walk without looking where I'm going and I have a reputation for running into people. Oh, and I owe you an apology."

"For what?"

"For staring at you the other night, when I walked in on Ladies Night."

"Well… yes… you did keep looking. I began to wonder just how bad I looked…"

"You are the most beautiful woman I have ever seen!" he blurted out.

She was caught of guard by his sudden statement. Then she started to laugh.

"And you saw me for a long, long time." she said still laughing. "Well, did you enjoy Ladies Night?"

"I'm so sorry. I don't know what came over me. I don't usually act like that. No one informed me about Ladies Night. I didn't know there was such a thing. I hope I didn't embarrass anyone. I'd be happy to apologize to each person if necessary."

"Oh, I don't know about that." she said. "It looked like you had a lot of practice at staring."

"No! Really I don't…"

"I'm joking. Just yanking your chain a little."

"Oh!… uh, I'm Eckelberry Cove." he said extending his hand.

"I know who you are, Doctor Cove. I'm Er…"

"I know. I know who you are also, Miss Aimsler."

She shook the offered hand. They started to get up off of the floor. Eckelberry jump up and offered his hand again, and helped her up.

"I don't think apologies will be necessary. None of the girls are really very shy. Of course, this puts me at a disadvantage."

"What do you mean?"

"Well… you've seen me completely naked, but you had shorts on when you came into the room. I think there's an imbalance there that needs to be corrected."

"Uh… are… are you… are you suggesting that I drop my pants so you can have a look at me?"

"Well… that would be the only fair thing to do, don't you think?"

Cove stood wide eyed, stammering and at a loss for a response. Erika started to laugh again.

"Relax Doctor. I'm only joking."

Relief came over him, and he started to laugh also.

"I may be out of line," he said, "but I was wondering if you would have dinner with me tonight."

"In the Solarium?" she asked with a big smile.

"I would feel more comfortable in the cafeteria." he said, blushing.

Erika laughed at the irony of his being the one who was embarrassed.

Chapter 20

Test Flight and Other Things

1

December – 2014

"… Checklist complete."

"Roger. Checklist complete." said Smith. He pressed the transmit button on the joystick controller. "Flight Control, this is Folly. All preflight checks complete without discrepancies. We are ready for launch." He took his finger off of the transmit button, which switched his mic back to the ship's intercom. "Are you ready for this, gentlemen?" Washington and Califas gave him a thumbs up.

The three men were working smoothly as a team now. The hours spent in the simulator and on dry runs in the cockpit were paying off. Smith and Washington had become as proficient in using the Ganaphe' equipment, as Califas had in using the systems of the Folly. That was the way the Ganaphe' trained their crews, so that in an emergency any man or woman in the same section of the ship could do the job of any one else, at least at a basic level of competence. Moon Base Commander Travellor liked that idea, and adopted it for training 361 personnel.

Also on the ground, and facing the Folly was Orysta's shuttle number one. They would act as chase plane, and follow the Folly on its voyage. There were two reasons for this. First was to act as a safety backup ship in case something went wrong with the test flight. Second was that the Ganaphe' had a personal interest in how Cove's new engine performed. Looking at a data stream wasn't the same as watching it with your own eyes. On shuttle one, those eyes belonged to PIC Mersuul-sil-Vaana, copilot and technical observer Benua-sil-Plessa, and in a previously non-existent (and not required) post of moon base representative was Delores del Rio, who herself had suggested the creation of the position.

Del Rio had many friends on the base, and a small request like this wouldn't be denied. It also helped that on her own time she had been learning to fly the Ganaphe' shuttles by studying the flight manuals and by going out with as many shuttle flights as she could snag a ride on. As she became better known to the Ganaphe' she was given more time in the copilot's seat, watching and learning and asking questions. She could already fly the shuttles. She just couldn't land them. No one had a problem with her being there, and Mersuul and Plessa were quick to assign her small tasks which freed them to concentrate on the main mission.

"Folly, this is Control. Stand by." said Balfour. "All systems are up and ready to track the Folly sir. Chase ship is ready, and the Orysta will be monitoring telemetry and comms."

"So they went with Folly as their call sign. I'm not sure if I should be insulted or not." said Travellor.

"Sign of respect, sir. Those men know you have their backs."

"Are you ready gentlemen?" asked Travellor, looking at Farber-Chatwell, Ramsdel, and Cove. They all nodded. "Initiate the flight Commander."

"Folly flight, this is Balfour. Launch at your discretion. Good luck everyone. We'll be waiting for your return."

"Roger control." came Smith's voice over the comm. "Folly flight, this is Folly leader. We are a go. Folly chase, delay for ten before following. See if we leave any pieces behind."

Cove's eyes went wide at hearing the last statement. He looked around at everyone in the Control Tower.

"What does he mean pieces? There won't be any pieces. That ship is solid." he said confusedly.

"Relax Doctor. That's just small talk between the crews. Just

Smith's way of telling the shuttle to remain a safe distance behind."

There were a dozen people in the control tower, which was designed for a normal occupancy of four. That didn't leave much room for moving around, but it was the best seat in the house. Everyone watched as the forward landing gear on the Folly began to extend. It kept getting longer until the ship's nose was at a thirty degree nose up attitude. The ship was designed to take off without a runway if necessary, and that was one of the functions to be tested. The directional nozzle of the main engine was pointed at a downward angle for the takeoff. The glow of the main engine grew brighter as the throttle was pushed forward. The ship rolled forward less than ten feet, came off of the ground and began to climb. A blast trail from the engine's powerful thrust went back about three times that distance until it hit the surrounding blast shields, and was deflected upwards. Everyone watched as the Folly's landing gear retracted and folded into the body of the ship, and the flight path slowly curved up until it was vertical to the surface.

"Control, Folly is off the ground. Throttle at thirty percent." came Washington's voice over the comm.

The ship seemed to be slowly floating up and away. Ten seconds after the Folly had left the ground the shuttle rose vertically – effortlessly – upward to follow it, then changed attitude to face the other ship.

"Folly, shuttle one is up and in position. Ready to follow your flight plan." Mersuul was heard saying.
"Roger shuttle one." came the reply. "Initiating constant acceleration in five… four… three… two… throttle forward."

Even though they had been briefed on what to expect, none of the moon base personnel in the tower were ready for what they saw, except for the Ganaphe'. To them it was normal. The Folly's engine glowed brighter and whiter until it was a beacon in the sky, almost too bright to look at.

Then, within seconds, both ships began to shrink in size and were suddenly gone from view.

"Thrust at forty percent." came over the comm. "Fifty percent... sixty... seventy... seventy five and holding. Shuttle one, did we lose any pieces?"

"Why do they keep saying that?" asked Cove indignantly. "Nothing is coming off of that ship!"

"Folly, shuttle one. Everything looks good from our position. Specialist del Rio thought she saw a slight variation in the color of your exhaust stream, but she is not certain."

"Confirmed!" replied Califas. "I measured a small variation in thrust. I suspect it was due to a contaminant in the fuel. We will have to investigate when we get back to the base. You have very good eyes specialist del Rio. Most people would not have been able to detect that."

2

The telemetry from the Folly and shuttle one were being received and analyzed back at the base for the two hours the mission had lasted so far. The Folly maintained seventy-five percent thrust throughout the first phase of the flight. They tested every system short of firing the guided missiles they carried, opened every hatch, cover, vent, and panel that was designed to do so during flight. Everything they checked opened, closed, pivoted, and met operational specs at worst. The ship was solid. Weapons systems deployed, operated, and recovered as designed. Sensors and analysis systems sensed and analyzed. Monitoring systems monitored and reported. Systems intentionally overloaded were automatically shut down by the safety systems. With each test the crew of the Folly became more confident in their ship. They even started to refer to it as 'Our Folly'. Even Califas, who was used to ships that were much more technologically advanced began to feel appreciation for the craft. His main interest was the engine, and so far it worked as expected. But he was waiting for the final engine test – fully power for almost twenty mirlots. It wasn't a drastic test, but it would yield valuable information – information that would tell if the Orysta and her crew could go home again.

Everyone on shuttle one was also beginning to appreciate the Folly. Realization set in with del Rio that if testing continued to show such positive results the Folly soon would not be a one of kind ship. There would probably be a fleet of at least a half dozen, and they would not be tasked with staying near the moon base. These ships would be the first real exploratory vessels and they would be heading out to the other planets. Del Rio suddenly knew without a doubt that she wanted to be on one of them, and she started to think about how she could accomplish that. She would have to retrain in another field. Her electro-mechanical background would help. She was sure each ship would require an on board engineer. Someone to repair equipment and correct faults. Then she realized that most of the equipment on the Folly was custom designed by Cove. There were no other experts on them. Engineers for these ships would have to be trained from scratch – and that was her way in! As soon as her feet touched ground again she would file her request to cross train.

3

Most of the observers in the control tower had left after the first hour, leaving Balfour, Travellor, and two technicians monitoring the deep space radar and the communications channels. There wasn't anything that anyone on the base could do right now other than wait and listen. The Folly and shuttle one were far from the Moon. Even if they turned around right now it would still take them hours for the return journey. The telemetry from the test flight was distributed to several locations on the base and the Orysta. The comms channels from the flight were being fed to the base intercom and personal comm devices so that base personnel could listen in if they wanted to. As the minutes passed people slowly tuned out of listening to what they knew would be fairly routine. It was an Eckelberry Cove designed ship after all. There might be a glitch here and there, and

372

someone would recommend a modification or three, but all that could be caught up on later.

4

"Shuttle one, this is Folly. Ready to begin phase one of full power engine testing. Are you going to be able to keep up with us?"

"Folly, shuttle one." replied Mersuul. "Doctor Cove's projected maximum speed should not be a problem for us. We are ready when you are." She looked over her shoulder at del Rio, who was standing behind her. "You should be in your seat for this next test Delores. Even though inertial stabilization is active, the expected rate of acceleration will be felt."

"What about the Folly? They don't have IS on the ship. Are they going to be OK?"

"Doctor Cove has designed limits in the engine that will not exceed what can be tolerated by the body. They will be highly physically stressed, but no physiological damage will occur. The medical staff should find the crew's biomedical readouts very interesting." Mersuul smiled as she looked forward again. "I believe that Tahn-grilik Califas is actually looking forward to the experience. We do not normally get exposed to such forces with our ships."

The computer on shuttle one was linked to the computer on the Folly. Mersuul would not have to touch any of the controls when the test began. Shuttle one's computer would control its speed and tracking to follow the Folly, and could easily keep up with the lead ship.

"Are we ready gentlemen?" asked Smith, of his copilot and Califas. "Instruments ready to go Tahn-grilik?"

"Hit it!" said Washington.

"All instrumentation is ready." replied Califas.

"All right then." said Smith as he pressed the radio button. "Beginning test, shuttle one. Here we go."

Smith checked his instrument panel to make sure everything looked correct. Slowly and steadily he pushed the throttle forward until it was set for ninety percent of maximum power. The Folly picked up speed. It wasn't anything out of the ordinary at first, but the rate of acceleration was not linear. In a few seconds they were feeling the G force pushing them into their seats. The rate just kept increasing faster after that. At first Califas didn't think the force on his body was much worse than what he was expecting – but it kept getting stronger. Before he realized what was happening it got much worse than that. He knew something was wrong. He tried looking at the others but could barely move his head. His body was pinned against the seat – something had gone wrong, and he was going to die! They were all going to die – and there was nothing he could do about it. He couldn't control his body. He knew instinctively that he only had fracins left to live.

All three men were thinking the same thing. Smith didn't understand why the ship's computer hadn't shut down the engine when this dangerous situation occurred. Then their bodies began to catch up to the speed of the ship as the rate of acceleration and the pressure on their bodies diminished. Slowly they regained control of their limbs. Their breathing, which had been labored, was getting easier. A few seconds later, their bodies and everything else in the ship had reached a constant speed. They could move again – think again – talk again. The primary engine shut down. The Folly had reached its selected speed and was holding steady. The training of all three men kicked in and they started checking systems to make sure everything was still functional. Then they looked around, checking on each other. All was right with the world – or more accurately all was right with the Folly.

"I have never felt such acceleration in my life." said Califas. "I was sure something had gone wrong with the ship."

"I thought the safety system had failed." said Washington.

"I'm going to kill Cove when we get back!" said Smith. "He never told us anything about this, and I know the SOB had some idea of what would happen."

"He knew." said Califas. "He knew how much our bodies would be able to sustain. I am certain he had run tests. He never thought to try to explain it to us."

"I wonder if his test subjects wanted to kill him too." said Smith. "When we get back we're going to have a talk with him. Just the three of us and him."

They continued checking the ship's systems as they talked. Everything seemed to be normal and operational.

"Everything checks normal." said Washington. "Holy shit! Look at our speed!"

"Yes." said Califas. "It is very impressive. My instruments confirm your reading. On my planet we have studied many peoples who have developed space travel technology. The rate at which you Humans are progressing is impressive. Your Doctor Cove is truly a genius. I think that rather than kill him, you should make sure nothing detrimental happens to him."

"Well..., I didn't really mean I was going to kill him." said Smith. "But you gotta admit, he should have warned us about the acceleration. Maybe I'll just punch him in the arm – real hard."

"Folly, this is shuttle one." came del Rio's voice over the radio.

"Shuttle one, Folly – go ahead."

"DO YOU KNOW HOW FAST YOU'RE GOING? I want one of those ships for my own." said del Rio. Her excited words brought some laughter to both crews.

"She does beat anything else in the fleet," said Washington, "but before you put a down payment on one of these you may want to feel what the acceleration is like in this thing. It's a real eye opener."

"Were there any problems or anomalies?" asked Plessa.

"Not a one that we are aware of. Tahn-grilik, anything on your instruments?"

"I detected no problems or deviations from the expected

performance."

"OK then." said Smith. "Let's push this puppy as fast as she can go. Time for the full power test. And shuttle one, call me a worry wart if you want, I think you should leave a greater distance between us on this part of the test."

"As you wish Captain Smith." replied Mersuul. "I shall maintain twice the previous separation."

5

Travellor slowly sipped his coffee as he listened to the chatter between the Folly and shuttle one. He was actually hearing their words several seconds after the actual conversation took place. The delay was caused by the time it took for the radio waves to travel from the ships to the moon. The Ganaphe' had a method to send their signals much faster through space, but it was against their regulations to use their equipment on the Folly for anything other than monitoring and recording purposes. It was just a few seconds. It wasn't that bad. *'Still,'* thought Travellor, *'it would be nice to know exactly when they initiated an action.'*

Balfour and the technicians were busy tracking, recording and analyzing the telemetry from the flight. Their concentration was on their jobs. All the test data coming in was normal, and they soon fell into the routine of it. No one noticed the explosions going off outside the window until they were close enough to shake the building. Then the alarms went off.

6

"One-eighty K." said Washington. "I knew Cove said it could do it, but I still had some doubt."

"And I haven't fire walled it yet." said Smith with a huge grin that matched the one on Washington's face. "I am feeling a bit on the cautious

376

side – but it's NOT fear! You got that. I am NOT afraid."

The three men cracked up with laughter. They were all a little bit afraid. Even Califas was feeling the nervousness that filled the other men. The Folly was not a tested ship using proven Ganaphe' technology. This was a ship from back in his grandfather's early era of space travel. A time when new technology was being tested, and people losing their lives was expected, if not openly expressed. It was something Ganaphe' of Califas' generation never thought about – never had to. Space travel for them was almost as safe as local travel back home.

Califas found himself back in time, and the fear and excitement was everything he had secretly expected. He was now experiencing what only the generations before his had known. This was time travel in every way but the date. They were all putting their lives on the sharp edge of success and failure – and failure here more than likely meant death.

"Push it!" said Washington. "All the way. Go for it! Let's find out what this ship can do. Let's find out if Cove is the genius we all think he is."

Smith looked at Califas, who nodded his agreement.

"Shuttle one, Folly. All the way to the stops now. Here we go."

He slowly move the throttle control all the way until it was physically stopped. The speed readout climbed. He watched as it read one hundred and eighty-five thousand. Then one-ninety. One-ninety-five. Then right up to two hundred thousand miles per hour. Then it kept climbing!

"Is that right?" he asked excitedly, looking at Califas. "Are we doing better than two hundred K?"

Califas checked his panel and nodded affirmatively. They watched as the indicator climbed higher and stopped at two-zero-seven. Then the computer shut down the engine, as it was programmed to do.

"Son of a… He IS a genius!" screamed Washington. He activated the radio. "Shuttle one, are you with us?"

"Shuttle one is with you Folly. We read your speed as two hundred and seven point two thousand."

"Easy for you to say." he replied with laughter in his voice. He realized that the Ganaphe' shuttle could far surpass their speed, but this was an Earth ship – their ship – his ship, and he was thrilled with it. He removed a thumb sized camera from his zippered pocket and took a picture of the speed indicator.

"Folly, shuttle one. Say your intentions please. Are you going to maintain speed?"

"Roger shuttle one." replied Smith. "Will maintain speed for the duration of the twenty-five minutes, per mission profile."

"Shuttle one will maintain separation and follow." said Mersuul.

"Thank you shuttle one. We appreciate you staying with us." He released the PTT and switched back to the intercom. "Mersuul is one very competent lady. I'm glad to know they are right behind us as backup."

"Yes," agreed Califas, "she is an excellent navigator and an accomplished pilot."

The crew of the Folly checked and rechecked their instruments. Everything was stable. At this stage of the test flight the crew was mostly along for the ride, monitoring instruments, and making sure everything was working. This was the final phase of the burn-in of the ship and its systems. If anything was going to fail, there would be an indication of it during this final period.

The timer on the display panel counted down the minutes. After this phase, the flight would turn around and head for home. On the return journey they were to increase speed using the Forced Ion Pulse engine, and measure the rate of acceleration.

"Hey. I just thought of something." said Washington. "Why is there no test of both engines at the same time?" He looked at his companions.

"There would be very little to gain from such a test." said Califas. Compared to the main engine, the Ion Drive generates a relatively very small amount of thrust."

"It would be like a burp in a wind storm." said Smith.

"Yeah. I realize that, but I'm curious. Isn't it worth having the data even if it just proves it's not worth doing?"

Smith shrugged.

"I suspect Doctor Cove has already run such calculations and found it to be of little benefit." said Califas.

"Yes, but Cove isn't here. He's not the one flying the ship. Shouldn't we at least know first hand what it does?"

"It couldn't hurt." said Smith. "Now you've got my curiosity up. How much time left on this phase?"

"Four minutes."

"What the hell. Let's give it a try." Smith keyed his mic. "Shuttle one, Folly."

"Folly this is shuttle one. Go ahead."

"We are going to deviate slightly from the mission plan. For the last few minutes of the full power phase, we are going to turn on the primary engine and the Ion Drive. Both engines will be active."

There was silence for a few seconds, and they knew that the people on shuttle one saw no purpose to having both engines running, and couldn't figure out why they would want to do it.

"Very well Folly. We will monitor you."

"Roger shuttle one. Restarting primary engine now."

The engine came to life, and Smith checked his engine instruments. All readings were normal.

"Commanding full throttle on the primary engine." said Smith. He didn't expect anything unexpected, so he decided to let both engines run until they reached the turn around point on the flight plan. *'Oh well. Guess nothing unexpected happening beats being blown apart.'* he thought. "All instruments show normal." he continued. "Starting Ion Drive now."

The procedure to turn on the Ion Drive took less than twenty seconds. The instruments on the Ganaphe' shuttle detected the ion stream, but saw only a negligible change in the Folly's rate of acceleration. The same thing was noticed aboard the Folly – everything was working as would be expected. Progressively, the Folly's speed increased, as did its rate of acceleration.

Slowly, the crew of the Folly began to feel the acceleration forces on their bodies again. As their speed increased, the computer on shuttle one increased the shuttle's speed to follow.

7

"Well that was anticlimactic." said del Rio. "I was hoping Cove had built in some surprises."

"I do not believe that Doctor Cove is the type of person who would build surprises into his work. What he says he will do is what he will do."

"Yeahhhh… I was just hoping the Folly had a few more horses under the hood."

"My interactions with Doctor Cove and his past work indicates to me that he is very precise in his specifications." said Plessa. "That is a characteristic I value, especially in a person who has built a ship that has to keep me alive."

"I know. I know. Don't get me wrong. I admire his work. I was just hoping that since he designed an engine that can go this fast he might have added a nitro button. You know… a big red button with a label that says 'Push Only In Emergencies' or something like that."

"Like in a science fiction movie." said Mersuul, smiling.

"Exactly," said del Rio, "and... HEY! What's that glow around the Folly?"

Mersuul and Plessa turned back around to look at the other ship. Glow wasn't exactly the correct description of what they saw. They recognized it as a low level energy field that lightly danced over the skin of the Folly.

"It is... It is not possible!" said Plessa.
"It can not be." added Mersuul.
"What? What is..."

Del Rio never had a chance to finish her sentence. She went silent, with her mouth still open. The Folly was gone.

"Whe... WHERE'S THE FOLLY?"
"You saw it, didn't you?" asked Plessa.
"Yes. I did. I do not believe it." said Mersuul.
"Saw what?"
"The light emission surrounding the Folly" said Plessa.
"I do not believe it." repeated Mersuul.
"What about the light?" asked del Rio.

They both looked at her.

"When our people were beginning to travel through space, as your people are now, we lost many ships. The reports from those that observed what happened said that the lost ships began to emit light and then disappeared. It was a long time before our science advanced to where we understood what had happened. None of the lost ships were ever found. But it can not be! Your propulsion systems are not advanced enough to cause this!"
"Cause what? What is that glow?"
"It is the first sign of high energy free particles being drawn into

381

the ship's propulsion stream." said Plessa. "In space there are high energy particles traveling freely away from their emission sources. They are everywhere within the dark matter of space, but travel haphazardly without any specific purpose. In a way you can consider them to be free and available power if you know how to utilize them. When these particles contact the outside of the ship they change energy states and release photons that create the glow you saw. They also collect on the skin of the ship and act as a magnet that draws even more and stronger forms of free energy. The stronger energy particles collect in a second layer around the outside of the ship, and then combine with the propulsion energy generated by the engine, adding to it and creating much greater total energy levels than what the engine is itself capable of creating. But the Cove engine can not cause this effect. It is not possible."

Mersuul looked at Plessa.

"It was not possible for our early ships either. Yet they did it without knowing how. The Folly must have done it as well." said Mersuul.
"So where are they? What happened to them?"

Mersuul and Plessa were silent for a while.

"We don't know."
"But… can't we track them? Your instruments must show you something."
"No." said Plessa. "This shuttle is not equipped to do so."
"They disappeared! How did they disappear?"
"They did not disappear. It only looked that way to us because the ship jumped into FTL – Faster than light speed. Just in the time we have been talking about this they have traveled a great distance. That is why it seems like they disappeared."
"We have to notify Moon Base." added Mersuul, as she changed the comm frequency for one better suited to voice transmission.
"So they are OK?"

"If the Folly has not been destroyed by the stresses imposed they should still be alive." said Plessa. "What is wrong?" he asked, seeing frustration on Mersuul's face.

"I can not establish a voice channel with the moon base."

"Is it the delay? We are far from them now."

"No it is not that. I am receiving only noise. The time synchronization data stream they continually transmit is gone. We should use our own communications system and contact the Orysta."

"You know we are not allowed to do so. We can only use the moon base radio system. Even acting as the safety ship for this test flight is bending many IGT laws."

8

Ships passing in the night

The wide area scan of his ship's automated defense system alerted Dhona to another vessel moving towards him at high speed, but the normally infallible system was unable to identify it. Sometimes ships were so heavily modified that they no longer matched anything in the database records. Camouflage and defensive systems were automatically turned on by his ship's battle computer. He watched as the vessel got closer. It wasn't coming directly at him but would be close enough to capture an image of it. He touched the control screen and the ship went dark and silent. With his engine shut down he was just drifting on his momentum. The battle computer was continuously calculating intercept points for the imaging system to record the vessel as it went by.

He was now relatively close to the moon of the third planet, which at first made Dhona think that this must be one of their ships. But that wasn't possible. There wasn't much known about the planet called Earth by its inhabitants – there was little need to. It was tanrhas away from practical space flight that would bring it into contact with its galactic neighbors. Occasionally a ship full of sociologists and anthropologists would go there on a field trip to observe the planet, update their records, and look for any anomalies that do come up in the development of all species. For a fee, talented amateur scientists could also come with them, which would help offset the cost of the expedition.

Dhona watched his display panel and when the ship was in visual range he looked out but saw nothing. That wasn't surprising considering the speed the other ship was moving at. His defense systems were well capable of doing what his eyes were not, and almost immediately images of the vessel were sequentially displayed on one of his screens. He was very surprised. This was not a known vessel design and it was not one that was modified. This unknown vessel was a sleek and beautiful ship that looked like it would be able to hold its own in a dog fight. This made no sense. The Earth people had not reached this level of technology, yet this ship could only have come from that planet. Analysis of the exhaust stream it left behind was more confusing. It indicated by-products of combustion as well as an ion stream, both occurring together – which was ridiculous. No one would do that. Even more confusing was that neither propulsion method was capable of propelling a ship at such speed.

Then a memory of his school days popped into his mind, and he remembered something he had learned about the early days of space flight and vanishing ships. *'What was the name of that...'* he thought, *'the Gol... Guul... no, the... THE GUUVASIE EFFECT! That was it – the Guuvasie Effect, named after the physicist who discovered it and was finally able to explain why ships would suddenly vanish.'* It was the basis for the development of propulsion systems that allowed his people to travel across galaxies in short periods of time. Those first generation interstellar engines are considered archaic by today's standards. *'Could the Earth people have developed a Guuvasie engine. Can't be possible – can it? Could the crew of the Orysta be alive, and have violated the IGT by giving the Earth this technology? Could they have been forced to?'*

Dhona transmitted this new information back to the Eowaar, and continued back on course – but this time at inter-galactic speeds. It was normally not recommended to travel at this speed within a solar system, but the questions at hand were too serious to ignore, and they were also the

384

basis for authorization of his action. He looked at his ships indicators and watched as temperature, stress and performance monitors climbed to their maximum indications. If he wasn't flying one of the latest IGT fighter designs he would not be able to maintain this level of performance for as long as would be needed. His fighter was one of the first production models of the type, and he was about to find out if it truly could do what the designers said it could – or probably blow up in the process.

9

Intul-sil-Califas felt like the skin was separating from the rest of his body. He had trouble breathing. Having been turned in his seat while checking his equipment, the sudden tremendous acceleration had caught him off guard. Now his right arm was being crushed against the back of the seat by his body. The cushioning material of the seat had been compressed from a thick foamy material to a paper thin solid, and offered no protection or comfort. The G forces on his body kept him from turning around, and he couldn't see the other two men. He tried to call to them, but the force pressing against his torso, and neck muscles, made it impossible to speak. Still, his mind was functioning and after some thought he had a good idea of what had just happened. Now there were only two questions in his mind – Would he live through this, and was this actually what he thought it was?

Since he heard no sounds from the other men he assumed they were feeling the same influences that he was. On the positive side, no body parts had come off. On the negative side, he was beginning to black out. He didn't know if this was due to low oxygen levels from his shallow breathing, or from the blood being forced from his brain. His vision narrowed and everything was getting quieter. Then he heard it, just before everything went black and silent. It was a scream of horrible pain. He couldn't tell who had made the sound.

10

"HRRRAAAGGGHHHH !!!!!!" came the sound that John Smith forced from his throat, as he tried to maintain consciousness.

He couldn't believe the force he was feeling against his body. Warm fluid ran from his eyes, nose and mouth, and he only knew what it was because he could taste his own blood. They were all about to die – he knew that. But he wasn't going to give up without a fight. He was being crushed to death, and knew the others were also. His years of training kicked in automatically, and his mind went through the minutes before whatever happened had happened. They had been running for some time with the main engine at full power so it probably wasn't that. Then they had engaged the Ion Drive engine which ran without much effect for just a couple of minutes, and wasn't likely to have caused this. There was nothing else that he could think of. There just wasn't anything else. Even when the Folly's main engine was running at ninety percent there was nothing out of the ordinary. They flew faster than the other base shuttles, but still no where near the speed the Ganaphe' shuttles were capable of. *'Undo the last steps one at a time.'* he thought. That was what he was trained to do – undo the last steps before the S-H-T-F and hope you can reverse the situation before you die. It was a tried and true methodology – a few people had even lived through doing it. The last step had been the Ion Drive.

He tried to reach for the drive controls mounted on the lower center console but couldn't move his arms. They were pressed hard against his seat. He tried turning his head to check on Washington but he couldn't do that. Worry crept into his mind. *'How long has this been going on?'* he wondered. *'How much longer can I stay conscious?'* He tried moving his legs and found he could inch them forward. The larger leg muscles had enough strength to overcome the force pushing them back – just barely. He pushed – and pushed – and kept pushing them to the side, nearer the control console. His body felt hot, and breathing was hard. Progress was very slow.

He wondered if he would die first. After what seemed like a very long time, he had his knees against the console, but the throttle was higher than they were. He was able to force his left knee under the right one, and locking them together used their combined strength to slide up the side of the console. There was too much friction for his muscles to overcome, between his pants and the console. Then he remembered to breathe.

He tried to jerk his body forward to get his knee to slide against the console, but it was such a small movement. He did it over and over, gaining fractions of an inch. Smith took a slow, labored breath into his lungs. Then another. Then one more, and with all his will he forced his legs to move upward until they were touching the throttle. Another pair of knees came into his peripheral view, and he knew that Washington was trying to help him. They were both in contact with the throttle handle. They had to get the throttle back beyond the overthrow position that kept it in place. When they stopped pushing forward with their legs, the same force they had had to fight against was now pushing their knees backwards, bringing the throttle with them.

Chapter 21

Encounter

1

Faoul Mahna had been a dhrojja for most of his adult life. He considered himself to be an intelligent man who never could fit into the restrictions of society. He didn't understand why people had looked down on him for torturing small animals when he was a child. He thought it was great fun. And didn't these same people raise animals to slaughter for food. What hypocrites! Then later, in his early adulthood, when he would beat young women into submission for his sexual gratification, the same society tried to put him on trial for what they called crimes. But didn't these same people go home every night and beat their wives and daughters for the same reason. Mahna had no doubt that they did.

The so called legal trial was nothing more than other men trying to show they were superior to him, which Mahna knew they were not. It was their game, by their rules, but Mahna didn't play. Escaping prison wasn't very hard. He only had to kill three guards to do it. Once free he was able to steal a ship and flee. Luckily the ship he stole was very new, and fast, and easy to power up. Over the decitans he had modified his ship by adding weapons, armor, and the latest technology that he could steal. Even today he could remember the faces of all the people he had killed to do this, and it always brought a smile to his face.

There had been many people from many planets and galaxies. The ones he enjoyed killing the most were the free thinking fantasists that thought they could talk him into leaving them alone because they offered him their understanding. They understood his situation, and they understood his anger, and they understood where he was coming from, and they understood his being misunderstood, and it all could be worked out peacefully with talk – and more understanding. When Mahna thought about those people he almost started laughing. They were the easiest prey.

Mahna was a hard worker. Over the decitans he worked hard at his trade, and now he had accomplished something no other dhrojja had in history. He had brought together the largest coalition of dhrojjas ever seen by the galaxies. Dhrojjas were by nature suspicious of other dhrojjas, and rightly so. Mahna had killed many other dhrojjas to put this collection of ships and personnel together. Some he killed while sharing a meal, and others while buying them a drink. Some he killed in their beds while they were unconscious – that he reserved for the most dangerous ones. Some he had even betrayed to the IGT, and let them do the killing for him. It was all just a day's work. The work had paid off.

Mahna was now the unchallenged leader of a fleet of ships. Enough ships to challenge even some IGT security forces – IF they could sneak up on them. That was the reason why he was here in this unaffiliated galaxy, gathering the ships together, away from the eyes of the IGT. When he fortuitously spotted a mining ship in trouble in the same area, he knew it was a good omen. He didn't even bother following the damaged ship right away. He didn't think he would have to. He knew that they would leave a trail of emergency beacons that would point right to their location. Unfortunately it didn't work out that way. He had no way to decrypt the data stored in the beacons, and for some reason the trail of beacons ended at the outermost planet in this solar system. Even a relatively small solar system as this one is very large when you are looking for something the size of a mining ship.

Mahna didn't waste time searching for the ship – it was too big a job. Instead he sent out his dhrojjas in small groups to attack the helpless throughout the known galaxies. They would regroup back here, and while planning future attacks, he would assign some of the dhrojjas to continue the search for the mining ship, and what he was certain was by now a dead crew. His part time search over the decitans had turned up other beacons but they didn't seem to lead anywhere. Then two small ships were spotted flying away from the moon of the third planet. One was a shuttle of standard design, and the other was unknown. It was another good omen for his fleet of dhrojjas. He had left the two ships alone so that they would not alert anyone, and pointed his fleet at the third planet's moon.

2

     The alarms and warning lights went off simultaneously with the automated evacuation instructions that came over the speakers throughout the base. Strobe lights on the walls flashed continuously, while rotating red beacons marked the hallway intersections. The blaring horns intermittently stopped to allow the pre-recorded verbal instructions to be heard.

     "THIS IS A STAGE THREE ALERT! PROCEED IMMEDIATELY TO THE LOWER LEVEL SHELTER! THERE IS AN IMMINENT THREAT OF LOSS OF LIFE SUPPORT SYSTEMS!… THIS IS A STAGE THREE ALERT! PROCEED IMMEDIATELY TO THE LOWER LEVEL SHELTER! THERE IS AN IMMINENT…"

The message was repeated three times, followed by blaring of the horn alerts for thirty seconds, followed by a repeat of the verbal instructions.

     The evacuation procedures were all covered and practiced during orientation, and no one had any hesitation once they realized it was happening for real, and happening now. No matter how comfortable people got while working on the moon base, no one ever forgot the danger that existed just outside the walls. All it took was a look through the windows to see the desolation that waited for you. It even looked cold. Death waited outside the shell of the structure – cold, quick death – if you were lucky. There also existed the possibility of a slow death for those not so lucky.

     "This is Kibbee. All defense personnel to stations. All defense personnel to stations. We are under attack. Guns to hot. Wait for my command to fire."

     Travellor was the only person remaining in the control tower when

390

he heard Kibbee's command over the comm. It had taken less than five minutes for designated personnel to evacuate the upper structure. He wanted to be certain they were safe, and he knew how to confirm it. Only the Orysta's main computer could continuously monitor all personnel at all locations. The Orysta did this by monitoring the comm badges or wrist bands that were required to be worn by everyone. The Moon Base did not yet have that capability. He would have to get that corrected at the first opportunity.

"Orysta this is Travellor. Has the upper base structure been evacuated?" he said loudly before realizing the alarms had gone silent.

He watched outside as the ground randomly and silently exploded, leaving craters where the bombs had landed.

"*All non-combatants have evacuated the upper structure of the moon base.*" said a strange male voice. "*Defense stations are being manned.*"

"What… Who is this? Who's speaking?"

"*This is Orysta.*"

"Commander, this is Munen. We are under attack by dhrojja. They still do not know exactly where we are. They cannot detect us through the camouflage. Their strategy is to find us by bombing the area until something is hit and blows up. It won't take long for them to bomb the whole crater."

"What do you suggest Grilik Munen?"

"Hold all fire until Orysta's guns activate. We will know when they are in range. If we attack at the same time we will hit them from all directions."

"You've done this before." said Travellor rhetorically. "Kibbee, did you copy the Grilik's instructions?"

"Affirmative Commander. All fire control personnel, this is Kibbee. Acquire your targets and fire when the Orysta opens up. I repeat. Acquire your targets and fire when the Orysta's guns go active."

The surrounding area within the crater continued to randomly explode in no predictable pattern except for one thing – the explosions were moving closer to the moon base and the Orysta. Travellor was about to leave the control tower when he realized he wasn't in any more danger there than he would be in any other location.

He sat at the main control console and logged onto the computer. Username – Supreme Commander. '*No one would ever think I'd use that.*' he thought. Password – 75T#k8Htt4!3. The moon base's computer network wasn't any where close to the sophistication of the Orysta's, but it served its purpose. Once logged on he activated the program only he and a couple of software engineers knew existed – TERMINAL SERVICES. It was an appropriately name program.

The Terminal Services program performed only one function. He touched the screen where a red 'ACTIVATE' button was displayed, and looked outside. The protective half-dome located outside at the center of the crater opened up to reveal the quad fifty caliber guns salvaged from an old B-52D model bomber, and modified by 361 technicians to operate in the vacuum of space. Travellor preferred to be able to shoot back when someone was shooting at him, and these were his personal guns.

The fire control system for the weapon had been updated with the latest cross-beam LIDAR and optical targeting system available. Even ships with stealth technology could be detected. The best update was that the information from the targeting systems was fed to both the Orysta's computer and the dedicated local computer. Orysta's computer would easily be able to track and predict target position with its tremendous processing power. With the speeds alien ships were capable of achieving this would be a necessity in some possible situations. If connection to the Orysta was lost the local computer took over. But the moon base was a static target on a relatively stationary solar body, and in the attempt to achieve greater accuracy these attacking ships would be moving at much slower speeds than what they were capable of. Still, it was nice to have the capability there.

He switched the system to manual, and swung the guns left, right, up, and down to verify the hydraulics were working. The system responded normally. He switched back to computer controlled tracking. His computer screen now displayed LIDAR target returns. The bombs were getting closer now. He could feel vibrations being conducted through the ground from the blasts outside. The sky that had shown only stars a few minutes ago now showed lights that grew larger by the second. The dhrojja ships were within gun range, and getting closer. The bombing stopped, and Travellor suspected those ships were switching over to their guns for strafing attacks. In his peripheral vision he detected the Orysta's guns swiveling around and pointing upward. Her guns tips grew bright and slugs of electromagnetic energy were shot at the enemy. Then the base guns opened up and he joined them with his quad.

It was a target rich environment, and Travellor picked a LIDAR signature in the middle of the pirate swarm and locked onto it. With the touch of his finger he triggered the quad. As they fired, the recoil shifted the guns' position as the hydraulics worked to pull them back on target – it was a continuously repeating cycle. Because of this constant, slight change of the guns' position, a cloud of deadly projectiles spewed from the barrel tips to cover a wider area, making the weapon much more deadly to a group of attackers than if the bullets all followed in the same track.

Some of the targets on his LIDAR screen appeared to diminish in size and brightness of the return, as they broke apart, still in large pieces. Some of them fell back behind the advancing group, too damaged to continue their assault. Others just faded out completely, reduced to pieces too small to be detected. The reach of the bullets fired on the Moon was much farther than it would have been with the higher gravity and air resistance of the Earth, but there was one major restriction for the weapons modified for use here. On the screen of each weapon system's targeting display was drawn a circle. It was the seven second circle which marked the point where the internal timer would trigger the explosive that would blow up the bullet into a fine ceramic powder. Anything beyond that range was safe from the projectiles. Those bullets could travel a long way in seven seconds!

One of the remote gun emplacements was hit by enemy fire. There was a bright flash, and a puff of smoke which expanded outward for a short distance, then stopped and just hung over the site. There was no fire – there was no oxygen to feed it. That was it. The destruction wasn't a very impressive sight, all happening in silence.

3

"WHAT THE HELL HAPPENED?" Washington yelled before Smith could.

They both watched Califas busily checking the data on his instrument console. Their own instruments showed a spike in thrust output and speed, but nothing to explain why. All three men were breathing heavily as their bodies tried to readjust physically and psychologically to their near death experience. The adrenaline that had been dumped into their blood had them moving jerkily and aggressively.

"This cannot be correct." said Califas, with an almost nervous laughter.

Smith and Washington kept staring at him. Califas looked surprised and excited as he continued going through the data.

"Haha…, I… I cannot believe this."
"Believe What?" asked Smith and Washington in unison.
"Heh… you… you recreated history. OUR history!" Califas said, with a big smile on his face, as he looked at the others. When he got no reaction from the other two he continued.
"The Folly has gone FTL. You have broken the faster than light barrier. Hahaha. You will go down in your world's history. You will be famous. – OH!…," he said realizing the implications, "I will go down in your world's history. I will be noted in the historical records of another universe!"

394

Silence followed for a while as Smith and Washington tried to assimilate this information.

"I'm no Eckelberry Cove," said Smith, "but I know that this ship can't generate enough power to even get close to the speed of light."

"That is true." replied Califas. "Under normal circumstances it cannot."

"Please explain, before I jump over there, shove my fist down your throat and pull it out of you." said Washington, obviously still shaken up by the experience. He shook himself, and regained control of his nerves. "Sorry. Sorry. I... I'm still feeling the effects."

"Yes. You are feeling more than you know. The effects are both physical and mental. Everyone reacts differently. I will explain as succinctly as I can. Space is full of high energy particles and energy waves that are emitted by many types of galactic and solar objects. Now look at this waveform of the Folly's thrust profile that I recorded."

Smith and Washington stared at the display screen next to Califas. On it was a straight horizontal line that changed into an oscillating waveform, and then showed the waveform rising sharply in amplitude and level.

"This point just prior to the oscillation is where you engaged the Ion Drive. I am guessing as to what actually happened, but I base this on our own space flight history. Somehow the output streams of the two engines combined in a parasitic oscillation, the effect of which was to attract the high energy particles and waves. These particles were pulled to the Folly and traveled down the skin to the output streams where they combined with the existing output and increased the amount of thrust many times."

"But... how many times could it possibly increase the thrust level. I understand that you guys do it regularly, but my understanding is limited. This ship was not designed to travel that fast. Shouldn't power levels that high have destroyed the ship?"

"That is where it gets complicated." said Califas. "At a certain point after FTL the ship is no longer flying through space as an airplane flies through air particles. When that point is reached the surrounding 'bubble' of space travels with the ship, and is not flowing passed it. You can think of this as a protective layer of space that moves with you."

"Do you do this every time?" asked Washington. "Do you go through this … this torture every time you travel in the Orysta?"

"We do not. The Orysta and all galactic class ships have systems that cancel the effect if accelerated properly."

Washington tilted his head back against his seat and took a deep breath.

"I have to tell you, I thought we were dead. I had no doubt the ship was going to be torn apart and us along with it."

"This is odd." said Smith. "Must be something wrong with our gauges. This says we still have most of our fuel left."

"That would seem to confirm my theory." said Califas. "The ship's fuel was only being used to sustain the oscillation. The power for FTL travel came from the outside."

"How far did we travel?" asked Washington.

"I will see if I can determine that." said Califas, as various star charts popped up on his screen. He looked up and pointed. "See that large body over there."

"That oddly shaped – what is it, a moon without a planet?"

"That is known in your database as asteroid Vesta. It is considered by your people to be a small terrestrial planet because of its size and composition. We have traveled over ninety-seven million five hundred thousand larn. That is over one hundred and fifty-six million miles."

"Holy sh…"

"The shuttle!" interjected Washington. "They must be wondering what happened to us." He touched the comm button and spoke. "Shuttle one, this is the Folly. Over." When there was no response he repeated his message.

"If we have traveled FTL, which I am certain we have, shuttle one will not receive your message for some time. Your communications system emits signals that only travel at light speed. It will take approximately fifteen minutes before they hear you – if they hear you."

4

"Just background noise." said Mersuul. "It is as if all signals are being blocked."

"Could there be something between us and the base?" asked del Rio. "An asteroid or something large?"

"It is not likely." said Plessa. "It would have to be traveling on a path directly in line with this shuttle and the base to continually block out the signal. Something else is causing this problem."

"You said we could contact them on the shuttle's comm system." said del Rio. "It's only the base's frequencies that are being blocked."

"That would violate IGT law." said Plessa. "You know that."

"Yes, I know. I also know that our people have disappeared and we need to begin a search as soon as possible. Remember – it was an immediate search that saved my life. You were both there when it happened."

Her reminder triggered memories in the other two that made them uncomfortable, and brought back the feelings and thoughts they experienced then.

"It… would not be violating law if we contacted the Orysta instead of the base, to give them a report of our status." said Mersuul. "If anyone under Commander Travellor's command was there to hear our report it would not be a violation."

"That is correct," replied Plessa, "it would not be a violation. Do it."

Mersuul initiated the transmission. Then she tried again.

397

"What is the problem?" asked Plessa.

"All communications are being blocked. It must be being done intentionally. I have tried all frequencies. Something is wrong. This would only happen if…"

"Place the shuttle on course for the moon." Plessa said anxiously. "Maximum speed. Secure yourself in your seat Delores. You will feel this again."

"What's the problem?" asked del Rio as she sat back into her seat. "Why can't you raise the Orysta?"

The sudden intense acceleration of the shuttle pushed all of them back into the seats. The shuttle systems to negate these forces under normal circumstances were not completely effective at maximum acceleration. Del Rio remembered that the Folly had no such compensation, and wondered what the people in that ship must have felt. It was several seconds before she stopped feeling the effects on her body, after the shuttle's speed had stabilized. She asked again why they couldn't contact the Orysta.

"There is only one logical reason." answered Mersuul. "The base is under attack."

"Attack? By who?" asked del Rio. "There isn't anyone on Earth capable of doing that."

"Dhrojja!" said Plessa. "Pirates!"

"Pirates? As in 'pirates'? In space? Why would they attack us? We don't have any… OH!… Crystal-flow!"

"Yes. They want the crystal-flow – and anything else they can take."

Del Rio though about this for a while, and wondered if the base's defenses were good enough to fight them off.

"What kind of weapons do they have?"

"They likely have energy pulse guns, as well as exothermic bombs similar to Earth's."

"And our guns – can they take out their ships? Will they be effective?"

"Very effective." replied Mersuul. "The dhrojja will not be expecting projectile weapons. It is likely they do not know the moon base is there. It is probably the Orysta they are looking for."

"But the Orysta has been there for years. What brought them there now?"

"I do not know." said Mersuul and Plessa at the same time.

"Are the weapons on this shuttle working?"

"Yes. We have one forward mounted energy pulse gun and one top mounted turret gun." said Mersuul as she turned to look at del Rio. "This shuttle was not meant to engage in battle. Those weapons are mainly for defense."

Del Rio felt confused and angry. The base was possibly being attacked, and the Folly's crew were lost in space without any way to know where they might be. She felt slightly sick, but after a few seconds that feeling began to resolve into anger.

"What can I do?" she asked.

5

They had made a major mistake – understandably. The remaining sixty-two dhrojja ships adjusted course and headed for the location of the Orysta's glowing guns. They knew the mining ship was the only ship out here that was big enough to defend itself, which was partially correct. They assumed there was no other threat to them, which was wrong. It was Kibbee who first noticed their change in attack pattern, and he understood what had happened. He immediately came over the comm and ordered all base guns to hold fire and wait for his command. It took only a seconds for the dhrojja ships to get much closer together while also getting well within the fire zone of the bases guns.

He waited as long as he could without endangering the Orysta more than was necessary, then gave the command and all guns opened fire. Eight of the dhrojja ships were destroyed by the unexpected onslaught before the others realized what had happened and broke of their attack. Several others had been damaged, but were still operational. It only took a short time for the dhrojjas to locate all the guns and their remaining ships picked their target of choice. The seven Moon Base gun emplacements had been randomly located throughout the area – intentionally not placed in any pattern. Together the guns could cover all the visible area above the crater. This placement made it harder for the attacking ships to avoid flying into each other. The dhrojjas knew some basic tactics but didn't have the discipline of a trained military force. The sky became a dangerous criss-cross of single minded ships, serendipitously avoiding in-flight crashes – for a short time. Three collisions occurred after the first few minutes, causing five of the dhrojja ships to crash into the moon and one to limp away from the battle.

The dhrojjas were so involved with their attack, and trying to avoid crashing into each other, that they didn't notice the three smaller ships converging on them from the rear. The moon base shuttles had been on normal patrol, with their crews expecting a quiet routine mission when the alert came over their comm systems. Each base shuttle was equipped with two guns, modeled after the Orysta's shuttles. One was a forward facing gun that fired at whatever the shuttle was pointing at. The other was a turret mount that could rotate three hundred and sixty degrees around and pivot one hundred and eighty degrees in elevation, effectively covering the lower hemisphere of the ship.

Over an encrypted low frequency comm channel the shuttles quickly decided on a plan of action. They had all flown away from the moon until they were beyond the attacking dhrojjas, and then turned back towards the rear flank of the attacking ships. They would get one or maybe two shots at taking out an enemy ship before they were noticed. The dhrojja ships had slowed to more accurately aim at their targets. The base shuttles closed for the attack in a diamond formation and at their maximum speed.

The closure rate was high and in seconds they were in firing range.

The shuttles easily took out the three rearmost dhrojja ships, then immediately changed course to intercept their next target. In each shuttle the pilot controlled the forward gun while flying directly at his intended target. The copilot controlled the turret gun and fired on the first target of opportunity that came into his fire zone. The dhrojjas were still not aware of the shuttles when the secondary targets were taken out. Five more dhrojja ships had been destroyed or disabled. The shuttles were forced to maneuver drastically to avoid debris from the destroyed ships. The advantage of surprise was now gone.

More than half of the dhrojjas, not yet sure of where their enemy was, broke off their attack and maneuvered out of the attacking swarm. Not all dhrojjas are good fighters. Some will only attack when their target is unaware, and some will run at the first sign of resistance. There were a lot more of them than there were base shuttles, and the shuttles were soon on the defensive. Dog fights broke out with two to four dhrojja ships attacking each of the shuttles. What should have been an advantage of numbers for the enemy became one for the shuttles as too many dhrojjas attacking the same shuttle interfered with each other. Two dhrojjas ships were destroyed by friendly fire. The shuttle crews were all disciplined ex-military fliers, and what started as an outnumbered defense soon became one on one dogfights. The base shuttles were small and maneuverable. They could make tight turns and rapid heading changes. The dhrojja ships were larger, heavier, less maneuverable and more heavily armed. But having a lot of weapons doesn't do any good if you don't get to use them.

6

"WHAT THE HELL ARE YOU DOING HERE?"

"I came to help." said Cove.

"Help with what, Doctor? This is a gun fight, and all the guns are already manned. I have very clear orders that your safety is a base priority, and Farber-Chatwell is right. You are too important right now. GET

BELOW!"

"You're not using all of your weapons."

"Unless you know something I don't, we're sending everything we've got at them. GET BELOW – NOW!"

"The area lights! You're not using the area lights!"

The curse words were just about to leave his mouth, when Travellor realized what Cove was getting at. The area lighting fixtures were huge devices that put out an unbelievable amount of candle power. That much light was needed to illuminate this very large crater for outside work. They were capable of turning the entire area within the crater into a bright and sunny, Florida-like summer day. Everyone always joked that you probably could get a tan if you could go outside without your space suit. Travellor didn't know the exact specifications on the arrays, but newcomers were instructed never to look directly into one. Each array sat on a computer controlled motorized mount that could swivel their beams to point to any section of the crater. During maintenance the arrays were pointed straight up, and they could be pointed to almost every section of the sky. The enemy ships were attacking from low altitude now, which meant they were operating visually.

"How do we point them?"

"We can't, not the way we need to. But the Orysta can. Her computer can calculate the intersection angle of the beams for maximum effect."

"Grilik Munen, this is Travellor."

"Yes Commander. I hear you."

"Doctor Cove believes we can use the area lights to blind our attackers. He says Orysta can calculate and control their aiming. Is that possible? Over."

"The Orysta can generate her own code and create a program quickly. I will start on this now. It should only take a few fracins. Stand by."

"You should also get your other shuttle ready to launch. Inform me

402

when it is ready. Over."

"The shuttle is ready to launch now, Commander. We have been waiting for an opportunity to do so."

Travellor turned his attention back to Cove.

"Thank you Doctor. Please go back below now."
"No. I should stay here."
"I believe Erika would be very upset if something happened to you." said Travellor, trying to get a psychological advantage in his argument. "Go be..."
"That's pretty low Commander. I'm staying! Precisely to help make sure that nothing happens to Erika. You seem to forget that I am also a resource at your disposal. I may come up with other ideas to help."

Travellor felt frustration, and anger at the younger man. The feelings quickly changed to respect. He knew what Cove was feeling. When the lives of people you care for are threatened, you want to fight – and you want to kill the threat. Cove was right. The lives of a lot of other people might depend on just one good idea today.

7

"Are you sure we can do this?" asked Smith.
"I am calculating the time and direction of travel that should reverse our course and get us back to where we started." said Califas.
"Are you sure we can do it again – break into FTL?"

Califas thought about that for a short time before answering.

"Theoretically we have the same components that caused us to do it the first time. We should be able to recreate the same circumstances. I cannot guarantee it."

403

"And we're going to experience the same thing... the same pain... all of that?" asked Washington.

"There is no way to avoid it on this ship. However, now that we are expecting it we can position ourselves more comfortably. We should place our backs against the seats, with our heads facing forward, and our arms down at our sides."

"I'd rather not do it again, myself." said Washington.

"We have no choice." replied Califas. "We do not have enough fuel to make it back at normal speed. We are not equipped with food or water for an extended period. If we can not replicate the factors that put this ship into FTL we will die in space. The Orysta's shuttles searching at their maximum speed would be unlikely to find us."

"How do we shut it down? We were lucky the first time." asked Smith.

"Our luck is still with us, in that the Ion Drive control can be preprogrammed to shut down at a selected time. When the drive shuts down the parasitic oscillation should terminate, dropping us out of FTL."

Smith and Washington looked at Califas with some doubt in their eyes.

"It should work. I cannot guarantee it. Perhaps, as a secondary option, you should also place your knees in a more advantageous position this time."

Washington closed his eyes and groaned. Then a thought came to him.

"Hold on." he said. "The shuttle has probably headed back to base by now. You said they have no way to track us. What else could they do? So you should calculate our flight to get us closer to the moon, instead of where we started FTL."

"Good thinking." said Smith.

"I agree." said Califas.

"Is shuttle two ready Grilik?"

"Yes Commander. The shuttle will launch on your command."

"Good. Stand by." Travellor took one last look outside, then keyed his mic. "Arrowhead flight, this is Travellor. Report status. Over."

"This is Arrowhead one. Arrowhead flight ready for launch on command. Over."

"Roger. All ships, this is Travellor. Stand by for full power launch on my command."

He got acknowledgements from all four shuttles. The three base shuttles had been caught on standby, in the landing bay, when the attack started, as had the Orysta's number two shuttle. Now they were going to try to give those ships a chance to get off the ground without being destroyed. He turned to Cove.

"Are we ready?"

"All area lights are aimed and ready. Those pirate ships will be flying into a wall of light. They'll have to deviate over twenty-five degrees to be able to see again." said Cove.

Above them, the pirate ships were gathering into a wall of their own – a wall of attacking ships. Their intent was obvious. All ships releasing weapons at the same time would carpet bomb the crater. They didn't need to know exactly where the guns were located – everything in the crater would likely be hit. It would be devastating. It had to be stopped.

"Commander, this is Munen. They have begun their attack run. The clock is ticking."

"Roger Grilik Munen." said Travellor while looking at the two count down timers on his display. One was the time to turn on the area light, and one had five seconds more for launch time. "All ships stand by on throttles and brakes. Weapons hot."

Weapons hot was not a command normally given to ships still in the docking bay, but nothing about the next moments would be normal. Travellor watched the first timer count down. Seven… six… five… He knew all of the shuttles were also watching it. Four… three… two… one… The area lights bloomed together into a mini sun. Even the bleed-over light from the edges of the arrays was blinding.

"Arrowhead flight, this is arrowhead one – ENGINES TO FULL POWER!" came over the comm.

The metal structure of the building vibrated from the roaring thrust of the shuttles engines as they throttled up to the firewall. All unattached tools and equipment should already have been moved out of the bay, but there would still be a lot of damaged maintenance stations, and certainly a big mess from the heat and combustion byproducts of the engines. The Orysta didn't have to worry about those things. Her shuttle's engines didn't work on the same principle.

Travellor watched the second timer count down. Three… two… He couldn't see them, but knew the bay doors were opening as fast as they physically could – which was quite fast. He and Cove looked out the windows, both shielding their eyes from the lights with their hand. They saw three blurs, one after the other, heading away and towards the edge of the crater, and then upwards at an angle. They knew a forth ship also took off from Orysta, which they didn't see. They were running out of time before the enemy dropped their bombs.

9

The four shuttles engaged the attacking ships on their rear flank. Unspotted and unexpected they destroyed seven of the dhrojja ships before completing their traverse through the attacking formation. All shuttles had been equipped with IFF. It was one of the few 361 supplied systems the

Ganaphe' had fitted to their ships. The Identification Friend or Foe system showed which ships were friendlies and which were not, and displayed their location on the radar screens. They could see the first three base shuttles engaged in dog fights, but couldn't do anything for them at the moment. They had their own job to do – stopping the attack on the moon base.

The shuttles came back around behind the dhrojja ships. They spread wide, and at high speed, again flew into the rear of the formation. The element of surprise was not going to last and they took advantage of it while they could. Locking onto the lead dhrojja ships with their targeting systems they launched self guiding missiles just at the moment some of the other dhrojja ships became aware of the rear attack and broke formation. The evasive maneuvering of these dhrojjas was only helpful to the shuttles, making the path to the targeted ships less obstructed.

Everything was happening in such close proximity, and high speed, that in less than sixty seconds after launch several dhrojja ships in the front of the formation blew up. Any dhrojjas that hadn't realized they were under attack from the rear were now aware of it. They quickly took evasive action, which put an end to the massive bombing run. But not all of the dhrojjas were undisciplined, and three ships continued flying towards the moon. The dhrojjas that had scattered now targeted the four shuttles and a repeat of the original dog fights took place, with multiple dhrojja ships targeting a single shuttle.

10

Shuttle one came into detection range with their fire control systems armed and ready. What appeared on their display screen shocked them. It was filled with target detections, and only a handful were friendlies. At first they were confused by the number of ships being indicated, but they had no choice but to believe what was being shown to them.

Keeping their speed up, Mersuul flew towards the outermost targets. Three of them were marked as base shuttles. The others had to be dhrojjas.

Plessa controlled the turret guns, and del Rio was given control of the forward guns. Their plan was simple – pick off the easiest targets first and hope they could get most of them before they themselves were targeted. Mersuul and Plessa operated like a well trained team, working almost emotionlessly. Del Rio was angry – and ready to kill. These pirates were attacking her friends and her home. She intended to kill them all.

Mersuul headed for the nearest dog fight, and directly for the trailing dhrojja ship, while rotating the shuttle so that the lower part of the ship faced the second attacker. The fire control display went from red to green indicating their guns were in range. Del Rio could barely keep herself from activating the guns until the enemy ship was in her sights. When they were, she fired. The tips of the shuttle's guns glowed brightly and pumped volley after volley of cohesive energy pulses that proved to be right on target. The energy pulses didn't penetrate the target like a bullet would have. Instead they transferred their tremendous level of energy to the molecules of the material they contacted, disrupting the bonds of the material at an atomic level. The result was that the material fell apart, into its constituent substances. In the end, it was just a high-tech way of creating a hole – a big hole. A very effective, big hole.

Plessa had locked on to the second dhrojja ship in the dog fight, and his turret guns had fired shortly after del Rio's. He had aimed for the rear of the ship, and must have hit the energy conversion chamber. The rear of the dhrojja ship blew apart leaving only the front half intact and tumbling uncontrollably in space.

"Thanks shuttle one." came over the radio. "Base two joining up with you. Let's get some more of the bastards."

Base shuttle number two smoothly arced around and came up beside shuttle one. They quickly decided on their next targets. The plan was the same. Each would assist the other shuttles that were still engaged in a dogfight. With all four free, they could re-engage the enemy as a force.

"BREAK AWAY NOW! BREAK AWAY NOW!" yelled Plessa,

who had been monitoring the dhrojjas.

Both ships immediately pulled away from each other at maximum power. The fire from the enemy's guns traveled right through the space they had been occupying. Plans can often go wrong.

11

Mahna could not believe what he was seeing on his screens. It had taken him decitans to get this fleet of ships together. They were a formidable force – he had thought. They would be able to fly through any galaxy of their choice, and take whatever they wanted – he had thought. All they had to do this diest was attack one damaged mining ship. One lousy helpless mining ship! Before his eyes he watched as more than half of the dhrojjas were destroyed by a handful of smaller vessels. They weren't even fighter craft! They were just shuttles! What kind of incompetents had he assembled? He grew angrier with each passing fracin.

He wondered where the mining ship had gotten so many weapons. And most of those shuttles were not standard designs either. Where did they come from? The miners wouldn't have dared to contact anyone in this non-affiliated solar system. They knew the penalty for that was severe under the IGT. The so-called law abiding citizens of the IGT feared its laws and penalties. Then again, none of this really mattered. The truth was that those selfish, greedy, useless excuses for dhrojjas that he had gathered never bothered to better their ships or their weapons. He would have to correct that when this was over. He would kill a few of them and destroy their ships (after first taking anything of value) as an example to the others. No one would argue when he told them to spend their plunder on better weapons and armor. If they did he would kill them too.

Mahna watched as three of his dhrojjas approached the surface of the moon, ready to release their bombs. He couldn't see what they were targeting, but it had to be the mining ship. Even just three ships could release enough bombs to cause a lot of damage. He had to admire their bravery, to be getting so close before releasing their weapons. It would insure that they hit the target. They were close to the release point and would drop the bombs at any fracin now. His tension and anger eased a little. He was going to enjoy knowing the surface of this moon, and he assumed the mining ship also, would be blown out into space as dust and debris. A smile lifted the corners of his mouth. This would be a very good show. As he watched the display screen, his three dhrojjas flickered out of existence.

12

The Folly dropped out of FTL when the Ion Drive shut down as it was programmed to. The pain the men were suffering immediately began to diminish. If judged by their last experience with FTL it would still be a while before it went away completely.

"Everyone OK?" asked Smith, in a croaking voice.
"I am alive." replied Califas.

Smith looked over at Washington. His eyes were closed and fluttering, and he wasn't moving.

"WASHINGTON! WASHINGTON, WAKE UP!" yelled Smith while reaching over and shaking him. There was no reaction.
"He is alive!" said Califas, looking at the biometric data from Washington's suit. "Brain activity is not normal. He is injured."

Smith was about to unbuckle his safety harness when the view in front of the ship caught his attention. Debris was spread throughout the area. What looked like bodies floated with all the ship parts, some in space suits and some without. His radar showed too many returns to count quickly, and only a handful of them were friendlies.

"I see them also." said Califas, unbuckling his harness and getting out of his seat.

"What are you doing?"

Califas released the unconscious Washington's harness, and lifted him out of the copilot seat.

"The base is under attack. I can be more useful up here." he answered while securing Washington in the rear seat. He took Washington's seat and strapped in. He quickly looked over the location of all the controls and hoped he could remember what he had learned about them. "No one has detected us yet." he said pointing to the targeting screen. "Those three ships are heading for the base. We have to…"

"Got it!" interjected Smith. "Are you familiar with the fire control system?" he asked as he moved the throttles forward.

"I studied everything about this ship when I knew I was coming along on the test flight." He tapped the touch screen in front of him. Guns and rocket launchers extended outward from the fuselage and wings.

"Good man!" said Smith as he maneuvered towards the three threats. "I'll handle the guns. You lock on and fire those rockets as soon as you get target lock."

"I will. But how do I…"

Smith reached over and set the controls for individual targeting.

"When you get target acquisition one rocket will automatically be assigned to one target. They will both show the same iconic symbol to let you know which ones are paired up. Launch the rocket by touching it on the screen."

"Yes. I remember now. Thank you."

Nothing else needed to be said. At that moment target lock was achieved. Califas touched three of the six rocket symbols on the left side of the screen. There was another six on the right side. Each symbol in turn changed from yellow to red and the word 'Deployed' was flashed over them.

"Sometimes fate is on our side, and sometimes it is not." he said to Smith. "The test flight was designated to be carried out with all systems operational, and because of that we are fully armed. Today, fate is on our side."

Both men watched the exhaust trails as the three rockets closed rapidly on the attacking ships. All three hit their targets. Smith's eyes went wide when he saw the size of the explosions that resulted, and he wondered if that was due to the type of explosive in the rockets or something that blew up in the ships. There was nothing left of the enemy but shards. *'Something to ask about at a later time.'* he thought, and turned the Folly towards the nearest enemy targets.

That was when the Folly started shaking, and the dark coating on the left wing blistered and ablated away. Then the structure underneath turned red, and then white, with increasing brightness, and they could hear a rumbling followed by the sound of partially melted metal tearing as the wing completely separated from the fuselage. They had been hit.

The sound of liquids and gases escaping came to their ears, followed by multiple *'fip – fip – fip'* sounds of safety valves closing. The men quickly looked at each other, and then Smith pulled the ship up and to the right. He was surprised that he still had full control. The display panel showed the flight computer was automatically compensating for the lost thrusters of the left wing by adjusting the thrust direction of the main engine, and the output of the body and right wing thrusters.

"I LOVE YOU COVE!" Smith yelled, while looking where the missing wing used to be.

The targeting computer showed his attacker following close behind. It also showed another unidentified ship closing in on the enemy very fast. A second later the radar return of the enemy ship bloomed into a larger shape and then disappeared.

412

13

Joe Riley and Matt Pope tumbled through space, moving away from where their Moon Base shuttle had been destroyed. The small craft had taken a hell of a beating before the propulsion and life support systems failed (Credit to the ship's designers). Their ship had become the proverbial sitting duck, and several pirate ships were firing on them. There was nothing left to do but eject, which they did, one after the other and just in time. The shuttle was turned into scrap by enemy fire just seconds later.

Ejecting from a ship in space is not like ejecting from a plane on Earth. In space there is no gravity to pull back to the ground. Instead you just keep traveling in the direction you ejected, at pretty much the same speed you separated from the ship at. And of course you are continually tumbling. You're not supposed to tumble, but Hey! That's life. There is no air resistance to stop the tumbling. There was a parachute but out here is space it was useless. The ejection seats were designed to separate the person from the ship in a stable and straight line, and it probably works very well – on Earth. In space the slightest imbalance can affect the end result. Now the result was that Riley and Pope were rapidly flying through space in nothing but their space suits, still strapped to their ejection seats and tumbling at a slow and steady rate.

Riley pressed the release on his harness and pushed back with his arms and legs, separating himself from the seat which moved away from him a few yards but continued to follow him. Pope had done the same. Pope had been hired by 361 to pilot his own ship, but there wasn't one available at the time. While waiting for a new Base shuttle, Pope was temporarily assigned as Riley's copilot. Both of them continued on their way to open space, accompanied by their now separated seats, which traveled in slightly diverging paths. They both saw the energy pulses that hit one of the seats and sent it hurtling away, and both looked in the direction the pulse came from to see a pirate ship heading for them. It was damaged, with sections of the hull missing. It was moving very slowly, and seemed to be having a lot of trouble holding its course. The whole vessel would vibrate and suddenly change heading. Every time its nose veered off it was forced back towards them. That was the only reason they hadn't fired again.

Riley understood one thing about what he was seeing – the people in that ship wanted to kill them – strictly for revenge. They were waiting until they were so close they couldn't miss. *'He's going to blame me for this.'* he thought, glimpsing Pope as he rotated. *'If he wasn't given the temp assignment as my copilot he wouldn't be a defenseless target right now. He's going to be pissed if they kill us.'*

14

Giell-sil-Dhona dropped his IGT fighter out of tetra-space, close to the moon of the third planet. You never know what you are going to confront when you do that, and his ship, being one of the latest design IGT fighters, automatically deployed defensive systems and armed all weapons. His eyes locked on to a ship at a distance in front him. It had holes blown through its hull. Its internal gases and liquids were venting into space. Some of it was white, some blue, and some red. Some of it had frozen into ice and some was evaporating away.

He instinctively knew it was a pirate ship, as he also instinctively knew that the solid projectiles that made those holes were still intact and traveling directly at him. He had flown into the path of someone else's gun fire. The fighter's armor could protect him from most of them but not all. It all happened in a fraction of a fracin.

Thousands of heelas of training kicked in without thought and he went to maximum power in a direct vertical climb, just as he saw those projectiles explode into a fine powder. He released the breath he had unconsciously been holding and inhaled deeply, quickly performing a visual survey and then studying his weapons targeting system. The display showed two friendlies, five unknowns, and eleven dhrojjas. His battle computer located and identified the Orysta on the moon's surface. He knew

414

the Orysta was equipped with two shuttles. Where did the other five ships assisting those shuttles come from? The computer didn't recognize their design, but they were obviously fighting with the Orysta's shuttles against the dhrojjas.

"Send status report to Eowaar. Dhrojjas attacking Orysta and unidentified friendly ships. Orysta on surface of third planet's moon. Engaging eleven enemy ships."

"*Message and situation data transmitted to the Eowaar.*" said the computer.

"Give me targeting solutions on all dhrojjas engaged with friendlies and unknowns."

On his screen all ships were color coded. Red for the dhrojjas, green for Orysta's shuttles, and orange for the unknowns. Curved lines from the symbol that indicated his fighter were drawn to the enemy ships, each marked with the name of the suggested weapon to use. Dhona smiled to himself. He just loved this fighter. It was designated a multi-purpose ship but it could outperform any dedicated purpose fighter even in its designated role – and he was one of the few people who presently had one. Now he was going to probably be the only person to have the opportunity to apply many of its capabilities in actual combat.

15

"Matt... do you see that..., what's... going on?"

"Yes. Amazing. What are we firing at those shits?"

"I don't know. Must be from one of the Orysta's shuttles. I don't think we have anything that can do that."

"What about the Folly? Does she have it?"

"Not that I know of."

Every time their bodies rotated into the position where they could see the battle, they strained to maintain their view. Pirate ships were blowing up one after the other, like they had been programmed to self destruct. At first it seemed random, but it was happening so consistently you could keep time by the flashes. The pirates were scattering, and running scared.

"Their running! Those ass holes are running! They're scared now."
"Joe. The ship! It's almost on us!"

Riley looked back at the pirate ship that had been stalking them. It was so close now that he could see the joints and attachments on the skin. He knew it was just a matter of seconds now.

"I'm sorry Matt. For getting you into this situation. It was an honor fighting with you."
"What?… This is not your fault… not anyone's fault. Just the hazards of the job. Wish I had a gun. Even if it wouldn't stop the bastard, I'd still feel better shooting at the son of a bitch."
Riley chuckled at the comment. "Me too. Next time we carry guns… in big holsters… six shooters!"

They both broke into laughter as they watched the nose of the ship slowly move back in their direction. Then its forward guns glowed as a steady, regular pulse of deadly energy started flying out. The ship wasn't on target yet, and as Riley and Pope watched it seemed the pulses formed an arcing stream that moved closer and closer to them.

16

Shuttle one moved as fast as the calculated safe speed given by the computer allowed. It was going to be close – and dangerous. They were moving into the firing zone of the dhrojja, but there was no time left, and no other way to do it. Their turret gun had literally been shot off of the ship.

416

The damage to that gun had also made their forward gun inoperable – both guns were powered by the same, now damaged, energy source. They were out of the fight, and were about to attempt getting back to the Orysta when they spotted one last bit of good they could do in this battle. There was one very small chance of pulling it off without getting killed, and all on board had agreed to take the risk.

As it approached the targets, del Rio opened the cargo door, and Mersuul pivoted the shuttle so that the opening was facing broadside. There would only be one shot at this. At this speed, being misaligned would cause the death of their friends just as surely as the enemy's guns. The closure rate was very high, and Mersuul had to maneuver by eyesight, with very subtle touches of the controls. There were no sensors on the shuttle that could detect the two targets and allow the computer to fly the ship with the precision necessary. If she made a misjudgement, the men would suffer serious injury or a painful death.

"Five…, four…, three…," the shuttles computer counted down, calculating the time from it starting position, the distance to target, and speed of the ship. *"two…, contact."*

The impact shuddered the shuttle.

17

Riley and Pope never saw shuttle one approaching at high speed. They had been fixated on the approaching stream of deadly energy pulses from the pirate ship. It was a total surprise and shock when their bodies contacted the cargo net that had been strung across the opening of the cargo door. Del Rio immediately closed the cargo door as both men came through the opening. Mersuul commanded maximum speed, and the shuttle moved rapidly away from the approaching gunfire.

The net was normally used to hold down heavy cargo, and keep it from shifting inside the shuttle. It was made of a strong fiber that was not designed to be very flexible. It was not soft, and it was never intended to be used like this. The impact forces of the two bodies hitting it at high speed caused the net to stretch until both men slammed against the opposite wall of the shuttle. The impact was severe enough to break Pope's left arm, and knock Riley unconscious, with a concussion. As the net sprung back, it slung the men against the now closed cargo door, dislocating the unconscious Riley's right shoulder, while breaking Pope's jaw and cracking his right eye socket. Both were now slumped on the floor, unmoving.

Mersuul maneuvered the shuttle away from the stream of the dhrojja's gun fire. She and Plessa looked back to see if they were safe, and saw the pirate being cut in two by fire from another ship. The opened hull ejected three bodies which jerked around for a moment and then floated motionless in space. None of them had been wearing their helmets.

"Orysta shuttle, this is IGT interjection fighter pilot Lanor Dhona, off of the Eowaar. I am here to assist you."

"EOWAAR?" screamed Mersuul over the comm. "Did you say the Eowaar? The battle carrier Eowaar?"

"That is correct. Who am I speaking to?"

"This is Orysta navigator Mersuul-sil-Vaana."

There was a pause, and Mersuul thought her transmission wasn't received.

"Vaana? Mersuul-sil-Vaana you said? Is that correct?"

"Yes. That is correct. I am here with Chief Engineer Benua-sil-Plessa, and members of Earth's Trailblazer Moon Base."

"This is amazing!" said Dhona. "Is the rest of your crew alive? We thought you were all dead. Your uncle will be very happy to hear this. I'm transmitting a report to the Eowaar now."

Mersuul smiled and looked at Plessa and del Rio.

"My uncle is here. He brought the Eowaar!" she said, her smile almost breaking her face.

"That is excellent news!" said Plessa.

"What's the Eowaar?"

"The Eowaar is something you have never seen before." Plessa said to del Rio. "The greatest war ships on your planet cannot prepare you for what the Eowaar is. It will amaze you."

"He said it was a battle carrier. Is that like a battle ship… or an aircraft carrier?"

"It is all of that and much, much more. You have to see it to understand what it is. Are they alright?" he asked, looking at the two unconscious men.

Del Rio looked back at the two men on the floor.

"Oh God, I forgot all about them." she said, rushing back to unhook the net. Plessa got up to help.

Mersuul touched the display screen to pull up the biometric data on the two men.

"Be careful!" she said to Plessa and del Rio. "They need medical attention. They have broken bones." She tapped the comm button. "Lanor Dhona, I have injured personnel on board. They need a doctor. What is the status of the battle?"

"I have destroyed the remaining dhrojja that wanted to fight." replied Dhona. "Other ships are fleeing the battle area. The battle is over, Navigator Vaana. You are clear to go to the Orysta. I will accompany you… CRHAAKA! HOW THE BLEHM DID THEY GET ONE OF THOSE?"

"One of what?" asked Mersuul, responding to the fear in his voice. "ONE OF WHAT?"

With no input from her, the shuttle suddenly and automatically rotated and started moving away from the battle zone at maximum speed. The shuttle computer was responding to a programmed signal Dhona had just sent out. All IGT ships' computers were programmed to override flight crew control inputs and immediately move away from the designated area at maximum speed, when that signal was broadcast. Mersuul looked at her targeting display and saw that shuttle two had also received the override command. She tapped the comm button but was behind the other shuttle with her action.

"ALL BASE SHUTTTLES THIS IS ORYSTA SHUTTLE TWO. MOVE AWAY FROM THE BATTLE ZONE AT MAXIMUM SPEED. MOVE AWAY FROM THE BATTLE ZONE AT MAXIMUM SPEED. MOVE NOW!" came Mengu-sil-Valian's voice over the comm.

Several voices interfered with each other on the comm channel, asking what was going on.

"THIS IS VALIAN IN SHUTTLE TWO. NO QUESTIONS. MOVE AWAY FROM THE BATTLE ZONE AT MAXIMUM SPEED IF YOU WANT TO SURVIVE. DO IT NOW!"

Apparently hearing the warning the second time, and Valian's tone of voice, made the seriousness of the situation clear to the base shuttles. Mersuul watched as their symbols on her screen turned and flew away from the battle zone as they were told to do.

18

Faoul Mahna had never felt such rage as he was feeling now. His fleet of dhrojjas had been decimated by a handful of transport shuttles. Decitans of work had been destroyed. Then he realized what had really happened. This had been a trap all along. This was an IGT trap set just to get him! That was it! This was all about him. The IGT was worried by his intellect and effectiveness. The IGT was threatened by his leadership of other dhrojjas. They wanted to keep all the treasure and women for themselves. This was a conspiracy against him. They knew of the greatness of Faoul Mahna and they wanted to destroy him. These had not really been transport shuttles he was fighting. No! These were no doubt specially designed fighter craft made just to destroy him. Now he understood the truth. They had him fooled for a short time, but now he knew the truth. Now he knew that this was all about him.

Well as far as Mahna was concerned, that was alright. He had learned to plan for the future, and now everyone would know that he was someone to be feared. He placed his ship on a direct run for the moon, through the battle zone. He wasn't very worried about being attacked by any of the enemy fighters. His ship was protected by the best armor and energy shields that a man could steal. Certainly they would attack him, but for the short time this would take, his ship would sustain only relatively minor damage.

Mahna looked at the display screen that showed the battle zone with all the dead dhrojja ships, and the surface of the moon. The flashing symbol indicated his ship as he traveled towards the red dot that marked the release zone. It would only be fracins now. He watched as the two indicators merged together, then rotated his ship so that the cargo bay doors faced the moon. With a manic, gleeful smile that stretched the edges of his mouth, he released the hiddrothermic gas bomb, its momentum carrying it out of the ship and towards the moon. He immediately reversed his ship's direction of travel while breaking into laughter. '*They won't be expecting this!*' he thought as he continued to laugh, happy in his undeniable and soon to be victory. This wasn't the best or even a very fast way to deliver the weapon, but it was fast enough. His laughter grew almost hysterical as he watched all the ships on his screen fleeing the area.

There were a few ships that weren't running away, and he knew that they were what was left of his dhrojja fleet. It was too bad that they didn't know what was about to happen, but in times of war sometimes sacrifices had to be made for victory. Besides, he could always find more dhrojjas. When news spread about his victory here they would be begging to join him.

19

Dhona shook off the shocked surprise of detecting the weapon that now moved towards the moon. The hiddrothermic gas bomb was one of the most devastating weapons ever created, and there was no way for anything smaller than a class three battle vessel to stop it. If he tried to attack it with his fighter it would only trigger the bomb to go off, and none of the other ships were at a safe distance yet. But at the relatively slow speed the bomb was moving, there was enough time for one possible plan of action. He couldn't destroy the weapon or stop it from detonating, but he could control when it blew up. He activated his communication system and broadcast in the open on all frequencies.

"Attention all IGT vessels in the reach of my transmission. Attention! This is IGT interjection fighter pilot Lanor Giell-sil-Dhona. A hiddrothermic gas bomb has been launched at the moon of the third planet of this solar system. I repeat, a hiddrothermic gas bomb has been launched at the moon of the third planet of this solar system. Move away from the area at maximum speed." said Dhona, and then he set the comm to retransmit his message continuously.

That was stage one. Stage two of his plan required very accurate timing. He spoke aloud.

"Calculate detonation point of hiddrothermic weapon that will cause minimum damage to all ships in the area and the surface of the moon. Fire all remaining vectras to intercept the weapon at that point. Confirm."
"Interception point calculated." replied the targeting computer. *"Firing full vectra battery from present position in three point three mirlots from now."*

'Three and a third mirlots is a long damn time to wait to be killed.' he thought. At his present position he was well within the blast zone of the bomb. The thought of dying didn't bother him too much. Not being around

422

to find out if his actions had been successful, now that bothered him a lot.

"Can I move from this position to a safe location without affecting the accuracy of the vectras?" he asked.

"Movement at a speed sufficient to position this vessel out of the blast zone would introduce too many variables to maintain accurate control of vectras."

'*No surprise there.*' he thought. He was too experienced and familiar with his ship's weapons not to have known the answer before he asked – but what else was there to do while waiting to die?

"Upon launch of last vectra, initiate maximum speed withdrawal from blast zone. Confirm."

"Maximum speed withdrawal from blast zone course plotted. Maneuver will be initiated on launch of final vectra."

Dhona wouldn't have taken any bets on his chances for survival. A hiddrothermic gas bomb is made with a synthetic, extremely volatile gas, whose molecules have such a strong affinity for each other that they stick together like glue. It is the only substance classified as a gas that self compresses into a dense liquid at atmospheric pressure. Designed for only one purpose, the gas depends on the vacuum of space to pull those molecules apart and expand the substance into an extremely large volume cloud. When pulled apart from its liquid to a gaseous state and ignited, the energy released by the thermionic reaction is so sudden and intense it is like a small sun. It is a non-discretionary weapon, leaving nothing intact within the blast zone. It is such a destructive weapon the manufacturing or possession of one, or any part of one, was banned by treaty with a penalty of summary execution. The weapon is so devastating the treaty banning the weapon was signed by all the peoples of all the known galaxies, IGT members and non-members alike. He couldn't figure out how a dhrojja got a hold of one.

"Configure ship for impact survival. All energy shields at maximum."

He felt the vibrations of his ship physically reconfiguring itself, and indicators glowed to show protective energy shielding operating. It was going to be an interesting show. The launch of all the vectras would be like a fireworks celebration. *'A celebration of my death.'* he thought, *'Well at least I get fireworks.'* The almost instantaneous acceleration in an attempt to achieve FTL speed would be uncomfortable at best – but FTL wouldn't be reached before the blast hit the ship. It would all occur almost simultaneously. He hoped the others had made it far enough to be safe.

20

"Access door three closed and sealed!"
"… Access door seven closed and sealed!"
"… Access door five closed and sealed!"

Travellor listened to the reports coming in over the comm until all the access doors had sealed. *'Not enough time.'* he thought. All the lights went out and everyone became quiet and still, until the emergency lighting switched on. The power umbilical from the Orysta must have been severed. The underground structure then jumped and fell, accompanied by a low rumbling and an almost deafening boom. Travellor was knocked off his feet, as was everyone around him. He realized it wasn't the structure that had moved, it was all of the surrounding ground. The heavy and very strong moon base structure had just gone along for the ride. He heard people scream, and things crash to the floor. There was loud cursing, and calls for help.

It was dim, but you could see enough to move about safely. He had been on site as this structure was built into the ground. He knew how heavy and strong it was. He had watched them weld, and rivet, and anchor it into the substrate. He could barely believe it had moved as much as it did.

424

Whatever had impacted the surface had done so with the force of a very large asteroid. A few seconds later the backup generators kicked in and electrical power was restored.

"Kibbee, this is Travellor. Did everyone make it down? Did everyone make it down?"

There was no response, and Travellor was about to call again when Kibbee finally replied.

"This is Kibbee. I don't know Commander. We had to seal the doors. There was no more time."
"Did Munen and the others make it out of the Orysta?"
"I'll have my guys check. I didn't see them where I was."

Only a few minutes had passed since Grilik Munen gave the warning for everyone to abandon the surface, and Travellor could tell by the fear in his voice that it was a time to move now and ask questions later. The strange part was that he felt no fear for himself, but was worried about getting Cove to safety. He had kept thinking that no one would forgive him if he let anything happen to Cove. Then he had wondered how involved Erika was with the man. Cove was safe. He was safe. Everyone that was underground was safe – relatively anyway – for now. He wondered what kind of weapon had been launched at them. He wondered if Munen had made it to safety. He wondered if the Orysta had been destroyed. Then he felt angry. Very, very angry. Then the anger suddenly subsided as he thought about Mersuul. She was in one of the shuttles that had been fighting the enemy. He didn't know if she was safe, or if she was still alive. He felt sick for a second. Then he wanted to kill every one of the pirates – by hand – personally.

21

Mahna watched, safely out of range of the hiddrothermic gas bomb. He saw the IGT fighter launch a barrage of missiles, which caught him by surprise. He had no idea that any of their fighters could carry that much armament. It made for an interesting display, but he knew even that much firepower could not stop the bomb from going off. It would, in fact, only set off the bomb by triggering its proximity detector. *'How useless.'* he thought. *'What a stupid, desperate move.'*

Just as he expected, the vectras did set off the bomb. Mahna was completely surprised by what he saw next. In a fraction of a second the whole of space in that area changed from the familiar darkness to an instantaneous explosion of a small sun. He reflexively shielded his eyes with one hand, and felt an instantaneous searing heat cut across his body, that stopped just as suddenly as it began. *'Hah! Now my mind is playing tricks on me.'* he thought.

22

The Eowaar had dropped out of tetra space and back into normal space in full battle readiness – all weapons and systems were on line. Dhona's last transmission had served as both a warning and a call for help. Pirates attacking would alone have been reason enough, but a hiddrothermic gas bomb made it imperative to violate the safety protocol of not traveling at intergalactic speed within a solar system. Planna had some difficulty at first believing that pirates had acquired such a weapon. None had been made in tanrhas.

As soon as the Eowaar dropped to flank-speed-normal its computers and sensors analyzed the area and displayed several action plans. Planna had ordered flank-speed-normal be maintained until the strategic situation could be determined. Experience is the acquisition of knowledge through survival. It was his extensive experience in battle that allowed Kalinor Planna to react as quickly as he did. Experience that younger commanders who hadn't lived through an inter-galactic war didn't have. He had been a young officer in a time when hiddrothermic gas bombs were in frequent use, and the knowledge of them he had gained had remained unused for all of these decitans, but was never forgotten. They were devastating weapons, and important lessons were learned in those past battles – at the cost of many lives. Planna never thought those lessons would ever be useful again. He was wrong.

The Eowaar's Aligned Cohesive Beam Array is a weapon capable of placing multiple pulsed energy streams side by side forming a projected blade of energy. Like a blade, these energy beams slice through the target instead of just forming a hole in it. The weapon system polarizes coherent energy beams, allowing them to be bent and controlled. The alternating polarity of the beams draws and keeps them together so that they do not disperse at long distances. Planna activated the ACBA when he ordered the Eowaar into tetra-space. He wanted it operational at destination. It was a lesson learned in the last war, when hiddrothermic gas bombs were first introduced.

His battle field display showed him he had arrived too late to stop the bomb from being deployed. He saw the scattering of small vessels, most moving away from the blast zone as fast as they could. There were a few ships heading for a much larger one that was already at a safe distance, but they would never make it there. They were obviously dhrojjas with no identification beacons, and it seemed that they were not aware a hiddrothermic gas bomb was about to end their lives. The larger ship was not sending out any warning to them. Planna's next motions were more reflex than thought. There was no need to attack the smaller dhrojjas – they were as good as dead.

He placed his whole left hand on the sensor, which scanned and confirmed his identity almost instantaneously. With the index finger of his right, he touched the symbol of the ACBA and drew a line through the larger dhrojja ship, just as the hiddrothermic gas bomb exploded. The ACBA beam sliced the ship horizontally in two. It was a clean, surgical slice that caused no explosions. The ship merely opened up like two halves of a crilly shell.

23

After a few fracins Mahna lowered his hand and looked again, and he felt the air leaving his lungs. *'That's odd.'* he thought, *'It was a surprising sight but I didn't expect to react like that.'* He saw a man's arm float up in front of him. Then a leg! He looked around to see who had been injured. Several bodies floated into view, and he recognized them as members of his crew. He was confused when he realized that the floating body parts were dressed in similar clothing to his own. Then he saw that his ship had neatly divided itself and let the darkness of space in. *'Why the crhaaka would it do that?'*

24

Without looking to see the results of his first actions, Planna turned his attention back to the tactical display which showed the expanding cloud of destructive thermal energy that traveled outward at unbelievable speed. The Eowaar's computer had calculated the damage zone of the bomb. The surface of the moon would be impacted, but with diminished force. Planna hoped the people there had been warned in time to take shelter. Also within the damage zone was the debris of many battle damaged ships and several occupied escape pods, all of which would just be obliterated into space dust. That would be no loss since under IGT law the pirates would have been summarily executed anyway.

There was also one of his own fighter craft accelerating at maximum capability as it tried to outrun the explosion. It was Dhona's fighter – it would never make it in time, but it would get far enough away to escape the full force of the blast. He prayed that all the lives lost in the past war would now guide his hand in the attempt to save this one life. He drew another line from the ACBA out across the space behind the fighter craft. He couldn't protect Dhona completely, but he hoped that by creating a back-pressure wave between the expanding destruction zone and the fighter it would cancel out some of the explosive force. This action had saved lives in the past war – sometimes.

Planna looked over to the screen where Dhona's biometric telemetry data was being displayed in real time. Heart rate and blood pressure was high. ACTH and adrenaline levels in the blood stream were also high. All of it to be expected from a man in a life or death situation. Then all readings dropped to zero, and the display turned red and started flashing.

Chapter 22

Diplomacy

1

December – 2014

Earth's first battle in space, that no one knew about

It had taken almost two hours to clear a path to the surface, from the only still operational pressurized access chamber leading to the underground section of the moon base. Many sections of the base closest to the surface had been destroyed or were impassible. The five base shuttles, the damaged Folly, and the two Orysta shuttles sat at a clear spot near the center of the crater, their reflections coming off the fused silica that had been turned into glass by the tremendous heat of the bomb blast. With them were several fighter craft from the Eowaar. More ships and personnel from the battle carrier were constantly traveling between the behemoth war ship and the surface. It was only by chance that the Eowaar had stationed itself on the moon's far side, and could not be seen from Earth. Other Eowaar fighters had set up a security patrol, while still others went out farther hunting for any pirates that may have survived the battle.

The above ground structure of the moon base no longer existed, unless you considered the torn, twisted and melted heap that had been blasted up against the side of the crater to be part of the base. The Orysta was gone – literally. It had not been anchored to the surface, and speculation was that the tremendous force that had ripped the thick steel pylons which supported the base had also blown the Orysta out into space.

Eowaar search and rescue vessels were assigned to search for whatever was left of her and the four people inside. This was officially designated a rescue mission, but most believed it to be a recovery operation. Eowaar had calculated possible trajectories the blast could have sent the ship on, which defined the search area.

Base personnel were quiet, moody, somber, scared, and sad, but they all did what was asked of them. No yell for assistance had to be asked twice – someone was always willing to lend a hand. Cooks helped hold things steady while they were being welded or cut. Communications techs went to all levels of the remaining structure checking for pressurization leaks. Flight crews helped remove the surface obstructions with heavy machinery. Cleaning robots were put to new use as they moved through conduits to check for damaged cables and optical fibers. There was no worry about the essentials. All of the stores for the moon base had been kept in the underground part of the structure. The Eowaar stood by to supply anything else that might be needed.

A transport from the Eowaar had been sent to Earth to get Farber-Chatwell and Ransen Ramsdel, and the first group of construction personnel. Doctor Blin had been on planet and was also coming back, as were a few Orysta crew members that had been off duty. Several pallets of communications and office equipment had been put together by 361 logistics on Earth, to get the base back into operation as quickly as possible. Also being brought to the moon base on the Eowaar transport were miscellaneous packages and one very large, freshly cut pine tree. It was the morning of Christmas day.

2

Kalinor Gorheel-sil-Planna held his niece in a tight, crushing hug. It wasn't until this moment that his fears of returning home without finding her dissipated. He had received the report that she was alive, and he had talked to her over the comm. It wasn't until he held her that it all became reality. She had been lost and feared dead for a long time.

"I promised your mother I would find you and bring you home." he said with tears beginning to form in his eyes. "I was afraid I would find you dead after all this time."

Mersuul returned the hug, and held on to family. Holding her uncle was almost like being home at that moment. Her tears were already flowing freely.

"We wondered if we would ever go home again. We had the greatest luck. These people are not just allies, or friends. They have become our family here. It is because of them we did more than just survive. We lived productive lives." She moved back and looked up at her uncle. "You have to find the Orysta. Grilik Munen and the others could still be alive."

"Don't worry about that. We will find her and your crew. Everyone in our SAR section is working at finding that ship. Come over here and sit with me. I want you to tell me how you are doing, and everything that has happened to you here. When you are done, I'll tell you how scared for my life your mother has made me."

Mersuul laughed at his jest about her mother, who in truth was a very strong willed person. The top of her mother's head only came up to her uncle's chest. It was funny to think she could scare the commander of one of the most powerful vessels in the IGT.

3

36 HSB

36 HSB. That's how everyone on the moon base were noting time now – HSB – Hours Since the Bomb. Even Ganaphe' on the base were using that reference. It was now thirty-six hours HSB, and still nothing found of the Orysta.

Doctor Blin looked at the unconscious body in the stasis chamber of the Eowaar. She was here at the request of General Farber-Chatwell and Commander Travellor, who wanted a report from someone they knew and trusted. On the chamber walls, written in various colors of marker pen, were Get Well wishes, messages of thanks, prayers, invitations to recuperate at several family homes on the planet, and signatures of all the base personnel. Blin had before only seen one other patient whose body had suffered anything near this much insult – and she had survived. This case was worse. As Blin scanned the patient's medical record it seemed the list of injuries to the body was endless. This life was clinging on only because of the support machinery – internal organs were either not functioning or not functioning well enough to do the job. The Eowaar had the latest and best medical technology, as well as doctors experienced with the trauma caused by war. They were capable of growing new replacement organs, but that took time. She would not have been able to do better even if the Orysta was still available to her.

Dhona was being kept in a medically induced coma, to spare him the agony of his injuries and to allow his body to have a chance to heal. The force of the blast had splintered, twisted, and compressed his ship into a lump of metal and synthetic trash, pieces of which had been forced through Dhona's body. The damage to his ship was so bad that it had to be taken apart piecemeal to get to Dhona, who was barely alive. If Blin had to put a word to his prognosis it would be 'Unknown'. Even the medical technology available on this ship could only do so much. There were some similarities between Dhona's condition and what Delores del Rio had experienced. They both had suffered the force of a tremendous blast. Del Rio was protected only by her space suit, but had no penetrating injuries. Dhona was hit by a much larger force but had the protection of his ship and its systems to mitigate his injuries.

Blin looked around the outside of the chamber. There was a collection of gifts on the table next to it, from moon base personnel and flight crews. They had learned about his actions to reduce the force of the bomb while placing his own life at risk and they were more than grateful. Some of the items were expensive, and others were more personal. There was a small trophy with a dancing figure on top engraved with 'First Grade Dance Recital' and an attached note in technician Jenny Simmons five year old daughter's childish scrawl, that read '*My mommy said you saved her life. Thank you. This is for being my hero. This is your trophy now. You can keep it. You can come to dinner on Saturday we are having pizza.*'

Blin placed the trophy back on the table and headed down the hallway. There was another patient she had to check on. Personnel on the Eowaar recognized Blin as an Orysta crew member. They had all been surprised to learn the crew had survived. Everyone on the Eowaar had believed their journey to this galaxy was to find and bring back bodies. The discovery that not only had they all survived, but were in excellent condition mentally and physically was amazing. They greeted her as she walked through the ship, and asked if there was anything they could for her and the others. Blin thanked them and promised to pass on their invitations to the other crew members.

She turned into the next room in the ward. Slouched in the chair by the bed of the unconscious man was John Smith. He had fallen asleep, and the condition of his clothes indicated he had been there for a long time. Blin quietly touched the instrument screen and pulled up the patient's medical record. George Washington's condition was serious but stable. He had had an undetected brain aneurysm, which resulted in a subarachnoid hemorrhage, caused by the physical stresses of the second FTL journey. While being treated, doctors on the Eowaar detected two other aneurysms in his brain and were able to repair the weak blood vessels, eliminating any future chance of a recurrence. Some brain damage had occurred. He would have to undergo a long period of rehabilitation with speech and physical therapy, but his prognosis was good. Luckily his vision had not been affected, but it still meant the end of his flying career.

4

39 HSB

The moon base was as busy as an ant colony, as transports from the Eowaar set up a continuous schedule from Earth to the base. Where the Orysta had had two shuttles to transport people and supplies, the Eowaar had hundreds. Even with that many vessels traveling between the two locations, the Eowaar's transports remained undetected. What had taken months and years to bring to the base before, was now taking hours. 361 logistics personnel were living a nightmare, but none failed to come through with the supplies needed. The operation was on a war recovery footing, and Farber-Chatwell and Ramsdel made sure that those who needed to know that were aware of it.

Kalinor Planna used the situation as a real life training exercise. He had his engineers working with 361 engineers. His transport pilots were put under the control of Flight Commander Balfour, whose own small team was getting a crash course in working under pressure. Spare medical equipment was sent to the base where a field hospital was set up for the inevitable injuries that would occur during reconstruction of the surface structure. Language databases were updated on the Eowaar with the copy of the Orysta's data, that was kept on base servers. This made the battle carrier's translators more accurate and nuanced, and reduced misunderstandings.

5

70 HSB

The conference room on the Eowaar was huge – and completely practical. Except for the chairs there was no other thought given to the comfort of the occupants. The chairs, table, and other fixtures were secured to the floor, but had enough built-in adjustments to make them suitable for anyone's use – this was a battle carrier after all. Comfort was a secondary consideration in its design.

In the short time period between his arrival to now, Kalinor Planna had learned a lot about the people and the organization from the planet Earth that had established a colony on the only orbiting moon. Under IGT law this organization and its people were the legal authority on this moon. That alone made the interaction between them and the crew of the Orysta a legal and proper first contact situation. Even more important to Planna was the way they had accepted and nurtured the stranded travelers. Mersuul's connection to, and affection for these people told him the most important thing he needed to know – that they could be trusted. The Eowaar was the only instrument of representation of the IGT in this galaxy, and as such made Planna the authorized representative. It was a role he had played before.

At the request of his hosts, the Eowaar was kept camouflaged and on the side of the moon opposite to the planet's. Planna wasn't sure how helpful this would be as the satellites orbiting the moon must have detected the battle and transmitted the anomalous data back to the planet – but that was not his concern. Earth's business was the business of Earth's people. It was up to the 361 organization to deal with this.

Representing the moon base were General Robert Farber-Chatwell, Ransen Ramsdel, Moon Base Commander Anthony Travellor, Doctor Eckelberry Cove, and Flight Commander Brighde Balfour. From the Orysta crew were Tahn-grilik Intul-sil-Califas, Chief Engineer Benua-sil-Plessa, and Doctor Toisae-sil-Blin. Missing from that group was Grilik Artau-sil-Munen. Also present by Planna's own request was his niece Mersuul and moon base specialist Delores del Rio, the latter there to satisfy his curiosity about the person who had suffered some similar injuries to Dhona. She had agreed to let the Eowaar's medical staff scan and analyze her in the hope that something helpful to Dhona's recovery might be learned.

"I understand, Commander Travellor, that Trailblazer Moon Base has been renamed the Giell-sil-Dhona Moon Base. As Dhona's commanding officer, I thank you. Giell would appreciate the gesture."

"He will appreciate it, Kalinor, when he comes out of the coma. Then we will thank him properly. When the story of what he did got around to my people, it was as one mind to rename the base in his honor. We will tell him so when he awakes."

"Yes," replied Planna with a contemplative expression, and his eyes down, "when he awakes." He choked slightly, then continued. "We have a lot to discuss. Presently our peoples are operating well together, to the benefit of both the moon base and the Eowaar. My crews come back to the ship complaining that there is too much to do, then go to bed with satisfaction on their faces. I see them smiling when they go back to work on their next shift. The Eowaar doesn't face many situations that challenge her crew. Some times it can be boring and routine on board a battle carrier. Not many would dare challenge us. The sections that are working with your people end their shift with a feeling of accomplishment each diest. I have a list of requests from other sections asking that they be included in the…"

"Kalinor Planna, this is Kolaaho in Signals." came the interrupting voice over the comm system. "We have her sir, we have the Orysta!"

"WHERE?" yelled Mersuul, jumping up. "IS EVERYONE ALIVE?"

"Where did they find her?" asked Planna.

"Well that's the strange part sir. The Orysta is on the moon. We are getting an extremely weak comm signal from her. Grilik Munen is transmitting that all on board are alive, but injured."

Confusion lasted only for only few seconds before Plessa realized what had happened.

"THEY SANK HER!" he yelled. "They sank her. She's underground!" It only took a fraction of a second for the others from the base to understand.

6

76 HSB

The self-guided boring cables going down into the ground had finally attached to the Orysta. On the other end they were attached to two tugs from the Eowaar. Just one tug vessel would have had the power to do the job, but two would make it easy and much faster than the first time the Orysta had risen.

"You are able to turn the soil into a fluid?"

"Yes Kalinor." said Plessa. "The concept of Orysta's newest crew member, Assistant Engineer Erika Aimsler. She is the niece of Base Commander Travellor."

"She is a member of Orysta's crew?"

"By authority of Grilik Munen. It is all properly recorded in the ship's logs."

"Where is the Assistant Engineer?"

"She is on her way back here. She had talked her way onto one of your SAR vessels. Told them her familiarity with the Orysta could be useful when she was found."

Planna laughed at this.

"I want to meet Engineer Aimsler. I believe this fluidization process could be useful in many ways."

438

"I have no doubt she would want to meet Mersuul's uncle. The two have become very close friends."

The cables went taut as everyone in the area watched. Anyone who could get a hold of a space suit was outside watching. Camera feeds gave the people in the underground structure a view of what was happening. The ground changed from the static dry soil they had been watching to undulating, marsh looking land. The tugs began to rise higher, but there was nothing to see except the cables feeding out from the ground. Planna expected to see the soil become wet but it never did. A couple of mirlots later the ground bulged upward, followed by the Orysta penetrating the surface.

7

The Orysta had always been considered a large ship by moon base personnel, especially considering the internal capacity and industrial capabilities it contained. Compared to the Eowaar it looked more like a dinghy. It had taken over twenty minutes to cut a hole through its side, and Grilik Munen and the crew members who had helped him man the ship's guns hobbled out to hugs and shouts from the rest of the crew. Shortly after that they had the chance to look around at the destruction in the crater. Then they turned and looked at their ship.

Orysta sat on the ground, tilted to one side. Its port side landing gear had snapped. That was minor damage compared to the ship's hull, which looked like a Tonka toy that had a steel canon ball dropped on it. Even though the ship had been below the surface, the fraction of the tremendous force of the explosion that reached the Orysta through the soil had been powerful enough to cave in the center of the ship.

All four men had been rendered unconscious for hours by the shock of the blast. The only reason they were alive was their having worn space suits as a standard safety procedure when under attack. The internal pressurization and atmosphere of the ship had been lost through the many breaches in the dual hull.

The four were put on levitation boards and taken to the field hospital underground. Broken bones and torn ligaments were mended, and braces applied where needed. Medical scans showed no serious internal organ damage. Each was given a pain control wrist band and a monitor pill. The wrist band intentionally reduced the pain until it was tolerable, but did not eliminate it completely. Ganaphe' medical science believed that conscious awareness of pain helped the body heal faster. The pill could not be digested. It was designed to travel through the gastrointestinal tract for the next twenty-four to forty-eight hours or so, while continually monitoring and transmitting physiological data to a medical analyzer in the hospital, which provided real-time analysis of the patient's condition.

8

168 HSB

Plessa and the maintenance crew, supplemented by Eowaar personnel, were able to seal multiple sections of the Orysta, and re-establish pressurization. The ship had been righted and placed on temporary supports so that the floors were fairly level again, making it easier for personnel to work inside. The main computer was interfaced to the Eowaar, and the ship's logs and databases were transmitted to the battle carrier for storage. Power generation was still operational, and a new umbilical was run to the base for construction and every day use, which made life there a little easier and more secure for every one. The bridge, forward part of the ship, and rear sections of the ship were put back into operation, one section at a time. But the overall damage to the hull was too extensive. The Orysta would never fly again.

9

Inspection of the Folly's airframe, along with the crew debriefing, astounded everyone. Recorded data from the Ganaphe' equipment removed all doubt that the Folly had broken the FTL barrier. The data showed the ship had achieved low FTL speeds – nothing near the speeds that intergalactic ships reach routinely, but so very much faster than anyone thought possible with the Folly's design. The excitement level was very high as word got around about the accidental technological breakthrough. Cove was especially surprised. His mind was working overtime as he tried to understand the underlying physics to what had happened. He thought about how to design his next engine and ship, which would be specifically designed for FTL flight, but had a mental block that kept interfering with his thoughts on the matter. Cove was a great admirer of Albert Einstein and his theories. The specific Einstein theory that interfered with his thoughts was Special Relativity, which basically said that it was impossible to exceed the speed of light. He had studied it – learned it – believed it. Even contact with the Ganaphe' hadn't really changed his mind on the subject because he had never experienced it. After all, whatever the Ganaphe' had claimed, the Orysta had never been able to fly. It existed. It was there for all to see. It did have technology beyond anything on Earth – but it never moved. But now there was the Eowaar, and all the smaller vessels it carried – all capable of exceeding FTL by a large margin. Now he had flown in them himself. He had experienced FTL himself. He could no longer deny that the Folly had broken the speed of light.

The problem remained that they did not yet know how to cancel the injurious effects of such sudden high speed acceleration on the human body. It was one problem demanding a solution to another. Cove's initial thought was simple and direct. Physically mitigate the effects through the design of the crew seats, improving on what the Folly's crew had done by reconfiguring their seats for their return trip. This was only a temporary solution. Washington's condition clearly showed that the stresses on the body would be too drastic for this to be put into regular use. The second course of action would be to figure out a way to compensate for the forces as the Ganaphe' had done. Under IGT law the Ganaphe' could not tell them how to do this. They were not allowed to directly affect the technological advancement of another world.

While Cove worked on his new design, two more Folly design ships would be built to quickly get the base fleet back to normal force levels. One to replace the shuttle lost during the battle, and the second to increase the size of the fleet. After analyzing the battle damage to the Folly it was determined that missing and damaged components could be replaced or repaired, and the ship put back into service as a test platform for future innovations. All ships would be retrofitted with greater firepower capability. Space was no longer just a passive entity that coldly tried to suck the life out of you. Space was now a known potential harborer of enemies. The romance of space travel had run right into the wall of reality. It was a new era in the moon base's history, and limits to personnel and equipment were no longer in effect – the Ganaphe' were going home.

10

"… they expected a damaged mining ship to be an easy target that they could pick off whenever they wanted." said Planna, to the intent listeners at his table. "They destroyed the emergency beacons as they followed them, so that the rescue vessels that would inevitably come would not be able to find the ship. That is where they ran into a problem. Some of the Orysta's beacons had failed to launch and the trail was broken."

The new formal dining room in the Giell-sil-Dhona Moon Base was just as extravagant and beautiful as the old one. Three oval shaped chandeliers threw their glittering light over the central part of the room. The hand carved teak and old redwood table that ran the length of the room was actually multiple tables designed to be assembled as one long one if desired.

It was covered by a high-tech table cloth of woven optical fibers,

442

that subtle light pulses ran through, displaying random patterns. This was a formal affair, and everyone wore their best and most stylish clothes. At the head of the room-long table was the guest of honor seat. The name card at that location read 'Warta Giell-sil-Dhona', and the chair was left empty in honor of the man that remained in a coma. On the right side of that seat sat Kalinor Gorheel-sil-Planna, and to his right was his niece Mersuul-sil-Vaana followed by his command staff. To the left of Dhona's seat was Farber-Chatwell, Toisae-sil-Blin, Ramsdel, Travellor, the command staff of the moon base, and the crew of the Orysta.

Except for the skeleton crew that were required to man their posts, including the newly established Early Warning Defense section, all other base personnel, as well as a large contingent of Eowaar personnel, were seated in the dining room, enjoying a social event that was meant to form ties between the two peoples. Everyone was having a good time. Base personnel were enthralled by descriptions of space travel from the Eowaar's crew, while the battle carrier personnel were entertained by descriptions of vacation spots on Earth. Food, drink, and conversation flowed continuously.

"They had no means to decrypt the data from the beacons, even if they had not destroyed them all. The dhrojja were also not equipped to search a solar system for a ship whose comm transmissions had suddenly stopped. They had no way to track her journey. They considered the Orysta to be a prize to search for when they had the time and the inclination, since mining ships usually carried high value cargo." Planna continued, with the Orysta crew intently focused on his words.

"After the company realized the Orysta was overdue they notified the Inter-space Safety Organization authorities and a Search and Rescue operation was initiated. They knew the Orysta was headed to this moon, and came to look here first, but nothing was found. Even if the Orysta had crashed they would have found the debris – but there was none."

"Except we did crash!" said Mersuul.

"Yes." said Planna, smiling at his niece. "You crashed, and broke through the surface crust, and the ship was buried by the loose ground material and covered up. SAR found nothing. Not one clue pointing to your location."

"And our comm signals were being blocked by the debris as well." added Munen. "We could not transmit a call for help."

"Even if your signal was not blocked, your transmission would not have made it out of this solar system. SAR sent three different expeditions and found nothing. Your employer was not happy. He refused to accept that all on the Orysta had lost their lives while in his employ. When SAR called off the search after the third attempt, your company sent out its own ships. They also found nothing."

Munen closed his eyes and shook his head. "It was just bad timing. None of the search vessels came here when we were running shuttle excursions on the surface."

He shook his head again in disbelief. The others all showed similar expressions on their faces.

"Oh my God!" blurted Erika in a low voice, also shocked at the misfortune of the Orysta crew. "You could have all gone home long ago if not for bad timing."

"That is very true, Miss Aimsler." said Planna. "Sometimes fate works against us."

Everyone was shaking their heads in agreement, except for Travellor.

"You are wrong Kalinor. Fate wasn't against these people. It was their fate to find the Trailblazer crew. It was their fate to save Tonio's life. It was their fate to teach us about things we didn't know existed. Yes, they weren't able to go home, or contact their families. And Yes, many times they felt sad, and lost, and depressed. From my point of view their misfortune was a good thing. These people are friends, and have been accepted as family. I think fate was with them and with us – and now they will be leaving us, and when I think of that it makes me sad. I will raise a glass to fate," Travellor said, holding his wine glass high, "and drink to the fate that brought them here."

"I will also drink to that." said Blin, raising her glass.

"And I also." said Califas.

Everyone at the table followed by raising their glasses. Mersuul did also, but her face was troubled. She had been quiet and sullen for the past few days, and Travellor had not been able to find out why.

"To fate then." said Planna. "It is often a double edged sword."

11

Erika and Cove danced slowly to the soft, low music that emanated from all directions on the dance floor. She very much liked this unexpectedly real genius that couldn't care less about his designated status. Genius was only one of his notable attributes. Her uncle had filed an official report praising his bravery and composure under enemy fire. Farber-Chatwell on the other hand had cursed the proverbial blue streak at him when he read the report. She liked the way he held her hand when they walked, and the way he felt when she had her arms wrapped around him. When he was working on Earth, and she was on the moon, she felt a sense of emptiness.

When the music ended they went back to the table and sat together. The double rich chocolate cake with butter cream frosting tasted better when Cove fed it to her, even if he did intentionally get it all over her mouth. They were both enjoying the evening. She glanced around the dinner table and spotted Mersuul. Her friend had had a strange unsettled, almost unhappy look on her face for days now. Erika had tried to ask her about it but could not get a straight answer. Mersuul occasionally would smile at a remark made to her, but Erika could tell it was not a heartfelt response. Erika's uncle had also noticed the change, but he had not had any better luck at finding out what was bothering her. Then her friend stood up looking like a person who had finally made a serious decision, picked up her wine glass and tapped it with a knife to get everyone's attention. The room went silent to hear what she had to say.

"This is a special gathering of friends, and family, and friends who have become family." started Mersuul. "If I were back home, I would do this in the privacy of my parents' house, and in the presence of family only. But circumstances demand a change in custom."

She got up from her seat, and moved to the other side of the table. Standing behind Travellor, she placed both of her hands on his shoulders.

"I choose this man!" she said loudly.

It was a short and simple statement, but the reactions from the front of the table came immediately. Many of the base personnel looked confused. Many of the Eowaar personnel showed surprise and even mild happiness. Kalinor Planna looked shocked. Doctor Blin had a big smile on her face – she knew, or at least had suspected, and Farber-Chatwell leaned over to ask what was going on. Travellor looked shocked and surprised. He knew what the Ganaphe' custom meant.

"Oh my God. Yes!" said Erika in a low voice only Cove could hear.
"What's going on?" he asked.
"Mersuul just proposed marriage to my uncle. And by his reaction, I don't think they talked about it before hand."
"Really?"
"Really. Marriage is something the Ganaphe' take very seriously. In their culture the woman declares her intention at a gathering of her and his immediate families, that is normally prearranged by the two people involved. I can't believe she did it in front of all of these people. No wonder she was so moody lately. She never told uncle Tony she was going to do this, and she was scared he would reject her – which he wouldn't. He's crazy about her. She probably didn't even decide to do it until just now."
"I guess she considers you to be his family and the Kalinor to be hers. So what happens now?"

446

As if answering Cove's question, Travellor got up, and stood facing Mersuul. He placed his hands on her shoulders.

"I accept this woman." he said, then he kissed her on both cheeks.

It was done. Proposal and acceptance. Both acts done in the traditional Ganaphe' manner. The tension and fear in Mersuul's face disappeared, replaced by a big smile. Planna turned in his seat and looked away, deep in thought. Erika noticed his unexpected reaction, and wondered what was going on. Everyone else who understood the custom toasted the couple. Then realization set in.

"Oh… Now I understand."
"What?"
"Kalinor Planna." she said, turning to Cove. "Did you see how he reacted? I couldn't figure out why until it hit me. He came across galaxies to find Mersuul, and bring her home. But Mersuul won't be going home with him. She'll be staying here, with uncle Tony – with her soon to be husband!"

Chapter 23

The Journey Home

1

April – 2015

The last few months had seen an unbelievable and unexpected amount of activity, that strained the large resources of Operation 361. The above ground structure of the Giell-sil-Dhona Moon Base was seventy percent completed, and fully operational, thanks to the added manpower and equipment from the Eowaar. New fabrication techniques had been introduced by the Ganaphe' battle carrier's engineers that made the structure much stronger than the original. Sections left to be finished were additions that expanded on the original design, and would be used for the planned deep solar system explorations that would slowly be brought into operation when Cove's new ship design comes on-line. The sections of the underground structure that were damaged by the blast had also been repaired and re-enforced.

Communications relays had now been placed throughout the Vialactea galaxy by Eowaar's engineering team, and a reliable connection to the IGT communications network had been established. It was a rudimentary system not meant for heavy comm traffic, but would no doubt be able to meet the requirements of Vialactea for some time to come – unless the random factor called Doctor Eckelberry Cove came into play. The Orysta crew members had all been able to contact their families, many of which were shocked that they had been found alive and well after so many decitans of thinking that they were dead. A lot of tears and crying were transmitted over those calls.

The Project 361 organizational heads and Kalinor Planna had

signed a treaty agreement which allowed regular visits from an IGT vessel to be scheduled every 6 months. The ships are to enter the solar system camouflaged, will approach from the far side of the moon, and will maintain their position there. The first visit will be a return trip by the Eowaar, and after that by vessels from other galaxies that may be interested in establishing a relationship. This procedure would remain in effect until 361 determines the procedure is no longer necessary. The agreement wasn't anything major. Mainly it was an invitation to visit. Its implications though were huge. The transfer of knowledge, and potential purchase of technology, could advance moon base capabilities at an accelerated rate.

In the collective eyes of the people that lived and worked on the moon base, there was one thing that out shone all of these accomplishments. Giell-sil-Dhona was conscious again, and healing. His physical condition was extremely poor, due to the extreme reconstruction that had been performed on his body. But he was showing improvement daily. His brain had recovered completely and tests showed his memory to be intact. His speech sounded a little odd, and his body movements were uncoordinated. He would have to relearn control of his muscles and it would take time to strengthen his body.

Dhona had no lack of visitors, both friends from the ship and strangers from the base, and a strict visiting schedule had to be enforced since his recuperation demanded many hours of sleep. A rehabilitation program had already been designed for him, which he was expected to start in a few weeks. It would be a long, slow process.

Dhona had several video chats with his family. They had been informed of what had happened to him, what his condition was, and what was yet required in his treatment. They were just glad that he was alive.

2

May – 2015

"You made us your friends, and took us into your homes. You

taught us about your culture, and were interested enough to learn about ours. You allowed us to be productive in our work, and mundane in our leisure, and for that I cannot thank you enough." said Munen to the gathered moon base and Eowaar personnel. "Please raise your glasses with me, to toast the newly weds. To Anthony and Mersuul. May you have a long happy life, and may all your desires be yours."

Shouts of agreement went up from the wedding guests, and Erika noticed that Kalinor Planna was one of the loudest. His attitude was so very different from that on the night Mersuul had proposed, and Erika was very confused by the change. His conversion had only been over the last week or so, which Erika thought was rather sudden after months of seeming to feel the opposite. It was a puzzle she was determined to figure out.

The sunny afternoon on a green Swiss Alps mountainside made for a gorgeous setting for Earth's first inter-planetary wedding, an event that would go unremarked in the history books. Although the elevation wasn't very high, several of the Ganaphe' guests had small oxygen canisters strapped to their waists. It had been a simple ceremony in traditional Earth style. When and if the bride and groom visited Taloraicia, another traditional ceremony of that planet would take place.

Erika watched her uncle socializing with the guests. She was surprised by how comfortable he seemed. She couldn't remember his having a serious, long term relationship when she was growing up. Mersuul changed that. Now he was married. Mersuul had told her that children would definitely be in the future. That was something else she had never associated with her uncle – he would be a parent. Over the last two years there had been so many changes to what she had considered normal before. She looked at the man by her side, and remembered how young Cove had looked when she first saw him. He didn't look that way anymore. He just looked right.

3

June – 2015

"Commander, this is Delfin in comms."

Travellor reached over and activated the channel. It was a small break in the work day routine, and Mersuul, Erika and Toisae Blin were having lunch in his office. The smile cleared from his face – Delfin only called him when it involved something out of the ordinary.

"Go ahead Jibble."

"Sir, I just received a signal from the General. He is on the Kalinor's transport and on his way here. E-T-A seven minutes. They both request a meeting immediately on arrival."

"They BOTH request?"

"Yes sir. That's what they instructed me to tell you."

Everyone looked around at each other. They all knew that was odd. After a few seconds of thought, Travellor responded.

"Tell the General and Kalinor Planna that I am waiting for them in my office, if that is suitable."

"I'll relay the message." said Delfin.

Travellor leaned back in his chair, and looked at the others. They all had questioning looks on their faces. He took hold of the mouse and selected the landing pad camera on his computer, then sent the output to the overhead monitor.

"Now we can see when they touch down."

"Does the General always give such short notice when he comes

451

here?" asked Mersuul.

"Only one other time, when he delivered the Folly. He wanted to surprise me with it. But I don't think this is a social visit. Not with the Kalinor coming with him."

"If you ask me," said Erika to Mersuul, "Your uncle has been acting suspicious for the last couple of weeks."

"Oh? Do tell." said Travellor.

"You must have noticed that when Mersuul proposed to you he wasn't very happy about it."

"Ohhh yes. I noticed."

"Well I noticed that his attitude changed completely at the wedding. Why?"

Travellor thought about this for a while.

"I noticed that too, but I don't know why." he said, then looked at Mersuul and doctor Blin.

"He was happy for me." said Mersuul, as Blin shook her head to indicate she didn't know.

"Perhaps we should clean this up and leave, so that you can have your meeting." she said, nodding at the food on Travellor's desk.

"NO!" he said sharply. "Stay. They wanted to catch me off guard for some reason. I'm not going to give them what they expected. Let's throw them a curve ball instead. Besides, we haven't finished eating yet." he said with a big grin.

4

They were all either surprised or shocked as they let what they just heard sink in. Travellor sat quietly in thought, looking at Farber-Chatwell. Planna sat military straight in his chair trying not to notice the stares he was getting from his niece, Erika, and Doctor Blin. Farber-Chatwell sat casually slouched as he waited for Travellor's response.

"Ambassador?"

"Yes." said Farber-Chatwell.

"To Taloraicia?"

"Just a temporary assignment. For six months – until the Eowaar returns. The Kalinor suggested that you would be the ideal choice for the job. I believe he is right. We are new to all of this, and we both know enough about IGT law to know we have to get a more accurate understanding of it. You're the man I want. I know you will do it correctly! It will be a contingent of four. The others will be experts in legal, financial, and trade matters. I need you to tell me if something doesn't seem right. I need you to bring back the information that ties everything together."

Erika looked at Kalinor Planna with newfound admiration and amazement, as she realized why he had achieved command of such a powerful force as the Eowaar. To be the type of man to command such a vessel you had to know how to get things done – the way you wanted them done. That was what she was seeing here and now. He had come to find the lost member of his family, and keep the promise to return her home to her mother. He had found her alive, which was more than he had hoped for. Then she married a man she would stay with, and not go back home. And now he had found the way to get what he wanted anyway. Mersuul would not leave her Moon Base Commander husband – but she would accompany him as the ambassador to her home planet. This is why Planna had been happy these last weeks. He had figured this out before the wedding. He knew Farber-Chatwell would agree to his suggestion. '*Get what you want much?*' she thought, while looking at Planna.

"You like this idea?" Travellor asked Mersuul. "Do you think I should do th…"

"YES! ABSOLUTELY!" she replied excitedly, then regained her composure. "This is an excellent idea." she said, with happiness all over her face.

"OK then. I will let you know my choice for acting Base

Commander by tomorrow morning."

"Excellent." said Planna. "We leave in two Earth weeks."

5

The observation dome was the newest and tallest addition to the moon base. The crystal-flow dome was manufactured on the Eowaar, using the raw material mined by the Orysta crew for the 361 organization, and was optically perfect. It was worth a fortune in intergalactic trade value, but in practical value it would allow astronomers to view the section of space above them without any extraordinary protective measures for space radiation. The space under the dome was empty now, but floor space had been designated for two large diameter optical telescopes. At present it was used for star gazing and day dreaming by the base occupants. Various pieces of furniture had magically appeared, seemingly out of no where. No one complained. It would be months yet before it was occupied by the scientific community, and a permanent observation seating section had also been designated in the room.

Taking up a large part of the view now was the Eowaar. It was ablaze with lights, and as active as an insect hive, as various ships and maintenance personnel traveled in and out of her as she ran systems checks, in preparation for the journey home. From the dome the ship looked like a huge sword blade with its tip pointed directly at the moon base.

"Not many people get to see her this close, and from this viewpoint." said Dhona.

His speech was more fluid now, sounding more natural and less strained. He sat strapped into a levitation chair, braces on either side of his head – his muscles were not yet strong enough to support his body for long periods. A nasal cannula supplied the higher level of oxygen that he required. His color was bright pink, his body still swollen, and the pain control bands were still necessary – but each day was a little better. Now

454

carrying the rank of Warta by order of Kalinor Planna, Dhona would not be making the trip home with the Eowaar. His doctors didn't want to take any chances in his present condition. There was no need to. Everything that was needed for his continued recuperation was available here and on Earth. He would even have a Ganaphe' doctor to look after him.

"It is an amazing sight." said Doctor Blin. "Even as far away as she is from us, she still looks huge."

Blin also was not going home with the Eowaar. She would be Dhona's personal physician while he remained in this solar system. Farber-Chatwell had asked her to stay with him until the Eowaar returned. She accepted his invitation. He made her smile – more now than she had in a long time. She had not been this happy since the death of her chosen, which had been the impetus for leaving her medical practice and taking the job with the mining company. She had enjoyed the traveling through space, to strange and barren planets where the mining usually took place.

Now this man of Earth had woven himself into her life, day by day. She had not thought she could be this happy again, and she was very happy when she was with him. It was only for six months, which seemed a small amount of time more compared to the decitans they had been missing and thought dead. She wondered if in six months she would be as brave as Mersuul had been, and choose Farber-Chatwell. She wondered if he would accept. Six months would be a good length of time to find answers for all of these questions.

6

Intul-sil-Califas was staying in Vialactea until the return trip of the Eowaar – at least. The Orysta would never fly again and it was the mining company's job to salvage her, but that was not the real reason he volunteered to be the company representative here. He wanted to see the continued development of Earth's advancement into space – and he intended to insert himself in it whenever possible. His fascination with it was too strong to ignore. In the meantime, with most of Orysta's major functions operational, she would continue to support the moon base operations by supplying power, gravity, an advanced technology medical bay, camouflage, and two shuttles. The crystal-flow that was in her cargo hold had been off loaded onto the Eowaar, since it was a strategically important mineral. It would be delivered to the mining company on arrival at Taloraicia. It was an impressive load, and would make the company a very large profit, even after the loss of the Orysta. The load of crystal-flow would also be profitable for the 361 organization. No one had any doubt that they would use their share to bargain for leaving and maintaining the Orysta here on the moon – and there was also no doubt that the deal would be made. There was more crystal-flow to be mined here, and the company would want to maintain a good relationship.

Benua-sil-Plessa was also remaining behind, at the request of Farber-Chatwell and Travellor. He would be needed to keep the Orysta's systems working, and the arrangement also made Erika very happy – there was much more he could teach her. Plessa had talked to his daughter, who was not happy about his staying after such a long absence. He had a new grandson that he had never seen, and she wanted the toddler to know his grandfather. He felt that he owed his new family here some loyalty, and six more months would be small payment for all they had given him. In the end he had appeased her, and with the comm relays now establishing reliable communications he promised to call daily.

7

Mersuul and her new chosen had been assigned to one of the special guest quarters on board the Eowaar. It was a very comfortable suite, but Travellor didn't plan on spending much time in it. He wanted to see as much of the Eowaar as he possibly could, and the short trip to Taloraicia would not be enough time. Then there was the Ganaphe' wedding ceremony they would be required to go through to make Mersuul's family happy. Add to that the official duties and social events required of an ambassador, and it was going to be a very busy six months. He suspected that this trip would not be the honeymoon they had yet to take.

"I am sorry that Erika decided not to come with us, but it will only be six months and you will see her again."

"I know." said Travellor. "She's all grown up now, and it was bound to happen. It's not surprising. I guess it's just not what I wanted." He looked at Mersuul questioningly. "And what about you? After you go home and see your family again, are you going to want to come back here with me?"

Mersuul thought for a while. She sat on his lap and wrapped her arms around his neck.

"When I was trying to decide if I was going to ask you to be my chosen, it was the hardest decision I have ever had to make in my life. I knew it would mean that I would be away from my family, if not forever then for much of the time. That was what made it such a hard decision. I decided that in everyone's life there comes a time when you have to separate from the family and make one of your own. Now it will not be so difficult, with established communications and travel to your solar system. I will be able to talk to them whenever I want, and visit them. It will not be much more difficult than someone on Earth flying from one continent to another. I will go wherever you are."

8

Acting Base Commander "JJ" Jennings sat in the very comfortable chair in the base commander's office. He still expected someone to walk in and tell him to get the hell out. This unexpected, although temporary, change in status had him doubting himself a little. He swiveled the chair and looked out of the window at all the activity in the crater, then looked up and was once again awed by the sight of the Eowaar.

This was all so wrong, and so much better than it should have been. The original plan had been to live – no, survive – in a box while building a bigger box, and then more boxes. There would have been a lot of boxes by now. Instead there was this complex structure with sections above and below ground. All of this was an accident of fate. If the Ganaphe' had not crashed and been stuck here none of this would have happened.

He had often been given command of the base when Travellor was off site. But those times were short, and direct communication to Travellor was always at hand. There would be no calling for guidance now. For the next six months he had to do the job as well as Travellor had, and Travellor had done a very good job. The last official order Travellor had given as Base Commander was to have his picture removed from the reception area, and replaced with JJ's. There were two very large pictures there now. One of JJ, with a plaque reading 'Base Commander Jonathan Jennings', and another of Giell-sil-Dhona, with a sign above it reading 'Welcome to the Giell-sil-Dhona Moon Base'.

"Commander Jennings, this is the Eowaar." came the voice over the comm.

"Jennings here. Go ahead Eowaar."

"Commander, the Eowaar is departing the area. Kalinor Planna sends his regards and says he looks forward to seeing you again in six Earth months."

"Please express my thanks to the Kalinor and the crew for the assistance they provided. I look forward to your return. Jennings out."

It took several minutes before he could detect that the Eowaar was getting smaller in his view. The ship was backing away slowly, to put more distance between her and the moon. As she continued to move, the ship got smaller at a faster rate. Then it pivoted, and Jennings could see the glow of the engines.

END

Glossary of Terms
Including the Ganaphe' Language

arcleeson – unit of angular measurement approximately equal to one degree.

bliml – a cream like substance derived from the Blim plant. It is both a creamer and a sweetener.

crystal-flow – a crystalline material used by the Ganaphe' to create a radiation proof transparent material.

decitan – approximately equal to 1.4 years

dhrojja – space pirates

diest – one solar day

Distributed Registries Exchange – Intergalactic data warehouse maintaining copies of all documents related to commercial and political interests of IGT signatories.

ducifel – a multi-colored flower from the Ganaphe' home world, that are usually found growing at the entrances of caves and tunnels. They grow downward or sideways without consideration for sunlight or gravity, and are very sensitive to oxygen levels. Oxygen levels of eighteen percent or less causes the petals to immediately turn white.

FBO – Fixed Base Operator. The business that provides aeronautical services at an airport.

fracin – approximately equal to two seconds

Galya – the language spoken by the Ganaphe'

garva – a hot Ganaphe' beverage

gorbel – a sport similar to tennis.

gordaelate – a strong and flexible metal like material, having the flexibility and strength of steel cable infused with carbon fiber composite

GRAIL – A NASA satellite mission to map the gravity of the moon. Comprised of two satellites (GRAIL-A and GRAIL-B) given the names Ebb and Flow.

459

Grilik – Captain or Commander of a ship

heela – approximately equal to one and a half hours

HUD – Heads Up Display

IFR – Instrument Flight Rules

IGT – Interconnected Galaxies Treaty. The inhabited Galaxies that form a symbiotic union for their mutual benefit. It was evolved after centuries of early haphazard contact between species, which many times led to wars and genocides. Conceived by galactic survivors of wars that were so annihilative they had no other choice if they were to survive. These wars were so devastating, that the laws developed were specifically defined, and required that the punishment for violation was without leniency. In later times, as new galaxies and species were discovered, many were able to join without having suffered the devastation, learning from the terrible history of the founding members. Some galaxies chose not to join, but non-member peoples do not benefit from the mutual protection, technological advancements, and emergency aid supplied to members.

IGT Esploreesum – A condensed or simplified introduction to the IGT. For educational purposes only. Not to be used for legal application.

Ilmerts law – close equivalent to Murphy's law – "If it can go badly, it will go very badly"

Jade Rabbit (Yutu) – China's roving Moon surface explorer

Kalinor – Ganaphe' Military rank similar to Navy Admiral

LADEE – The Lunar Atmosphere and Dust Environment Explorer satellite

lanor – military rank equivalent to lieutenant

larn – a unit of measurement, approximately equal to 1.6 miles.

LIDAR – Light Detection And Ranging. A remote sensing technique that uses a pulsed laser to measure distance

liff – a unit of measurement, approximately equal to one liter

limm – a unit of measurement, approximately equal to one yard

LRO – Lunar Reconnaissance Orbiter satellite

mirlot – approximately equal to 1.4 minutes.

misoravis – An crystalline material, used in special applications requiring a stable explosive, that can be triggered by an alternating high voltage/high current signal in a specific frequency range.

MPO – Document classification Mission Personal Only. Only personnel directly involved in the designated mission are authorized to view the document.

nardle – needle

Orysta – name of the Ganaphe' mining ship

PIC – Pilot In Command

plebal – a measurement of weight approximately equal to 1.3 pounds

ploon – hay stack

quint – cubic

SFT – Sanction of Free Transit. An agreement among the IGT that gave inter-galactic vessels the right to travel through member galaxies without restraint. It requires that vessels to be equipped with specified identification equipment, and follow defined protocols, under automated/computer control that can not be interfered with or disabled by the crew. Destruction or removal of such equipment without proper authorization is punishable under ITG law, and is considered a serious violation. It also required that aid and assistance be given when possible, if it didn't endanger the responding ship.

sil – prefix meaning 'Of the family'. Used in formal form of person's name, and left out in casual reference.

SOP – Standard Operating Procedure

Tahn-grilik – First Officer of a ship. Literal translation is "Officer under the Captain" or "Officer after the Captain".

Taloraicia – name of Ganaphe' home world.

tanrha – approximately equal to 1.4 decades

vectra – high power cohesive energy burst

VFR – Visual Flight Rules

vheen – approximately equal to 10 days

Vialactea – Ganaphe' name for the Milky Way galaxy

Warta – military rank similar to Captain

DISCLAIMER

This book is a work of fiction. No information within this work violates the United States Espionage Act, 18 U.S. Code Chapter 37.

- Book Cover Credits -